I0822460

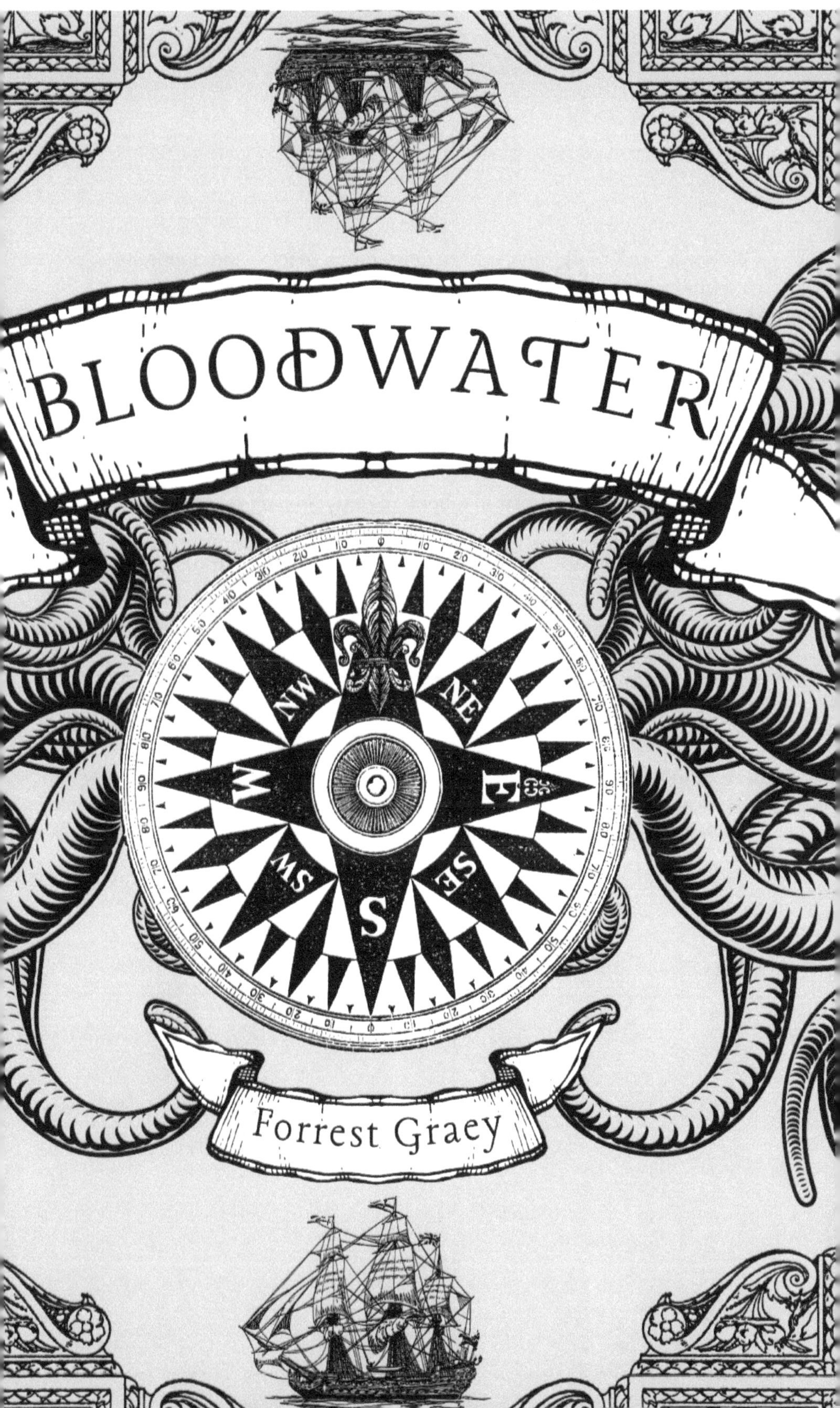

BLOODWATER
NW
NE
W
E
SW
SE
S
Forrest Graey

First edition 2025

Book cover design and glossaries by Forrest Graey. Images from Canva.com from CanvaPro subscription. Individual elements belong to their respective parties. Cover and interior art designs fall under CanvaPro's Content License Agreement.

Maps designed in InkarnatePro.

Interior art designed by Forrest Graey

ISBN 9798218774745

Published by Silvergane Publishing

To my Love.

Let me always face the current and chaos with you.

TRIGGERS & CONTENT WARNING

This book has graphic and descriptive scenes of:
blood, murder, abuse, gore, suicidal ideations, and fighting.

Foul language is used throughout the book.

Other potentially triggering content includes:
Necrophilia/mention of necrophilia (*off-page, but with occasionally descriptive lead-up*), abortion (*commentary, non-descriptive*), grief, mention of cannibalism, themes of colonization, themes of genocide, drug use, child death (*off-page/descriptive aftermath*), psychosis, disassociation, alcoholism, suicide (*non-physical description*), animal cruelty/death, illusion to rape, and racism.

Please note that this is a work of fiction and that the negative contents of this book are not examples of the author's desires.

The Uncharted Lands of Verdinum

Lusc

Lesser Syvon

Greater Syvon

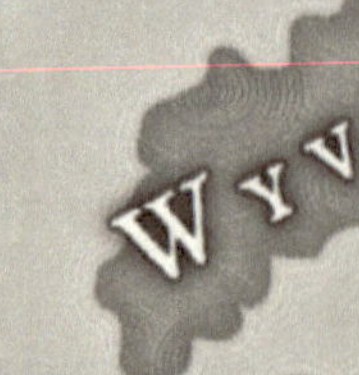

The Nameless Seas

Non

HANWE

PLUNNET

DEMIETAS

SAGEON

THE NONAN DIVIDE

THE CARORDTIAN SEA

The Monoliths

ITHERNATE REPUBLIC

ISLE OF DUNN

ETIAN STRAIT

EWILDES

NAMELESS SEA

DEATH'S ROOST
the Brimelands
Bastard's Keep
Fogwind
Neighweath
STORMSHALE
ESMAR
Farstone
PORT OF MA
CENTRUST
Crossmark
THE CROSSING
SOVIL
IGRISECT
RUINS
LANDMARKS
TOWNS OR HOMESTEADS

THANTIS
the Greenpeaks
VINRET
Vimhel
OT-AMOS
Onmont
ENWETH
Perry
Sherton
EENSPORT

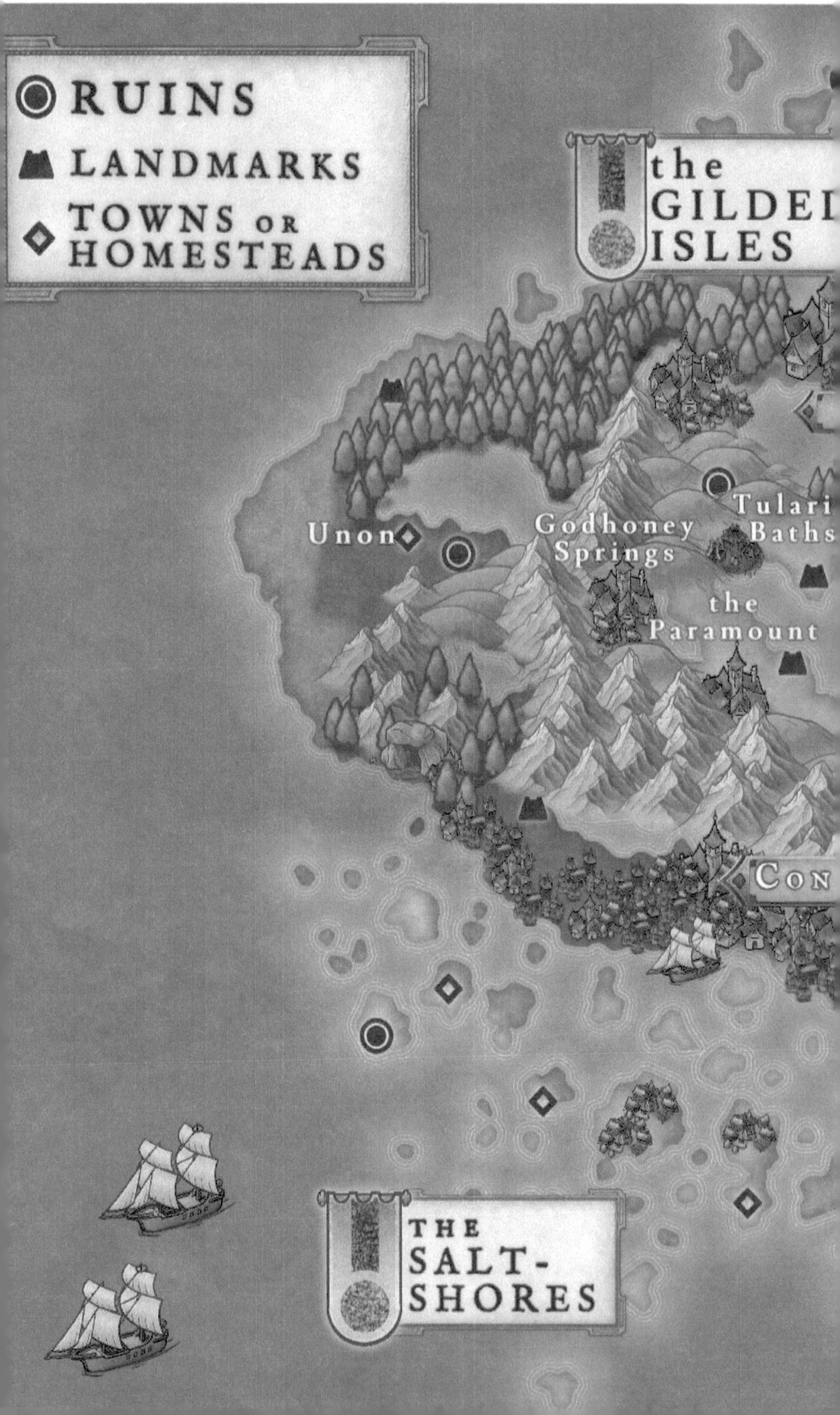
RUINS
LANDMARKS
TOWNS OR HOMESTEADS
the GILDE[…] ISLES
Tulari Baths
Unon
Godhoney Springs
the Paramount
CON
THE SALT-SHORES

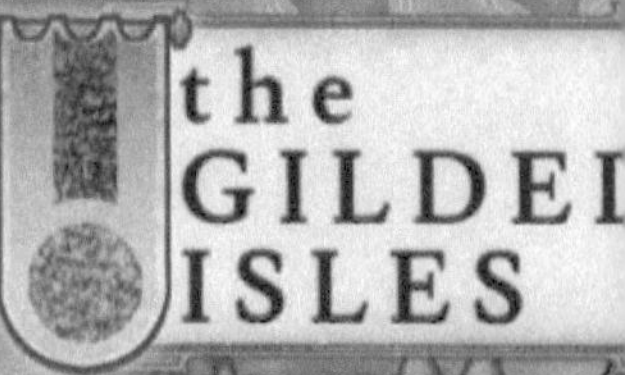

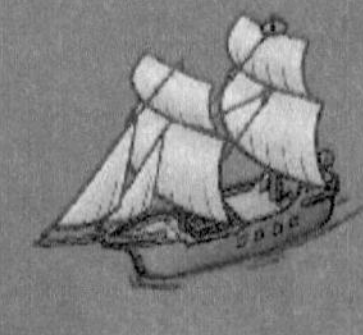

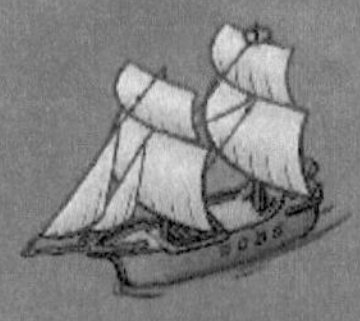

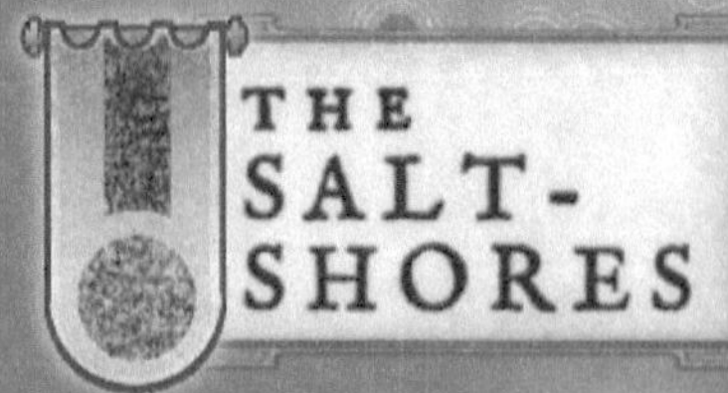

the
YeSara
Residence
YeKist
Estates
ne
Sara
r Homes
Murkthistle
Soapstead
rand
pian
MENTHIS
TRILABOLD
LINLOCKE

The Seasons & Their Months

As Established in the Age of Commodity

Sommet

The hottest season, and a time when many intercontinental holidays are celebrated.

Entash, Dutash, Tritash, Figtash

Wotag

The coldest season; regions within Lesser Syvon only experience mild temperatures

Ceitash, Hattash, Septash

Brite

The Blossoming Season, when temperatures begin to climb once more.

Votash

GILDONAIS

THROUGHOUT THE AGES

THE FORGOTTEN AGES

AGES OF ɔUSTRY

THE BOULDERFELLS

THE IRONFOLDS

THE AGE OF BRUTALITY

A warring Age filled with the displacement of the Kahun, first peoples of Esmar, and the establishment of the first Esmarin Monarch. Thantis attempts invading Esmar and Sovil, but is crushed by Sovilian berserkers. Revkyn are banished by law of the Solon Confluence, created after the Fangbearer Conflicts. The Gilded Clans contend for power and land during the Mage Wars.

THE AGE OF COMMODITY

Trade connects the world as people expand the edges of their map after the Ages of Industry and Brutality. Treaties, laws, and allyships are established throughout. The Syvons are created under the Solon Confluence. Dubbed "The Age of Fragile Peace" by historians as tension remains between Esmar, Sovil, and Thantis.

HE PLIGHTS

mage sickness" spreads roughout all known 'donais, called such for how ickly it ends the lives of own mages. It affects not ly people, but crops. herever one with the mage-kness dies, a blight begins, stroying crops and spoiling ll-water. People are burned stead of buried, or sunk at a.

THE DAWNING

The first morsel of calm after The Plights. Countries begin to reopen their trade routes after forcing a worldwide bar on trade to halt the spread of the mage-sickness.

THE APATHESIS

Tensions heighten as countries enact stricter policies on one-another for trade and travel. Longstanding treaties are either modified, or rejected.

THE CURRENT AGE

Characters & Peoples
Kahun: *kay-hoon*
Revkyn: *rev-kin*
Dua-Nythi: *d'wah nih-thigh*
Saltraroran: *sal-t'rah-roar-an*
Talamondin: *tah-luh-monn-din*
Pelagios: *puh-lay-jis*
Einar: *eye-nar*
Theon: *thay-on*
Mycin: *my-sin*
Chiflot: *chif-low*
Lanet: *Lah-nay*
Damalis: *da-mall-is*
Avenir: *ah-veh-near*
Neoma: *nay-oh-ma*
Urias: *ur-eye-us*
Koa: *co-uh*
Talaya: *taa-lay-uh*
Sulien: *soo-lee-in*
Inara: *ih-nar-ah*
Calily: *kay-lily*
Valeska: *va-less-ka*
Naseria: *nah-see-ree-uh*
Viorel Duhane: *vee-oh-rel do-hane*
Cyra Veles: *ky-ruh veh-lay*
Myrnn: *mern*
Omalia: *oh-mall-ee-ah*

Places
Gildonais: *gill-don-ay-is*
The Syvons: *sigh-von*
Carn-Duhl: *kharn-dool*
Dunhet: *done-het*
Con-Quary: *con-quarry*
Tularin: *too-lah-rin*
Kairdwillo-Nhan: *care-d'willow- nahn*
Amalak: *ah-muh-lack*

Houses
Demont: *dee-mon*
YeSara: *yeh-sah-ra*

Gods
Hecleon: *heck-lee-on*
Ma'Ceste: *mah-sess-t*
Duathi: *dwa-thee*
Khiro: *k'eye-row*
Hasild-Neht: *ha-sill'd net*
Hyyke: *high-kee*
Shaksa: *shock-saa*
Shakkan: *shaa-khan*

BLOODWATER
NW
NE
W
E
SW
SE
S
Forrest Graey

CHAPTER ONE

There were a dozen stories explaining why Esmar was sinking back into the ocean, though people favored the one of the Mad King. As the tale went, his bloodline desecrated the land with a constant disregard for humanity, so much so that the old gods sought to make the country anew. But no matter how much land was lost to the tide, the Mad King sat deep within his lone mountain surrounded by his court of gnashing shadows. Esmar slipped like mud through his hands, and the country placed carnal desire before the preservation of its society, the rot seeping up from ruined farmlands and burrowing itself within the hearts of its inhabitants.

No city under the Mad King's banner took advantage of his failing grasp like the backwater region of Stormshale.

In Esmarin terms, it was a blessing that Stormshale survived the long centuries of ravenous, thrashing waves and storm clouds so brilliant with lightning that the skies danced well into sleeping hours. Unfolding from the rain-slicked mountains of shalestone, the city stood as a testament to the country's unwillingness to repent. It faced angry, god-like weather since settlement, yet there it stood on rocky shores and stilted platforms made of stone and silverwood. And beneath the monument to thievery and vices the frothing, chilly ocean slammed into pebbled shorelines. It was a sound more familiar to a child born in Stormshale than their own mother's heartbeat.

People kept themselves warm in all manner of ways during the worst of the season, the brothels dry and inviting as their glass-cased lanterns swung next to signs painted with red everbloom roses. Their rooms, filled with feathered beds and heavy sheets all the way from Thantis, tantalized even the richest of folk. It allowed them to think they lived in *true* luxury, at least for an hour or two, before they were cast out into the drudgery of the dock town once more. But in a place like Stormshale, there were few ways to make the kind of coin good enough for those comforts.

Stealing was easiest, though the Watch occasionally proved serious enough to threaten cutting off a thief's hands—but only just, for anyone could be bribed into looking the other way. The fishing was carried out by grizzled spearmen, and stood as proof that some people in Esmar were lucky enough to dive into a storm and return with their lives. Iron-bellied, they maneuvered through the choppy waters to bring back their fat, glistening catches to sell along the docks.

There were few other ways to make enough coin to satisfy one's vices, though none as tricky or high-paying as climbing.

The gleaming, flat side of the mountain looked fearsome as remnants of a thunderstorm pattered out its last few drops of rain. A mist would soon settle over the shoreline, thick enough to catch in one's throat, but Dice paid as much attention to the future as she did to her inky, poorly cut hair.

Toeing to the edge of the sheer drop, Dice eyed the jagged boulders sticking out of the foaming blue waves, their gnarled fingers reaching out of a watery grave. A quiet, mournful voice churned in the back of her mind, rhythmic with the thrashing of the ocean on the stone.

Jump.

As soon as the tenor of sadness rumbled over her mind, she shut it away. An iron door, barred and reinforced, locked into place to keep those shadows in their dark corners. Once, it had not been so easy to quell the sense of slipping outside her body and into the fantasy of succumbing to the unforgiving ocean below. Now, she made it out only as a murmur of disquiet.

Let those thoughts rumble like stones before a landslide all they wanted, since in the end they were *only* thoughts.

Dice forced herself to look at the slice of shalestone climbing up the rock in a jagged strike, a shock of black lightning caught within the mountain. It might be obsidian, but it was too crowded by the gray to tell. Obsidian was not uncommon, though still rare enough for veins to be priced well, but Dice knew to keep her excitement reserved until she held the proof.

Glaring downward critically, the earlier storm left the rocky cliffside shimmering with streams of foam and salty rain. Dice knew it would not be an easy climb, or a quick one, and leaned away from the edge to seek out a firm place to set her first anchor. A climb was dangerous enough to satiate that earlier voice, but like a fingernail picking at warped paint it scraped at the edges of her mind. Where body and thought mingled in some dark, distant place, there it sat, picking, picking, picking.

Jump. You would feel so free in those last moments.

Short, choppy strands hugged flat against her skull, heavy with the previous rain, and she absently swiped the back of her hand across her forehead to adjust them. A few feet away from the cliff's edge, she bent a knee and slipped her bag of tools from her shoulder. On the ground, she lined up iron contraptions, cumbersome and awkwardly shaped. Dice knew the hand-cranked drill for the callouses it left on her palms, and set about turning the slightly rusted point into the surface by her knee. The weight of it brought her mind down from its foggy thoughts and back to a solid place, and once a decent hole was drilled she set up anchor, giving it a heaving tug to assure its stability.

While she daydreamed about jumping off of the shalestone mountains, *falling* was a different theme altogether.

Blinking away moisture trapped on her eyelashes, Dice reached into a different weatherproof satchel at her hip. The old leather bag felt soft under her bare fingers, the waxy surface sticking a little to her skin as she opened the pouch and removed a few strips of thick, stained cloth. Winding them around her palms, in between her fingers, and down over her wrists, Dice looked over the cliff's edge once more. Her gaze sought out the tiny footholds along the surface of the stone, small lips barely an inch wide.

It was enough, and only just.

Dice removed a round, thick tin from the satchel, popping the lid and scooping a hefty dollop of the dense mixture within. Silverwood sap was expensive, though Dice had not come by the tin honestly. A crisp scent that reminded her of apples tinged the air, the gummy adhesive making her skin tingle. Clinging to the fabric of the cloth strips and the pads of her exposed fingertips, the tacky substance would allow for purchase as she climbed and set in the other anchors.

After rubbing the sap on the toes of her boots, she rolled out her shoulders and took a step closer to the slanted rockface. The voice's urging cadence no more than a hum now, Dice removed a length of thick rope from her bag, taking a knee to tie a complicated, twining knot that was her barrier between life and the crushing weight of the waves. Pulling it taunt, Dice looped the rope through the contraption of her belt, feeding it through to hold in her left hand to guide herself down the cliffside. The tools returned to her satchel, and then Dice backed towards the edge, pressing the flat of her boot against the drop.

Her heels hung free, her entire body leaning at an angle over the raging waters below.

All Dice needed to do was let go, and it would be done.

The wind sliced across her backside, whipping her short hair like blades of grass across her forehead. There was something about leaning over open air, the sea raging below, that made her heartbeat gallop. Equal parts fear and excitement flooded her body, the dance of her blood thumping in her temples and fingertips. Dice's breathing labored, lungs struggling against the thrill of hanging so precariously over the unforgiving waters.

She loosened her grip on the rope for only a moment's breath—then she released it entirely. The weight of her body carried her backward, down, further past the cliff's edge. Every ounce of her blood roiled with adrenaline and fear in those seconds when her body flooded her mind with the need to survive.

Dice caught herself once more with a gasp, fingers locking around the rope so tightly that her knuckles throbbed with her heartbeat. Her father always said she toyed with death. If he were there, watching the smile spread across her pale face, he might even call her a fool.

Casting a look over her shoulder at the clouded horizon, a part of her wondered if Evander's eye saw her from *The Jolly Marksmen*. Such a weathered and worldly pirate must know which of the filthy cities she had run off to, yet if such were the case, surely he would have docked in Stormshale by now? Evander never missed a chance to prove to Dice that he knew her as well as the sunspots on his hands, but all of Sommet unrolled without Evander searching her out—and it was the longest she ever spent on land.

Maybe Evander was making a point to her *and* the crew.

Or maybe he finally grew weary of Dice's vanishing performances, leaving the young woman to face Esmar without his protection as one final lesson.

Roaring below, the ocean reminded Dice that there was a job to do. Letting out a ragged breath, she slowly walked backward down the cliffside, straddling the jagged vein of stone. The rope held true as she leaned one way, then another, boots searching for purchase so that she may be able to start on the next anchor. The thrill from endangering herself still hummed in her veins, heightening her attentiveness. Dice found the footholds easily, tying herself off to lean into the air.

She fished the screw out of her bag once again. Another anchor secure, a twist with the pliers driving it home. Thoughts of falling and letting go of the rope—or cutting it entirely—faded as her hands busied with preparing the line for future miners. Left over from the obsidian rush an age ago, a handful of companies existed in Stormshale and yet there existed only a few people in the city itself willing to move down the sides of mountains and cliffs like twitching spiders. Once a path down the mountain proved secure, people came in behind her to run their lines through them and swing tools much heavier than hers at the vein, and if it *were* obsidian she might get a chip for her troubles. But a vein this dense meant it could be another week before Dice saw any such fortune.

Salty spray hissed across the back of her breeches, slickening the tall leather of her boots. Though the mountain disappeared into the water plenty of feet further down, the waves were large and beautiful, their foaming heads smashing so desperately into the rock, trying to part it aside. Dice, setting the last anchor into a perfect wedge of stone, pulled herself up to spin and face the ocean. One heel found the iron loop as a foothold, her hands clinging faithfully to the rope.

The chorus of rushing waves filled her head. Dice's eyes beseeched the churning, dark waters, unsure of what it was she sought. Sometimes, the pull to fall into the ocean came like the waves—smashing and angry—but in other instances, it felt like *this*. An achy, longing feeling in the hollow of Dice's chest almost begged her to release the rope and return to the sea, as gentle as a lover slipping the shirt off her shoulders. She figured she missed her life on the *Marksmen*, surrounded by the only kind of family she ever knew, being rocked to sleep in her hanging cot in the quarters. It caused enough pain for her eyes to prick with moisture, her breathing shortened by the sting.

The depths called out to her, the sound layered with the hush of crashing waves… and something else.

Dice heard the song her whole life. Evander knew not of the layered, mournful tune that dug its way into Dice's mind, and she had no intention in any part of herself to reveal such a thing. If she ever told him what plagued her, Evander would ask what it sounded like, and for that there was no sensible answer. Sometimes, the music's bidding came on so strongly that Dice felt it reverberating throughout her body.

A chorus of bubbling voices layered with the feeling of the sea pulling the waters back in preparation for a great, dangerous wave that meant to come crashing down over her head at any moment.

Sea spray rocketed upward, the cold stinging her knees. It was enough to shock Dice back into her body with a gasp of surprise. Her boot slipped from the anchor, swiveling her around to face the stony cliffside.

The rope ground against her palms as she pulled herself upright, straightening her climbing posture and settling her boot atop the anchor once again.

"Alright," Dice mumbled to the moanfully desperate hiss of the sea.

She told herself she did not hear the groaning, deep and guttural, beneath the music of the waves. Instead, she climbed, replacing the desire to let go of the rope with the resolution of drowning herself in a bucket of barley wine.

Frying fish, the smell thick with butter, coaxed Dice out of her ambling stupor as she drew closer to the first platforms of Stormshale. The walk back from the jagged paths that split into the mountains, depositing miners at random crags of shalestone, was a steep decline. Sunlight hiding behind the gray storm clouds attested the late hour, a pale yellow turning to a faded purple. Dice's legs burned from the walk and the climb, weariness holding down her shoulders as she approached the fishermen's booths on the edge of the boardwalks lining the shore.

The fishermen prepared their catches next to the ocean in long, solitary booths where under each awning sat buckets of water filled with writhing bodies. While the market itself kept to the drier parts of the city, one bought fresh catches along the boardwalks. Ships bobbed in the unruly waters, but none of them were bigger than the *Marksmen*, and few made it across the basin to mainland country.

Salt filled the air, along with the charred smell of something burning on the wind. A platform jutted out of the side of a gray foothill, the rickety but deceptively sturdy staircase leading up to the platforms of the city. Beyond it stood the giant pillars of stone that held up those platforms, covered in mildew and barnacles from when the tide came in. Roads of wood overlapped like a puzzle throughout Stormshale, and Dice imagined that if she were a bird looking down the city would be nothing more than a pile of sticks. Some of the richer folk, the ones whose families lived there since the settlement of the island, could afford digging out homes into the sides of the mountain. People like Dice, like the fishermen who huddled under their booths, like the bawds and children and those who were the unlucky backwash of society, had to be all right with living half-damp.

Kaine grunted as she approached, which was the only sort of hello Dice or anyone ever got from him. A shallow bucket stained white with flour and spice sat on the stool at his hip, and gleaming, oily fish awaited their delicious transformation on a short counter next to it. The humble shack sat protected from the drizzle by a layer of a seal's hide that declined at an awkward angle over the cookfire. The crackling sound shut out the music of the ocean, the smell making Dice's mouth water.

"How much for a head?" Dice asked, knowing the exact amount of meager coin in her pocket.

"How much you got?"

Dice knew better than to be honest with her answer because to tell him what was in her pocket meant it would happen to cost *exactly* that. As good—and necessary—as food was, Dice needed to make sure the coin stretched the week.

"Enough for a fish head." She crossed her arms, meeting his steely gaze. "Don't you know better than to cheat a local?"

"You say that like being from here is honorable." Kaine grumbled, separating a fish from the pile and drawing out his cleaver. As the blunt edge chopped through the neckbone, his eyes locked with hers. "You ain't no local, neither. Best to keep your defensiveness to yourself."

"Leave the eyes," she quipped instead of proving his point. The wiry man huffed out his nose like a horse, shaking his head in mild annoyance as he battered the fish and tossed it onto the cookfire.

Kaine settled back into his routine, ignoring Dice as he sliced the belly of a fish to dump its guts into a chum bucket. She watched his deft fingers pry out the needlelike bones before turning her back against the shack's post. Above them, the sounds of the waking city echoed down in woodsy groans and clattering footsteps. While fishermen and miners woke with the sun, no matter how thick the curtain of storm clouds hiding it, some folks kept their shutters locked long into the afternoon.

Certain people settled in places like Stormshale, where the distance to any other civilization took a week of sailing. Shadows grew longer there, stretching wide and thick to conceal what transpired within them. Bodies went missing, and if the ocean did not spit them back up, bloated and rotten, then they were never seen again. People stopped asking questions long ago, even if it was their loved ones who found such ill fortune.

Growing unnervingly comfortable with the fact that any moment could be their last, the city did not protect anyone. So, everyone learned to protect themselves. If sleep hid them from those looming shadows, Dice did not blame them for closing their eyes and shuttering their windows. When one's living world is the stuff of most people's nightmares, getting lost in dreams was easy.

Walking up the staircase, the fish head too bony to provide any real sustenance, Dice ground her teeth against the bone to scrape away as much meat as possible. A couple passed her, descending the staircase while giving an odd look to each other as she gnawed away. The sounds of the ocean became only a murmur in the background when her booted foot hit the stretch of the first platform, and Dice tossed the naked fishbone over her shoulder.

As filthy as Stormshale was, it was life. She remembered this place from a rushed docking that Evander ordered some months ago when they found out they were taking on water. A plank was thoroughly rotten, and it took over a week to fix, but Evander called it luck. According to him, there seemed no better place to get things waterproofed than a city that was constantly under water.

Dice slipped her hands into the pocket of her waxy coat, searching for any eyes that studied her. The first tier of Stormshale laid flat, edges shaped like burned paper as the planks shoved into every crevice of stone the mountain offered. There were no shops on this level since the heavy, crisscrossed beams supporting the tiers above took up too much space; there was only dim light and corners thick with bodies. Eyes, glazy and yellowed, saw her but did not register Dice's existence at all, watching without understanding.

To her left was an alcove of stone, and underneath it stood a few men gathered in a half-circle. Their eyes as immobile as the city's vices, Dice's gaze jumped from each of their faces to count their numbers. The men gathering were nothing more than drunkard servants of the Watch, wearing immunity like a sleek coat. There were other ways to get to the upper tiers, but they were also carefully watched, and Dice did not like the idea of anyone being mindful of her schedule.

As she passed the men, she gritted her teeth against the urge to run.

A primal sensation of *knowing* twined in Dice's chest as she walked onward, weaving through the haphazard structure of beams and iron brackets towards another staircase on the right. Hungry gazes sought her out, beady and sharp. Men boasting a partnership with the Watch carried with them a repulsive stench, despair so thick it permeated the air around their waterlogged heads. Dice knew better than to meet those needing eyes as a woman, so she gave the dark corners a wide berth as their tittering scraped across the platform. Disembodied words dragged their ragged hands down her back and cupped her rear, so obvious the intent of their gazes and whispered growls. She felt them, Stormshale's shadows taken to the flesh, not for the first time sensing the fear of being without Evander's protection on land.

Her steady footfalls echoed across the boards. In the platform's four corners were staircases leading up to the other levels. During storms made from ballads and fables, the first tier and the one directly above flooded so severely that it took the next season to drain out to sea again. Dice found herself cursing the weather but had no urgency to change her surroundings. Even though it took considerable balance to remain upright on the algae that shined underfoot, Stormshale provided plenty of obscurity, something Dice treasured after growing up on a ship as the captain's favored ward.

She would face its horrors so long as she garnered the will to manage them.

The support beams were not so packed together on the next level, keeping to the center to bolster the weight of the city. On this tier, there were a few shops of fishing wire and buttons, and a small market that rarely carried anything nicer than whaleskin boots. Planks shoved desperately into every nook and cranny kept the stores upright, their slant bodies creating silhouettes of broken teeth. The stairwell spat Dice out next to the solid, hip-high barrier that prevented anyone from toppling over and plummeting three stories. People grew livelier the higher Dice climbed, and she almost decided to keep going until her eyes snapped to an opening doorway, and a swish of skirts.

One of the Ladies of the *Roses* slipped out of the haberdashery. Dice recognized her as Madam Leonora, hooking a hip to the railing to get comfortable as she watched with bored fascination. Leonora lorded over a three-rose establishment and rarely came this far down the platforms for fear of sullying her Thantis skirts. If Leonora had secrets, Dice wanted to see what kind.

Her eyes drew down the length of the older woman's figure, noting how the skirt hugged her hips before flaring out in the Thantis style around her ankles. It was a sullen gray color trying to fit in with the lower tiers but Dice was worldly enough to note the richness of the fabric. Even her plain blouse, a dull blue like the sky before a storm, was glossy in the weak light. Nothing bought or made in Esmar was so expertly tailored. It hugged Leonora's breasts snuggly, the billowing sleeves tapering at her wrists. The woman threw her cloak over her arm and turned to face whoever stood beyond the threshold.

A man exited the haberdashery, all outdated Esmarin finery that dulled in comparison to the madam's attire. Stirring around him was the air of someone who once thought themselves lofty but now hid behind a loathsome half-smile. Neither ugly nor handsome, Dice wondered which of Leonora's roses got in trouble with their client.

His hand cupped the madam's chin, and despite snatching it out of his grasp she did not step away from him. Acrid power tinge the shadows of his smile before he gave her a pert nod, finalizing their conversation before whooshing like a long-forgotten banner across the platform and up the furthest stairwell. Dice only had a moment to wonder to herself the meaning of the confrontation before Leonora's gaze narrowed on *her* like a lighthouses' beacon.

"You foul rat." Remembering herself, Leonora quickly threw on her cloak and lifted its hood over her tousled hair as she approached the pirate. "Why is it that every time I turn my back, you appear from the shadows?"

To say Leonora did not care for Dice would not do her anger justice. Once she arrived in Stormshale, Dice acted every bit like the pirates who reared her—all the way down to not paying for her lengthy stay at Leonora's *Three Roses*. The madam found her excruciatingly unbearable, especially when a few of her ladies refused to take any men to bed once Dice was barred. Leonora often sneered at Dice in passing, but being rumored as such a skilled lover bolstered her pride enough for the young pirate not to mind.

Dice lifted her hands in mock surrender, unable to help the easy grin lifting her mouth. "A coincidence, Madam, albeit a happy one. For me, at least."

"I suppose you want your debt forgiven?" Leonora huffed, crossing her arms over her full chest. "Or one last night of pleasure before I have the Watch toss you in the pit?"

The suggestion of such a foul punishment loosened Dice's smile for a moment. "If you wanted me drowned, you would've sent your men already. It's not like you'd ever want to be indebted to the Watch. And," she continued with a deceptively carefree nod, "believe it or not, Leo, I wasn't searching you and your lover out."

"He's not—ne'er *you* mind." A muscle twitched under Leonora's eye, her beautiful tongue rolling the Esmarin language.

Dice's gaze jumped to the stairwell the stranger ascended. True, it was not her business, nor Leonora her responsibility, but she did not care for the anxious way the older woman began to pick at her fingers.

"Let me escort you back to the *Roses*, Leo." She offered, a strange bubble of protection pressing behind her ribs.

"Oh, please." The woman rolled her eyes. "*Escort* me? Like you're not going to pick my pocket the moment you see an opening?"

Dice's lip twitched, the words coming up like bile. "If my recollection of my stay at the *Roses* is correct," she stepped in, relishing the cherry color blooming on Leonora's cheeks, "your door was as open to me as any other. I don't need to steal what you happily gave me for free."

Leonora's hand was fast, the sting it left on Dice's cheek patronizing, but she knew *exactly* how the madam might receive her words and let it land anyway. Anyone in Leonora's station would feel a morsel of regret about welcoming a pirate into her bed, even if the hours—and hours—were nothing short of blissful. Neither of them believed a bond outside of sex existed between them, but Leonora's ego was bruised from Dice cheating her out of a good pocketful of money.

"You—"

"Rat?"

Ruby lips trembled in frustration. Dice remembered their taste, the stain of rouge only a smear across Leonora's chin. A twinge of desire mingled with humiliation flickered in her belly, but Dice ignored it like she did everything else that made her uncomfortable.

"Forgive my debt, and I'll pay upfront from now on."

Leonora balked, a stubborn set to her jaw.

"Or I can just ask your friend from the 'dash to pay it for me." Dice leaned on the railing in casual indifference. "I'm sure he'd like to keep his secrets as much as you, yours. Seemed like you had a bit of a business arrangement... and we both know how I tend to shirk such things."

A thrash of heat passed between them, bitterness colliding awkwardly with the memories of rapturous pleasure. Leonora was a decade older than Dice, yet the latter had more experience. This meant something to a woman whose whole adult life revolved around the exposure and temptation of sex and desire.

Every raw sound Leonora had made echoed in the space between them as she considered Dice's offer. In a voice akin to pity, the madam whispered, "They *do* miss you. You were kind to them—not that I don't take care of my own, but… They liked your stories. And as much as I *despise* you…"

Other words settled, unspoken, in Leonora's statement. Her eyes flicked, and Dice knew they were thinking the same name.

Evangeline. Had she put in a good word for Dice after all this time?

Feeling a thickness in her stomach, Dice simply asked, "We're square?"

The woman sighed after a moment, defeated. "Yes. We're square. So long as you keep your mouth shut, and let my business be mine, then… you can come back. I'll let my boys know not to pummel you the second you get too close."

She opened her mouth to thank her but Leonora turned quickly on her heel. Hidden under the dark hood of her cloak, the madam blended into the shadows before disappearing up the furthest staircase. A prideful feeling swelled in Dice's ribcage, and it was enough to tamper down the sick sensation that lingered as Evangeline's name echoed down her spine.

As more people began to fill the platform, Dice shifted her mind to finding something more sustainable as her stomach growled. Evangeline was a bliss meant to be felt in privacy, and she meant to enjoy the feeling later.

Fishermen climbed the steps, and people descended from the more refined levels above. With enough bodies to cover her, Dice managed to pick a few coins as she made her way through the growing crowd, but people on the lower tiers never had much to steal.

She stole enough to buy a little bread, the texture crumbling like sand in her mouth as she ripped through it with her teeth. Climbing to the fourth level, Dice swallowed the last bit of it down before approaching the doorway of *The Far Sailor*. Shoving the creaking mass of wood open exposed a low ceiling, a few tables, and a short counter behind which the bookkeeper and innkeeper sat. The bookkeeper did not sign her name at the sound of her entry, and the innkeeper only glanced over her person. Without lifting his lips from his dark pipe, he ignored the bag of tools slung over her shoulder as he checked for any obvious weaponry. And, finding nothing else entertaining about her, he returned to staring blankly ahead.

The dankness of the inn, gloomy and punctuated by the smell from the innkeeper's pipe, enveloped her. Remnants of breakfast hung stalely in the air, and she slid across the floorboards with her shoulders hunched forward. Only a few patrons woke in time for the meal, some of the breakfast plates still littering the table. Dice's quick fingers scraped up the cold remnants of thick porridge that clung to the sides of bowls. By the time she made it to the split staircase, she was satiated.

Dice did not have the proper coin to satisfy the innkeeper, but after drinking her money and beating a man twice her size it was decided that she could have the storage room in exchange for being extra muscle on busier nights. The room was half carved into the mountain, so small that the walls brushed against Dice's fingertips when she stretched out her arms. Some of the wood underfoot was too rotten to hold up any crates or barrels of ale, their creaking worrisome enough for her to make a hammock out of a fishnet and not stand on them longer than a handful of moments.

Exhausted from her work, and eager to gather her strength for the ladies under Leonora's roof, Dice rolled into the hammock with her boots still on. Hanging the weatherproof satchel on a nail left over from the room's more useful days, she settled in with a sigh.

Swaying in the net, she found her body being tricked into thinking she was back aboard *The Jolly Marksmen*. A strange feeling stirred beneath her ribcage, one she tried to avoid at all costs.

Crossing paths with Leonora left her feeling guilty. Though Dice tried her best to shut it out, the quiet of the room forced her to look at the interaction… and Evangeline.

Then, she was thinking about leaving the ship without telling a soul of her departure, stowing away from a port in Esmar and across the basin to Stormshale.

You rat. Leonora's voice strained with regret and frustration in her mind.

"Rat," Dice murmured to no one, thinking about that sinking feeling she experienced when hanging above the thrashing waves. The voice came a bit louder now, only promising to quiet once she closed her eyes to welcome sleep.

CHAPTER TWO

A bedraggled messenger arrived at the foot of the gate a little after sunset. Mud obscured the colors of his tunic; if one of the archers had not recognized him, an arrow might have found its new home in his chest. The call went up, commanding the archers to relax their bows, and the cold metal of the gate moaned in obedience as the chains began to turn.

The drawbridge lowered, and the messenger slipped beneath the still-rising iron gate beyond. He wasted no time, scuttling like the hard-shelled beetles found throughout the castle. Knowing the way through the winding, torchlit halls of Carn-Duhl perfectly well, he came upon the knights guarding the throne room like a phantom, and they observed him for only a moment before shoving the doors open.

On the opposite end of the hall stood a roaring fire in a hearth large enough to burn a man alive. Favorites of the king wandered mindlessly around the room, their gowns or tunics pressed and simple in the manner of Esmarin threads, the layers offering protection from the cold but the fabric too nice to survive mud or rain. Upon a dais stood the throne, its iron and wood molded into the shape of a tree split by lightning. In its shadow, sitting upon a simple wooden chair, was the advisor left as steward in the king's absence. He picked underneath his fingernails, half-lidded gaze watching the messenger's quick approach.

Watching him approach the steward, the court flittered to their seats. They postured themselves along the edges of the throne room, conversations dying in their throats. Wringing their hands, their eyes bounced around the candlelit room. Tension hung so thickly in the air that not a word passed their thin-lipped mouths. They watch in rapture as the messenger bowed at the waist to whisper his message into the steward's ear.

"The gods do not allow peace for long, it seems." He murmured, the words solid despite the color draining from his features. The messenger blinked, knowing that such a comment was treasonous, but did not argue.

Straightening, the messenger gave a single proclamation loud enough for the rest of the company to hear: "His Worship requests his son and Her Worship, the Beloved Queen, to be ready to meet him upon his arrival."

With a deep swallow, the young man concealed his worry, a flicker of disgust behind his eyes. Quirking his jaw and giving a single nod, the steward rose from his seat. Hands disappearing into the sleeves of his robe, he stepped off of the dais and approached the middle of the room. He seemed overcome with thought, taking a moment before he called a pair of footmen hidden in the shadows.

"Ready the young prince." They scurried off, and he addressed the court. "You will show *great* joy in the presence of your *great* King, and will welcome him home like a mother welcomes her child into her bosom."

His words gave them something to hold on to in their uncertainty, despite the angry, desperate cadence of his voice. Fluttering dripped through the air as ruffled skirts adjusted in their shallow seats. People rolled their shoulders as if preparing for an altercation rather than greeting their king. Their eyes settled on the closed door to the throne room, bodies alight with anxiety as the fire created monstrous shadows along the walls. It would be some hours before the king returned to Carn-Duhl, but there they would stay in fearful obedience.

Protected by the safety of stone, the castle's main and lower baileys had gardens, courtyards, stables, and roofs made of heavy clay shingles. Carn-Duhl morphed outward from the inland side of a solitary mountain like a disembodied hand digging through the stone. Lording over the city, it continued deeper into the craig, hiding away lightless grand halls and the private rooms of the king and his courtiers.

Beyond the thick, gilded doors and dreary mazes of halls and rooms, past the grand courtyard and hefty bridge, a city unfurled from the edges of the surrounding wall.

People with threadbare clothing huddled together to keep warm, some homes sheltering three or four families. Displacement followed the marsh's overtaking of the fields, its water thick and unyielding in its approach from the sea. All of Esmar suffered this extreme shift of earth, of solid ground turning to uneven wetland underfoot. Parts of the country sat wholly severed from one another because of widening rivers and streams, the narrow strips of land between them like dangerous bridges with no guarantee of a safe crossing. The king held on to these spits of mud with a fast grip, unforgiving towards nature's claim on what he considered his birthright. But rule must remain, and the small towns and villages separated from Carn-Duhl appointed councilmen to stand as leaders for their isolated communities outside of the king's reach.

One such city, overrun with descendants of the ancient Kahun, dared to appoint a monarch. Such defiance refused to be brushed aside like the tiny council members made up of sheepherders and farmers. For one to claim any right in the ruling of Esmar alone was treason, but the fact that this delegate came from the blood of the druids who cursed King Einar's family was another creature entirely.

It was a beast that claimed every drop of the king's attention, more than the sinking farms, and it had been worthy of a full battalion.

When the people of Farstone spied the messenger running deliriously fast towards the castle gates, they peeled themselves away from their fires to stand shivering in their doorways. No man would be caught ignoring the return of King Einar, son of Mycin, no matter the weather or one's ailments. If they could fill their lungs with breath, then they were expected to use that breath to welcome their fearsome ruler.

Hills overrun with more marsh than farmland turned a purple-gray as the sun made its way below the horizon. Backlit by their fires, the people of Farstone stood as inky, flickering shadows. Crooked noses and withered gazes appeared more inset on ancient faces. Even the children, cheeks round with youth and eyes sullen with despair, looked wicked underneath the cover of restless shadows. Nothing more than expectation held these slivers of people upright, for their animalistic need to survive outweighed their desire to fall victim to hunger and cold and be rid of this world altogether.

Far away, lights climbed over the hills. Madness possessed any creature that lead a battalion through the marshlands in such weak light, but Einar cared for nothing outside his desires. If he wished to be within the castle walls before the deepest hours of the night, then it happened. Neither the council of his closest advisor nor the wisdom of his esteemed general had the power to change his mind.

The people of Farstone watched as the lights grew closer. Some winked out, harboring the fate of their bearer through the darkness and into the city without uttering a word. Marshland claimed a body as quickly as a sigh, the wet ground giving away suddenly to deep water. It took the longer part of two hours for the battalion to arrive on the edges of the castle-city, their faces obscured by shame. Whatever crimes Einar forced them to commit under his reign hung over the knights like a mourning shroud, their guilt as palpable as stone.

Leading the procession on a great warhorse towered their king. Upon his head sat chain mail, shimmering beneath his crown in the scattered firelight. The people cried out their blessings in broken voices, rumbling like weary crows croaking with thirst and fear. On either side of the king rode his general and advisor, both on simpler steeds and wearing traveling armor. Pelagios, the general, gave a relaxed appearance in his saddle, the weathered face beneath his helmet almost entirely hidden by shadow. Every other moment, a flicker of the fire exposed his bearded, marred features.

The nervous glance to the iron-barred cage that followed showed his true discomfort. Pulled by exhausted horses, the wheels ground in the mud in protest. The cage was large enough for only the single occupant within, and miraculously survived the trek through marshland.

Chained to a hook in the floor kneeled a young man with reddish hair like blood in the minimal light. Upon his capture, Einar ordered him to be stripped of any clothing, an insult to the time where the Kahun roamed Greater Syvon in little more than bolts of calfskin to cover their intimates. In the cool air, his sunburned body shivered, yet even in his embarrassing state pride radiated from the cell. The shadows bent their knees to him, wholly and mournful. Unobscured by the darkness, black ink riddled his body, the birth-language of Esmar recalling a time before kings.

Even with his head bowed, the figure commanded respect.

Pelagios' gaze settled upon the accompanying advisor, Damalis. Neither of them let out an easy breath, not until the king dipped his chin in a silent decree.

Pelagios straightened his posture in the saddle. Lifting one hand, he let out a booming call: "Release!"

The knights took their time ambling towards their firelit homes. No sounds of happiness rang through the air when mothers welcomed back their dirty, tired children—nor was there a single note of mourning when the arms of mothers and fathers remained empty. Still, they lingered in their doorways, fatherless children and childless fathers ever faithful to their king.

Einar lifted his bearded chin, the gray streaks in his mane of russet brown like threads of silver. The warhorse stomped its path through the muck of the city streets, its massive nostrils huffing out globs of liquid. Though it ate better than most people, the beast was sick. It struggled to carry Einar to the gate, its mud-covered legs shaking. The king ran the horse ragged in their return to the castle before night fell, and many of the other horses suffered the same exhaustion. Somehow, it endured the long journey, blood-smeared armor clanging as its muscles twitched viciously underneath.

Not a soul in Farstone breathed with relief in their lungs until the king's procession disappeared behind the rising drawbridge, the clanking of the lowered iron gate echoing within.

Though the castle once glimmered as the pride of the Esmarin peoples in the days before Einar's brethren took it, Carn-Duhl's receiving courtyard reflected the rooms within. Cracks as wide as a finger spiderwebbed across the floor, their depths varying, unknown. Each scar disrupted the surface of an intricate mosaic made of pure obsidian, faded paints, and dusty red stone. In the center of the piece sat a figure upon a rearing horse, engraved lines of tarnished gold paint spilling outward in a spiral from their head. Their clothing was of the old fashion, no more than a simple unisex gown with a studded belt, and in the hands raised above their head sat the sheath of a great sword. At their feet were studded flowers, petals made from marble and green aventurine. In a perfect circle, coiling outwards like the rings of a great tree, sat hundreds of other images depicting scenes that ranged in severity, from a gory childbirth by the sea to a man standing in a window above crashing waves.

Grandness echoed out of its brokenness, a beacon of something that promised to withstand the reign of any king. It was there before Einar's time, and so it would remain long after.

Pelagios avoided looking at the figures in the stone as he dismounted. All of the faces gazed up at him with looks of admonishment, sharp and cruel. The child within Pelagios wanted to beg them for forgiveness. The adult wondered what could offer such a blessing as washing his soul anew after all his time as the king's general.

Servants peeled themselves from the shadows, grasping the reigns of the horses to guide them towards a massive archway leading to the covered stables. The cart drawing the iron cage wheeled into the courtyard with a sinister groan. Sitting still, head bowed, the naked figure did not lift his gaze to observe his new surroundings. The tired horses were unhitched from the cart as four knights flanked the cage, swords eager at their hips.

Pelagios' horse went to the stables eagerly, as did Damalis' steed, but the warhorse remained where it stood on shaking hooves. The servant's glance widened as it flicked back and forth between the unruly beast and its master, who stood immobile above the figure at the center of the mural. The servant desperately tried once more to get the beast to move, but it shook its head, ripping the reigns from his grasp. The leather straps landed with a loud enough *thud* to bring Einar out of his stupor.

Slowly, the king turned his face to the servant. A distance settled over his features, a stare so void of compassion that it made the very concept of sin feel ashamed. Pelagios, unwilling to lift a hand to save the meager life of a servant, watched the king step closer. His coat of arms groaned with every move, the long cape attached to his shoulders by iron brooches hushing over the broken stone as he took graceful steps forward. Pelagios equally feared and admired the elegant way Einar walked, even if it was the stalk of a hunter toward its next kill.

Einar's fingers wrapped neatly around the leather grip of his great sword. In one step he unsheathed the mighty blade and plunged it through the folded armor of the warhorse, piercing it in the heart. Those witness to this act stood immobile in only mild shock. Fear kept them steady, for as the great sword was drawn out of the horse and the king spun on his heel to face his company, a spray of blood followed.

Pelagios held fast to his belt as it hit his shin, thumbs hooked in its loops in a faux posture of relaxation. With only a sigh, Damalis adjusted his own robes, looking away when the horse collapsed with a resounding *clang* onto the courtyard floor.

Silence filled the room, no one daring to speak before the king. Einar's gauntlet held fast to the weapon, its edge scraping across the stone ground as he walked back to the center of the courtyard. Every eye trained on the blood glistening on the edge of the blade. Servants quickly disregarded the horses that pulled the iron cage to help their companion drag the warhorse out of the courtyard and into the stables. A pool of blood seeped into the crevices of the mosaic, outlining every panel, every crack. Despite himself, Pelagios' eyes dropped slowly to the image of the gory birth, stomach turning as the horse's blood surrounded the twisted face of the woman. Her eyes sought him out, holding his gaze before she was swallowed in blood.

"That *beast*," Einar lifted his tired blade to point at the receding group of servants, "was not fit for a king. Who allowed such a monster into battle? Who allowed such a creature to carry their master?"

King Einar turned about the room, his dark, wide eyes surveying every face, burning their features into his mind.

With a certain bravery Pelagios admired, Damalis replied. "My Esteemed General, it is your horse master who provides the steeds to be sent into battle. This horse specifically was a gift from House Turrant on the eve of your naming day."

"House *Turrant*." The word came out of Einar's mouth on a stream of spittle. "Of course. I should have known." At his feet, the blood of the horse cascaded like a gentle bolt of silk around the edges of his cape. The red took hold of the fabric, spreading upward like the bare branches of a tree.

Einar did not notice or did not care. Tossing his great sword unceremoniously to the ground, he unclasped his belt and sheath. The items followed the weapon, and without another word, the king vanished into the inner chamber.

"Bring the speck of shit," he commanded to Pelagios over his shoulder before the shadows laid claim to his body.

The knights guarding the young man did not need the general to repeat the order. Iron scraping against iron filled the room as they drew their swords and aimed at their captive, one knight unlatching the door and swinging it wide. Even when his shoulders were grabbed and he was yanked out of the cage, the young man did not lift his head in defiance, nor drop his shoulders in defeat. Pelagios admired the youth's strength of will, though his admiration quickly turned sour as he imagined what the king might have planned.

"There is no House Turrant."

Pelagios glanced over to the advisor, whose steady eyes remained on the massive pool of blood. "It doesn't matter, I think, either way. He'll forget come morning that he ever possessed such a beautiful creature."

Damalis made a croak in his throat as a response. The man was not as old as Pelagios, who sat beside Einar's father, but flecks of gray turned his blond hair ashen. Unlike the general, who was entirely gray and no longer boasted of his strength like in his youth, Damalis passed for no more than forty.

"That was wise," Pelagios added as an afterthought. "The horse master is a decent man."

The advisor lifted a shoulder in dismissal. "There's no need for another senseless murder of someone who is actually of use to us. With His Majesty's insistence on applying pressure to the borders of *both* Sovil and Thantis, we cannot lose another man to a petty annoyance."

Petty annoyance, thought Pelagios, *or madness?*

They all knew the rumors spreading like the marsh sickness throughout the country. Unsurprisingly, some of them began within Einar's own court. It was expected, since the king's health had been declining for years and it was becoming harder to determine whether his actions were out of cruelty, or confusion. Pelagios imagined that every country in

Greater Syvon heard the tale of the Mad King, and though it was not a term he cared for Pelagios knew that, to outsiders, Einar indeed appeared senseless. He was the stuff of nightmares, and Pelagios stood as nothing more than a calloused old man pretending he could keep the shadows at bay.

Mycin failed to make it to his fortieth name day before the confusion and fear swallowed his mind entirely. By then, Einar already did exactly what was expected by killing each of his seven brothers and laying claim to the throne as the final, legitimate heir. Einar surpassed his father's reign by a decade, and Pelagios fell in line behind his king, as was his duty and promise to Esmar but more to keep himself alive. The history of Esmar's kings was rich with the blood of their own court, and Einar, like his father before him, intended to use his power to keep tradition.

Now, Pelagios' hands were stained with so much blood that even the marrow of his bones ran crimson.

"Lord General."

Damalis' voice sounded impatient. A servant appeared without Pelagios noticing, scrubbing the horse's blood on his hands and knees. The cage stood empty, the prisoner long been escorted into the belly of Carn-Duhl. How much time passed with him standing there?

The old man swallowed hard. Gaze refocusing, he stared at the mosaic's panel of a man standing on some sort of platform high in a tower, blue pebbles depicting a thrashing sea at his feet. The figures arms were outstretched, the stony gaze empty.

An uneasy feeling stirred deep in Pelagios' belly, a twist of knowing, of fear. With a glance up to Damalis, he wondered if the king's favorite advisor meant to say something about his strange behavior to Einar.

"It is best we join the others." Damalis' eyes remained steady. Pelagios wanted to ask how the younger man stood so calmly—and immediately felt ashamed of his weak belly. Pelagios felt soft in his age.

Pelagios removed his helmet as he walked onward, passing the advisor and disappearing with a fixed look of agitation into the darkness.

Strands of silver and gray hung in the air. Einar swiped away the cobwebs with a restless hand that he dropped to his side, shaking out his fingers.

Twinges of fire raced down his arm. He felt alight, consumed by flames. Around his body, the air shivered with nothingness, with less than nothingness, with darkness unending. Small stars glittered in this powerful void, casting a bit of warmth on Einar's face when he turned toward its light. Flames of golden orange echoed a song, the deep hum of something ancient that called out to Einar's soul.

He did not touch the fire, but his hand burned with radiating heat.

Murmured voices pulled the king's eye away from the dancing torchlight. Hallways branched out on either side and in front of him. Behind was only darkness, miles of it between himself and the next torch. A yellow dot twinkled there in the emptiness, and when Einar turned around again the paths at his feet multiplied in number. His armor glowed, reflecting the torchlight that embedded itself into the metal of his breastplate. It swirled around, a snake writhing in its nest. With a humming, high-pitched song the snake opened its mouth, alighting the path to Einar's right. The other paths faded as he walked, his armor aglow.

Looking at his hand, he saw flames licking at the skin. More light spilled out from his fingers as the golden tendrils made his soft flesh bubble and split. Muscle unraveled to reveal the white bone of his fingers, fat and skin dripping like wax onto the floor.

"My Lord King."

The torch in Einar's grasp wavered in the air as he turned to face the stranger concealed by darkness. After a moment, the man stepped into the torchlight and Einar recognized the stranger as Damalis. The man wore his traveling armor over the steely blue of his advisory robes. Muddied boots made gentle steps as the advisor approached him gingerly.

"My Lord King," Damalis repeated, bowing lightly at the waist. "Your court eagerly awaits your presence."

"Of course. I am their king."

Damalis inclined his head in reverence.

I am their king. Einar nodded, walking around Damalis with a hand on the stony wall for purchase. Great mosaics rose high above them, the roughly hewn pieces of the stone tableaus scraping against his calloused fingertips. Torches sat in the sconces, spaced to illuminate the worn paths that branched out in four directions from the center of the antechamber. The one from which Damalis materialized echoed with the sound of clinking metals that scraped slowly into low, guttural moaning.

A pale foot, its toes blackened with rot, stepped out of the shadows. Its slim ankle was concealed by layers of fine silks that glowed and shimmered in the torchlight. Barely stepping out of the dark hall, Einar shifted away from the partly concealed figure to face Damalis.

The advisor said nothing, his brow furrowed. Einar understood something was wrong about the advisor's unawareness of the rotting figure, but could not state what it was. A ball of pitch stuck to the insides of Einar's throat as the quiet sifting of gentle movement stopped directly behind him.

Coolness broke through the shield of his armor like a frost climbing up the heavy fabric of his cape.

With his hands lifting from his side, Damalis folded together his fingers. He inclined his head once more. "Our time is yours, my King."

Einar sensed the chilly breath of the creature kiss his neck, a cold finger across his skin. The air stirred with motion, and he envisioned the figure reaching forward, branching the space between them, curling into the hair at the nape of his neck in admiration for the tender ringlets.

"Let us continue, Damalis."

Damalis stepped aside and opened his arm for the king to pass first. The king moved on as though the chill was not hanging like an inebriated hum over his limbs. Deep darkness expanded on either side, and the halls wound further into the crag. Damalis walked with an even pace, the creature shuffling behind their small procession, concealed within the shadows.

Einar continued to hear its whispering skirts and barefoot steps on the stone floor even after he and Damalis approached the doors to the throne room.

Upon revelation of their king, the courtiers and gathered advisors stood from their low benches to clap and cheer. Their voices like an onslaught of carnage, Einar's face twisted first in a manner of disapproval. It was too much, too loud, the shadows heavy with incense and body odor.

They cheered louder, unfaltering, as he stepped forward into the middle of the room and approached his throne. Pelagios stood to the left of the dais, his eyes fixed on a kneeling, naked man guarded by four knights.

Anger stirred in Einar's belly, the inky language dancing across the naked man's skin like silk caught in the breeze. The knights did not notice the quivering symbols, nor did the general, and as Einar took his seat upon his throne his eyes remained transfixed on the vision. A hissing of steam filled his ears, moisture clouding around the false king as though the languages inked on his skin were so hot that they turned the water in the air to fog.

Einar fisted his fingers on the armrest of the throne, the groaning of metal scratching the surface of his mind. Kahun magic controlled the elements. Was this fool daring to cast in such a public setting? Was he ready to condemn himself so freely?

With a start, something leapt onto Einar's lap with a giggle. Hair like pitch shimmered in an inky cloud around the boy's head, curling above his ears and across his forehead. A reflection of Einar's eyes gazed up at him in admiration, but it was the queen's smile that brightened his face.

My son. Esmar's last prince.

The emotion behind Einar's ribcage was unfathomably strong, twining itself around the edges of his heart. He forgot, for a moment, about the false king as he took the boy into his arms. The memories of the boy felt distant, mist slicing through the space between Einar's fingers. Moments passed but with every beat of his heart, panic climbed through the king's chest.

Slowly, the mist cloistering Einar's mind began to dissipate, and what he desperately sought as he held the prince winked like embers in the dark. *His tumultuous and lengthy birth, Einar showering the queen with rubies like the droplets of blood on the birthing sheets, and then, finally, a name.*

"Theon." Einar let a hand rest on the boy's head. Blinking, he saw his fingers covered in metal and dirtied with blood, having forgotten he was dressed in riding armor.

Staring not into Theon's eyes but at the dried flecks of brown, he asked, "Where is your mother?"

One of the advisors stepped forward. Gaelis, balding and red-faced, cleared his throat to call attention. Bowing low, he kept his gaze on the ground. "My Lord King. The Beloved Queen is still ill, and remains in her bedchamber."

Einar's breathing shallowed. His son squirmed on his lap, uncomfortable sitting atop the armor. Over his head of inky curls, the king glared down at the back of the advisor's balding scalp.

"You mean to tell me that even a king's coin cannot buy decent healers?"

A spider dropped into Theon's hair. It burrowed down into the boy's scalp before Einar chanced brushing it away.

Gaelis kept himself prostrate. Little beads of moisture collected on the shiny part of his skull as he took a moment to answer. They glistened like crystals, hitting the stone floor with gentle clacks.

"My Lord King, I—the Beloved Queen is quite ill."

Along the edges of the throne room, the courtiers, officials, and other advisors kept their steady gazes on the sweating advisor. Through the slits of windows at the highest point of the surrounding walls, a half-moon winked in and out behind plum-colored clouds. Silver light eased over the room, plunging half into a ghoulish pallor as it collided with firelight. Armor amplified its sheen, a bolt of silver slicing across Einar's angular chin and brow.

Of all his brothers, he had been the handsomest. Of all his brothers, he had been the only one brave enough to raise a sword to his own kin.

Theon protested as his father lifted him from his lap, setting him gently down in front of Pelagios. The old general clasped the prince's shoulder when he lurched after Einar—and the lad gave Pelagios a disturbingly murderous glare. Theon did not inherit his mother's temperament, and was familiar with abusing the castle staff.

Einar felt glad that Pelagios could be there for Theon, just as the old general had been there for him. He looked back at his son with a grin of assurance before the smile turned wickedly towards the advisor.

Gaelis did not dare lift his head. When Einar's metallic boot halted beneath his nose, the advisor fixated on the warped reflection of his face. Sweat dolloped the metal as he began to shake, streaking through the mud and gore.

Einar clasped his hands before him, the metal clanking together like a death bell. The diamond sweat clinked against the metal of his boot. *Plink, plink.*

"I minded your kingdom in your absence, Lord King." The advisor's voice warbled. "I am your servant. I do what you ask—"

"I asked you to fetch your queen."

Silence.

Every word uttered between the king and advisor jumped across the stone, filling the room.

If any eyes dared to break from Einar, they would have seen the face of the captive for the first time since he was stripped and shackled. Eyes like golden coins glinted in the torchlight, shimmering, intent on the king and the advisor. A firm, strong nose with a slight hook on the end sat between them, and his cracked, thirsty lips were pulled into a thin line of dissatisfaction.

Einar felt the weight of many things, some of which he could not name. He felt the heaviness before a storm, the chill before the first snowfall. Most of his life bore the weight of his father's legacy, the heft of the crown upon his brow. *He* was heaviness itself. Einar was the shade, the slivers of moonlight, the clouds that concealed and created both. This heaviness—of his head, of his armor, of his crown—made him tired. It was his father's weariness, and his father's-father's weariness, all congealing inside his chest. Some days, he thought himself more cursed than cruel, too exhausted to differentiate between the two outside of the moments where gore flickered across his receding memory and he wondered, *what sort of man could do such a thing*.

Einar grew weary by staring down at the sweaty, balding head of a man whose face he did not care to remember. He kept looking down, feeling the pressure of the world and the sins of his father pushing on his mind. He felt the eyes of those around him, his loyal subjects, and the eyes of his son. If the queen had been well enough, he knew he would feel the weight of her gaze, too.

As soft as it was when it fell to him, Einar felt her beseeching stare more than any other.

He fought against this weight as he lifted his folded hands upward, driving his gauntlets down into the soft skin of the man's neck.

The advisor stumbled at the initial strike, shocked, remaining folded either out of fear or pain. Einar lifted his hands overhead once more, dealing another blow against the back of the man's skull.

All was silent. Einar did not grunt or growl, and the court watched with their bellies flipping like waves. Only the sound of metal striking flesh echoed through the room as the advisor received each striking blow until he collapsed before the king.

Einar heard the hush of silks across the stone floor, though the door remained closed. Such a barrier was not enough to dissuade the rotting body of the woman as she lurched towards the show of murder, a string pulling taunt and dragging like to like. She wore layers of fabric arranged in the winter fashion, moths and other creatures destroying what might have been beautiful.

Stopping before a courtier, she gaze up at Einar but her face was wrong. Its shape was smooth and featureless, no indentations for her eyes or hills for lips or cheeks. It stared up at him nonetheless, eyes that were not eyes watching Einar closely.

After the advisor hit the floor, a groan escaped him. Einar took this painful sound as an act of defiance. He did not strike with his fists for the final blow but with the spur attached to his heel. Dark flecks of his warhorse's blood stained the barb, and there was a gurgling sound when Einar slammed it down. A vein in the advisor's throat opened, much like the warhorse from before, and blood pooled at the foot of the dais.

The man's body was carried out before the women of the court retrieved the handkerchiefs in their sleeves. Sickly sweet smells hit the air as they covered their faces with the perfumed cloths, hiding the iron tang of blood from their delicate noses.

Einar opened his arms, and Theon went running. A smiling, joyous look flowed out of the king's face, a stark contrast to the empty gaze he possessed when killing the advisor.

"Pelagios."

The general stepped forward, a perfect figure of detachment.

A sharp edge slid into Einar's gaze. "Bring it forward."

Pelagios obeyed. Stepping into the throng of knights who stood around the young man, he gripped the muscular bare shoulder. Moving with a slight limp, the man stumbled as Pelagios forced him to the feet of the king. Einar took his seat on the throne, wrapping a gentle arm around Theon's waist to hold him close.

"Look at him, my boy." The king inclined his head to the captive as if he were showing off a boar he killed in the hunt. His ink no long stirred across the surface of his skin, but now gold rivers of tears fell from the Kahun's eyes. The gilded tears dripped onto the floor, turning into coins with a gentle *clink*.

Theon glared, something innocent bouncing around in his gaze. "Why does he have paintings on his arms, Papa?"

"A wise question!" Einar barked toward the room. The court scrambled into agreeance, their high-pitched shouts like the cawing of birds.

They fell immediately silent as their king continued. His voice, to them, was gentle as he told his story, a father murmuring tales to all his little children.

The rotten woman turned, shuffling away, no longer interested. Einar spoke, his eyes trained on the wet footprints she left behind before she slid through the wall.

"A long time ago, people like *him* roamed Esmar with no real king, no real cities." He gazed down at his son and wiggled a finger against his ribcage, teasing a laugh from Theon. "Your great-great-great-grandfather, the Ironclad King Germain, conquered them. He gave them homes and fields and bread and wine and *true* gods, yet they refused to honor the hands that fed them. They kept up their blasphemous altars to the sky, the earth, and the ocean. It was *Germain* who toppled them and gave them the great Father and Mother, and their son Hecleon. Our lovely castle was once their temple, but your ancestors reclaimed it for a greater purpose—to be the seat of kings."

Theon's eyes lit up, bright with rapture. Another spider, then another, dropped onto the child's face. One scurried across his open eyes while Einar bat away the other, but it disappeared into Theon's hair.

"But all great kings fall," Einar nodded after a moment. "The Kahun used magic, calling up beasts in the earth. Their magic is what killed the Ironclad, and his son, and his son's son. It is what killed your grandfather."

In a flash of hatred, the prince whipped around to face the man kneeling on the stone. Screeching, his pitch voice grated out, "Murderer!"

Pride swelled in Einar's belly as he barked a laugh, the court screeching in their seats. All he saw in the world of ember-colored light and silver moonbeams was the round face of his son, the heir of Esmar, ready to leap out of his protective embrace with fury. Einar remembered this first spark of hatred for those who wished to steal his crown, recalling how his father stoked the embers. Within him now blazed an unrelenting fire, one he intended to stoke in his only son.

"They said this monster is the son of the old Kahun, and the true king, but that is treason. *You* are the son of the *true* kings of Esmar."

His next words came out like a prayer to the shadows. Einar leaned in, whispering into the boy's hair. "What do we do with murderers, my son?"

Theon's voice sounded resolute. "Kill them."

The king's heartbeat quickened. "And heretics?"

"Kill them. Kill *him*."

Einar grinned. "Pelagios, my father's most trusted general—give me your dagger."

Without delay, the general unsheathed his blade and passed it hilt-first to the king. But when Einar shook his head, Pelagios' confusion eked out onto his features.

In a flurry of annoyance, Einar motioned to his son. "Give it to the boy, Pelagios. Let him know what it's like to carry true steel."

Pelagios was an obedient man, no more than a beat lapsing between the order and the action. The general carefully extended the weapon to the child, bobbing his head in respect for his prince.

Reverence filled the child's gaze as he took the blade from Pelagios. Intricate metals twisted around the hilt in the pattern of curling tentacles, an ode to the sea villages where Pelagios' ancestors lived in a time long forgotten. Despite this, the blade looked fresh and sharp, glinting the firelight onto Theon's eager gaze.

"Go on." Einar urged when the prince's gaze flicked to his father, uncertain. "Go on. You're nearly ten. I killed two men already by that age. The deaths of those men made *me* a man. Go on," Einar ushered once more. "It is time for you to become a man now."

CHAPTER THREE

Pelagios' gaze met Damalis' over the head of the king, thinking about what the advisor said only moments ago in the receiving courtyard. Though the man attempted to avoid a senseless death, senseless death still found them. Perhaps it was inescapable within these walls, which ran red through centuries of war. Maybe in the heat of madness, there was some truth to Einar's paranoia. Carn-Duhl, of all places, seemed the breeding ground for curses and misfortune.

Pelagios wished he knew of the mind better than he did the sword, for he was as unequipped with Einar as he had been when standing next to Mycin.

Sometimes, it felt easier to call it all a curse—and who was the old general to say it was not? Feeding Einar's paranoia with every agreeable nod left behind the acrid twinge of guilt in Pelagios' chest, but what could he do? Einar's mind was receding from the solid world, but his body was that of a highly skilled warrior. It took only a few beatings of his fist to kill the advisor, and Pelagios saw men cleaved nearly in half with one strike of the king's great sword. And liquid medications concocted secretly, dispelled into Einar's wine at dinner, calmed him enough for sleep but radicalized his hallucinations.

It was exhausting, the charade of practicality amidst a sinking country.

The old man realized with a start that cracks ran across the surface of his face, revealing that his indifference was a façade as the prince stepped forward with his ancestral blade. Quickly, the general painted his features with a look of interest and respect for young Theon.

The captive, too, kept his eye on the prince, but it was not fear or anger that marred his features.

A tear escaped the Kahun's golden eye, then another.

"What sort of king shows such weakness at his death?" Einar shouted, laughing with insult. Dark shadows along the wall joined him, their pearl teeth glinting in the dark. A thousand gnashing monsters sat hungry for the man's blood.

Pelagios knew why the Kahun cried. Innocence held a knife in its firm grasp, a plague generations old worming into its skin like maggots feasting on putrid flesh. Perhaps young Theon was infected long ago. Perhaps he was ill since birth. But the prince was doomed to die in the same way as his ancestors—and no one except the king had any right to stop the rotting inevitable.

The Kahun did not raise his hands to stop the child, despite his shackled forearm alone carrying enough weight force the prince to the ground in an instant.

Pelagios glanced to the floor when Theon raised the blade.

A wet, solid sound broke the intense silence, and a gentle sob escaped the captive king.

Another heavy thud as the blade cracked bone.

Another.

Another.

Pelagios wanted to drink himself numb the rest of the night, but Damalis sent for him well into morning hours. Having been able to get a few pints into his belly, the old general stumbled through the corridors of the official rooms in a hazy cloud. Plainclothes adorned his fit form, simple but still lush enough to feed any peasant in Farstone for an entire year. The blood which purchased such finery tinged the air with iron, making Pelagios' stomach roil as he thought of how many people he killed during his time serving Einar.

Enough to afford his velvet slacks and cotton shirts without batting an eye at the price.

What did the blood of a woman equal? Maybe a brooch, or a nice cloak. What of a child, or a man? An entire family? Pelagios envisioned a wardrobe of families in his private rooms, and countless perfectly preserved specimens in the surrounding marshlands.

Pelagios stayed to watch the Kahun's body, bleeding and twitching, be hauled away by six men. Though the general did not take his life, it was *his* blade that stole those final breaths. While Theon ran into the arms of his father in celebration at his first murder, and Einar lifted him onto his armored hip and disappeared into the furthest halls, Pelagios stayed. Courtiers filtered out of the room, the king and prince long since vanishing into their chambers to console the queen on her sickbed. Safe for the evening, they dispersed into their own rooms, not bothering to glance in Pelagios' direction.

All he could feel was his family's blade in his grasp, darkly shining with blood. Soon, only the knights who guarded the chambers stood with their Lord General in trained silence. Some time passed before Pelagios wanted a drink, the urge strong enough to rip him away from the bloodstain on the floor as a servant appeared from the shadows to clean it.

During their months of travel alongside the king, Pelagios and Damalis conspired, sharing words that might kill them if any other ears heard. It was Damalis who confided in the old general first about the true state of Einar's mind. Evidence of his receding awareness as he chased some intangible curse only served as proof of how little time the king truly had. They had hoped that upon arrival at Carn-Duhl, Einar's mind might find ease in the familiar.

Pelagios felt his throat grow thick with shame. For years, he stood at the wayside and watched his kings deteriorate. Unable to do more than obey every order in the hopes that it relieved some part of Einar's mind, he chipped away at his own soul in some vain attempt to save another's.

Stumbling, Pelagios pressed a calloused hand against the stone wall. When did those dark spots and rivets of veins appear? Oftentimes, Pelagios forgot his age until he caught his reflection in the silverware, or noted the texture of his hands when they passed in front of his face. How many people did those hands strangle or beat? How many were ordered to die by Pelagios' blade simply because they stumbled upon their king in a foul mood?

The ale in his stomach soured for a moment before reason sought him out in the dark. He was a *lord* general of great esteem, with years of weathered experience under his belt. Throughout the decades, he gave uncountable orders to children only a little older than Theon, so why did he hide away his family's blade tonight? Why did the shame and guilt accumulate *now*, and not in his youth, or a time where he might risk change?

The sound of the blade breaking the young man's collarbone slid into Pelagios' ears. Darkness, still and bated, hung around him. A sconce sat lit some paces away, but between it and the one Pelagios stood beneath drifted an expanse of black pitch. He blinked away the haze in his vision, glaring deeply into that stretch of dark that separated him from the next torch.

As if any monster within it might fear him, Pelagios grimaced.

Behind him crackled the sound of splintering bone. It was the same sound his family's blade made when it broke the neck of the false king.

Spinning to face it, Pelagios unsheathed the short sword at his waist, heartbeat in his throat.

"Come to me, coward!" His voice boomed out into the corridor, the echo dancing further and further until it faded into nothing. Anyone daring to sneak up on the lord general was indeed foolish, for he was second only to the king in swordsmanship. There yet proved to be anyone in Esmar who outmaneuvered him in combat.

Even then, fear gripped his wrists and made the sword heavy. Pelagios' blood rushed into his head, ears ringing slightly with adrenaline. Did the drink and the excitement make him see rotten black toes pushing forward into the dusk of the torchlight?

Pelagios blinked, forcing away the sound of rustling silks.

"My Lord—"

In a flurry of barely discernable movement, Pelagios swung his narrow blade around, pressing it against the speaker's neck. Yet, it was not a thief or cruel specter but one of Damalis' errand boys.

The young man trembled, his soft hands lifted in submission. Blue eyes the color of stormy waters flicked down to gaze at the blade in Pelagios' grip.

After a beat of awkwardness, the general dropped the sword, returning it to the sheath. Nothing was said by manner of apology, the man dipping his head as he asked the general to follow him swiftly into the head advisor's chambers.

The torchlight was not so dingy, nor the space between the sconces so dark as Pelagios followed the man through the winding spaces. Great mosaics of complicated stonework spread the length of entire walls, climbing upwards towards a hidden ceiling. The young man, wearing Damalis' house colors of soft orange and white, wove through the corridors with practiced grace. Upon reaching the door to the head advisor's private rooms, the man did not enter after Pelagios but, bowing deeply, disappeared down the corridor.

Beyond, Damalis' receiving room stood with a vast table at its center, highbacked and padded chairs encircling its shining wood. Other advisors loitered around the room, helping themselves to a long shelf of wines and heavy clay vases of dark alcohol that tinged the air with a syrupy aroma. Simple tapestries, thick as carpet, hung on every wall save the one which led into Damalis' bedroom and bath.

No one other than Damalis turned to greet him with a nod. The general shifted on his feet, ambling closer to the drinking and glasses alongside an assortment of tiny wedge cheeses and buttered rolls. Carn-Duhl's stores would last for years, but no wheat or wine would touch the lips of the starving villagers in Farstone.

"Friends," ushered Damalis, and suddenly every advisor shifted into a chair around the table. When Pelagios stood alone, the head advisor nodded to the empty one at his left—one that belonged to a now dead advisor, and seemed a death sentence in itself.

"Welcome, Sir Lord General Pelagios Yan of the Fishmen Gales." Damalis motioned once more to the chair. "Please, sit so we may begin."

An air of discretion drifted into the room, stifling with mystery. Pelagios took his time pouring a drink—something that no one protested, even at his lengthy drought—before sauntering over to the empty chair.

Confusion addled his mind. The general sat in on plenty of meetings before, though none within the advisor's private chambers. A not so small part of himself wondered if the king knew of this, while an even larger part scowled. Every advisor and member of the court owned a handful of servants for the sole reason of observing others, and Pelagios possessed a fair share of his own eyes. How had *this* evaded *him*?

The advisors observed him, waiting as Pelagios rested the cup on the table and sat.

As soon as his satin-covered rear touched the bench, Damalis faced the group. "We are here to honor Gaelis."

Heads tilted towards the candles in reverence. Remembering the sound of metal striking against flesh, the general bowed his head in muted respect.

After the moment of silence, Damalis continued in a solemn voice. "We are here to speak on the matter of the marsh sickness." He placed his palms face-down on the table. In the center of the table sat a grand candelabra, the only light source in the room. "We are here to discuss the event of the murder of the last Kahun king."

Pelagios' face did little to hide his surprise. As the general looked about the room, there was not a single raised eyebrow or offended grimace. Men and women, advisors to the crown, nodded solemnly, their faces lit from underneath by candlelight. It appeared that only Pelagios felt his equilibrium shifting to another continent.

"What is the meaning of this?"

Twelve pairs of eyes slid to him. A woman sitting across from Damalis answered, folding her ebony hands on top of the table. Her kinky hair was twisted in the elegant but formal style of court, the candlelight shimmering in the gold clasps that held the intricate braids together. Strands of silver like tiny rivers struck through them, her age marked by thin crinkles between her brows.

"This is a *meeting*, Lord General." Kana's voice sounded impatient when she spoke. She, along with a few other familiar faces, was one of the rare advisors who survived Einar's court without running away or being bludgeoned to death.

"Of course—"

"I beg forgiveness, Pelagios, for not explaining myself during our journey." Damalis interrupted before any words got too heated. "We spoke briefly about the state of King Einar's mind—of how he often makes decisions, and forgets them moments later?"

Awaiting the general's acknowledgment, Damalis did not continue until Pelagios nodded. "Some months ago, after the tragedy of the Queen's illness, King Einar enlisted a sellsword to kill the wife of Councilman Tribet in Thantis. By the blessed Mother and Father, one of my men intercepted the sellsword on the high road before he entered the marshlands."

Drink forgotten, Pelagios leaned back in his chair. Concern etched his features, brows furrowed and covering his eyes in shadow. One of his hands lifted to stroke his beard in thought as Damalis observed him.

"We narrowly avoided a war." Another advisor, a man with a thick, braided beard, pointed out. His voice rumbled like the depths of a mountain. "Certainly, one sellsword alone doesn't have the power to break through the defenses of a High Councilman, but only a fool wouldn't look to Esmar as the perpetrator. Councilman Tribet is no fool."

Damalis inclined his head towards the bearded gentleman. "Riven and I first proposed that you be informed of these meetings, Lord General, for among us you have the most wisdom when it comes to war—and how to prevent one."

"You seem to do well enough." The general mumbled a bit gruffly, his ego bruised. Still, he envisioned what a war with Thantis might be like, and every outcome meant failure for Esmar. The country was too broken, literally by the marsh sickness and politically by the king's own slipping rule. With Einar's mind drifting further down a path Pelagios could not follow, any war underneath his banner meant uncountable deaths.

Around the table, advisors waited patiently for Pelagios to digest the information. Pelagios slid his gaze to Damalis, finding the advisor already looking to him. "You want to avoid more *senseless killing*."

Everyone around the table nodded, not just Damalis.

"Then," snarled Pelagios, "why not just *kill the king*? Hm? Come now," the general spat when the advisors finally looked surprised. "You sit in the shadows at your table, discussing for who knows how long about the best path for Einar. For the country itself. Now," he leaned forward, locking eyes with each of them, "would his death be senseless?"

"No," Kana admitted with a solemn sharpness in her gaze, "but Theon's might be."

Pelagios stilled in his chair. She smiled at him, sadness in the tilt of her mouth. "What do you think happens when a king dies? His heir claims the throne. The illness that consumes Einar's mind, and the mind of his father and forefathers, will eventually claim Theon. This is truth, however awful it may be. Einar is a man afflicted but that does not make his actions excusable… As such, whatever riddles the blood of the kings of Esmar will claim Theon in time. Our assumption is that it may even be perpetuated by the sudden death of his father. Imagine that?" She shook her head, the lonesome smile still on her lips. "This illness or curse striking down a *child*. Mycin neared his fortieth year before it destroyed him—Einar may have until his sixtieth. We cannot risk a child being consumed by this madness, let alone rise to a throne he has not been taught to rule. So," she sighed, "we *cannot* kill the king."

Until then, the accompanying advisors were respectfully silent. It seemed the decision as to whether or not they let the king live was a matter not fully decided. Words flittered across the wavering candlelight, the closest thing to an argument Pelagios saw all evening. Eventually, Damalis lifted his hand. Conversation petered out until silence once again enveloped the table.

"I must agree with Kana. Allowing Theon to claim the throne after his… *eagerness* tonight means simply replacing Einar with a younger version of himself. Curse or malady, it will be strong for years before it claims Theon's faculties."

"Though we are not above killing children," Sevrit of Neighweather added from the shadows, "it is only as a last resort."

"Pelagios." Riven tilted his chin to the general, who was staring thoughtfully into the darkness until that moment. "This is much to take in. We didn't agree to admit you to these meetings simply to overwhelm you. As Damalis mentioned, your wisdom is needed to help us to prevent any more warring on behalf of some artificial curse. Though," he let out a breath, "it is not *only* your wisdom we seek."

A beat passed but that was all Pelagios needed. He was no youth, and experienced a number of covert operations in his time as lord general. "You want me to feed you information."

"You are Einar's greatest confidant. After Mycin's death, you were practically his father."

A sword plunged through Pelagios' chest, striking him down to the bone. Remembering his drink, he gripped the cup tightly and brought it to his lips, downing the contents in a single gulp. The advisors awaited his response as if this entire night were organized for him.

Pelagios ground his teeth, thinking. "If we kill both Einar and Prince Theon, we could establish a governing council like in Thantis. There are some members of the court who are relative enough to the crown that they may volley for the position to rule, but—"

Kana lifted her hand to interrupt him. "These are all things we've already considered. We—most of us—have chosen not to kill Einar or the prince not simply because of the headache that comes with establishing a new governing body, but because of his zealots."

One of the counselors *tsked.* Obviously annoyed by something Kana stated, he leaned forward in his chair to meet her gaze. "They are as mad as Einar. Carn-Duhl can withstand any number of zealots—"

"What of his followers within his own court?" Kana snapped, the twitch of her brow standing out against her professional façade. "There are young men and knights who would still fight for their king even in death. Am I wrong, Lord General?"

The eyes of the advisors snapped to him once more. In his belly, the thick syrupy drink clotted and turned. Pelagios shook his head, feeling both like he might throw up and pass out. He knew, though, it was not just the drink making him feel this way. All around him sat proof of the world as he understood it tilting off its center. Treason, which he was now an agent of, had been slinking through the halls for months—possibly years—and he suspected *nothing*.

Someone else began, but Pelagios' voice cut off their sentence. "Kana is right. Killing the royal family would result in outrage from those who worship Einar like a god. There are men who I have seen in battle gazing up at him like a Child sent by the Mother and Father. So," his fingers gripped the armrest, bulging knuckles turning white. "What am I to do, then?"

His words landed with surprising confidence despite wanting to become ash and blow away on the wind. In what could only be a faint manner of protest, memories of Einar as an innocent young boy flicked across his mind. *He laughed like a bell, clicking a wooden sword against Pelagios' shin guards as he wove between Pelagios and Mycin's feet as they took a turn about the garden. Black hair, a smile so open to the world, trailed by the eyes of a king, a father, who only occasionally recognized him.*

Damalis' hand lighting on his shoulder brought him back to the reality of Einar's misdeeds. That young boy existed only in the past.

"What are *we* to do," the head advisor corrected, "about our king, and our country?"

"There is little to be done about the marsh sickness," a woman next to Riven murmured. Lanet tucked a graying strand of hair behind her ears as she continued. "However, I want to propose an idea on how to handle the king without laying *all* of the pressure on Pelagios' shoulders."

Earnestly, the general nodded his head to her.

The woman took a breath before saying, "We find a mage, a true one, and enlist them to be the king's confidant. If Einar is so certain there is a curse upon his bloodline, then let us turn his attention away from innocent people and towards trying to break it. There is some danger in feeding his hallucinations and paranoia…"

Everyone waited as she trailed off, Lanet pressing her lips in uncertainty. Pelagios felt the idea settle in the air, filter into the minds of each person at the table. No one spoke as they took their own positions of thought, leaning back in their chairs or holding their chins. Were there any mages left in Esmar? After the first official murders of the Kahun some years ago, the practice of magic disappeared with the fleeing tribesmen. Magic itself had been returned to the soil for Ages, unable to be coaxed out of bookish spells or bloodlines. Only the old families in Lesser Syvon possessed a whisp of power, so what hope did Esmar have in breaking a curse?

"It is something to consider, surely?" She muttered, glancing around the room. Her companions picked at their nails, avoided her gaze, stared into the candlelight. Desperation clung to every word. "It is not a cure, I know. We shall not stop giving the king his medicines, nor halt our other proceedings. But if we can manage to hold his attention, even for only a few more months? Well," she nodded firmly, "then those are months of… not true peace, but the closest Esmar can get despite the marsh sickness."

"Which reminds me," interrupted Chiflot, a man who was known to lift many things from the king's own coffers. "I have some idea about what we can do for those who've been displaced. The more isolated communities, I'm afraid, should be left to themselves for the time being." He grimaced, the next words leaving an acrid taste in his mouth. "My rats returned with news of debauchery under the banner of House Pargus, out on the edges of Neighweather. Horses are being used for more than transportation."

The disturbed tone in his voice needed no elaboration.

"We should consider the option of the mage—" Lanet tried to continue.

"There are more pressing matters, like the displacement of entire farm villages and how the king's money is being spent." Sevrit, who did not appreciate Neighweather being mentioned so poorly, narrowed his eyes at the gilded Chiflot.

"We should consider, too, what to do for the Wotag season. Too much land has been lost to the water to provide enough grain for entire providences." Riven half-murmured.

"*Damn* all those who've divided themselves from Esmar. They won't get a kernel."

Voices collided, each arguing which event was more pertinent. Pelagios watched them war with one another, their voices level but firm with each statement. The energy proved very different compared to the war tents and encampments Pelagios was used to, where each commanding officer spoke a little louder to have his opinions heard first. If Damalis had not slammed his hand down on the table to demand order, one or two advisors may have tried to settle their arguments with their fists.

"*Every* issue brought to this table is important," the head advisor chided, his steely gaze landing on each of them. "*Every* matter discussed here has the potential to aid us in our cause to protect this country. Now, in reference to hiring a mage… I think, given the king's current distaste and distrust of any magic-user, it is unwise. However, it isn't foolish. Lanet," he nodded to her, "if you have the time, consider how we can move forward with the idea privately. Because of Einar's rampages over the years, any mage who once resided in Esmar has either fled or is far into hiding. *You* are responsible for this idea's fruition, but we will not be acting on it until every person at this table agrees."

Lanet nodded, content with Damalis' instruction. Pelagios was beginning to understand why the position of authority fell to Damalis. Even though the title of Head Advisor meant power in the court of the king, he did not speak haughtily but with an air of practicality and respect. Damalis commanded the room simply because his mind proved the sharpest, while his ego remained in check—at least, for a court official.

The night ended with little circumstance, the advisors slipping in to conversation that sat beyond Pelagios' breadth of understanding. After some time, and another drink, the general inquired as to whether or not he was allowed to leave.

"Of course." Damalis nodded.

Kana looked up at the general from her conversation, meeting his gaze as he moved to bid them all a good day.

"We will call upon you again to detail your requirements, Lord General." Then, smiling kindly, she added, "You still have to earn your place as a turncoat, after all."

Pelagios closed the door unceremoniously behind him. The words sent a ringing sound of finality through his body, for in a span of moments he rejected a lifetime of devotion to the Royal House of Esmar. Was his loyalty so weak that a candlelit meeting with spoiled, finely dressed members of court turned it?

No.

No.

Pelagios did not believe his heart changed so easily. Yet, Einar was too displaced to receive any news of the treason. It was his whole advisory court, after all, and such a revelation would cripple him. For the king's sake—and for Theon's—Pelagios considered that it would be best to play Damalis for a fool. Speaking to relieve the burden on one's mind, which is what Pelagios did during the frustrating hunt through Esmar, was different than outright mutiny.

Pelagios decided to have no part in the treachery other than to be an ear for the king. If Damalis and the others planned something that brought about an end to the Royal House, then it was his duty to stop it. The group was correct in saying that Pelagios was the king's closest confidant—and so he would protect Einar and Theon.

Decades of service cannot be bought with the promise of saving a nation already lost.

CHAPTER FOUR

Sen tilted their face to the sun, eyes closed against the warm breeze as they deeply inhaled the drifting scents of perfume and baked bread. As the ferry drifted closer to the docks at Dunhet, the smell grew stronger and more punctuated with the odorous tones of the city. Yet, there was still something blissful about the notes of musk colliding with the scent of vanilla and wheat.

Dunhet stretched across the curving shoreline, glistening stone buildings fitted against the towering, broad leaves of tropical trees. Pearlescent, the bleached white buildings were intermittently struck through with the pale sheen of silverwood. Buildings withstanding the grand test of time held emerald sloped roofs with golden figures facing the points along the horizon where the sun rose and set. These were the buildings of Sen's ancestors, rising out of the common, quickly constructed city that sprawled around them like great pillars of history. Even from their place on the boat, Sen noted the hanging lanterns and wide, linen walls. Streaks of gold and red flags whipped in the air, the symbol of a crane mid-flight sparkling in the middle. Dunhet was the shimmering pride of the Gilded Isles, a cacophony of languages and music, thriving with merchants from as far as Sovil in Greater Syvon. The scent in the air smelled like life, the mixture of sounds a siren's call.

It smelled like *home*.

Leaping from Murkthistle to Dunhet could have been avoided if Sen's family sent an escort, but their return home was a surprise. They enjoyed having another few hours to stitch together a tale elaborate enough to be believable.

Picking at their fingernails, Sen wore away the dry skin there. A new callous sat on the inner side of their finger, marking the efforts of their last few months at the Amalak as their studies of minor magic proved as fruitless as their expensive private tutors. Even the teachers, with all their historical knowledge of book-learned *and* bloodline magic, wondered why the YeSara Clan possessed such a weak connection to the two despite having such powerful ancestral mages.

Harnessing the ability to radically shape the natural world through bloodline magic was as much fable as the dreaded sea monster, the Duathi. Sen could not control a ship by coaxing the wind into its sails or do more than light a candlestick, but they were proof that the YeSara clan harbored elemental capabilities—and that those capabilities once existed in the ancient original settlers of Lesser Syvon. It was not a curse upon the YeSara Clan that the magic faded over the Ages, but some cruel joke on what remained of the world.

The Ages of magic were gone. No Mother of Wolves or great Fangbearer could change that, for now they were only stories.

As one of the oldest families to still exist in the Current Age, the YeSara Clan treated the magic in their bloodline as leverage throughout the country. The goal *was* to eventually have more power through Sen's abilities to control the wind, waters, and flame. Their time at the Amalak *was* meant to usher forth whatever laid dormant, though the schooling proved to be little more than stuffy historians pushing quills across parchments and calling it *education.*

The teachers should have expected Sen's withdrawal from their sheltered, isolating environment. Murkthistle stood as a lone town of only the Amalak, a few farmsteads, and an inn-and-tavern. It was an endless procession of waking, bathing, and breaking fast with four others who were not mentors, followed by hours of listening to Ser Keed drone on about the sacred blood rites that were performed centuries ago to appease gods Sen did not believe in. And every time Sen managed to bring one of the barmaids or farmhands past the Amalak's receiving gardens, they were thwarted by a mouth-breathing sellsword.

Then, once Ser Keed realized the sellsword found deeper pockets, he took it upon *himself* to roam the gardens. Ser Keed grew frustrated enough with Sen to threaten expulsion, and shame like that brought with it the potential to ruin Sen for an entire season in high society.

So, they left.

Naseria YeSara refused to be disgraced by anyone, knowing that her sisters would bring the family to ruin if she was humiliated enough to step down as the clan's matriarch. Sen left on their own because of this—*before*

Ser Keed, or any of the other instructors, chanced sending an unfortunate letter to their mother.

The more selfish reason for their escape was that they were bored to *death.* Their family estate, sprawling to consume an entire island, stood within eyesight of the extravagant city of Dunhet. Brothels, booths, silks, and foods that Sen could never dream up were only a short boat ride away, the nights offering endless entertainment. Those nights unfolded their temptations like a lady slipping off her silken gown, urging Sen to take hold of the soft flesh and drink in every experience it offered.

Life happened in Dunhet and on the YeSara island—and not the tasteless, boring kind with which farmhands and historians seemed content. Sen needed to feel the joyous haze of stumbling drunk out of a bar, their arm slung around one rich, casual friend from high society or another. They wanted desperately to flash their coinage, baring their teeth at anyone who doubted the YeSara coffers.

It was a good thing, their return. The only other option was slipping into madness the longer they stayed confined within the Amalak.

At the docks, thick-shouldered people awaited the ferry. Sen leaned against the railing of the wide boat, squinting against the setting sun. It was not the grandest of ships, meant to only travel along the coastline, but the midnight blue paint shined splendidly, and it did not smell of fish nor tar. Sen gave the captain an extra gold piece for ferrying them out that evening since he said that the later part of the day was his busiest, but he seemed a fine enough old man with no end of sea shanties in his reservoir. Sen actually enjoyed the drift along the coastline with his warbling voice in the background, to their pleasant surprise.

One of the dockhands watched attentively as the captain tossed coarse ropes over the railing, eyes roving over Sen's expensive canary yellow silks. They particularly liked these threads, with the migrating swans decorating the garment in bold shades of blue and green, scattered across the breadth of it. The hem and cuffs shimmered, a trick of the dyeing process that made the fabric shine like spun gold. Fine hairpins of gold the length of Sen's forearm held up their mass of black hair, sticking out of their rich locks like sunbeams, delicate charms made from rubies and pearls dripping off the ends and singing a rich tune as they turned their head to observe the unloading of their items.

As the young traveler took the offered hand of the worker, another started hauling their luggage into a cart.

"There's a gold piece for you if you get that safely to the YeSara residence."

Face paling, the man bowed before assorting the luggage, treating the heavy leather cases like delicate porcelain.

"You." Sen spun on the worker, giving the man's hand a teasing squeeze before slipping a gold piece into it. "Flag a rickshaw down for me, will you?"

Once the YeSara name passed Sen's lips, it took the dockhands little time to prepare their way. Sen wiped away the grime collected on their palm from shaking the hands of the workers on a square of fabric. They lamented the stains on the golden thread tossing it over their shoulder, not bothering to watch it drift through the air and hit the top of the water. Small waves quickly absorbed the handkerchief into its dark maw, disappearing the fabric in moments.

A rickshaw with an overhang was flagged down after the cart of Sen's luggage was instructed to go ahead to the private YeSara dock. The captain of the little ferry refused to take Sen any further up the coastline than the first piers of the dockyard, which irked them greatly since now they had to pay for extra transportation through the mile of fishmongers and merchant stalls.

Although, a rickshaw ride through Dunhet sounded romantic. Sen chose to enjoy the return as they situated themselves on the thin padding of the rickshaw's bench. The broad woman pulling it turned to meet their eye over her muscular shoulder, just as Sen flicked open a wide satin fan.

Not making eye contact, Sen gave instructions from behind the fan. "Second Courtyard, the Lacunar."

With a jerky start, the rickshaw lurched forward. Sen reflexively grabbed the armrest with a startled gasp, the woman's shoulders bouncing with a chuckle.

Oaf, they sneered to themself. A prickle of shame lingered behind that unspoken insult, which they brushed away like a frayed piece of lint before it had a chance to linger.

Sen leaned against the back of the seat, fanning themselves as they rolled away from the soft, open winds of the docks to the shadows of Dunhet's gleaming stone buildings. Merchants erected their stalls close to the water and incoming ships, eager to be the first introduction to any newcomers. As Sen paraded through the streets, the woman navigated wide pavilions and narrow passageways. People on either side called out to them like the rhythmic cawing of birds. Gold silks like theirs caught any trader's eye, desperate for their attention and coin. Sen paid little mind to the trinkets, their local knowledge diverse enough to know that most of the stalls closer to the docks peddled gold-painted tin and silks with mistakes all throughout their patterns. Only those who lived a boat ride away in the Saltshores fell prey to the indistinguishable charm of a merchant desperate for a fool.

Sen kept their fan up for most of the journey, eyes jumping around to absorb the life they so desperately missed. A fishmonger reached down into the ice-packed cart where she kept her fresh, scaly wares. Grabbing the tail, Sen watched with delight as she whipped it out of the cart, circled it around her head, and smacked it right into a man's face. He scrambled off howling about how awful a woman she was while the monger returned the fish to the ice.

Winding out of the market streets and busier pavilions, the rickshaw turned down a lane as wide as six horses. Sleek cobbled pathways stood free of any unsightly piles of dung or screaming, sun-burned peddlers. Tall doors of white-gray silverwood sat underneath intricate moldings and flat alcoves, their wares depicted in red paint on a stone tablet next to the entrance. A needle and thread for the seamstresses, a button for the haberdashery, a pair of shoes for the cobbler. The buildings were struck through with the remnants of Sen's history, wide linen screens thrown open to reveal low-tabled tea shops and steaming bowls of hand-kneaded noodles.

Those who parted around the rickshaw inclined their heads, comfortable enough in life to not shout for any prospective customer's attention. While clotheslines crisscrossed above one's head near the docks, there were only banners and elegant silk flags in this section of the Market.

At the end of Merchant's Lane sat an enormous fountain surrounded by palm fronds and flowers with wide, flat pink and white petals. The icon in the middle lifted a dish with both her hands, calm face gazing towards the docks. People meandered around the basin of the fountain, splashing each other with water or sitting on the edge to chat in the evening sunlight. Smaller statues of the same figure stood along the coastline, depicting some goddess or another—Sen cared little who it was, and other than marveling at the detail coaxed out of stone for a brief moment, forgot its existence once the woman turned the rickshaw down a branching street.

Dunhet's inner city reflected much of the same simple, clean architecture as Merchant's Lane. The First Courtyard was a great circle almost as large as the YeSara island, with numerous fountains portraying different gods and goddesses slaying sea monsters or resurrecting ships out from under great waves. Sen disliked this Courtyard the most since the religious air made it feel like judgment personified, and avoided the insistent gazes of the zealots who looked up at them from whispered prayers. Though the overhanging garden of white lilies and pale pink flowers gave an innocent aroma to the Courtyard, Sen could not help feeling like the obstinate praying concealed something darker.

The doors lining the walls of the First Courtyard led into extravagant apartments for those who worked along Merchant Lane, or families that were part of Dunhet's high society but not as wealthy as the original clans. The religious iconography was only a part of the vast expanse of the Courtyard, with a covered pavilion at the center for musicians and artists to gather. Surrounding it sat permanent food stalls, low walls of stone encapsulating firepits that roasted meats and vegetables at all hours of the day. Mingling with the hum of muted prayers floated a lute and lyre, a melodic, feminine voice singing in a language Sen did not recognize.

Moving easier now, the woman pulled the rickshaw along the outer edge of the busy crowd until they approached the curved archway marking the entrance into the Second Courtyard. The street was narrower, and the layout did not host a bevy of statues or a pavilion. A few food stalls crowded the center of the Courtyard while some of the employees of the surrounding establishments bought their dinners of fire-baked sweet bread and grilled mutton. The woman stopped the rickshaw just before the tablet painted with an image of a locked chest.

Sen dismounted without thanking her. When they did not immediately reach for their purse, she straightened herself to her towering, broad height. Beads of sweat speckled her forehead and upper lip, but she did not appear out of breath, or even winded. She would not dare strike a YeSara, but there were no laws against intimidation.

"I'll only be a moment," Sen promised. "I'll pay double your fare if you wait to take me to the YeSara docks."

After glancing down over Sen's elegant attire, the hardy sandals, and the jeweled pins in their hair, she nodded. The woman got comfortable, leaning against the rickshaw with her muscular arms crossed over her barrel-sized chest as Sen headed into the treasury.

After counting out their last silver pieces for the rickshaw driver, Sen turned to face the dockmaster. He was a scrawny but well-dressed fellow who wore ruby studded hoops in his ears. Assuring Sen that the luggage had continued onto the island without a problem, he stepped out onto the dock.

Beyond, the lazy waters rolled against the edges of the YeSara homestead. On the border of the sandy beach encircling island, sandstone and silverwood towers reached skyward to brush against the plum purple clouds of the evening sun. While some of the older architecture honored the generations which came before Sen, the newer additions reflected some of the modern styles noted within Dunhet. Underneath bright golden flags with swordfish dancing on their colors, the emblem of the YeSara Clan kept watch over villas and blooming pathways lined with flowers. A massive glass dome reflected the sunlight, the greenhouse a spectacle of money as it stood twice as large as the governor's own homes inside of Dunhet. Palm trees bowed in the gentle sea winds… Sen could nearly hear their rustling against the stone of the buildings and felt their heart twinge with homesickness. From where they stood, the isle felt distant and proud, gladdened by the half-mile of water separating it from the mainland. They imagined their family within, the entire YeSara Clan wandering about their equal divides of the island, lounging in the common rooms gossiping, pouring the clear expensive liquor made of rice down their gilded throats.

"Where's the boat?" Sen felt anxious, a mix of dreadful eagerness stirring in their belly.

"It should be arriving shortly, young Seram." The dockmaster responded easily, pulling the end of a rope out of the water. "Ferris is rowing this day."

Sen rolled their eyes. "*Wonderful.* Is anyone going to tell him that retirement means he doesn't have to work?"

Something shifted in the dockmaster's eyes, the smile remaining steadfast on his lips as he tossed the rope down onto the planks. "Perhaps old Ferris simply enjoys the exercise."

The heir to the YeSara estates was smart enough to pick up a tone of distaste, but calloused enough by high society not to care what it meant. They leaned a hip against the tall iron lantern that marked the private dock. YeSara money spilled into the streets of the Dunhet, and here the dockmaster lived in his own private rooms next to the water. A gold banner drifted beside the apartments, and Sen met the eyes of the swordfish emblazoned upon it.

"Ah, Blessed Ma'Ceste. Your chariot approaches!" Motioning, the dockmaster pointed out the boat leaving the dock of the island. The water deity's name often fell from the lips of servants of the YeSara Clan, since according to one myth or another, the YeSaras descended from the goddess herself. To the servants, invoking her name not only meant her favor, but the Matriarch's.

Sen picked at their fingernails as they waited for the old man to paddle close enough for the dockmaster to lend him a hand. It took some time for the old rower to adjust himself properly against the siding of the dock, long enough for Sen to release an impatient huff.

"You can go home now, Ferris." Sen unfurled their fan, batting it at their neck. Their slanted eyes roved over the old man, wondering how such a wiry, muscular person moved so slowly. Releasing him from another journey might save his breath, which would likely please the old man.

Ferris and the dockmaster exchanged a quick look, one that often passed between the servants in Sen's presence. Despite their desire to argue—they always wanted to argue, Sen knew this—Ferris only bowed his head. Smiling, he accepted the dockmaster's hand to help him from the boat. Dressed in the regalia of a simple servant, the threads still finer than any footman in the city, Ferris shuffled down the dock and up the hill.

As if in afterthought, he paused at the twin lanterns. "Seram? Am I to get my full day's pay?"

Sen waved their free hand in his direction. "I'm sure you will—and then some. Now," they put on a smile that many in Dunhet's high society witnessed, full of equal parts venom and disinterest. "Go rest your weary, weary bones."

The answer was enough for Ferris, so after he bid Sen and the dockmaster a good evening he continued his shuffling walk up the cobbled hill.

After making sure his apartments were locked up, the dockmaster helped Sen step into the wobbling ship. His callouses snagged against their soft palm, sending a disgusted shiver up their arm. The feeling did not reach their face, hiding behind their fan as they settled in.

Since the YeSara coffers overflowed to the point of being annoying, fine silk padded the benches of the dinghy, and solid gold lanterns alight with oil hung from either end. Sen reclined easily, leaning against the cushioned seat as the dockmaster rowed over the gently surging waters.

They gave the man a judgmental once-over before staring out at the shoreline of Dunhet. Lights blinked to life in the windows, people and parties rearing awake. Night's approach meant the revival of music, of people who spent the day sleeping finally waking for another midnight adventure. Sen felt eager to return to those tawdry dens filled with padded furniture, the smoke of pipes and sweet tar in the air.

For a moment, there was nothing to break the traveling silence except the dip of the oars—whale bone, with intricate carvings in the handle—into the water, the slap of small ripples on the belly of the boat.

"So," the dockmaster's voice sounded coarse against the drip of the water, "you have returned from the Amalak."

Sen cut their gaze to him, saying nothing. They leaned against the edge of the boat, chin propped up in their hand as they gazed over the sea. Murkthistle stood next to a lake, but Sen had missed the great, unfolding ocean. Golden sunlight dappled the waves, diamonds sparkling on the surface of the water. Fat clouds rolled overhead, their plum and pink underbellies struck through with pale yellow.

"Your family must be thrilled at your early return." Continued the dockmaster in a way that seemed more than just noise to fill the space between them.

Sen could not help but roll their eyes, both at the man's amity and his statement. They had plenty of time to think about how *exactly* their family might respond to their impromptu arrival. But was is their fault if only the sparsest bit of magic existed in the bloodline? Some of the original clans spent generations marrying only family, but even then the elemental magic ended up weaker than Sen's. There was no way to cheat the reality that magic was fading from the world. Soon it will be gone entirely, ending in the next generation.

However, Naseria still tried to fight the inevitable. She believed that lessons and study and meditations with the brightest historians might win against evolution, though Sen's twenty-three years showed how none of it actually worked. They were a ticket to power since accidentally lighting their bassinet aflame, little more than an icon for their mother to set on a high shelf. Naseria love them, in her own way, but it felt hard to see it past the duty she piled upon Sen's head. Even though the YeSara Clan stood as one of the oldest families in Lesser Syvon, the title alone coming with power and generational wealth, Naseria remained unsatisfied.

"Do you have family?"

The dock master seemed shocked at the question. "I have a brother in Menthis, and he a child in Soapstead."

Sen smirked. "A relative in the soap-making business? I'm sure they'll go far." The impoliteness felt light on their tongue, their voice dripping with mockery.

"My brother works the lumber mills in Trilabold," the dockmaster murmured as a response, not giving any evidence of noticing. "His child had no desire to spend their years grinding away at silverwood trees.

Soapmaking is a gentler means. They are happy, the both of them. That is all I can ask Ma'Ceste for."

They are happy.

Sen felt the prick of discomfit climbing up their spine. Sen was happy, of course they were. What else could jewels and silks buy if not absolute contentment?

Quiet settled over the boat, awkward as a tense, depressed energy bloomed from Sen's distant gaze. When they finally settled against the dock to the island, the sun was mostly set, and the lanterns lining the hundreds of pathways throughout the wide-leafed trees were lit. Servants rushed forward to lift Sen from the boat, exchanging their well-worn traveling sandals for thick, plush ones meant for meandering. The dockmaster lifted off as soon as Sen's feet hit the dock, not another word passing between them as they split off towards their distinct lives.

With the servants fluttering like butterflies uncertain of where to land, the young seram of the house let their feet guide them. Generations before, Sen's ancestors walked the very same paths underneath shaggy heads of coconuts and trees with long, spikey leaves. Feather reed grass hushed in the wind, heads bowing in advent respect as Sen passed.

Despite their inability to fully submerge themselves in elemental magic like their ancestors, the world still recognized the ancient echoes of power within Sen's veins. Leaves rustled in conversation, their whispers familiar to the young person but still profoundly distant. It felt as though Sen tried to see those elements through frosted glass, only receiving shapeless blobs of color or indistinguishable words. Still, the living grass and the breath of the wind continued speaking to Sen in hushed tones, hoping that they may understand one day.

They played with a leaf in the air in the meantime, partly to show off for the servants but mostly to keep their hands busy as they walked. Nervousness settled into their muscles, and as they threaded the leaf through their fingers they approached the main house with a pit in their chest. Incense hung on the air, thick with veneration. Someone had lit it for the family shrine, and, like the earth at their feet, Sen felt the ancient pull of something beyond themselves.

At the end of a wide, flat bridge curving over a pond stood an intricate archway indicating the start of the matriarch's estate. Drifting lazily in the water were dozens of pink flowers, not yet in bloom and nestled on top of lily pads. Sen glanced down for a moment at their reflection surrounded by the pool of the stars winking awake in the deep blue sky overhead. The island came to life at night in a way Sen never could describe, pulsing with old memories. The stars were the first illuminating call that woke its archaic generational charm.

Unfolding from the archway and its carved stone pillars were sturdy walls that stood long before Sen's grandparents. Narrow, glassless windows hewn out of the rock stood equally apart, and in each of the spaces sat a familial guardian who looked towards the city of Dunhet and the coastline. Sen knew their open maws and raised daggers and snake tongues well, considering they plagued their nightmares as a child. The familiar hum of disquiet hushed over Sen for a moment as they continued across the bridge, the servants falling silent in a line behind them.

Across the pillars of the archway was a slated roof made of clay shingles, their edges dipped in gold and shining even in the low light. Two bulbous lanterns hung from their rafters, the shimmering brasswork dripping with suncatchers that threw rays of candlelight across Sen's face in a rainbow of color. Beyond stood the courtyard, its flourishing garden interrupted by small footpaths.

Sen's slippered feet touched down onto the slatted walkway that lined the perimeter of the courtyard. Glancing around, they noted that all of the six sliding doors were open to the night air, their linen screens revealing the soft glow of the lanterns within. Their eyes jumped across each amber brushed rooms, starting at the study on the left and ending with the tea room on the right. No breath other than that of the wind's drifted through the receiving rooms despite there being enough time before Sen's arrival for their family to be notified.

Grimacing, Sen lifted a hand, dismissing all of the servants without a word. They were not expecting a party, but a greeting at the gate was more than customary. Worse than any highborn gossiping behind their fan was the feeling of returning to an empty home.

Across the courtyard was the altar room, where family greeted one-another. Large, beautiful cushions sat in front of a gilded shrine that stood layers high, every surface decorated with fruit and jewels, the paintings of Sen's ancestors gazing out with quiet judgement. The oil lanterns on either side of the shrine burned low, dowsing the gold and food in amber. Incense burned in the tray, and judging by the ash only a little time passed since being lit. Some of the cushions, Sen noted, were still limp with indentations.

In the quiet, Sen felt the world press in. They adjusted their fine silks as they lowered, pressing their knees into the cushion as they sat before their bloodline. Dispelling their anxiety for a moment, Sen pressed their palms to the wood floor and bowed, forehead lingering on their knuckles for a long breath before they rose.

It was not until they stepped away from the cushion that bitter resentment climbed from Sen's chest to settled in their mouth, the taste acrid on their tongue. The lack of not only their mother's presence, but their sister's, felt like a plain show of disapproval.

Sen thought it petty of their sister to act out in such a childish way. Lon was still part of the richest family in the Gilded Isles, possibly in all of Greater and Lesser Syvon. Ancient clans often outranked royal families in money alone. Their sister never wanted for *anything* yet she possessed enough audacity to blame Sen for consuming the attention of their mother and father. Servants waited on them hand and foot, and still that was not enough for Lon.

"They've gone to dinner."

Standing in the entryway, coaxed to life by Sen's thoughts, stood Naseria. Her house garments were simple but no less fine, the black satin robe stamped with shimmering golden lilies and long, thin reeds. Her fingers peeked out of the long sleeves, clasped professionally over the wide belt of crimson fabric cinched around her waist. The layered neck of her robe barely exposed the matching red lining underneath, and her hair sat in a twisted bun at the nape of her neck. Pinned to her left shoulder sat the emblem of the Matriarch, a blooming white lotus made of pearls set into a plate of black tourmaline. Tiny chains of gold dripped from its gilded setting, one for every child she bore.

"No one thought to greet me?" Sen griped back, staring at the five drips of gold hanging from the brooch. Only Sen and their sister remained, Naseria's body unable to withstand other pregnancies after Lon's complicated birth. Still, they were forever memorialized as children of the Matriarch.

Their mother's face stared forward. Unpowdered, the smallest swipe of rouge across her lips, Naseria exhibited no shame in the weathered lines on her sun-kissed forehead or nestled into the corners of her eyes. Before another word passed her lips, she stepped into the room and approached the second cushion. She bowed, just as Sen had, lingering on the floor for a beat longer as she whispered a prayer to her predecessors.

When she rose, adjusting her sleeves, Naseria gazed at Sen as if waiting for them to realize. Then, after another beat of silence, she sighed. "I'm the one who received the messenger. I waited for you, and sent our family off to eat."

The thought of Naseria wanting to be the first to speak with them crossed their mind during their traveling, but Sen hoped Lon might provide a boundary of civility. Despite their sister's solemn nature from her years at Dunhet's naval academy, her presence alone typically softened their mother's words.

Sen crossed their arms, the hush of their golden sleeves breaking the silence. Being in their mother's presence sent every excuse out of their head. Their heart thrummed anxiously in Naseria's quiet, waiting energy. She looked on, not quite frowning, opening the space for her heir to speak first.

"I decided to come back early," they found themselves saying, dropping the defensive posture. Letting their arms hand at their sides, Sen lifted a shoulder carelessly. "The Amalak is fine for a school, I suppose, but everything to be said was already taught to me by all those tutors you hired."

Naseria raised her chin, thoughtfully studying her child.

"You might be surprised, but I did rather well. See?"

Their mother watched as Sen raised a hand, palm facing the twisting smoke of the incense. In moments, the smoke ran upwards in a straight line, all the way up to the ceiling. Sen brought it down, curving until the tendrils of smoke made the outline of Naseria's lotus brooch.

Naseria looked on, unimpressed. Sen felt their anxiety rising, the judgement wafting from their mother in waves.

"I'd do more, but I'm *so* tired—"

Reaching into the sleeve of her robe, Naseria withdrew a letter. As she unfolded the rich parchment, her child looked on with fear climbing into their eyes. Sen forced their face to fall flat, hiding the shaking in their hands by crossing their arms again.

"*Esteemed Matriarch; I regretfully write to inform you that your honorable heir plans to return home without finishing their studies. While I am uncertain as to the date, the servants, who upon your advice have been instructed to inform me of any changes, stated that Seram YeSara packed most of their luggage and sent it to the docks*."

Sen balked. "You told him to *spy* on me?"

"*While I was rigorous in my teachings*," their mother read a little louder, "*it did not seem enough to advance your heir's abilities in any notable regard. I also regret to inform you, Esteemed Matriarch, that should Sen YeSara leave without honoring their studies, they will no longer be welcomed within the sacred walls of the Amalak. This was decided by the Tribune this morning. Despite my failures, I hope this news will not force you to reconsider your sizable donation to the Amalak. Signed, Ser Keed.*"

The silence was palpable as Naseria folded the letter slowly, returning it to her sleeve. Every lie that Sen considered fell dead on their lips, and they shrank under their mother's gaze.

"I… if you tell anyone about that," Sen dared, earning a wary glare from their mother, "then it's just—it's going to be shameful. Absolutely awful."

Their mother *tsked.* Though they did not truly care about being banned from such a morose place, Sen knew that the moment the news reached the other clans, embarrassment followed. Sen wanted nothing more than to vanish, or turn into smoke and drift away with the incense on the breeze.

Naseria spoke once the flicker of anger in her eyes dissipated. With all her strength and fearsome energy, she never struck out at her children. It made it that much harder for Sen to despise her, or her instruction. Sen might allow themselves to hate her more if she was a monster, and not simply a woman doing her best to spearhead her entire Clan through a world that did not always acknowledge its ancient history.

"I've considered what to do once this news reaches our peers. As you know, we never shame our own publicly, no matter how public the shame."

Guilt stuck in Sen's throat. They swallowed hard, nodding. A simple, silent assurance that they will do whatever their mother decided. As much as Sen hated anyone commanding them, their entire life being orders and instruction, they knew that to get back into Naseria's favor meant obedience. Everything blew over, eventually. Sen planned to return vicariously living as soon as their mother was satisfied.

The anxiety in their lungs finally settled, then their mother continued. "Lon will be your chaperone until I decide otherwise."

The world tilted for a moment. Sen's words fumbled out, the startled, "What?" shaky on their breath. Naseria repeated the order, which was how Sen knew she was proud. She *hated* repeating herself.

Lon, born after Sen, deserved the power—everyone knew it but what could be done? Fate made its decision, Sen's destiny laid out for them as Lon's path was laid before her own feet. Lon studied war and battle strategy, as there were numerous relatives who trained at Dunhet's naval academy. With her level head and natural drive, Lon brought honor to the YeSara Clan as the youngest captain to command her own ship. She did her best to act like the perfect sister, a proper scion of the esteemed YeSara Clan, but on the island Sen was invisible to her.

Next to her, Sen, in all their trained grace, felt foolish and clumsy.

"For how long?" Sen whined, immediately regretting it as their mother glowered.

This time, she did not repeat herself. Instead, she picked up the front of her robe, lightly stepping to the side. Sen gazed at their mother's profile, her soft jaw and slanted eyes sliding to them when she noticed their gawking, angry stare.

"Since I have no intention of punishing your sister, she will be your chaperone only until I find a guard you *can't* swindle from me."

An invitation to dinner did not follow, as Naseria suggested Sen had such a long journey and may feel better eating in their private rooms. When they arrived to the wing of the house reserved for them, the beauty of the rich wood furnishings and embroidered linen walls fell dead. Nothing about the soft lantern light and rich, sweet smell of incense pulled Sen out of the haze of angry guilt roiling in their chest.

Sen's favorite dessert awaited them, a sticky bun filled with thick red bean paste. Anger boiled over in a startling wave of anxiety and bitterness. Sen grabbed the dish with the sticky bun and threw it against the wall with a scream that matched the shattering of the plate. They kicked over the remaining food until it went splattering across the floor. Thick creams and specks of rice clotted into the rug at their feet, the evidence of their tantrums suddenly so embarrassing that Sen ordered a servant to carry it all away immediately. Food stuck to the end of their beautiful golden robes so they ripped it from their shoulders, tossing it onto the servants who hurried to clean the mess.

"Get out!" Sen's voice frayed, crackling as the tears filled their eyes and blurred the world. "*Get out!*"

The servants took the robe and the rug littered with food into their arms and vanished, neatly closing the linen screen as they went. Hot tears streaked down Sen's cheeks, evidence of their frustration hidden away from anyone else. Apparently, it was not enough for their decisions to be ruled over simply because of an ability they did not ask for. Now, they must be monitored like a child, and for what? Because they, as an adult, left a stuffy and limiting place that offered nothing more than books and sideways glances?

Sen collapsed into their bed, ignoring the grime of travel clinging to their body. Had Lon agreed to this out of spite? Did she wish to be their chaperone just to tell their mother lies as a way to get back at them? Sen knew their parents paid more attention to them than their sister, but this would be the first time anyone went out of their way to make them suffer.

All of this muddled their head—the weariness, the regret, the frustration at being wholeheartedly dismissed from dinner. Even the dockmaster's placid kindness earlier seemed to allude, in hindsight, to some awful confrontation that he tried to soften with conversation. If Sen had been able to look past their fan, perhaps they might have noticed that the man had been worried about more than filling his pockets.

In the recesses of sleep, an idea slinked into Sen's mind from the shadows. Lon did not walk the streets of Dunhet as often as her elder sibling, going strictly between the naval academy, the Upper Courtyard, the fine merchant district, then home. She possessed limited experiences with the *entertainment* the city offered its nighttime travelers.

The tears were still drying on Sen's cheeks as they fell asleep, smiling as the idea took form.

It was good to be home.

CHAPTER FIVE

Grief, Neoma decided, felt something like sickness. In the twilight, her mind wanned like the moon still hanging in the sky. Overcome with the shadow of heartbreak, slivers of herself were engulfed by the traitorous, empty sensation in her chest. Neoma's bones ached right down into the marrow in such a drilling, weary pain that she wanted to dig into her skin to relieve the pressure of sinew and muscle. As though swallowed by a fever, her mind felt light despite every thought being clotted behind one sallow truth: Koa, her son, was dead.

Bit by bit, the world faded during the passage of the last few days until it all stilled in the apple-colored morning. In what became the shattered definition of normalcy, Neoma woke well before the dawn to sink into the chair nestled against the largest window in the sitting room. Her black skin held to the shadows until finally touched by the gold of morning, and even then she refused to move. She had no desire to fix tea or break her fast, or do anything other than stare out into the sea. The sun, a gilded coin lifting out of the pocket of the ocean, was the only warm thing in the days leading up to Koa's farewell ceremony.

Neoma's stomach cramped, the sharp ache slicing through her from navel to spine. It was not dissimilar to those first contractions twelve years ago, when Koa arrived too early and her husband had to run into the village to fetch their midwife. In the time it took for Urias to return with the pruned woman, her apprentice trailing behind, Neoma was holding their baby boy.

What an excited fellow for one so early. The crone's haggard voice rumbled in Neoma's memories, those weathered hands cleaning Koa's little body and gently prodding his tiny, kicking legs.

Yes, she agreed, the blood on her dress and the floor riddled with the pieces of herself that kept Koa alive while he stirred inside her belly. *He is perfect. Ten chubby fingers, ten little toes*. The woman passed the baby to her outstretched and waiting arms, mouth shaping words that faded into the air as Neoma gazed into the half-lidded eyes of her son. Leaving the apprentice with them, since Koa needed more care at first than the average baby, the midwife joked how the boy must have been eager to meet Neoma with how he refused the safety of her womb for another two months.

Urias, before the love left his eyes, called Koa brave for wanting to face the world so soon.

A sobbed wracked through her chest. Clapping a hand over her mouth, Neoma waited for the whispering sounds of soft feet on flagstone. After a moment passed, heavy tears slipping over her fingers, it seemed Urias remained in bed.

The sun watched her cry silently. It did not judge Neoma when her hand fisted, knuckles digging into her doughy thigh, or when a rivulet of snot dribbled down her chin. In the silence of the morning, in the warmth of the first rays of light, Neoma's tears were met with the gentle hush of the ocean outside.

As Koa grew, he taught her a new love for the ocean, one surpassing the comradery she felt as her family grew their salt farming business. In trills and flailing hands, he would lurch towards the ocean in excitement, ready for their days in the sun and her stories. His mind at first was not as quick to understand the world around him, and the midwife told her that while he was healthy, his early arrival might give him pause. Yet Neoma saw the sparks of understanding in his eyes when she read to him, or sat with him on their blanket by the sea and told fables about pirates and the Duathi. Koa only spoke a different language when he was little, one that her family and their friends came to understand over the years. Each trill was unique in its meaning, every hum distinguishing between satisfaction or disgust. She was an avid student, and his fiercest translator in a world that was not often eager to be patient with him. After his sixth nameday, he did finally grasp the Common Tongue, even interjecting it with sayings from Neoma's traditional language.

Neoma stood suddenly from her chair by the window, a dazing sensation from the memory trickling down from the top of her head. Heart thrumming in her wrist, the numbness continued until it flowed down into her toes. Her eyes slid across the room—filled with the clutter of life brought to a halt, a kitchen on the opposite end littered with jars of salt, and herbs that she smoked into the salt to add flavor hanging from the rafters, still and fuzzy in the morning light—until it landed on the shut door to the bedroom.

She realized she did not want to be in the house when Urias awoke, gripping the shawl hanging on the back of her chair fiercely. Everything in her wanted escape, but Neoma's feet were iron. The grief sank her down into the chair again, the sensation fleeing as quickly as it arrived. Gazing up at the moon still clinging to the bluebird sky, Neoma watched the receding darkness. With crooked hands it took her shoulders, pinning her with icy heat to the seat in which she had nursed her son.

Why did she want to run, anyways? Urias never hit her, though his words often felt like the thrashing limbs of an unsatisfied child. He never hit Koa, or said a foul word to the boy even on his more tiresome days. Where did this urge come from?

"There is only bread." Urias' voice, clotted with the raspy sound of drunkards, grumbled. She had not even heard the door to their bedroom open.

When she said nothing, eyes transfixed on the whitecapped waves, he muttered something under his breath. Sounds of cupboards opening and closing filled the room as he sought after the butter jar and skillet. He struck a fire, and slowly the scent of cooking bacon filled the air.

Food made her sick. Anger roiled in Neoma's gut when she wondered how Urias managed to stomach a single bite.

Between them rested a solid expanse, one filled with unspoken words that neither were skilled enough to voice. When separated by sleep, it was easier to ignore, but with her at the window as he silently prepared his meal it rang out with every breath.

The distance had been growing for years, but neither dared to admit it.

After the excitement of infanthood rolled into Koa's frustratingly difficult toddler years, Urias all but surrendered his paternal rights. Neoma knew it would be harder with their son's delayed speech, yet she expected Urias to stand with her as they navigated helping their child. It was not permanent, after all, yet he acted as though Koa might never talk, and that they failed before they began.

This isn't what I expected, he once told her on one of those candlelit nights where they tried, desperately, to find connection through sex. It was interrupted by Koa's violent screaming, a yell Neoma associated with nightmares or bedwetting.

And, though Neoma never planned to admit it, it was a relief. Sex to her felt like the last thing a person should do when they wanted reconnection with their loved one, but she relented after Urias pointed out a year passed since their last time in the marriage bed.

Where are you going?

She had risen from bed, and remembered the feeling of utter loneliness when she looked down at him.

To help my *son, she murmured, and left him alone that night to wrap Koa in her arms and coax him back to sleep.*

Urias did not have what it took to not only be their son's father, but a caregiver—that night revealed as much in so little words.

A plate appeared over her shoulder, the sickening aroma of meat wafting up her nose. Urias proffered it forward, waiting for her to take it. A disapproving sound escaped him when she refused.

"You've got to eat something."

"I'm not hungry." The words scraped out of her throat. She spent the night crying, her neck tight from stifling the noise.

Urias dropped the plate on the windowsill. The smell was so overpowering that Neoma felt she might vomit. Glaring at the plate, she waited for Urias to take it away, or do anything to keep him from standing over her shoulder.

His eyes bore into the top of her head, their heat pulsing through her skull.

She wanted him to leave.

She wanted him to drop to his knees and take her hand, crying.

She wanted him to walk out into the ocean and drown like Koa.

The tide came in so swiftly. I looked away for only a moment. I almost drowned, diving in after him. Why would he do that? Why would he keep walking into the tide?

"Damn it all to the Aether, Neoma. Eat *something*."

Looking up, she met the watery gaze of her husband. The moments where he looked at her with admiration were so far in the past; all she saw now in the green of his eyes was an empty hopelessness.

Urias filled that space with drink. Neoma pretended it did not exist at all.

Extending her hand, Neoma took the plate to set it on her lap. Stomach twisting in disgust, she pinched the greasy strip of bacon, bringing it to her lips. Urias watched her eat every bite, knowing that however wide the distance between them, and however blank and empty they felt, she would do what she could to keep the peace.

Once, Neoma wished for something closer to the village. She grew up next to the waters and briny beaches of the Saltshores, her family's salt farming business thriving to the point of enlisting her help at only eight. After meeting Urias, her work fell off after the expectations of family life settled on her shoulders, and he built their home on the edges of Linlocke. Months passed before Neoma acclimated to the solitude since her childhood home put beehives to shame, but on solemn mornings like today she cherished the privacy. Hearing the ocean without the underlying hum of conversation made the water more ethereal, sacred.

In quiet moments before Koa sang in a yawning note that announced his awakening, the ocean drew her in. Sometimes, Neoma felt as though the sea tried to ask her a question—though like Koa's private language when he was young, she often missed the meaning of its words.

In some ways, the silence encapsulating their flagstone house was a blanket of peace, yet at the same time it felt like buzzing in the back of Neoma's mind. Maybe she *did* want to wake up to the song of her parents in the kitchen, their jaunty laughter and tittering mingling with the clatter of pots and pans as they started on breakfast, but for some reason she thought grieving meant solitude.

When it happened, after the screams made her throat raw and breathing ragged, and her hand stopped shaking only enough for her to get out a few lines on parchment, she had begged her family not to come. *Say your rites but leave us to grieve*, she wrote.

And her family listened. Not a letter came as a reply, not until Urias decided things needed to start moving, choosing a date for Koa's rites and farewells. He apparently asked her family to prepare the rites themselves, though immediate kin traditionally did it.

Of course, her mother replied, the distaste palpable even in her scrawl.

Time slipped through Neoma's fingers this last week, but it stilled on the morning of her son's rites. She found herself growing angrier as they walked the sandy path cutting through the hills towards the beach, thinking of how Koa preferred to go out on First Day but Urias chose the Fifth for the ceremony. Food often accompanied ceremonies like these as well, yet he said nothing about preparing a meal for their grieving relations.

Neoma felt stripped bare and placed under a glass dome. Everyone gawked at her nakedness, her shame, but no one was allowed to come close enough to cover her.

Pulled towards the beach by an invisible thread, Neoma wondered if Urias wrote his *own* family about the accident. Neoma only met his mother once, and she was a violent spit of a woman, thin as a branch and mean as a viper. They invited her to dinner to reveal their engagement, and the woman pointedly asked if Urias really wanted to marry a sifter *who spent so much time in the sun.*

Neoma stopped urging Urias to bring his mother closer than arm's length afterwards, the comment lodging itself behind her ribcage. Otherwise, she only knew of a brother somewhere off in Con-Quary, and a father living in Esmar, and Urias told her nothing about either of them visiting for the ceremony.

Though the sun set in a white-gold starburst that promised a balmy evening, thick storm clouds clotted the horizon. Their fluffy tops streaked with the white of the dimming light made their dark underbellies even more threatening as the wind pushed them closer. Cresting the hill, feeling a pit in her stomach, Neoma saw her relatives before they noticed her or Urias—who, she noted, walked at least six paces behind. His fear of the ocean after seeing his son drown repelled him, but still he walked on, and for that, at least, she admired him.

Her family stood dressed in simple clothes, meandering in a circle around an unlit firepit dug into the sand. Only six made it, the other hands needing to keep an eye on the fire that smoked the flavor into their salts, but the familiar faces of her parents eased the tightness in her shoulders.

Calily turned, and Neoma's empty chest flooded with a sense of relief when her mother noticed her on the hill. A moment lapsed where only their eyes met before Calily's wiry, muscular arms opened. Love slipped over the distance between them, and Neoma realized that the end of the thread guiding her sat nestled behind her mother's breast.

She ran then, like a child—like Koa might have in another life, muscles pumping in his legs and the wind sliding over his kinky hair—colliding into Calily and wrapping her arms tightly around her mother's waist. Thrumming against her ear danced an unwavering testament of love. That same kind of music hummed in Neoma's chest for Koa.

"My girl," Calily murmured into the large twists Neoma managed, with weary resolution, to fashion from her hair. They were similar to the row of small, beaded braids hugging Calily's scalp. "My sweet girl. My only child, who says goodbye to her own child this night. *Ocean, carry our Koa safely to the new shores of the next life…*"

Neoma choked out the sob she stifled all the way down the path. Tightening her arms around Neoma, Calily pressed a gentle hand to her face. Tears sat in her amber colored eyes, a startling contrast against her skin. Neoma wished she bore that same jeweled tone, but as her father stepped forward to embrace them both she remembered who she took after, and the love he had for her in his midnight eyes.

They stood like that for a while. Roland held both Neoma and her mother easily in his embrace, his chin resting on top of Calily's head. Both of them smelt like the brine of their family home on top of one of the thickest salt deposits in the Saltshores, but Calily carried with her the air of fresh rain underneath. Roland held with him the wafting aroma of lavender; he must have been preparing the floral salts that very morning.

When her mother pulled away, Neoma almost protested before she followed Calily's gaze towards the sand bank.

Urias stood with his hands hidden in his pockets, the gold and gray of his hair whipping in the wind. Weariness sat underneath his green eyes, though something else made his gaze hard as he stared back at Calily. He quickly approached his fortieth nameday, Neoma her thirty-sixth, but she never realized just how weary he looked.

He's so thin, Neoma thought, still in the embrace of her parents.

As if reading her mind, Urias' gaze cut briefly to her. Instantly aware of his distance, the awkward distrust that pervade his relationship to her parents made him shift his stance. Uncertain of where the animosity bloomed, Neoma only managed to prune back the weeds of discomfort when they gathered—and, with an exhausted anger settling in her throat, she realized her son's farewell ceremony was no different. Neoma guessed correctly that no one from his side of the family meant to be there, and while that made her pity him, she was also angry that he refused to be consoled by *hers*.

However, this was not the place to talk about such things.

Moving outside of her father's grasp, Neoma made her way back to her husband's side. Urias only welcomed her with a thick hand set between her shoulder blades. It reminded her of the first moment he introduced her as his betrothed.

Ribbons flying overhead—a flute on the wind. Celebrations for the turn of the season, and a handsy merchant who reached out for Neoma's rear when she turned away from the apples. Urias caught him by the wrist, a look like venom slicing into the man. The protection without an air of possession wafting off his reddening face as he spit the words, "Do not touch my wife-to-be, lest you loose the hand you sully her with."

Where had his passion gone? It had fled long before Koa.

"Urias." Calily nodded kindly, though Neoma knew it pained her mother to speak in any soft way towards her husband. Urias stole her away from home, after all, though she suspected something else made Calily distrustful. "I'm so sorry for what's happened."

The tension abated for a moment, the words genuine, and Neoma felt Urias' hand fall away. But he said nothing for a moment, glancing around at the people there who were not *his* family.

"Thank you…" he cleared his throat, emotion lodged there. "Thank you for doing this."

Calily nodded. Roland spoke, his voice husky with tears. "No parent should ever know the grief of outliving their children."

His hand covered Calily's shoulder, and her fingers rose to cover his. The pain of losing their children in stillbirths before Neoma, though not a story frequently shared, was common knowledge in their family. When Neoma survived, Calily spent weeks giving offerings to the Sea in gratitude. *The Ocean filled me with the saltwater that carried you here*, she often hummed throughout Neoma's childhood. *It brought you all this way, from sky to sea to me.*

"We…" Neoma's voice hitched, eyes glancing to the fire pit. Usually, it needed to be large enough to burn the body so that the ash may be returned to the sea. But Koa's body drifted somewhere far out in the water, unable to be laid to rest. Neoma hoped this gathering was enough to ease his spirit.

His bloated face, peeling skin and pitted where fishes ate at him, flashed across her mind. Neoma squeezed her eyes shut, everything falling away as she tried to shake the image of his waterlogged body from her vision.

It persisted, half-eaten, half-rotten, sinking slowly into the darkness of a bottomless ocean. Out there he floated, alone and with his arms outstretched to the glittering surface of the water, forever waiting to be lifted from the depths.

"We should begin." Calily finished for her, patience in her eyes when Neoma finally opened her own.

She opened her mouth, closed it. She wanted to ask Urias to place his hand on her back again, but before she found the words he stepped away from her. Walking towards the fire pit, Neoma's relatives stepped aside as he approached its edge. A beat passed where he only stared down, hands returning to his pockets.

Lifting his head, Urias faced the sea. Shoes hushing over the sand, the small salt deposits crunching underfoot, he walked through the gathering and towards the wet shoreline. No one called him back as he stared out over the ocean, sinking into the malleable sand as a tiny, foaming waves rushed forward, kissed the toe of his boots, pulled away.

Slipping backwards into her mind, Neoma felt the entire world stretch away from her body. Urias grew long like saltwater taffy. Sand gave way underfoot, but Neoma barely noticed. It felt as though her spirit lifted outward, the real world dropping away as the grief threw her into that first month, that moment she knew her body changed forever.

Was it her present state of mind that made the memory of that pink morning sky so much brighter, or had the dawn truly been so resplendent? Urias even complimented how bright and airy she seemed, floating around the kitchen as she prepared bundles of herbs to be strung from the rafters.

"You're golden," his dreamy, loving voice said in her mind, the tenor of unwanted sensuality beneath. "You look like the sun, you're so radiant."

His words clicked together something in her mind, the moment of realization as heavy as a crashing wave. Fear and excitement and joy rushed over her all at once; she was so overcome with emotion that when she started crying, Urias asked her several times if she was all right. It was not until she placed her hands lovingly over her stomach that he realized what changed.

Despite never being as eager to approach the marriage bed as her husband, Neoma had *wanted* a child. It was not a feeling of obligation that spurred her to deal with Urias' awkward advances, or even a selfish need to create a replica of herself. For Neoma, there was so much love stirring in her heart, and it was a type of love not fit for her husband or her family. Having a child to pour all of that love into felt *right*.

Where would all that love go now?

Rites varied from family to family, especially in seaside villages close to the merging cultures that passed through the harbors. Generations of one story crossing over another produced something that, to Neoma, felt beautifully unique. While some people burned favored items of the deceased, Neoma's family threw herbs into the fire. Herbs, and the thick salt deposits on their family homestead, were the foundation of the family's riches. To them, having your loved one burn with the season's first sprig of lavender was better than being buried with gold.

Calily lead the rites, a woven basket filled with rich smelling bundles hanging from the crook of her elbow. She spoke about great Ocean, and how a person is a raindrop returning to Its vast waters. Neoma's eyes did not leave the fire as the flames ate the wood, climbing high past the edges of the sand pit.

"Koa," Calily's voice was thick with unshed tears. "For you, I burn the star anise, for you fulfilled my wish of becoming a grandmother."

A swelling sensation pressed against the lower half of Neoma's ribcage, the cramp in her stomach jarring her backwards into the month before Koa arrived. In real life, Neoma's fingers splayed out over her pudgy belly, spiderwebbed with deep, silvery marks beneath the fabric of her dress. Proof that Koa was alive once, eager to greet the world, decorated her skin forever.

The morning he made his adventure through her and into her arms, Neoma rose with bristling unease. Everything was too slow, body drifting through the day. She splayed her fingers and wiggled her toes, wondering why her limbs tingled with anticipation. She went on her daily walk alongside the shoreline, as recommended by the midwife, a hand delicately on the swell of her belly.

When the contractions began, she was on her way back home, ripped from a daydream about pirates as hot lightning flashed across her hips and down her legs. Her water spilled, breaking out from under her, and a wave hushed over her bare feet as it sank into the sand.

Salt to salt, sky to sea to me.

Neoma felt Roland's warm hand bring her back to the present, to the rites and their gentle words. Calily held the dried anise gingerly, rubbing her thumb over the surface before dropping it into the fire.

"May the star guide you across the Ocean, my sweet boy. For you I burn basil leaves, for you filled our lives with the riches of your smile."

Pain drove up from her torso again, forcing out a sob. Her father grasped her shoulders, pulling her into his chest supportively. Calily burned lemon balm, fennel, and lavender. She held a dandelion between her fingers, gazing down at it as tears clung to her lashes. Neoma, as the grief filled her chest in a cloudy fog, swarmed with gratitude as her mother carried the emotional burden of leading the rites. As she cried against Roland's chest, nothing but heartbreak filled her throat.

"Koa, your grandmother burns for you a dandelion for selfish reasons. It is the simplest, most unassuming flower—" a sob cut off the sentence, and Calily's amber eyes lifted to the darkening sky. "Some even call it a weed. But it was always a flower worthy of blooming, just as you were always a boy worthy of living."

Koa loved to swim as a child, even more so as a young man. It made his death that much more fierce. Neoma would carry her son in her arms—he was so light, his legs kicking against her rear as she threw him over her shoulders—down to the beach. If the tide was in, Neoma threw the blanket over the brittle grass that grew along the banks and sat there, but Koa always wanted to be close to the water. Calily, when visiting, often said she knew Koa was a gift from the Ocean because of his desire to be nearer to it.

Neoma never feared the water, or drifting in it with her son. He was so much lighter there, his back leaning against her chest and his head nestled into the crook of her neck as they drifted in the shallows. As he floated, she kept her arms firm and supportive, never letting his chin droop. She would cradle him like a baby, and his head would roll back, dark eyes gazing up at the clouds. Swaying back and forth, back and forth, Neoma watched the water caress his face as he opened his arms to the sky.

When he died, Neoma dreamed that he was a sailor, the captain of his own ship with legs quick as a spider clambering up the rigging, jumping into the crow's nest with a gleeful shout. Wind tossed aside his linen tunic, whipping at him so high up, and the sun was a glob of white light in the sky.

Utter joy and immeasurable pain stirred her awake from that dream, tears already wet on her cheeks. To comfort herself, Neoma believed it to have been a vision of his next life.

It did not make sense that he walked into the ocean, turning that future to ash. It seemed impossible to come to terms with how his time in this one was finished. Over.

Gone.

Raising her hand over the fire, the small yellow head of the flower trembled in Calily's grasp. She held it a bit longer than the others, closing her eyes and releasing the flood of tears there. Neoma watched it drift into the flame, sensing her body drifting with it. Her father caught her as her legs gave out, dropping to his knees to cradle her against him. To signal the end of the rites, Calily threw a fistful of salt into the flame.

Ocean, whose salt we bear. Ocean, who carries us to the new shores of the next life. Salt within, salt without.

Beyond, the waves shushed over the sands. Urias stood there with no intention of moving, trousers wet up to the ankles as the waves came in. Outlined in the gold of the sunset, bright and harsh against Neoma's eyes, his ash-blond hair whipped in the wind. Those dark, buttery clouds finally released a bellowing roll of thunder, and Neoma turn her face upward to the dimming sky.

Some time passed before Urias turned, his face hidden by the glare of light from behind him, suggesting they make their way home.

A letter awaited them, weather-worn and shining in the basket in their doorway. Urias' eyes gleaned over it, noting the wax seal, promptly ignoring it as he entered their painfully quiet home. Neoma dipped down to retrieve it, not saying a word about its sender as she closed the door behind them.

On the wax seal was pressed a grain of barley. Her husband's family did not have a business as profitable as Neoma's, rarely stamping their wax seals with anything whenever they decided to send a letter at all. Part of her dreaded its contents, so she hid it underneath her shawl as she dropped the fabric onto the seat of her chair.

"Are we hiding things now?" Urias, with his back turned to her, lit a match. His eyes crystalline in the light of the flame, they roved over Neoma as he lit the candle in the window.

There was not a word in the Common Tongue that described the exhaustion in her body. Tears were heavy burdens, as taxing to release as they were to carry. Neoma's muscles felt stiff from shedding them, yet deep in her chest she felt the healing take root. Decades may pass before she assumed any sort of normalcy without Koa. After all, now she must live her life as a mother without a child, despite her body bearing the marks of carrying her son.

But the ceremony did what is was meant to do. Neoma said a proper goodbye in the arms of those who loved her and Koa, of those who shared her grief just as strongly. It had not been solitude she needed, but a love that overflowed into her empty cup.

A love Urias all but refused to give her. Then again, had she ever loved him in that way? Had he, her?

Neoma started, realizing Urias spoke to her. Shame blushed her cheeks. However the thought entered her mind, she tried desperately to push it away. Of *course* she loved Urias, and of course he loved her. It no longer looked the same, since these years revolved around being caretakers for their son, resulting in certain sacrifices, but they loved each other—they must. If not, then what was all this for?

"You're leaving?" Fear leapt up her throat when Neoma's mind finally circled around what her husband said. "Tonight? But I—"

She stopped, not because Urias interrupted her with words but because the look in his distant gaze was so earthshakingly broken that it startled her. Red lined his eyes, raw and gleaming. A single tear escaped as his eyes went from staring at her to gazing at some distant point.

Guilt, thick and rancid, made Urias surrender himself fully to the comfort of its shroud. Neoma watched his features change as it pulled him deeper, further away from her until he stood an on island.

It was no longer simple distance between them, but a chasm.

Even so, Neoma struggled to give him any kind words of assurance. Yes, she loved him, but now he was the man who let their son drown.

"I…" He started, struggling with the words. "I looked away only for a moment. A *moment*. He is—he was twelve. He knows—knew—not to go in at high tide. I… I won't be back in the morning."

The last part he murmured, cutting off the tremor of emotion hanging on his words. Neoma, in her daze, only then noticed the packed bag resting on the edge of the table.

Did he put a bag together as she was preparing to mourn their son?

Anger roiled inside her chest, white-hot and stinging. Urias was already halfway out the door when the world came into sharp focus, each sound louder and every candlelit shadow watchful.

"Go!" The word roiled up, a crashing wave against the shoreline. "Go then, you wretch. You—you *killer*."

She did not see his face or hear a single word before the door slammed shut. Enclosing her in the deep and deafening silence, Urias disappeared into the night with no inclination of where he may go. All that surrounded her was the echo of her words.

Killer, killer, killer.

Neoma screamed again at the panels of the closed door, the sound clambering from deep within her, glad to finally be released. She cursed Urias and the Ocean as her tears rolled in scorching streams down her cheeks. Anything immediately next to her ended up on the floor as she spun, striking at every item nearby until her palms throbbed. After an unknowable amount of time passed, Neoma laid on the floor atop the items strewn about her home. Rain, she realized, pattered against the window.

She hoped it came down upon Urias, since wherever he was going was more important than comforting his wife.

The sound of the rain eased the bitterness in her chest. For a time, Neoma remained in her uncomfortable position on the floor listening to it. Eventually, the chill of the room slipped beneath the fabric of her clothing and, shivering, she rose to start a fire. She wiped away the snot and tears with the back of her hand, glancing around the room for the matches when she noted the letter once more.

Ripping it open, she scanned the words. Then, with a start, she reread them as a rotten kernel of shock settled behind her chest.

What son of mine would be so foolish as to watch his own kin drown? You are a worthy candidate for suffering, and an even unworthier father. We knew you'd be no match for that monster you called a son, just as you are nothing more than a farm boy who acted above his station. You married someone too sunbaked to give you a healthy child. I warned you as much, never mind how kind you say she is. It's a shame her family didn't dissuade her from the marriage as I tried to you. They sent a girl off to marry a shit scraper and threw their name down the ladder's rung. I'm certain this is all just her blessed "Ocean" making a point. You try too hard, Urias, to be more than you are. Consider Koa's death a lesson in remembrance of that. You weren't meant to be a father. You've got too much of your own father's blood in you to be satisfied with only one woman. Don't write me again unless it's to say you've came to your senses and will be returning home.

Gaping, Neoma dropped the letter onto the starter log in the fireplace. It sat unsigned, but she recognized the sharp bite that belonged to Urias' mother. Silent, her heart aching more now than before, Neoma lit the fire with an eager strike of the flintstone. Watching the letter burn brought her some small joy in knowing Urias would never see its words, and as its crisped edges charred and turned to ash, she tried to straighten her little world.

You've got too much of your own father's blood in you to be satisfied with only one woman.

Is that why Urias left? To prove those words true?

Even though it was only paper and wicker baskets, the tidying of small things eased Neoma's mind. Distraction was needed from the contents of the letter as well as the eerie silence of her home without Koa's liveliness in it. Her body raged as it needed, and she felt no shame at releasing its anger and frustration at the chaos of the world.

The words she flung at Urias stilled her hands. He vanished, possibly to drown the guilt with something too sharp and strong, maybe even to do what his mother accused him of, but his eyes told her that in no way did he willingly let their son drown. Urias confessed more than once that this was not the life he expected—that this sort of parenthood stole more from them than they wanted to admit—but when did Neoma let that fester into a willingness to blame him for murder?

Beneath the surface of it all, something distant riled and stirred. With the feeling came the vision of Koa sinking into the dark water again, so Neoma tried her best to shove it aside. Whatever that uncertainty carried, she refused to allow room for it to take another part of her life.

She wanted safety. She wanted to mend things with Urias, but that foreign language of the ocean carried its whispers on the rain and spoke of things she did not yet understand.

Just like the tide, the foreboding sensation slipped away in the water. There were too many things to worry over without spending time musing about the chaos on the edges of her world.

CHAPTER SIX

"I thought I'd find you here."

The crystalline voice was a clear bell in the dinge of the crowd seeking out their evening respite in *The Far Sailor*. Every mumbling tone rolled like stones down a hill, clanging together in shouts or laughs, but that sardonic Thantis lilt to the sharper Esmarin tongue was unmistakable.

Dice knew to whom it belonged just as she knew the breath in her lungs. Every bubbling vowel stuck to her like fresh ink on skin, filling her with shame.

She stood to win her active card game with two gentlemen—one with a wooden eye and another who did not have his middle or forefinger on his left hand—so Dice choose to ignore the woman a moment longer. Let her shift on her feet or feel a dredge of awkwardness. Dice earned the right to ignore her for as long as she wanted, even though she craved to drink the woman in.

Thumbing the weathered edges of the tavern's playing cards, Dice sat forward. Gluttonous smells of roasted meat spilled out from behind her where the swinging door to the kitchen fanned the delicious scent into the room. It settled over sweating bodies, stabbing the air with cooked flesh and grizzle. Dice's stomach growled, a noise thankfully hidden beneath the rumble of a neighboring table launching into a fistfight. A woman with a gray braid and her rival, a man with hooped earrings all the way up the rim of both ears, were hauled out by the sellsword Jaque. Jaque, who worked the one night Dice did not, gave her a surly quirk of his brow before returning to the stool by the door.

Resting on the table between the card players sat only a few coppers, yet it was enough money to entice Dice at the start. Blessedly, the cards in her hand sang with victory. Their faded paints depicted an empress sitting on a low throne, blonde hair set with a wreath. Nestled next to her in Dice's hand stood her companion, the emperor, and while the other cards—a row of painted swords—would have been formidable on their own, she planned to win the handful of coins on the next turn with the matching set.

Firelight climbed up the edges of the darkening walls. A bit dizzy with ale, having stolen the last dregs from forgotten cups on the tables around her, Dice drummed her fingers on the wood. The man with the fake eye, after painstakingly lifting the cards to his good one, finally came to a conclusion.

"I've got a fox," he said, laying the flimsy card down with the painted side hidden.

Dice opened her mouth, but the man with missing fingers spoke first. "Cheat."

"Ah," mused the voice from before. "So *that's* what you're playing. You're good at lying, Dice. I'm surprised there isn't more at stake."

Her mouth twisting into a grimace, Dice remained facing the men even though the thrumming in her chest grew louder in her ears. A little closer now, the woman let out a delicate laugh that dragged seductively across Dice's neck. Perfume rolled off her, taking Dice a bit by surprise. Never before had the woman taken to anything stronger than rosewater. The colognes in Stormshale's markets faced weeks of travel from the mainland with a price reflecting its journey, and such frivolity never came before bread or mead.

Perfumed lilies, sweet and sharp, beckoned Dice to turn in her chair and take note of what else must have changed about Leonora's most expensive rose.

"It *is* a fox," the wooden-eyed fellow forced out. Skin clung to him, a wet blanket hanging from a skeletal frame. People like him got stuck in ruts like Stormshale, specifically backwater dregs like *The Far Sailor*, because of much stronger vices than gambling. "On my life."

"*Cheat*," the other parroted. Placing his mutilated hand on the tabletop, he leaned in, squinting at the ragged sailor. "And yer scant life ain't much to be bettin' now is it? So's I call *cheat*. Show us your cards."

Most players with bad hands in the game of Cheat were never quick to turn over their cards. Dice tapped the edges of her own winning hand, spiders of impatience climbing up and down her arms. Behind, she felt the woman drawing closer. It was then that the man with the missing fingers noticed the surveyor of their game, his black eyes going wide as they roved over her figure. Half the tavern must be gazing at them now, the card table nearly central to the room. Anything not clotted with smoke or rank from ale drew the eye of patrons hungry in ways that bread never satisfied.

Desperation created a thin sweat across the sailor's forehead. Once you were found out in Cheat, you lost any right to continuing the hand and wining back your money. While the man, Dice assumed, did not have much coin, he still managed to keep up with the increasing sums for each round. Dice felt gladdened by the man's losses because her own purse grew rather light during the game. The vein she found some weeks ago was unfortunately not obsidian, so the Lordmine only gave her a handful of coppers for the trouble.

"Gentlemen—"

Before another word fell from Dice's mouth, the wooden-eyed man jumped up from the table so quickly that his chair skittered backwards. It hit the floor with a loud crash while the other man tried to reach across the table and grab him by the scruff of his neck. Dice dropped her arms over the money to keep it from falling tragically to the floor and through the gaps in the wood. Cards rained down over her as the two disappeared, more intent on fighting than continuing the game. As was the way at *The Far Sailor*, the point of the evening had been lost in a drunk, firelit haze.

Dice felt a mass of layered skirts brush against her shin as the woman walked around the table, righting the chair with a resolute *creak*. The skirts rustled as she lowered herself down into the spot. Heat radiated off the woman, warmer than the fire in the hearth and softer than the sweltering, sticky heat of the bodies which surrounded them. Emotion lodged in Dice's throat, tasting of spoiled memories and bile. Slowly, she lifted her head to gaze at the woman with an annoyed look that masked a deep, unabated longing.

Evangeline changed. When Dice paid for her pleasure, her pitch colored waves were always a tangled braid. Now, her hair sat in perfect ringlets that framed her long, narrow face. A red velvet ribbon encircled her neck, a teardrop of real obsidian glittering against her pearlescent skin. Dice's eyes found the more precious things instantly—the necklace, the matching drops in her ears, the brooch nestled comfortably between swollen breasts. Her ears were not pierced when Dice first arrived in Stormshale and set about looking for pleasure, nor her figure so full and happy with rich food. Dice figured that alongside the new drapery Evangeline ate well now, the softness coming from tasting things Dice never had enough money to even sample.

While she was glad to see Evangeline radiant from not having missed a meal, bitter resentment ticked behind her heart. The echoing annoyance was cavernous as it sang above her empty belly.

Thinking Dice stared at her breasts—which she was—Evangeline adjusted in the rickety seat. Even in her fine attire, she still enjoyed lewd attention.

Evangeline never felt *forced* into her work, surprising Dice in the beginning with stories of experimenting with couples on the higher platforms above them. Once her infatuation grew into mild obsession with the gentlewoman, Dice bartered stories from others who knew Evangeline from before her time at *Three Roses*. Apparently, her parents did rather well in trading wool, and there was a life of money awaiting her should she grow tired of her work.

Lilies, mixed with that powdery smell, cut through the body odor that sat thickly in the room. Taking in the layers of red wool, designs of golden sea birds handwoven into the sleeves of the cloak, Dice noted the tension around Evangeline's waist.

"Are you wearing a *corset*?"

Delight flooded Evangeline's features as she laughed. Despite her new fullness, the sharp lines of her face darkened in the shadows of the fire; once, she told Dice a story about a father who shared Evangeline's sharp nose and thin, ruby red lips.

The world around Dice blinked into golden starlight when Evangeline laughed, growing dull once more when the rapturous sound dissipated. She placed a hand on the piles of cards beside her in the flirtatious way people did in order to draw attention to their fingers.

"I *know*," she smiled, picking at the edge of the card but not turning it over. "It's the worst thing, but apparently its all the fashion in Thantis. My mother is happy to finally see me in *respectable* clothing."

Talking to her called up a mixture of pleasure riddled with embarrassment. Before Evangeline distracted her, Dice swiped the coinage into her open drawstring bag.

"You said you wouldn't wear something like that even if it meant never having to bed a drunk sailor again." Dice checked the table for more coins, then drew the string taunt when satisfied. "I suppose a lot's changed since you left."

"No," Evangeline rolled her eyes, crossing her legs under the mountain of skirts. "A lot's changed since *you* left."

"I was banned." Dice clarified, winking with a tomcat smile.

"A point you really seem to enjoy making, by the way." Evangeline ribbed. Putting her elbows on the table, she rested her narrow chin on top of petite, folded hands. Instead of continuing her remark, the young woman gazed at Dice.

It seemed Dice's turn to shift in her seat. One of the men had been drinking during the game, she could not remember which, but she grabbed the half empty mug and sipped. The bitter, sour taste hit the back of her throat in a sloshing wave, the unexpected tartness making her eye twitch. When she glanced back, Evangline's gaze remained steady on her.

"So."

"So-o," Evangeline sing-songed. "Aren't you going to ask me how I found you?"

"Leonora told you where I stay." Dice sipped, bracing a little for the taste. The second time around was not nearly as foul. Shrugging, she added,

"Or maybe it was more colorful than that. She told you where I blackened my heart or lost all my money or something."

"Or something."

Dice blinked, since she meant that as a joke. Though, remembering their happenstance interaction a few days ago, her and Leonora were on as friendly terms as a fish with a hook.

"Well," the perfumed lady pushed the conversation onward. "You should at least ask what a woman like me is doing in a place like this."

"Is this because I haven't gone back to *Three Roses*?" Dice sniffed. Part of her wanted to add that a place like *The Far Sailor* was exactly where a woman like Evangeline thrived, but paused. Whatever the man from before ordered, haziness already seemed to be clouding her judgement and halting every other thought on her tongue.

"I've not had the money, Eva," she managed. "I swear I've not forgotten you. Though," she glanced over Evangeline's attire once more, "you seem to be doing plenty fine for yourself, what with those new rags. Leaving the *Roses* did you good. Are you back home?"

"Oh, gods no!" Evangeline laughed, despite it being a reasonable guess. There was a tenor of fear in the sound, loud enough to catch Dice unawares. "I just… I got a better offer. Besides, it's bold of you to think that I came all the way down the platforms just because I missed your tongue between my legs." Evangeline grinned devilishly. "And I would greatly appreciate it if you did not call my new gifts rags, thank you."

Must be some *gentleman caller*, Dice thought. Overskirts, a coat, petticoats, a corset, probably more layers since the chilly season of Wotag approached; not to mention the jewelry. The man must be out an extra fifteen gilded pieces.

One of the things that Evangeline enjoyed most about her work was the gifts—after the sex, and knowing that Leonora's men were paid enough to toss any unfavorable patrons out with just her word. Men paid her to keep things secret from their wives, their wives paid her to stop seeing their husbands. Evangeline's room at *Three Roses*, from what Dice recalled, was more furnished than the madam's.

This hunger for extravagance was the greatest barrier that kept Evangeline from accepting any sort of romantic offer from the shipless pirate. Though the woman swore they parted as friends once Dice admitted her feelings, Evangeline placed a considerable distance between them after the sore rejection. In some ways, Leonora banning Dice from her establishment helped clear her head.

But with her in this space, so close that Dice's leg kept brushing against her skirts, the perfume flooded her lungs as heady desire rushed back. Evangeline proved harder to quit than any vice Stormshale offered.

Dice tried to match Evangeline's smile as she sipped. The wound of rejection still made it hard to fully embrace the distance between them. "I never said anything about tasting you, Eva-darling."

"It was implied. I was never allowed off my back with you."

Emboldened by the drink, Dice murmured loud enough for only Evangeline to hear. "I can't help myself. I liked the sounds you make."

The low tenor of Dice's voice brushed over Evangeline, eliciting a very obvious response as the woman's cheeks reddened slightly. Nights of twisting in the finest sheets on the softest bed appeared in both their minds. Feverish, encouraged by a bottle of red wine, they tasted the drink on one another's lips until gray morning light spilled through the window. Dice still remembered the shape of Evangeline's breasts, and the birthmark like an ink smudge underneath the left nipple. She always kissed that marred spot before taking Evangeline's breast in her mouth.

After a pointed look from Evangline signaled the end of such musings, Dice rolled her eyes. Folding her arms on the tabletop as she leaned in, Dice met the woman's gaze.

"Now," she murmured lowly, "what's a gilded woman like you doing in a place filled with cutthroats like this?"

"Well, Dice," she started, "I've come to ask a favor, actually."

Evangeline's tone slipped into formality, carrying that same strange, nervous tenor from before.

Such quick stiffness made Dice uncomfortable. Taking up the deck of playing cards, wondering if she had just been played as well, she began to shuffle them in order to stay busy. When she flipped the wooden-eyed man's card over to see that he really did have a fox, she paused for a moment to study the animal's wicked, painted eyes. Every card in Cheat represented some creature or item associated with thievery and lies. Foxes, swords, badgers, gulls, kings and queens. The point of it all was to get away with lying, steal cards from your neighbor, or "kill" one of the animals or royalty.

An honest man never had a good time playing Cheat.

"I'm not much of a sellsword." She quipped, enjoying the *thwap* of the cards on the table.

"It's not that kind of favor. Dice," Evangeline's hand settled on Dice's forearm, stopping the shuffle midway. "Do you remember—oh, this must've been forever ago, and you've probably hocked it—but do you remember that little locket made from silverwood? It had all sorts of bobbles on it."

It took a moment for the memory of the trinket to come back, but once Dice knew what Evangeline meant she nodded. "I remember it. You said it was some stupid gift, that I could take it if I wanted. What of it?"

“Did you sell it to anyone? Do you still have it?” Evangeline’s eyes feverishly jumped around the hills of Dice’s face. Great saucers studied her with a distant, harried look that sent a pang of understanding through Dice’s chest.

Whatever filled Evangeline’s blood was stronger than ale. Thinking about the languid bodies on the platforms below them, stuck in the prisons of their minds, Dice stopped shuffling in order to fully study the woman. At first, Evangeline thought she was just being admired, sitting in her chair with a proud air.

Dice *did* think her beautiful. Evangeline could swell or shrink or even lose a tooth and still, she had Dice wrapped tightly in a knot of infatuation. But without quips or tawdry comments, Evangeline realized the truth of Dice’s scrutiny quickly. Nervousness cracked through Evangeline’s flirtatious, pleasant demeanor as her nimble fingers started drumming on the tabletop. She offered no desire to confirm Dice’s fear, or deny the existence of any substance lingering in her nostrils.

“I remember it,” Dice repeated, deciding she had no right to scold or control Evangeline—and that she was the least qualified person to give advice. “I’m not sure if I have it or if it’s been sold, but I can look around and bring it to you later.”

“You can’t look around now?”

Dice furrowed her brow. While a space in her heart stayed empty for Evangline, her eagerness put a bad taste in Dice’s mouth. Suddenly, she wanted to retreat when moments ago she would have given the last of her coin to be in Evangeline’s arms again.

“I’ll bring it to you when I find it, Eva.” The tone in her voice shifted from playfulness to warning. Despite the rambunctious crowd, the sound was unmistakable.

The young woman cinched her jaw to keep back the spiteful words floating behind her eyes, rigid in her chair. Eventually, she relented. “Fine. But if you do have it, you must bring it to me no later than tonight.”

Silverwood all the way from the forests of Menthis fetched at least three gilded pieces. If Dice buried it somewhere, forgetting to sell it, it would be a miracle. However, if the locket still sat among Dice’s possessions, then in no manner would she release it for *free*, not even to Evangeline.

She smiled at the woman, the sharpness of it making Evangeline lean away in discomfort. “That’s a lovely necklace, Eva. Is that real obsidian?”

Scowling, Evangeline reached up to untie the ribbon, dropping it into Dice’s outstretched palm so quickly one may think her open hand an open flame.

Weighing the little teardrop in her palm for a moment, Dice slid it into her pouch with a nod.

"Ah," she sighed, feigning destitution. "It *is* a shame to break up a set."

Evangeline blinked, offended. "Are you seriously implying that this favor is going to cost me—"

"I always paid *you* for favors," Dice winked without pleasure, something else more vicious twinkling in her eye.

After Evangline gave the pieces over with a loud huff, she placed her fisted hands in her lap. Dice was about to remark on the ruby band around her finger when, with a start, she realized it was a marriage token.

The world slid to a stop, the golden halo around Evangeline shattering enough to let in the dark, rank air of the tavern. All at once, the perfume and the cloak and the jewels made sense. These were not gifts from a man to his *Three Roses* lover. Evangeline sat dripping with symbols of her new status, the wife of some count or merchant, which might explain why no one in the tavern had dared to touch her yet.

Such finery meant there was someone guarding her, and Dice's ale-muddled gaze jumped around the room before she found a man thick as a barrel watching her with threatening severity. He frowned when she noticed him on a chair by the bar, but kept his gaze on them.

Her superior demeanor changed, slipping away like the tide and replaced with growing humiliation. Evangeline wore a wicked smile when Dice faced her again. Forgetting about the jewels, she placed the ringed hand on Dice's forearm. The stunning, simple piece glinted in the firelight, the ruby as large as a teardrop. Such a fine thing sitting in the middle of the dinge of the tavern howled insults at Dice.

You never would've been enough.

"I suppose I should explain a little," Evangeline sighed, the sound like nails hammering into Dice's ears. "The locket, you see, is meant for my new husband. Silverwood is so hard to come by this far from Menthis. A locket like that is meant for someone *special*."

In mere seconds, every gentle and lovely thing about their connection—the sex, the sly jokes, the easy smiles, the wine-stained kisses—vanished. Evangeline's glamour, once so enticing to Dice, revealed the insatiable desire in the woman's eyes. Hate blossoming into remorse radiated down into Dice's limbs, but she kept her hands on the drawstring purse.

Every muscle wanted to grip the edges of the table, to throw it against the wall in violent anguish as a testament to the shame and embarrassment flooding her, but she forced her shaking hands to simply reattach the purse to her belt.

"He lives in a big house on the upper platform. It has real stone steps leading up to the doorway!" Evangeline smiled, proud of her status even though with such comfortable parents she was already more established than half the port-city. "You can just leave it in the flower pot by the door. Make sure he doesn't see you—it is the house with the iron fish above the doorway."

Unable to speak, or even look at Evangeline, Dice stared into the fire past the throng of bodies. She managed a single tilt of her chin to let Evangeline know she understood. The woman said another lilting comment punctuated by an airy laugh before drifting away. Dice barely heard it, the words *Thank you, darling*, stabbing into her like shards of glass ricochetting wildly through the air.

She reappeared for a moment, a cloud of lilies. "I knew I could count on you," she said, planting a wet kiss on Dice's cheek before vanishing.

The ember-hot feeling against the corner of Dice's mouth grew, a wildfire spreading across her face and down her neck. Evangeline's last touch scorched her, searing the reality about their relationship with brutal certainty. All these months of longing and friendliness amounted to nothing between them in the end, even though Evangeline enticed Dice every step of the way.

Despite rejecting her, Evangeline welcomed the money, the company, and the companionship. If it meant nothing, if she got bored, then all she would have needed to do was call one of Leonora's men to toss Dice away—but that never happened.

I can't stay away from you, Evangeline said before Leonora's judgement was final. *I don't think I ever want to.*

Downing the sour ale, squeezing her eyes against the swelling anger, Dice threw the empty mug across the way. It hit a table, spraying droplets of what was left across a man in a long coat who seemed too drunk to care. When she stood, the world titled sideways. Dice clutched the edge of the table until it leveled enough for her to walk to the bar. The barrel-chested man vanished, no doubt escorting Evangeline to her new estate.

"What'll this get me?" She asked the barkeep, tossing her copper winnings in front of him. Not drunk enough to brandish the obsidian jewelry in a room crowded with desperation, Dice figured the coin alone may be enough to tip her over the edge and into that separate, intoxicated oblivion.

The man poured a pint, filling it from a barrel stationed on its side behind him. Froth sloshed over the rim, splattering the bar top as he passed it to her outstretched hand. Not thanking him, all cordiality gone, Dice faced the busy room as she drank in large gulps. Anger still sat in her bones, mixed with a certain type of guilt women often harbored in their chests when they felt slighted by their own. Had Dice really imagined everything between them? No one warned her about Evangeline's appetite, but then again, they were both adults. Issues between them needed to be settled between *them* alone, but that did not stop the feeling of the world dropping out from underneath her feet.

"Married." Such a foreign word sat weighted on her tongue. *Married.* Locked into a single person for the rest of one's life did not sound *un*appealing, but Dice never imagined it was a path meant for her. People wanted security, that she understood, but what about those couples who stay married after one or the other—or both—cheated? And what about those who married prostitutes, or a rake? How did they form that trust?

Ah... but who even dares to trust a pirate?

Dice slugged the rest of the drink quickly before the thought had any more chance to point out the hypocrisy in her judgment. Yellow-orange firelight softened the edges of her blurred vision, the brown streaks of shadows like ink smudged across her eyes. A faceless person whistled, probably at her, as she thought carefully about putting one foot in front of the other.

Married. Locket.

Evangeline.

Is she happy?

Happier without me.

CHAPTER SEVEN

A balm settled over the night as Dice climbed the stairways to the higher platforms. Her legs were unreliable, that last ale slamming through her blood as she tried to focus on staying upright.

Someone re-pitched the stairway, the tacky residue clinging to the softness of her palm as she broke away from the railing, only to stumble without the support. It may take another week before the lower floors received the same weather proofing, despite the season of swelling storms and rising tides a more present threat to those who could not afford higher ground. The unfairness sent a new wave of anguish through her, the overwhelming emotion leveling her vision enough for Dice to get an idea of her surroundings.

Higher levels kept to themselves, the homes built into the Slate Mountains with only their doorsteps resting on the wood of the platform. Shops sat a few levels lower, and as much as the merchants and well-off families tried, they could not justify building a second market for themselves. So, some of them mingled with the lower platforms as they bought their wares and fish from market, or sent a servant. This was the first time Dice walked the higher platform without running into another person who eyed her like she was a walking barnacle.

She had found the locket at the bottom of her knapsack, tangled up in a thread of old fishing wire. Its square body did not look fine enough to be a gift, but for all she knew about this new Evangeline, the whole tale about her husband could be a lie. If Evangeline was spending her money on that sweet tar that bloomed on the end of long a pipe, then the locket could easily get her more.

Evangeline... what happened to you?

Why had Leonora not said anything about the marriage, what with Evangeline being one of her finest girls? It was unlikely that the woman wished to spare Dice's feelings. What changed in the months since Dice last saw Evangeline?

The woman had never touched tar before—was it possible her gentleman forced it upon her, or did she choose it?

Either path broke Dice's heart.

Fog drifted up from the lower platforms, unfurling from the staircase as the balm turned chilly. Homes with blazing oil lanterns cast hazy orange light from their doorways, the carved stone awnings set with iron symbols of distant Esmarin nobility. Since the mainland began to sink, the icons stopped carrying as much notoriety, but the expensive designs remained as testament to times past.

Every step she took rang out, heavy boots thumping on the boards. Evangeline said her new husband's home boasted an iron fish above its doors. Such a rich symbol meant a long line of money and, once, a place in the king's court. Esmar's royal symbol was a school of fish under a crown, so any family who was blessed by the kings of old took on a part of the image for their own House.

When Dice finally found the iron-wrought design of a single curving fish chasing its tail in a circle, she did little to hide her scowl.

Three steps led up to the door, the stone awning carved smooth and flat. Dice ran a hand up over its supportive pillars, callouses not catching a single blemish. When she flattened her palm over the stone, its coolness seeping into her arm up to the shoulder, she glanced down at the twin flower pots by the door. Stormshale grew little in the way of decoration, and some part of her felt gladdened by the raggedy bundles of thistle packed together, failing to give the appearance of a bouquet. One could only go so far to change their surroundings before being reminded that they, too, were locked in an awfully remote, rainy city on the edge of the world. No amount of money changed that unless one decided to leave, searching for something better than Stormshale's listless gray.

Out in the world, there were many places finer than Stormshale. Dice wondered, staring at those thistles, why she bothered to stay so long in the first place? Maybe this confrontation with Evangeline, which exposed the truth of their rotting relationship, meant to jostle her into leaving. Perhaps it was time to find the *Marksmen* again, to discover whether or not Evander cared to welcome her aboard after their latest skirmish.

The skittering sound of feet rushing over the wooden boards made Dice turn, albeit too quickly. Vision swimming, relying on the column for support, she stared into the gray-green fog that consumed the platform when she was not paying attention. Lanterns cast a circle of orange light in the mist, every other detail obscured by the plumes. A glob of a lantern swung in the breeze, its creaking hinge screeching across the night.

Hair raising on the back of her neck, Dice fully turned to face the dimness. Even drunk, she knew the difference between a rat darting across wooden boards and the weight of man's step. She waited for a few heartbeats, the anticipation of who it might be draining the ale from her mind until her vision sharpened in the low light. Growing up on a ship meant knowing when the time for enjoying the flush of drink must come to an end.

Dice placed a ready hand on the hilt of her dagger, wavering vision jumping to the darkest points of the night. Without a proper sword, she felt pitifully unprepared, but only the Watch was allowed to carry such weaponry. A flintlock was ideal, but that was an expense Dice may never afford.

A foreboding sensation stirred in her chest, the kind which Evander taught her to pay attention to as she got older. *It could be the difference between losing men to a maelstrom, or to the blood-eaters*. The advice reverberated down her spine as she pressed her back fully against the wood door, deciding to release the dagger from its sheath.

It took a moment for Dice to notice that though the lantern swayed in the breeze, she no longer heard its creaking hinge. Looking down to her free hand, breath braced in her chest, she pushed her thumb and middle finger together and *snapped*. Though she felt the motion in her hand, the diluted sound did not scrape the otherworldly silence settling over her.

Over the whole world.

Dice snapped again right next to her ear, hand shaking when the sound died, cut off in the middle.

The world went quiet, absorbing every groan of wood or hush of wind. Dice snapped by her ears again, realizing she could not even hear the sound of blood rushing through her head.

Before terror chanced taking root, the night was ripped apart by the bellowing of a horn, its guttural, ancient sound a call from the depths of the darkest parts of the ocean. The echoing, elongated note, one that could not be pulled from the lungs of any human, sliced through the quiet. It rose from an unnamed place, a sound ancient yet so familiar to Dice that she felt it calling to her very marrow.

The reverberating sound conjured images of writhing bodies dragged from the shining surface of the water to the blue-black nothingness of the deep.

Dice covered her ears, mouth open in shock, unsure if she were screaming or trying to catch her breath. She felt her mind call up a memory that was not hers, the images slicing through her consciousness.

A boy with black skin sinking into the darkness.

Legs unable to kick, lungs unable to scream.

A hand locked around the ankle, warm but cold, too.

Crushing pressure, water in my belly.

Fear shivered through her muscles. She cramped under the weight of terror, shoulders hiked up to her jaw, fingers gnarled around the shape of her ears. Climbing up her feet, shaking her very core, the sound lifted in volume until Dice collapsed under its influence.

Red swam in her vision, the gray-green fog tinted ruby. Blinking, she saw a figure standing in the middle of the platform. Backlit by the lanterns that shook underneath the echo of the deep horn, the body remained upright, undisturbed. Dice blinked again, opening her mouth to call out only to see an empty space.

Just as the sound seemed as though it meant to split her skull, it vanished.

Her surroundings winked out, impermanent shadows against firelight twitching as a solid floor formed beneath her boots. Dice closed her eyes so tightly, stars sparkled against the black of her eyelids. She felt the heat of the air, the soles of her boots leaden. Every sound heightened, her ragged breathing like the scraping of tree branches against bare rocks.

At her back, warmth from a fire spread into the otherwise cool room. Logs in its hearth popped steadily, the sound easing Dice into gentler breaths.

A cold hesitation sapped the warmth of the fire from her limbs.

Dice opened her eyes quickly, startling backwards into a sloshing puddle something pungent at her feet. Solid stone walls, the inside of a home, caught the light of the fire only to spit it back onto the slick red strikes of blood on the weathered rug before her. Its pattern disappeared in the drenches of iron tang, long stripes like finger marks dragging down its edges. Life pooled in the ridges of the flagstone, droplets dotting ancient fabric-backed chairs, dripping down their wooden legs in thin rivers. It clung to her hair, her chin, and Dice gagged as the smell of an open carcass filled her nostrils.

She knew the scent of a flayed body, understood skinning a flank of meat and splitting the guts of a fish to rid her meal of innards and bones. A similar rankness, hot and putrid, blossomed around her. Confusion beat at Dice's temples as it begged her mind to recall the last steps that led her into *this room*, which otherwise had materialized around her blood-slicked body.

So much blood… *but where did it come from?*

Shaky hands searched her drenched tunic—she lost her coat and coin purse, somehow, and the fabric of her top was so weighted with blood that it hung off her arms like melting skin. The front of her thighs were damp, but most of the gore covered her torso. Dice's dizzying mind ricocheted in no organized pattern, eyes jumping from the open decanter on the table before her, to the two glasses sharing its brandy. Her search brought up a missing dagger, vanished alongside her coat, and Dice felt a garbled, broken sound escape her lungs.

The odd noise shocked her into the present. Dice's searching fingers did not find a puncture wound, so the blood cooling on her skin did not belong to *her*.

After a world of silence, every sound felt sharp. Under her breath, beneath the deceiving comfort of the popping fire, another inconsistent noise pattered against the flagstone.

Liquid hitting liquid, dripping from one lofty surface to *plat, plat, plat* behind her. Terror formed a solid lump in Dice's throat as she turned, the very air pushing against her, wanting no part in the revelation.

Heartbeat dancing thunderously in her chest, Dice steeled herself, fingers squeezing into solid fists, and turned to face the fire.

Stuck clean through was a man's head, pinned with *her* blade to the middle of a great mural of gore, the hilt sticking out of his open mouth. Thick pink entrails spiraling out from his head like festive garland shimmered and glistened in the firelight. Part of the rotten smell clotting the room was the contents of his intestines sloshing out of open ends, sliding down the edges of the wall. The arms of the disemboweled stranger were cut at shoulder and elbow, breaking the limbs into four sections that pointed skyward, downward, and to either side like a gruesome compass.

A slick covering of muscle and skinned flesh dressed the mantle resting underneath the man's head. Dice felt her stomach cramp, bowing forward to vomit into the hearth. All that came was bile and bitter brandy, sizzling in the fireplace and adding to the wretched stench as it burned. Her limbs protested this unnatural revelation of flayed skin and severed arms, white bone a pearl in the middle of slick, exposed muscle. When she finally looked up again, horrified by the dismemberment but unable to rip her gaze away, it felt like she were praying at an altar of carnage.

Forcing herself to stand on shaky legs once more, she searched in a vain attempt for anything that might revitalize her lost memories. All that complimented the pounding in her head was an unraveling blankness that gave no answer to how she appeared in the middle of *this* room.

Her eyes instead found the fingers of the man, severed at each knuckle and lined up in a jagged sentence of broken symbols atop the unraveled flesh on the mantlepiece. Staring down at them, swimming in the darkness of uncertainty, a single, intolerable question rose:

Had *she* done this?

Dice shot her eyes upwards, gazing at the face of the stranger.

A startled inhale raked her chest as she stared with aching recognition, and recalled the man who grasped Leonora's chin at the haberdashery. Here, he was flayed, bulging dead eyes open in shock, but she could place that sordid grin he gave the madam on his pale lips. What did she have against the man, other than being the pocket that could afford Evangeline a different life?

With emptiness pervading her mind, her last recollection was playing cards at *The Far Sailor*. The possibility of this being done by her hand created a violently new perspective to the mural of gore. Such a masterpiece of brutality was unlike anything of which she thought herself capable. The very concept of stringing up the entrails, their soft, slick skin in her hands, made her feel ill.

Leave—she had to go, run, *leave*.

Dice grieved her dagger's resting place for only a flashing moment, knowing that such a common wooden hilt carried little by way of identifying *her*. Every step leaden, her boots left prints of blood on the flagstone as she stumbled out of the poorly lit room and into the darker hallway beyond. It was only then that the idea of servants slipped into her mind, quieting Dice's footfalls despite every sinew raging for escape.

Luckily, the sitting room broke directly off of a long hallway leading to the front door. It sat locked, so either Dice broke in, or she had been welcomed into the home.

Two glasses, she remembered as she slid the bolt out of its hitch. There were *two* glasses next to the decanter of brandy, which she tasted as it made its way back up her throat. Something alluding to acquaintanceship, but how? And if the man was *Evangeline's* husband, then what did Leonora have to do with him?

Shoving the door open, Dice stumbled past two pots of thistle that twitched in the breeze. During the storm season, it was hard to tell how close the sun was to rising, but that morning the clouds peppering the sky were a deep, beautiful red.

Dice glanced behind her, back into the darkness of the house, waiting for a servant to discover the body.

No scream split the hallways, no pattering footsteps on flagstone echoed into her ears. Her jumpy, feverish gaze flicked up to the iron fish above the archway, a new terror at the symbol rooting into her mind.

Across the platform, the warning of an opening door jolted her into action. Never mind the drenched fabric, her missing coin purse, or the clots of matted blood in her hair—she had to vanish for long enough to pull herself into one piece. Whatever happened inside of this house, whether it had been her fault or if she was still reeling from witnessing something horrendous, Dice needed to act. If she stood there thinking, remembering, then the shards of her mind might splinter and shred the last of her sanity.

By the time the woman across the platform stepped out into the unusually bright morning, Dice was no more than a bloody boot print on wood grain.

CHAPTER EIGHT

Sleep gave Pelagios little respite. As a younger man, he accomplished great things after closing his eyes for mere moments. Battles were won on sleepless nights, his back arched over a map or his mouth between the legs of anyone who, like him, was too terrified of the morning to sleep.

Age belittled him, wore at the space between his knuckles until opening and closing his fist on a cold winter's morning brought pain, not relief. And as he aged, so did Einar, the monarch of Esmar, *the Mad King.*

Pelagios despised the label, but what could be done of it? Einar faded quickly, his mind receding into a world from which the old guardian could no longer protect him. Age was destined to kill Pelagios, if nothing else chose to strike him down sooner, but in the rotten race towards death he knew his path stood to be the easiest of them.

Graciously, the mutinous actions of Einar's council—which were now in part Pelagios' actions, too—relaxed into little more than knowing looks exchanged in passing. Everyone acted particularly interested in the summoning of a mage, despite the protest of a few, but the organization of such a plan had to be done slowly.

Pelagios hardly compelled himself enough to return the nods, the roiling thoughts of anger and guilt casting his face into a constant scowl. Nerves settled in his gut, making mead sit like iron in his belly. Food was little comfort, though his years on the field made Pelagios particular towards simpler breads anyway.

Why Pelagios decided to both betray his king *and* protect him must have been decided by the gods, for the old general considered himself well past the age of subterfuge. Nor was he entirely surprised the night of Damalis' calling, since betrayal ran rampant in Einar's courts. Pelagios seemed at a loss, though, in trying to map in his mind exactly how he should appeal to Damalis and the other counselors in a way that still allowed him the ability to protect the king.

Maybe there was no need for this worry, and the reason Einar called upon Pelagios was to accuse him of that which he was guilty.

Maybe these were Pelagios' last moments within Einar's court.

Death soaked the shadows of Carn-Duhl. Pelagios was never a lyrical man, but it seemed poetic that he should die there. It stained the inside of his nose, drifting like a perfume off the walls and up from the battlements. Pelagios' lungs filled with the stench of the marshlands, riddled with decaying bodies of humans and unlucky animals alike as he made his way across one of the exterior balconies that overlooked the lower courtyards. Pelagios rarely went this longer route to the vestibule of the king's meeting rooms, but for some reason the torchlit halls of Carn-Duhl felt suffocating. Pelagios could only explain the sudden fear of those dark halls as carnal apprehension, the exact reason for concern slipping past his fingers like water.

Thinking about walking in the pitch of an eternal night made Pelagios shiver as the guards pushed open the doors for him, expecting his arrival. Beyond stood a room with the most intricate masonry found anywhere in the monument of a castle, with vaulted ceilings interwoven with stone and silverwood braiding together above his head. Words—for they must be words of either protection or enchantment—sat immortalized along the arms of stone and wood. His eyes, beckoned by their inviting shapes, found the symbols as he entered the private room. It must have been a sacred room in the distant ages before Esmarin monarchs.

The arch of the stone ceiling dripped down into the creases where the walls began, seamlessly melting together into dishonestly soft ripples. Pelagios knew that if he laid his palm to rest against those gentle ridges, cold rock, not soft silk, would meet his skin.

In the classic fashion of Esmar, the chipped ridges of flagstone and pebbled grout were covered by a handstitched rug. While noble families commissioned pieces speaking of their Houses and their titles, this one told the tale of Einar's ancestral claim to Esmar. Pelagios noted how the expert threading did *not* depict the decades when Einar's lineage fled the shores of the country to escape a coup. Or how afterwards, Esmar became a small collection of elect-led villages, the rule and favor not being limited to the men. Matriarchs guided the country's upbringing for six decades before Einar's great-great-grandfather reclaimed the Esmarin throne.

On the other end of the room taking up the entire expanse of wall was a long, low fireplace. Its mantle came to the knee, and atop its roughly hewn surface rested a variety of furs. Heirlooms sat haughtily on these puffs of fox's skin and lines of bear pelts, from chalices molded from the first bounty of the mines to petrified barley from an ancestor's first yield.

At first, Pelagios did not notice the king standing amongst these things, his body still against a tapestry in a manner that made the old general first think a statue stood among the oddities. Dressed in a long, layered robe with flouncing heads of wheat sewn into the neckline and weaving up the belled sleeves, a vast measure of Einar's handsomeness broke through his often tyrannical appearance. It softened, in a strange way, the shrapnel edges of his features. While donned in his armor, the king made a fearsome silhouette, but he seemed almost feminine in the softness of his day robes, his dark hair loose about his shoulders. Only the iron circlet, a simpler monument to his kinghood, depicted his station.

Einar forgot for a brief moment that he called someone into the chambers. A glassy look faded from his distant gaze, which slid across the brightly lit room to find Pelagios, rigorous as a guard awaiting instruction. Standing on the opposite end of the grouping of cushioned chairs, Einar took a steps forward to placc his hand upon one's shimmering wooden back.

"Have you dealt with its body?" Einar's fingers curved around the chair's edge. Encircling his middle finger in a thick band of silver, nestled in a bed of gemstones as clear as water, sat his wedding token.

The queen's family, noble but not extremely wealthy, had little to pass on in ceremony. Aletta, young and bold, encased a lock of her hair in a glass bead. It was Einar who demanded the gaudy surrounding for the otherwise simple gift, and the bead looked like a raven's eye in the middle of stars.

It stared at Pelagios as he masked his confusion with an inquisitive lift of his chin. "Whoever has shamed you with their insubordination has surely already been delt with, my King."

"We cannot risk any other Kahun finding it—who knows what unnatural magics they may use. They once livened a creature of mud and stone to attack *my* ancestors in battle." Einar sucked his teeth, his grip on the chair tightening. "What matter, then, would be raising a body?"

His last words pitched low, directed almost entirely to himself. Pelagios kept his stance firm and unwavering, his brow furrowed over his searching gaze. To the old general's knowledge, the only Kahun they interacted with recently was the one Theon killed with Pelagios' blade.

The event transpired some weeks ago now, and the shadows molded into something more sullen, as if despairing the death. It was impossible for Pelagios to walk the halls without seeing the Kahun's golden eyes in the dark, or look upon his family's blade without feeling a draw of wrongness in his stomach.

Damalis, when discussing Einar's increasing issues with the concept of time's passage, advised that it may be best to be agreeable when these discrepancies appeared. It was the wisest course of action to not push against an already crumbling obstacle, a mix of fear and heartbreak in the agreeability.

Pelagios hinged slightly at the waist. Drawing together a righteous tone, he said, "My King, the Kahun has indeed being disposed of in the marshland. Whatever is left of his people, they would be fools to seek after his body—or act against any perceived wrong. Your walls are high, and your subjects more than willing to enforce your justifiable decision."

For a long moment, this did not ease the scowl on Einar's face. "A fool makes for a good warrior."

Pelagios opened his mouth, uncertain as to whether or not he should ask the king to elaborate on the lucid thought, but pressed his lips together as soon as the idea came to him. While Einar had yet to move against the old man in any threatening manner, the experienced general knew better than to assume he had complete leeway to speak freely.

Catching the light from the fire, the king's wedding token tossed a beam of light across Pelagios' eyes. Einar's hand flicked back and forth, thumb rubbing the pad of each finger as though lost in counting, the motion causing the gemstones to flick the speckles of light across the room.

"My wife…" began the king on an exhale, "asks after you, Sir. She is a little better this day, and wished at breakfast that you may visit with her."

Pelagios' heart skipped, a thread of desire needling into his chest. He tried to keep his voice even, wary of the excitement there. "I am glad the Queen is well enough to ask after me at all. Yes," he added, voice light. "I would be glad to say hello after these long months of praying to the gods to cure Her Majesty."

Though less of a praying man than most, Pelagios kept his humble icons of the Mother and Father dusted, a bowl of wine always set between them. It was the first matter he tended to after the secret meeting with the advisors, and Aletta's name was always on his lips when he bowed in prayer.

Did he look presentable enough? Would Aletta talk with him, or simply smile in that soft way of hers?

Wearing simple but fine riding leathers, no more than a decorative and dull short blade at his hip, he shifted on his feet. When addressing the queen he preferred to wear finer threads. His mind brought up the blue embroidered tunic specifically, iridescently white thread outlining infinite crashing waves along the chest and arms.

Interrupting his thoughts, a servant opened the door to bless the stifling room with a draft of cool air from the hall. Laden on their palms rested a tray of warm bread, a bowl of soft cheese, and a fat bushel of grapes that were so dark they reflected Pelagios' hungry gaze. He recognized the servant, recalling a small dinner where she served the wine.

The servant kept her eyes averted as she placed the tray down on a short table in the middle of the cushioned chairs. Once everything was righted, the servant folded her hands neatly at their front, taking shuffling steps backwards so as to not disgrace the king by turning her back to him.

Her long skirts, the hem dirty from walking throughout the castle, caught on the heel of her shoe. Seconds merged together into one quick moment, so seamless it felt preordained. Pelagios watched the servant fall, knowing better than to attempt to soften her landing. Einar's rage descended upon the servant, a hawk dovetailing to catch a mouse in the fields, for as the servant fell she turned her back to brace for the impact.

Einar, clearing the space of the room in five long strides, kicked his foot down onto the space between the servant's shoulder blades. He stood large and proud even without armor, the thin servant only managing to turn her head and press her cheek against the handstitched rug.

"You dare turn your back to me?" Einar's voice was a hiss, spittle raining down as he leaned his weight into the foot that pinned them. "I have men who take blades to their chest rather than turn away from me, but *you* are so weak that you fear a short fall?"

Tears flowed freely, the servants mouth a tight, silent line. Her plaited hair slinked across the floor, a beautiful dark rope that Einar reached down and *yanked.* A gasp of pain escaped the servant's mouth, her defiant silence over.

Pelagios looked on, pretending not to notice the pleading flick of the servant's eyes before they closed in vindication. With her palms pressed into the rug, knuckles white with fear, both figures looked like a statue depicting some violent capture as Einar towered over her.

Sometimes the king killed with such beautiful anger that the murderous action carried the same intensity as thrusting into a lover.

Einar continued pulling on their hair while keeping her pinned. The moment Pelagios realized what was happening, his mouth gaping but silent, a sickening *crack* resounded through the room.

Death did not readily take them, so when Einar removed the weight of himself from the servant's back a gurgle escaped her crooked throat.

"Your Queen is expecting us, my friend."

Kindness reserved for a rare few made the energy of the room shift into a corrupted sense of comradery. Pelagios moved his gaze from the twitching servant, face smooth and uncaring despite the roiling in his stomach. His king, backlight by the warm orange fire, folded his hands behind him in a picture of laziness. Broad shoulders blocked out the light, dark hair pitched in blackness. Logs popped, crackling as they ruptured and collapsed in the hearth.

A chill of understanding settled across the general's skin.

Einar extended a hand towards what Pelagios knew to be a secret door leading to the king's private rooms. Gold grain on the belled sleeve shimmered, the wall behind the king speckled with the reflection of the gemstones on his ring. Pelagios swallowed, forcing his gaze to remain on the king's shadowed face and not slide to the twitching, gurgling body on the floor.

She must be suffocating now, her neck twisted and spine crushed.

A part of his soul shivered, surprised at the calloused census, but a larger, louder part of himself snuffed out the shame. For the last few weeks, since the death of the last Kahun ruler, this voice often clamored over its empathetic counterpart.

"After you, my King." Though Einar stood by the door, Pelagios extended his arm. He waited to lower his outstretched hand until Einar shoved the secret stone panel, its old hinges swinging a part of the otherwise solid wall into a dimly lit corridor.

Passing under the etched words, Pelagios felt the tremor of a finger dragging down the base of his neck. Gooseflesh jumped to the surface in response, and the old man turned his head swiftly around the room. Noting little more than the still body on the floor, Pelagios relaxed his sword hand.

Dropping it to his waist, he gave a careful look down the length of his arm.

Blue lips sat in a pool of dribble. The arms of the servant were splayed oddly, one outstretched above her head, the other tucked under her body. Raven hair gleamed a deep blue, the reams of the firelight sending slants of orange light across the mussed plait. Pelagios thought of the guards waiting outside, and the rumors of desecrated bodies that churned frequently throughout the court. As soon as that secret door hinged shut, the guards would either have their way with the chilling corpse or sell it to the next dignitary who craved the icy companionship.

And that was being considerate. Pelagios figured the men outside may do both, cleaning up the evidence of sacrilege like skillful undertakers preparing a body for its farewell ceremony.

The general said old words that sputtered up from the memory of his father's funeral, which felt out of place in the world of courts and kings.

"A bounty of fish to feed you and yours."

Motion stirred in the corridor—the king.

Before Einar had the chance to see the uncertainty testing Pelagios' steely features, he shook away all care for the discarded servant. Designating one's self to the amenable service of the King of Esmar was an honorable task rewarded with a roof over one's head and food in one's belly.

There was nothing better than to be dismissed by that same hand.

Pelagios closed the secret door behind him, offering a meager but believable apology to Einar. The iron sconces set an arm's width apart were smaller than the ones which held massive torches in the public halls, where even their blazing lights did little to reach the distant ceilings. Einar's body dipped into shadow, and Pelagios began to forget the room—and the body—behind them as they walked.

Fiddling with his sleeve as he tread across the flagstone, the kind of nervousness he had not felt since he was a young man drifted up from the hollow of his belly. How much time had passed since the queen fell to her knees at Theon's naming banquet, blood speckling the bone white cloth she held to her lips? Einar's fury and fear that night challenge his ferocity on the battlefield. He did not sleep, did not eat, until every court physician stood at Aletta's bedside.

Age only wrapped Pelagios in a threadbare blanket when Aletta first came to court—his hair, at least, was not fully gray yet. He would be a serpent to claim he never imagined Aletta marrying *him* instead of a king. As the right hand of King Mycin, Pelagios often found himself as Einar's chaperone. Seeing the budding pair smile and titter softly set a knife between his ribs that he had yet to be rid of, and it felt that when Aletta whispered things to Einar, she was whispering to him, too.

I trust no one else, friend, Mycin once said, the phrase repeated often towards the king's final days. *You are my eyes, ears, and my firm hand. Guide him well, as soon I cannot.*

Once the two were married, the general figured his obsession with Aletta might fade, naively forgetting how much more tempting she may be within Carn-Duhl. Drifting in every corridor he ambled in quiet, watchful pursuance of her lingering the smell of sweet mead and pepper. It intoxicated him, chastised him, hardened the space between his legs.

But even with his station and respect in the court, the general might have met the butcher's blade if he did not stop shadowing the queen.

Aletta grew, both with child and in matured beauty. She kept the softness Pelagios so lusted after, round cheeks blossoming with rosebuds as she gave to Einar sons and daughters. In his darker moments, shut away in his chambers, Pelagios gripped himself to completion as he thought about spilling seed inside the queen, wondering in delirium how *their* child might look. Some release was found in women who mirrored Aletta's figure, but it all fell short of ecstasy.

The hall ended, depositing them into a round chamber. Einar strode confidently to the door set within the opposite wall. Pushing it open, the king called within the well lit and warm room, his voice like a young man's. Loved dripped from Einar's throat as he called for the queen again, laughing to himself a little as he stepped in.

Pelagios spied the chambermaids standing by the door. At first, everything about their stature seemed natural, their hair plaited and fashionably wrapped around their heads like twin crowns, their matching blue and silver gowns reflecting the colors of the queen's House. With their eyes cast demurely towards the carpeted floor, it took a beat for the general to see the reflection of teary rivers running down their cheeks.

Turning half-aside, Einar beckoned Pelagios to follow. No longer steeped in shadow, the king shimmered with the warmth of a hearth that sang of popping logs and crackling flames. Finding some comfort in resting his hand loosely on the hilt of his sword, Pelagios wore a relaxed grin despite the rising apprehension in his chest.

"She has complained of a slight chill, but nothing more."

The room was the tallest of the private chambers in Carn-Duhl. Reaching up overhead stretched the inside of a mighty spire with a circle of open windows high above. It was a marvel that the room felt as warm as it did with such an expansive ceiling, but not a chill tinged the air.

When his eyes finally leveled to the rest of the room, Einar was lowering himself into a chair by the wide bed. It's four posts built of stone supported tapestries that were tied away with thick cord, and the mountain of cushions supported the wheat colored head of the queen.

Pelagios let out a shallow breath, his nerves settling when he gazed upon the queen. Half concealed by Einar, she sat nestled under the hefty blankets.

Whispering in a sweet tone reserved only for her, Einar's voice drifted through the room. A cadence of affection, it ruptured into something bitter in the air and stirred a jealous bile in Pelagios' stomach.

"Come here, friend." Einar did not bother glancing at the man when he spoke, taking Aletta's free hand that rested at her side.

The general cast the sobbing chambermaids a strange look as he crossed the room. One of them raised her head, glistening eyes tracking his movement. Perhaps the queen had worsened. Maybe the spark of energy which caused her to ask after him was but a fleeting moment of hope. Oftentimes, Einar only heard what he wanted, so it would be no surprise to Pelagios if the royal physician spoke more ill news than good.

Approaching the royal bed, Pelagios graciously kept his chin lowered until he could do a proper bow. He caught Aletta's familiar scent of pepper and mead. Smelling Aletta, even in this state, stirred a shameful sort of longing in his chest. He wanted to mount her and hold her, thanking the Mother and Father for her prosperous health as he kissed her.

Startling his senses and unceremoniously pulling him from the inappropriate daydream was the sharp tang of wilting flowers. As he rose, he noted their decaying petals sprinkled across the top of the blankets. His first assumption being the apothecary placed the dying flowers to mask the smell of poultices and medicines, Pelagios thought nothing of it until, finally, with a smile of genuine desire on his lips, he turned his face to the queen.

Sharpening into a grating pitch behind him, the chambermaids sniffled to keep back their tears. Einar kept Aletta's pale hand in his large, battle-scarred one, the beginnings of decay only small specks of bruising along her wrist and forearm. Half-lowered lids gave the appearance of a near-sleep, of fighting against that dark wave of unconsciousness so as to not miss a single moment of life.

Pelagios' heart shattered behind his tunic, a sound so loud and sudden that it made him waver on his feet. The king's eyes snapped to him, the trance of his heavy-lidded wife breaking for a mere moment. A fever laced his gaze that when he stared up at Pelagios, the general felt the look pass right through him.

"Is that any way to greet your queen? Your *friend* of all these years?"

Bile gurgled in the old man's stomach, threatening to rise. Naivety lost, Pelagios smelled clearly what the flowers so desperately tried to mask. Rot twined its fingers into the bones of the woman he wished to bring back, if only to ease the shattered mind of the king.

What did this mean for Einar now? The king suffered greatly, speaking to the quiet body of his wife as though she responded. Voice muffled, Pelagios did not try to hear or understand the words whispered to the corpse. Fractured as it was, the king's mind must be splintered.

Aletta was gone, and his doting could not bring her back. Did he bring Theon into this chamber to speak with his dead mother in the same way? Did the prince humor his father, or did he believe that the queen was only a little ill?

Remembering his orders, Pelagios did not rip his gaze away from the spotted, veiny face of the queen until he bowed too low to see her. His voice slipped past his quivering lips in a miraculously level tone: "My Queen."

Einar *tsked*, annoyed. He offered Aletta's limp, pale hand to him.

Pelagios steeled himself, gazing down at the raw quicks of her nailbeds, the jagged edges of bitten nails that she must have worried between her teeth in anxiousness. He thought about how Einar kept her from seeing anyone during these last weeks. So much anguish must have settled over her in those final moments with no one but the physician and her chambermaids to ease the burden of dying.

My wife asks after you, Sir. She is a little better this day, and wished at breakfast that you may visit with her.

During these weeks, had Aletta truly called for him to visit with her?

Pelagios thought a hundred things as he bowed, sadness mingling with frustration in his throat. Aletta took ill only days before Einar set out to hunt the Kahun leader. With the marshes quickening into the mainland, the battalion did not get too far into Esmar before it became too dangerous to continue. Another few weeks passed, their return marking the start of

Ceitash, but the councilor told Einar she was still only ill. Was it their fault for prolonging this hopeless optimism, planting the rejection of her death into the king's mind? When did she *actually* die?

Had she asked for Pelagios with her final breaths?

Anger glinted within him, bearing its shimmering teeth. It grew white-hot when the general pressed his dry lips against the hand of his queen. Her skin was a little warm from being in Einar's grasp, giving the illusion of life, and a fresh wave of sadness rose high enough to quell the anger.

For now, at least.

CHAPTER NINE

Sixty days in Ceitash slipped past Neoma, no heavier than a sea breeze. Urias moved around her, a ghost in his own home.

No. *Home* was the wrong word. It stopped feeling more than stone and mortar the moment they lost Koa.

The letter she burned some weeks ago left its hashed cursive on her mind. Every time Urias turned from her in shame or anger, she thought of the mother who felt comfortable enough condemning her own child to misfortune. Whoever Koa might have become, Neoma did not have words like that within her, iron spikes filled with the desire to make Koa stumble.

Focusing on her husband's ill upbringing distracted Neoma from the fleshy, raw wound behind her breast. She wore the passing month as though it were a great tapestry hanging from her shoulders. Everyone possessed a story so dark that shadows balked in discomfort—Neoma's just happened to become visible. Grief made tangible, the dark of her skin no longer glowing with the vibrancy she adored in her motherhood. What she managed of her hair was simple, but she no longer kept the braids her mother taught her to weave from a young age. Her arms were too exhausted to define each plait.

What is the point? The shadows inside herself grumbled, and so she relented to a tight knot at the base of her neck. *A woman with a sad husband. A mother with no child. Nothing more than a shell of herself, see how she no longer smiles?*

Still, Neoma praised the strength it took to gather herself together for long enough to walk all the way into Linlocke. An easy footpath wound from their house on the shore straight to the waist-high stone wall that encircled the friendly if small island-town. Walking up the gentle hills proved more exerting that Neoma wanted to admit, yet the wafting smell of bread on the air stirred her. Blood pumped gratefully through her body, heartbeat treading in her throat, eager for the exercise.

A few well-meaning mothers found her in the crowds, giving her small smiles, their hands lovingly squeezing her elbow or shoulder when she walked by. These small gestures were strong enough to bring Neoma to tears. She was not as famous as the families of the Gilded Isles, but people knew the salts she made and were grateful for the money it brought into the Saltshores. In a strange way, the mothers who passed took on a bit of her grief with every gentle touch. *I see you.*

Every Fifth Day, the baker in town put out seeded bread that she never was able to mimic, and Neoma was all but weeping when she asked the baker for a loaf. The old woman, skin pitted with sunspots and palms rough from a life of salt farming in her younger years, placed a small jar of whipped butter next to the loaf. She refused to accept payment.

Warmth seeped into Neoma's side from the fresh bread, spilling into her chest to caress the wound of her heart. Linlocke may never be as large and thriving as Trilabold or Con-Quary, but each person on the island town must be worth ten, at the very least.

Why had she agreed to move closer to the shoreline? Her and Urias' first home on the edges of the thatched roofs and public fires seemed private enough. With their gated plot, they were still close to market and the ferry boats that tutted between Linlocke and the Gilded Isles. How had Urias justified the move all those years ago? It seemed so distant now, but Neoma itched to recall their conversation.

The plague on her mind distracted her on the walk home, though a part of her remembered to brace her heart for the silence that stood, waiting and impenetrable, within those walls of her house.

Then, Neoma was struck with the fiercest sensation to *turn around.*

She drew up short, breath quick in her chest from the first long walk in weeks. Rolling down and out before her stood the sandy dales, reeds and coarse grass nodding in the breeze. Gold spilled out from the sky, sunlight warming the cool earth, the clouds thick with what might turn into a storm as they drifted out to sea. On her left, the dunes began to wither into a shoreline where foam hissed against the white beach, dragging its watery grasp backwards to lazily crash down once more. The briny smell of salt clung to the air, making her think of tough meat and heavy stews riddled with potatoes. Just over the hills sat the stone wall surrounding Linlocke, the first dips of thatched roofs broken by columns of smoke from the cookfires.

So much beauty unfurled around her shattering senses. Aching wonder continued to bless the world with its waving grass and lyrical beaches, simultaneously feeling as though it taunted her pain, and wished to heal it.

Lay down, the grass murmured as its stalks brushed against one another. *Go to sleep*.

The sound of shifting sand and loosened pebbles drew Neoma out of her daze. Eyes blinking open, wondering at which point she closed them, the world sharpened. Coming up the path behind her was the familiar face of the laundress of Linlocke. Thick straps crisscrossed her chest, a satchel half her size against her back. Black ringlets escaped from under her cap, and when she noticed the other woman on the path she gave a startlingly kind smile. It was not the sort of pitying kindness Neoma was on the receiving end of these last few weeks, but one that said, *Hello, friend.*

"Aye, it's a lovely day for it, hm?" At the top of the hill, the woman stopped next to Neoma. She could not recall her name, though Neoma often watched her saunter to the freshwater pools further inland.

A gentle sheen of sweat speckled her brown forehead. Looking out in roughly the same area, her radiant smile never wavered. A crooked tooth stuck a little further out than the rest, tugging her bottom lip down, but it shined like an earthbound star. Strong shoulders easily relaxed at the view despite the hulk of freshly laundered clothing strapped to her back. The woman glowed, purpose spilling out of her, its happy edges brushing the darkness of grief cloaking Neoma in a way that sent a tremor down her spine.

Neoma realized a beat late that the laundress likely expected a response. Words clicked together a bit awkwardly, hitched as she cleared her throat. "Erm—yes. It's beautiful."

For the woman, that seemed an ample enough reply. "I never tire of this view. I lived in Trilabold for a handful of years. Now, I don't mind silverwood trees—all trees are lovely—but this?" She waved a hand out to the sand, the golden sun, the clouds. "I could never tire of *this*."

"I've not seen a silverwood tree." Noema surprised herself saying that aloud. A cloak of embarrassment added to the tapestry of grief hanging around her arms, its tang of pitifulness sharp in her ears. Neoma approached her thirty-sixth nameday, yet in all those years she never found reason to leave the Saltshores. Trilabold stood so close to the island town of Linlocke that she often spied its harbors and could pick out the House symbols of the boats docked there. Yet, for whatever reason, she never bothered to make a day of exploring the neighboring isle of Menthis.

The laundress raised her eyebrows in response. "Well, Trilabold is right next door, sweetling, and only a ferry away. You aren't missing much, though."

Sweetling. The woman gave out the nickname easily, causing a flush to climb Neoma's neck. "I've… I've just never had much reason to travel. My husband didn't—well, it's hard with our son. It *was* hard."

"Oh."

Such a small word, yet it thumped heavily down between Neoma's shoulder blades. Bracing herself, Neoma waited for the pitying words that echoed around her these last weeks.

"I see," the laundress nodded. "I knew I recognized you. I was on my way back from Linlocke after dropping off a delivery when I saw your farewell ceremony. It looked small. I mean, not *small*, but—gods above. I'm sorry." She adjust the straps across her chest, glancing back out at the picturesque landscape.

Neoma's hand carrying her basket became weighted, her shoulder aching. It was not the usual condolences, and she found some respite in the woman's floundering, but mentioning that day only made the pain feel raw again. The heaviness of the ceremony pressed down, its memory pungent, spoiled as fish left too long in the sun.

"I've never known agony like that. I'm sorry it's something you carry now."

Strangely, a tone of admiration threaded the laundress' words. Her dark eyes met Neoma's, the gentleness there reaching a distant part of herself that laid dormant all of Ceitash. While Neoma tended to brush off the kind words of near-strangers, she pulled these ones in tightly.

After locking them away, she nodded. "My name is Neoma."

Letting out a breath, smile returning to her lips, the laundress returned the nod. "Claramond—but only my mother calls me that. I prefer Monty."

Neoma opened her mouth, at first meaning to ask why not *Clara*, but Monty quickly added, "If there's anything I can do for you, please let me know. I can launder for free until you're on your feet again. Or, y'know," she lifted a shoulder, which was impressive considering the size of the bag, "if you just need a friend. I imagine friends are good for… this. *That*. I live past the hill, and if you don't mind, I'm gonna get going before I put my foot any further in my mouth.

"Lantern at your feet, Neoma." Monty added, a thread of companionship in her tone before she continued along the path.

Running into Monty on the footpath hugged close to Neoma's mind into the next evening. Unlike Neoma, the younger woman appeared satisfied with even the simple life of a laundress. Reading a person from the outside-in rarely produced an accurate depiction, though no matter what sort of palled history Neoma imagined, Monty came out untouched by grief. After all, how could someone so ready to speak to a stranger on the path, eager to offer the service of their livelihood *without pay*, be made from heartache?

These imaginings at first worried her, the fixation on the stranger causing shame to nestle quickly in her mind. Eventually, she rationalized them by telling herself that she was only curious about Monty in the way anyone making a new friend would be. Never mind that her beaming smile, as well as her floundering sense of words, stirred a mixture of relief and comfort in Neoma's chest.

Comfort did not live long in her house anymore. Despite leaving at the first beams of dawn on the Second Day to go fishing, Urias came back smelling more of brandy than brine. He stumbled through the door, ushering in the cool breeze that marked the only sign of Wotag the Saltshores would have all season.

Blond hair hid the gray easier than Neoma's, an ashen lock falling over one eye as he studied her. Urias was in desperate need for a haircut and a good shave, the stubble along his chin on the verge of a beard. Ceitash passed with them drifting around each another, guests in one-another's lives. Most of the mornings were so silent that it felt their home was abandoned.

In a way, it had been. Urias lingered in doorways when he thought Neoma did not see him, the energy swirling around his head with words unspoken. Eventually, he turned his back to her, slipping out the door without so much as a farewell. It seemed unfair to Neoma that he left, disappearing into the shadows his own despair pulled him under, leaving *her* to manage the home without any help whatsoever.

While he drank, Neoma was expected to keep the shambles of their life tidy.

While he ignored his pain, *she* was left alone to ask all the questions.

This angered her more than she had the energy to express, but she knew the burden of tidiness would not be removed by her husband. She hated leaving things for too long while Urias paid them no mind. So, she packed away Koa's things with tear-filled eyes, wishing desperately for her own mother to quell the ache in her chest. Neoma cried loudly, and *hard*, as she pulled a disused trunk from their storage shack, thinking of those awful caskets people in Menthis used to bury their dead. Her people preferred burning, their ash mixed with the ocean or with sand and kept on the altar in the family home.

Until that point, clothing and shoes sat scattered on the floor, waiting for Koa to pick them up and don them again. She stored these thing mindfully, but the clothes she held to her nose for long breaths. All his shirts were in the same crystal blue color that he loved.

Neoma was almost glad for having passed along his baby things to a cousin once Koa outgrew them, for if she saw those tiny socks that fit in the palm of her hand, the grief very well may have drowned her.

She placed a bundle of lavender on top of the pile of items, though it took Neoma a long, sullen moment before she let the lid drop.

A knot loosened around her heart once her son's belongings were lovingly packed away. Neoma refused to bear the idea of them rotting in a trunk outside, so she ended up pushing it to the space at the foot of his bed. This was enough; this was *healing*, however small.

And so, Neoma found herself with little patience to indulge Urias' self-pity. Neoma ground the beady heads of lavender in her mortar. Lavender salt aided in numerous remedies from nerves to baths. This batch felt important, considering how for the last month Neoma barely bothered with her herbs and dried flowers.

She attributed this burst of energy to Monty, wanting to offer the woman a jar of the lavender salts in gratitude for her kindness. But with Urias now home, she worried her displeasure might bleed into the salts, and stopped grinding altogether.

Dusting her hands on an apron that got moth-eaten since she last wore it, Neoma braced herself on the counter. Urias placed his hat by the door, attempting to do the same with his coat. It missed the hook entirely, landing heavily at his feet, but Urias either did not notice or chose to ignore this.

He turned to her, swaying a little. "Is that for supper?"

He sniffed the air, a hound searching for meat. Disappointment rose to his face when he smelt neither cook fire nor roast. Urias did not notice their son's thing were away, or he was too drunk to care. That hurt Neoma more than any insult, the perceived carelessness burning in her mind.

As if her husband already washed their son away, already blotted out the toys and the clothes, Urias acted unperturbed by the change.

As if they never had a son at all.

As if Koa had not walked into the sea right in front of him.

"No." Neoma's voice felt too gentle. Anger threatened to make itself known, the underlaying current of betrayal rushing in her ears.

How could you be away like this? Why won't you talk to me?

This is all your fault.

Since darkness stretched beyond the windows, Urias scowled at the fact the dinner went unprepared at such an hour. He looked more like a disgruntled boy than an angry man. "I should've stayed out."

Neoma felt the muscle in her jaw tighten.

Urias ambled to the sitting chair by the window—*her* chair. Countless hours she spent in it, staring into nothing until the sunrise shaped the world anew. His long fingers stretching down to brush over the upholstery, Urias stood there, lost in thought. Torn between wanting to know those thoughts, and wishing him away, Neoma grabbed the pestle.

Frustrated, she put it back down. When she looked up, Urias was staring at her. Distance pulled his gaze, eyes roaming her face in confusion.

"My mother wrote."

These were not the words she expected. Still, they seemed to ease the tense silence. The letter she read and burned had long lost its sting. It made sense that his mother sent another, if only to chastise him more.

You are a worthy candidate for suffering, and an even unworthier father.

Words bubbled up to her mouth, popping loudly in the air: "She's wrong."

Urias straightened, hand resting fully now on the chair for support. Maybe this was the moment both of them found a way to talk, to *listen*, to one another.

Neoma dusted her hands again, just to have something to do. Now that Urias' gaze rested fully on her face, clear despite the brandy, discomfort muddled her next words. "Your mother can be… Well. She didn't even say her farewells to her own grandchild, only to then call you a poor father. Neither of us knew how Koa would be different when he was young. Neither of us were perfect—"

"You're gentler than me." Urias suddenly interrupted. His eyes glassed over when he glanced away. "Were. *Are.* You still are, somehow."

Finally, he collapsed into the chair. Chest rising and falling heavily, the drink sank him lower into the cushions. Those boney fingers that Neoma always thought beautiful dragged down over his face. Neoma loosened a breath from her chest, walking around the butcher block and her crushed lavenders to step closer to him.

Another emotion often stood alongside the anger when she considered her new relationship to Urias. Regret, like a weed, grew unnoticed until Neoma came across a token of hers from their courtship. She found it while packing away Koa's things, hearing its plink against the flagstone when she upturned a pair of his trousers. It made her smile, thinking it caught Koa's attention so much that he hid it away and to carry with him, but the memory of the token itself made her heart break.

It was a stone tossed smooth by the tide, triangular in shape, with a perfect circle worn through its middle. Whatever the stone was, she had no idea, but it glinted with golden veins in the candlelight. People often exchanged tokens if rings were not attainable, and Urias' livelihood at the time relied on fishing, not only for his own food but to sell in the market. Their meeting was little more than chance, their drunken tangle in the fields of dry grass on the edges of Linlocke nothing but a drunken accident.

Neoma recalled the Festival of the Well, a celebration around Linlocke's establishment, and her family's stall of salts and spices. Yet, her memory of bedding Urias smeared across her mind. She wanted it, just to have the experience, but the desire was overshadow by her drunkenness and a sliver of disillusionment. Was he someone she wanted, or a passing curiosity?

Urias did as any respectable man would, and offered the token in marriage. No one pressured her to accept, but it felt proper, if not exactly right.

She wished she could slip through time to reject the proposal. Maybe then, her son might still live on. Koa would be a different man, but he would be alive.

"What do you mean…" Urias' voice hummed, the slur of his words pulling her from the stupor, "that she called me a *poor father*?"

Blinking, Neoma leaned against the table. Echoing those horrid words made her uncomfortable, but undoubtedly not as uncomfortable as Urias might be after reading them. "That's what she said in the letter the first time. How she has the nerve to send another is incredible, even for her."

"She never said such a thing. Her letter here," his hand slapped his trouser leg heavily, "requests I come home to help with the harvest. When did she say that I was a poor father?"

Realizing her mistake came too late. Urias took no time in understanding that, at some point, there was a correspondence which his wife did not pass along. Leaping up from the chair, and immediately bracing himself, he pointed at her with his free hand.

"You hid a letter from me? My *mother's* letter?"

Neoma let out an offended huff. "Believe me, Urias, it wasn't a letter you would've liked to have. But… yes. After our farewell ceremony." A weave of panic made her palms damp. "I thought you noticed it?"

"You don't read *someone else's letter*, Neoma." The shame rumbling through his tone hit like a fist. "How could you? You've never read my letters before. You never— Nothing's the same. *You're* not the same."

"Our *life* is not the same." Neoma's voice shook, her lip quivering. The panic behind her breastbone shifted, releasing a heavy stream of tears. How did he manage to find such despicable words? Of course nothing was the same anymore. Koa *died*, and death, for all its reliability, unwove every thread it touched.

Her last bit of resolve began to crumble. As she spoke, her words flew out with biting fury. "Our house is not the same—*I am not the same!*"

"That's what I mean—"

"*No.*"

Urias startled as if she hit him. Power behind such a simple word could be felt in the very stone of their house. Her husband seemed smaller afterwards as he fumbled to find his words.

She took advantage of his shock, a wave of bravery hushing over her. "No. No, Urias, I am *not* the same. I'm a childless mother because *you* couldn't mind the tide. I have lost everything about myself. I've lost... *everything*." When she lifted her hand to rest it on her heart, she felt the anxious thrumming through her clothes.

Neoma glared at him, the truth beating within her spirit. "Strangers at the market care more for me than my own husband. I went there only yesterday—I went there for the first time in a *month*, Urias—and women whose names I don't know held me like... like I was someone to them, not a stranger. They saw me and saw my hurt clearer than the father of the child I lost. It kills me that those strangers are the first people to hold me since my mother at Koa's farewell ceremony. It kills me that you don't even hold my hand through this—that we don't hold *each other*. Why not this, of all things?"

Wet rivers of tears stained her cheek, dripping down her neck. At some point, her words went from powerful to wavering as the reality of her loneliness crashed down. Her hand was a pleading fist against her chest as she tried to keep the pieces of her heart together.

In all his shock, Urias just stared on. Something within him did break, judging by the wetness in his eyes, but not a word of respite or apology or even acknowledgment left his lips.

Silence choked out the honesty in Neoma's voice until they settled in the mortar of the walls, the cracks in the wood. Those words meant to live on in the crevasses of that house. Could *she* live on, surrounded by such things?

As if thrown back into his body, Urias started forward. Not in a threatening manner, but a stupefied one, yet Neoma still took a stride backwards. This offended him, briefly; then the emotion slid off his features. She felt guilty thinking he might strike her since it was never something that happened before.

He turned from her and into the bedroom they had not shared since Koa's passing. Neoma stood in the main room, overwhelmed with a mixture of relief and uncertainty. Her heart did feel lighter, her truth out in the open now, but even after everything, she worried for Urias.

After a few moments of stomping feet and a trunk lid slamming shut, Urias reappeared with a sack slung over his shoulder. Sobriety hit him squarely, his steps even as he picked up his coat from the floor.

"I'm going to my mother's to help with the last of the harvest."

Neoma's mouth opened slightly, stupefied. After revealing her pain, he chose once again to leave her to suffer it alone.

He did not look at her as he grabbed the handle of the door.

Then he paused, and Neoma hoped against reality that he meant to close it to sweep her into an embrace she so desperately needed.

"I know you think it's my fault. I *know* nothing can be the same. And I know I can't make you love me again after—" His voice broke. Clearing his throat, he worried his lips together as though the words clotted in his chest.

Urias let out a short, shaking breath. "I know you think I hated him. I could've been better for you both, but… I never expected to be a caretaker."

"Urias. What did you think having a family meant?" Neoma whispered. Emotion tightened in her throat, making her sound raspy. Everything within her felt raw, sensitive.

Still, this was the most Urias had spoken to her since Koa's ceremony.

"I didn't have the greatest examples. I don't know what I was expecting…" The knot in his throat bobbed as he swallowed. "But I loved him. I did. I just didn't know how to… I loved him. *I lost…* I loved him."

The door shut behind him quickly. He was gone.

I lost a son, too. She heard those words without Urias ever finishing them.

In the stillness that followed, the air settling after being so charged with fury and resentment and pain, Neoma slipped a hand into her skirt pocket. Urias said nothing about when he planned to return, but Neoma no longer felt she wanted to be there to welcome him when he did.

If he did.

She placed their marriage token on the tabletop, the clack of stone on wood loud to her ears. In a way, leaving it there was her farewell.

The climbing, soft sensation of numbness worked its way into her bones as she began to pack.

CHAPTER TEN

During the beginning of Wotag's season, when the last tepid days of Ceitash bled into the early mornings of Hattash, the island smelled like honey. Music spilled out of one hidden veranda or another, the sharp notes of a long-necked instrument twanging expertly across the wind—or poorly, depending which relative snatched it away in a vain attempt to regain the spotlight from the player. Sen spent the early mornings with a hand thrown over their eyes as the pallid light consumed their rooms. Their mother despised closing the windows during the cooler months, ordering every servant to throw open each towering pane to greet the fresh air and white-gold sunrise. Dunhet's bleached silver spires, interjected with reams of gold and red banners, sparkled across the way.

Since their arrival on the island, Sen dreaded their eventual return to the restless harbor city. Not forgetting their shame, or allowing Sen to hide from it during the family dinners, Naseria YeSara made it all the more difficult for them to find the courage to alert their entourage of a mainland trip. Any letter sent by their hand or addressed to their name passed first between the nimble fingers of Naseria's faithful couriers. The events at the Amalak eventually reached the ever-tuned ears of Dunhet's high society, so the servants were indeed busy rifling through gossip and nosy lines of questioning.

Sen only received *those* letters once Naseria read them—an invasion of Sen's privacy for certain, though she claimed her roving meant to keep an eye on how out of hand the gossiping may be.

Most of the statements proved harmless or laughable. *Did you really climb out of the window and bribe highwaymen to guide you all the way from Soapstead?* As if Sen ever bothered to go long distance by foot and ruin their brocaded shoes. Either way, despite being scion of the YeSara Clan, Sen felt they earned fewer and fewer freedoms during the passing weeks.

Lon kept her distance, too. Sen was not expecting trumpeting when they arrived, but their younger sister made it clear that she cared little for Sen's presence. Weeks later, Lon still turned in the opposite direction when they both happened down the same hall, and Sen was too unbothered to chase after her.

Groaning, Sen rolled out of the tangle of plush blankets and gossamer sheets. While Lesser Syvon rarely felt the harsh chill of Wotag, the nightly temperatures dipped low enough for the light covers to be topped with exquisite bolts of hand-stained satin. Their hand brushed over the soft, dark shapes of blooming flowers, a contrast to the season, before they stood, naked. Sen paced about the room, swiping long fingers through their hair, working out the tangles until it ran smoothly down their back. Donning a house robe, fabric pooling around their feet like a fountain of liquid emeralds, Sen only just knotted the waistband at their hip when the door to the room flew open.

"I've come to free you!"

Valeska sauntered into the main room, a flurry of vanity that brought with it the thick cloud of confusion. Only just blinking the sleep from their eyes, Sen wondered how their friend managed to not only get on the island without an announcement, but into their *rooms*. And, after an awkward beat, Valeska lowered his dramatically raised arms to place bronze fists on his hips, disappointed when he did not receive the expected celebration of his entrance.

Beyond, where guests typically waited on large cushions and slinged chairs until Sen was fully dressed, the silk-paneled door remained open. Light spilled in, and the guard who was meant to keep an eye on their private rooms leaned her head around the frame.

"Erm…" she began, shrinking into her leathers, "I'm sorry, Seram. I am not certain of your friends title."

"Valeska Demont… of *House* Demont." Valeska called over his shoulder, jaw audibly clicking as he made a frustrated grimace. Then, smiling as though the insult to his station bore no mark, he pointed at Sen. "You've not been keeping the lessers informed. I am your closest friend, and yet I had to bribe my way onto the island."

Looking over at the guard who quickly vanished to inform Naseria that someone in the ranks had been pocketed, Sen let out a drowsy sigh. They despised how the silk-and-leather-clad harpers who wandered the island were called *guards*. Armed with a short-sword and a horn in case they needed to sound an alarm, none of them were shielded in more than a leather jerkin and tall, overly-buckled boots. Just like the many gardens, terraces, and gazebos on the island, they were little more than a show of the YeSara wealth. Only a handful were rigorously trained in combat at the Dome in Sovil, but *they* protected the matriarch alone.

"You have my mother to thank for that." Sen grumbled, twining their hair like a rope.

Valeska *tsked.* He walked about the room, ambling near Sen's vanity as he fingered a gilded comb, index finger drawing a line down its pointed teeth. "How you put up with that woman is beyond my understanding. You are the scion of the oldest Clan in the Gilded Isles—"

"*One* of the oldest."

"Still." Valeska jerked his chin towards the door where the guard once stood. "You should have more than a lapdog watching after your rooms, and more control of your own damned life."

Relief and pride made Sen suddenly glad for Valeska's early morning intrusion, even if the man was ranting before breakfast. Most likely rallying only a handful of hours before, Valeska himself probably woke in a throng of limbs and fabric. House Demont owned little land, with many scions to lay claim to its harbor on the edge of Dunhet. As the youngest of seven, Valeska knew his chances of rising to any noteworthy station, as well as any right to the family estate itself, were thin. His older brothers made sure Valeska remembered his place as the runt, but it also meant the youngest of House Demont could do whatever he pleased.

Valeska owned a life Sen lusted after. He wandered Dunhet so often that no one else was the better guide. Every crack was known to him, every shady dealing or delicious morsel of gossip shuffled into a deck of cards to be pulled out at whatever party he managed an invite. In another life, the youngest of House Demont might have been a smuggler with how at ease he seemed in the shadows.

Most of all, there were no shackles to keep him in his family's home, waiting for his mother's permittance to leave. Since all eyes were on Runerth, the standing heir of Demont, little Valeska rarely brought enough shame upon the House for anyone to look his way, least of all require a chaperone.

The uninvited guest took a seat on the low chair in front of Sen's mirrors. "I never understood why you must see yourself from every angle." To drive the point, he flared his nostrils unattractively.

Not yet determined to make conversation, Sen made a noise in their throat. Off their sleeping room spanned a closet with vibrant streams of silks, cottons, leathers; silk brocade robes in the fashion of their mother's people sat in boxes that slept in a narrow shelf, only to be brought out on ceremony; slippers, satin-heeled and meant only for the lightest walks, ran the length of the floor. At the other end were some pairs of heavy leather shoes wrapped in fur meant for those rare few days in Hattash where Lesser

Syvon got flurries of white snow—but that had not happened since they were little.

Sen ran a hand down the length of the hanging fabrics that cost more than all of House Demont's combined wardrobe. Whispers of embroidery kissed their fingertips until they settled on a silken tunic of pale blue, matching velvet trousers in a darker hue, and a long burgundy sleeveless vest. The leather vest shined, freshly oiled as if the servants knew Sen might choose it that morning. It was not until they decided on a tall pair of boots, bending to reach them underneath the longer garments, that they noticed Valeska waiting in the doorway.

Watching.

Behind him, the sun broke through a cloud and cast a beam of light into the room. If Sen did not know better, they might have thought Valeska some chosen warrior, or at least *desirable* in the divine lighting. But just as the Runt of Demont's eldest brother stood to be the only one to inherit anything important, Valeska sorely lacked natural beauty. His eyes were too small in his long face, paired with a crooked nose that, to be fair, was the result of a skirmish with an elder brother when he was but a child. If not for that, Sen thought Valeska *might* have been handsome. While the Demonts had little by way of station, most of them were oddly beautiful, with blinding white hair that made their brown complexion that much more striking.

Though Sen never planned to say as much to Valeska's face, it was the man's actions—and his small coin purse—that made him detestable, and the least attractive of all Sen's potential suitors.

How they became friends came across like a fever in their mind. Had Valeska been invited to Sen's naming ceremony when they were declared the scion of Clan YeSara almost a decade ago? More than likely, Naseria forced Sen to have a good relationship with House Demont during some function or another, and Sen took to the scrawny boy. Valeska was still thin in adulthood, but as a child he was even less threatening in stature. Though, on occasion, his eyes sharpened with a look that warned Sen not to let down their guard for too long.

Despite being caught staring, Valeska remained impassive, unreadable. The white of his hair consumed the sunlight, creating an alluring halo around his head.

"You said you were going to save me?" Sen caught the flirtatious note in their voice before they got too zealous. Valeska was not the sort of person they wanted to waste *that* attention on.

With an unbothered tone, they added, "How do you expect to do that?"

Valeska raised a shoulder while a mischievous grin took over his lips. "I figure it may be a moment before your dear old mother finds the guard I bribed, so we can go out the same way I came in."

"Like rats, then." The imagery did not conjure up the same feelings for Sen as it did Valeska. The former preferred to be shown around on the gondolas and ferry boats, making sure every person was aware of their arrival or departure. Their counterpart favored his quiet disappearances. Secrets floated around Valeska, ones of which even Sen barely reached past, and it made the unsightly man somewhat more interesting to keep around.

"Yes, quite like rats." Valeska smiled. "I figured a day slinking around Dunhet was a proper welcome home."

Sen remained unimpressed with the offer. Picking off a grain of invisible lint from their sleeve, they sought after a distraction. Valeska always attempted to be in charge of their goings-on when they tramped around the city, from when they arrived at an establishment to what they ate, but Sen enjoyed reminding him whose coin they always used.

Glancing over the fabric jerkin Valeska wore, the discomfort of walking around with a societal companion so underdressed made Sen shift on their feet.

"And… you plan on going on this venture in *that*."

A dark, dangerous glint slicked through Valeska's eyes. Sen relished the contained emotion, sensing the power of being the scion of one of the oldest clans on the continent roiling under their skin. It was so easy to remind people of Sen's power, they did not even need to bother casting a flame.

What was more powerful than a name, after all?

Resting a palm on his chest, Valeska bowed, revealing exactly how much the comment irked him. The man *never* bowed, not to Naseria, nor any other matriarch. Even though Valeska showed his distaste, and potentially his regret, at being in Sen's company, the seram smiled when the guest straightened.

"If something is ill-fitting about my attire, then by all means," he motioned to the swaths of fabric. "I am but a doll in your hands, Seram."

"My heir always broke their dolls in childhood."

Sen froze in their closet, blinking wide-eyed at Valeska. Their guest turned into the room, facing the entourage Sen knew awaited them.

"Naseria!" Valeska's voice rang jauntily, though anyone practiced in conversation heard the annoyance at her arrival. "You look absolutely *radiant*."

The YeSara Matriarch ignored him. "Sen?"

After letting out a sigh, Naseria's eldest peeled themselves away from the bolts of cloth. Their mother stood at the threshold of their bedroom, her entourage sitting in the receiving area beyond. Dripping from her shoulders were glass beads with impossibly small flowers painted on their surface. Each bead glittered like rain in the morning light, and when Naseria faced Sen, they clattered together with the sound of pebbles underfoot. The pieces at Naseria's shoulders made her half as wide at the door's opening, the burgundy of her robe hidden underneath the beads. Wide sleeves concealed her hands, which she kept elegantly by her side. Sen was surprised to see her face painted a chalky white with dots of red just beneath her pupils, and black kohl darkening her lash line and brows.

Naseria met them in ceremonial garments, face painted in a way that meant she was receiving a distinguished guest or communing with the ancestors. Even her long, thick hair was woven up to support a golden half-circle at the crown of her head. Usually, every member of the matriarch's family got a letter notifying them of any arriving dignitaries, so she must be visiting the massive shrine central to the island.

Had their mother informed the others, leaving Sen out to make yet another point of her ill favor? Why were *they* not invited to commune?

Perhaps, came a gentle voice that tried to reason with their ego, *that is why she got to your rooms so quickly. She was already on her way to escort you to the shrine.*

One of Sen's aunts eyed Valeska as though he just spat in her path. She, too, sat in a ceremonial garments and makeup that mimicked her older sister's, though without as many embellishments on her person. Naseria seemed less than pleased with the smaller House's uninvited presence, but kept most of her disgust hidden.

"Do you plan to leave the island today, then?" Her narrowed, displeased gaze remained on Valeska, who continued to smile in pageantry at her, but the question was directed at Sen. That gentler voice within them urger Sen to be patient in their response.

They hinged at the waist. While the professionalism felt foolish, especially in front of Valeska, there were certain ways to approach the matriarch in her officiality. Sen knew these rules, rules that would be expected of them once they were in charge of the Clan, and dared not break them. As frustrating the game was with their mother and her favor, Sen knew better than to shame a longstanding practice.

"If it pleases you, mother."

Naseria barely contained a humorless laugh. "There is still a long way for you to go before anything pleases me, Sen. Yet," she sighed, "it may be a wise choice to spend your time away from the island today."

The inclination stung, letting the heir teeter between disheartened annoyance and ancestral understanding. Sen's eyes roved over their mother's attire before reaching her face, the questions bubbling at the back of their throat. Naseria, however, met their curiosity with a lifted chin. If she were in simpler garb, she might have jerked it in Valeska's direction, but Sen grasped her meaning still. Whatever meant to happen on the island would not be discussed in front of *anyone* other than family. Sen desperately wanted to berate their mother with questions now that something was finally happening on the island, but they knew their place—and Valeska's presence, though a buffer, made Naseria all the more eager to remind them of it.

Valeska elbowed them lightly. "I think that's a yes, friend. I assume, Naseria, that means we can take a boat out?"

Sen cringed at how directly their counterpart spoke to the Matriarch of the YeSara Clan. Naseria being in her garb drove an even sharper tone of ignorance into Valeska's behavior, yet was that entirely his fault? Sen had no memory of ever bothering to explain their practices to him, mostly because they figured Valeska was from too low of a House to ever get an invitation to their festivals or ceremonies. Why bother with expending that sort of energy on someone who would never bear witness?

Naseria bore poorly concealed ambivalence. "A boat is the better option, yes. The bilge rat you *somehow* managed to bribe is no longer employed. Retracing your steps is no longer an option, Demont."

Anyone with a working pair of ears heard the shame rattling in those words. The direct insult to Valeska's own funds echoed in the room. How *did* the Runt of House Demont manage to bribe a guard from the YeSara Clan, whose own daily pay was more than his yearly allowance? The better gossiper knew that it was not only money Valeska offered, but what experience offered could barter passage?

Both young people knew their place, though, and remained silent. Despite Valeska visibly shaking in embarrassment, and Sen wishing they could think of a retort in his defense, Naseria tipped her chin at them. The way she managed to keep the half-circle upright on her head spoke to her perfect, practiced motions. It mirrored her distance to Sen perfectly. Ever the matriarch spearheading a longstanding family, cool and practiced even towards her offspring.

"Ser Demont. Sen," her painted white lips stretched into a kind smile, "do not forget to let your sister known that you are leaving."

Sen bowed, stomach sinking as they recalled Naseria's conditions on their adventuring. Lon was not the first person Sen, or anyone, wanted for company on a day meant for drunken mindlessness.

Valeska corrected himself once Naseria turned her back, not completing the bow. His eyes trained on the back of her decorated head, jaw slanting to one side as he worked the muscle there. Sen frowned, finding even *their* tolerance for him growing thin. But if Naseria had noted the disgrace, she likely would have pocketed her retort for later. What were words shared in a private chamber when she had the opportunity to bring down his entire House because of his insolence?

In a glittering cacophony, the entourage kept their eyes on the ground until Naseria passed. Power effortlessly hushed over the room as she glided to the door. She possessed no magic but wielded the authority of the YeSaras like the ancient mages of renown. Sen's aunt slipped in place behind Naseria as she passed, as did the others according to their station, until the gilded parade of painted faces and clattering beads disappeared.

Sen's shoulders deflated. The hateful look in Valeska's eyes vanished, and he clapped Sen on the back. It felt strange knowing how quickly his mood changed, how expertly he concealed his anger. But Sen found the man's worldly knowledge enough to overshadow his shifting temper.

"Now," Valeska smiled, properly showing off his crooked incisor. "You were about to loan me something more presentable?"

Valeska enjoyed attention, positive or shameful. Yet, despite Lon being his least favorite of the YeSara Clan, he managed the utmost decorum. For him, this meant efficient swearing, the classiest of his barbaric jokes, and minimal comments about Lon's weight. Not for the first time, Sen wondered where the man got the stupid courage to pick at Lon, considering her revered swordsmanship that garnered her numerous awards during her time at Dunhet's naval academy.

Still, Valeska prodded her icy wall with a silver tongue and serpent's smile. Sen watched with no small amount of interest as Lon visibly grew more exhausted with each of Valeska's insensitive comments, keeping their own mouth shut for most of the outing just to see what happened. Lon was often the more argumentative, and Sen felt justified in letting her have a bit of her own testy behavior.

"I don't understand why it was so important to buy something from that specific stall, is all." Valeska peeled away the wax paper that protected long, freshly battered salmon flanks. Their crispy skins, glowing with oil and dusted with salt, crinkled as he picked at one. "There must be over a hundred gods-damned fish friers in Dunhet."

Sen bit into theirs, the crunch a delicious song of perfectly cooked flavor. Butter, salt, and oil flooded their mouth, the sharp taste of salmon as relieving as a cup of water in the desert. It took them hours to agree on where to break their midday fast, Lon despising the idea of eating indoors on such a beautiful day while Valeska refused to go anywhere that was not serving a particular brand of mead from Trilabold. If Sen desperately tried adding to the discourse with their own opinion, it was effortlessly scuffled aside. When Lon and Valeska competed to be the loudest or the most controlling, no one else possessed the strength to interject.

At least it was entertaining.

Their sister made a face. Explaining anything to Valeska taxed her patience, so she steeled a breath before replying. "They were from *Venret*."

Both Valeska and Sen waited to see why that mattered.

"Half of our own meals in the Isles come from Venretian tradition! No one can fry, sear, cook, or sell a fish like them. Honestly," she flicked her long braid over her shoulder, "it's ridiculous how little you two actually know about this city."

Lon experienced the more manufactured side of Dunhet despite her interest in the traditions the Venretians and ancestral YeSaras built, but Sen could not help chuckling at her statement as she bit down into her own fried salmon flank. Their sister might know the curated surface of Dunhet as well as anyone who dwelt in the harbor apartments of the naval academy, but Sen knew from her letters during that time that she rarely experienced the city after dark.

With a glance to their friend, Sen witnessed what seemed like a private moment as Valeska chewed thoughtfully, the oil glistening on his lips. Flecks of salt clung to the corner of his mouth, and his eyes roved over Lon as she turned to face the passing crowd, standing on her toes to see if any of the stalls across the road piqued her interest. It was a gaze vivid with desire, and yet the look behind Valeska eyes reminded Sen of a butcher's knife. So sharp, it severed meat from the bone in a long, solid swipe.

A twinge of irritation nudged the back of Sen's heart as they quietly studied Valeska. Sen made a point not to watch him directly, enjoying their own food as the twining feeling in their chest formed a knot. The look passed in a handful of moments, though it seemed Valeska stared at Lon for hours.

Words bubbled in their throat, a desire to forewarn their sister swallowed down with bitter annoyance. Lon already knew the Runt lived up to his doggish nickname.

Valeska peeled his eyes away to look at Sen. "Do you figure your mother sent guards, or is *she* meant to be your protection as well as your chaperone?"

Valeska jerked his chin at Lon without speaking to her directly. Mood shifting from argumentative to strangely palatable, he glanced between them both. It was valid question that came to Sen's mind as well. YeSara nobles rarely faced kidnappings, their bloodline entrenched in

Dunhet to the point that even the brigands wished to be on the family's better side. Getting a favor from any of the oldest Clans also resulted in a form of immunity, and it was really only Naseria who walked with a full guard. As the matriarch, she even relieved herself with the entire bathhouse surrounded.

Thrown off by the question, Lon took her time responding. She crumpled the wax paper, elegantly dabbing the corners of her mouth with a handkerchief before giving Valeska the attention he so badly desired.

"Our mother has eyes everywhere, Demont. I feel you often forget just how far her hand reaches."

Valeska smiled. "Oh, I've certainly heard tale of her firm grasp."

Lon paled, eyes widening at his vile implication. Even Sen, who did not have the most wonderful relationship with their mother, felt their stomach drop. No person was safe from insult or rumor, not even Naseria, yet this was the first time anyone made such a rancid remark directly in the presence of her heir and second-eldest. Most of high society possessed enough decorum to titter behind their fans or wait until the YeSaras left, but Sen should have assumed Valeska would not act any better simply because Lon was there.

Continuing to finish his meal, Valeska licked the salt from his fingers, tossing the wax paper over his shoulder instead of seeking one of the public fire pits to burn it in. Dumbfounded, Lon remained silent, her gaze set on a distant spot down the road. Sen watched her fingers flex, and imagined she was praying to Ma'Ceste for a sword.

"What say we find something to wash this all down, hm?" He threw an arm over Sen's shoulders. Lon dove out from his grasp before Valeska managed to bring her in to his side with his other one, and he gave her a sad pout, bottom lip sticking out like a child.

Lon crossed her arms. When she spoke, she looked only to Sen. "I want to go home."

"Aw," Valeska sighed, his tone less than empathetic.

She ignored him. "Sen?"

Siblings often spoke without words. Familiarity crafted a whole other language, no matter how distant Sen otherwise felt from their sister. Valeska's comment about their mother was unnecessary, and Sen understood why she wanted to leave, but the thought of returning to the island after spending so long in the Amalak, then cooped up in their rooms, made their chest tighten.

Just as Sen noticed her own unspoken words, Lon's shoulders tightened before they even spoke.

"This is the longest I've ever seen you go without a drink in your hands," they laughed to Valeska, trying to make their decision lighter with a joke.

"Well, let's remedy that."

Lon pressed her lips into a thin line, the disappointment clear on her features. That bothered Sen more than Valeska's comment about Naseria, more than the fact that Sen knew his friend had no intention of returning the silk shirt and fine trousers he picked from their wardrobe. It seemed so easy to disappoint Lon, to disappoint Naseria, that nothing Sen chose mattered. Whatever Sen did, it made someone upset, so why not choose the things that made them happy for a while? If everything they did was wrong according to *someone*, then why bother to try and do good? Would their mother not just twist the outcome in the end to show Sen how much they failed?

Heat pulsed in Sen's palm, startling them enough that Lon noticed. She glanced at their hands, brows furrowed. Naseria, according to the one servant the scion managed to buy out from under their mother, revealed to Lon that Sen learned next to nothing at the prestigious coffin for books and dusty historians. The power her sibling possessed remained weak despite the symbolism it carried for the YeSara Clan, but it was difficult for her to hide the jealousy that broke through her trained façade.

Sen once burned letters from some Sovilian merchant who Lon swore meant nothing. It was jealousy over the life Lon was able to choose for herself that lead them to searching out those parchments, not rage, but that damage was final. Despite the beauty and honor of a magical lineage, an ancestry Lon might have been proud of, she sneered at the mockery of fire along Sen's skin.

Grinding her jaw, Lon watched the little sparks in her sibling's palm. All she had the right do to was talk, especially when faced with Naseria's own orders to chaperone her sibling. Sen held the power, both as the matriarch's heir and the last of their family with any elemental magic.

"Lead the way." Sen ordered Valeska, flexing their wrist in an attempt to dissipate the heat. Showing off at a tavern was one thing, but they did not wish to control the flame in such a crowded street.

Their friend glanced between them, shrugging when he decided the secrets passing from the siblings were not worth the hassle of questioning.

Lon trailed behind—Sen knew she did not dare to plan to leave them.

Thinking back to their first night home, the rage and frustration pulsing through them, Sen glanced back over their shoulder to make sure she was not listening as their thoughts brewed something devious. It was not the neatly cobbled streets or the manicured stalls that they wanted to experience with Lon, but the very rot of the city.

They leaned into Valeska when she appeared distracted by a throng of people. Valeska met them halfway, brow quirked in interest. "Do your friends still skulk around *The Dovetail*?"

Grinning, Valeska shot a vicious smile to the unassuming Lon. “Of course! And they’ve nothing better to do than make your sister’s acquaintance.”

Sen matched his wicked grin, ignoring the warning from a gentle voice within.

CHAPTER ELEVEN

Dunhet liked the pretense that came with being the jewel of the Gilded Isles. Its boastful architecture was an arrangement of designs from the Common Age erected around the what remained of histories long passed, their silk screen soft interruptions in the bleached stone and silverwood spires. The unhoused did not starve, for food sat on every corner, some offering the option of a meal paid for by work or a favor instead of coin.

Members of Dunhet's society may increase their riches, but no one grasped the same level of superiority as an older Clan.

While the YeSara island stood as the city's closest example of preserved history, its long sloped roofs fringed with ancestral statues, there were still places within Dunhet that rivaled it in age. In this way, the city and its people enjoyed pretending that Dunhet was too glittery to hide any sort of rough underbelly. It was simply too old, too refined, to house betters and gamblers and, gods forbid, successful whorehouses.

Just as the Clan homes preserved the ancestral history of each ancient family, *The Dovetail* worked hard to remind Dunhet's people of more sordid transgressions. While the governor's home was being erected half an Age ago, the plan for his death unfolded in the corner of *The Dovetail's* tavern. Ironback, Dunhet's first hero, once slammed the head of a patroness into the corner of the stone counter, leaving a bloodstain that lasted until the masonry needed to be replaced. According to the story the owner is forced to tell at least three times a night, Ironback paid off the woman's family to keep his good name.

Cities needed places like *The Dovetail* to remember where it all started. People from across Greater and Lesser Syvon lamented not spending their days on the shores of the Gilded Isles, or in the bath houses where Votives served every whim, however devious the request. For some reason, the shining structures of Dunhet lead people to believe they might be untouched by misfortune. They possessed no real idea of how dangerous the bath houses may be, or that Votives killed for their patrons if given enough coin and a good escape.

People were still people—liars, thieves, murderers, betrayers—no matter how far on the map one traveled. And the darkly lit *Dovetail* provided more than enough evidence to show how Dunhet's attempt to thrust those people into the shadows only gave their wickedness the concealment it needed to thrive.

Hours ago, Valeska sauntered into the tavern with a dramatic flail of his hands, much like how he presented himself in Sen's rooms that morning. Only this time, a cheerful *hoorah* went up upon his arrival. Before the three of them made it to the end of a crowded table, the first round of their drinks were bought by a man with a missing eye. Valeska lifted his flat dish of rice liquor in thanks while Lon and Sen dipped their heads, polite but tight smiles on their faces. Other than the free alcohol and the admittedly welcoming cheer, they drifted into the fringe, another set of faceless strangers in a crowd.

It took little time for Valeska's friends to arrive. Lon made her distrust of the new additions apparent as they all made room for them at the table. A few of the faces were ones Sen remembered from numerous other late nights roving the streets with the Runt of Demont, yet despite the comradery of drunken adventures the names of Valeska's friends evaded them.

One who looked every bit a noble spoke with the tilted accent of a lesser-born, making himself comfortable next to Lon. His shoulder-length hair was decorated with small beads that Sen knew were not real pearls, just as they saw through the vibrant jacket and scarf. Such brightly dyed leathers fell out of season in Sen's youth, so it might be pilfered from an old woman, or he might have found it in a nobleman's trash. Nights in the Isles began to cool only recently, so a scarf looked like a dramatic choice for an accessory. If Sen cared any more about the stranger or his fashion choices, they might have publicly ridiculed him for posing as someone of a higher station.

Sen turned when their sister shot them an annoyed look, acting as though they did not notice her hardset mouth. The other three people clamoring to be the loudest in the conversation—and in the tavern, it seemed—were a handful of years older than Sen and Valeska. A man with a few strands of gray, smiling easily, did not make the mistake of his companions by pretending to be more than his name. He wore the black riding leathers of a graveyard watchman, belt slung with only a short dagger and his coin purse. What the man donned was his total worth, and there was a careful air around him that Sen made a note of before turning their attention on the two others.

Drinking twice as much at the group since he sat down loomed a sellsword. Scars littered the back of his massive hands, which cupped the flat saucer of rice liquor gingerly as he drank. The sellsword offered loud quips at his companions, voice booming over the ruckus of the tavern in a manner that seemed uncontrollable. His shaved head boasted inky tentacles of a squid, two curling arms sliding down each cheekbone and up around the sockets of his eyes like a mask. Of the others, Sen found him the most physically interesting.

Valeska dipped his head to speak quietly to the last, a wiry man sharing the highborn's narrow frame. Plump lips sat crookedly on the man's mouth as though his jaw did not fit in his skull. When he noticed Sen watching them talk, the man gave either a grimace, or a smile. Sen did not feel confident to guess which, and went back to drinking. Since it was extremely likely that Sen would be expected to pay the bill, they meant to drink their share.

The older man slammed his cup down, sloshing the remainder of its contents over the rim. The party cheered as he slapped it on the table three more times to get their attention, smiling feverishly.

"Here's to good company," he wiggled his eyebrows at Lon, who sneered at him, "bad drinks, and the Mad King."

"Here!" Everyone besides Lon cheered, slamming their palms down on the table.

Sen knew their sister struggled to be softspoken. She gripped her own untouched drink, knuckles popping against the flesh of her hands.

When she found her voice, it came out like honey. "Why do you cheer the king of Esmar?"

Like the insects they were, starved for any morsel of sweetness in their lives, the men scrambled to answer. Only Valeska sipped his drink thoughtfully, admiring the way Lon shifted the attention when she desired. Even Sen found it amusing how only the peacocking stranger paid her mind until the tinge of her voice interrupted their childish roistering.

"We like to think the Mad King represents fellows like us," the older man got in first. His smile made Sen think of rancid meat. "He takes what he's owed."

"*Tsk*, it's not so simple—or brutish." The handsome, younger one chided. He threw his arm around Lon's shoulders, which very nearly destroyed her feigned look of interest. "The Mad King is an *idea*. He's a symbol of freedom from the binds of the archaic structure of diplomacy. He is a king, yes," he raised his index finger pointedly, "but he doesn't confine himself to the expectations of one."

The man at Valeska's side spoke up then, his voice nasally. "We also enjoy the irony in celebrating a man so despised. Almost as despised at us."

Everyone, save for Sen and Lon, gave a heartfelt *here, here* to the self-inflicted pity in the man's words. Their sister rolled her eyes when the other men lifted their dishes to take a drink.

"He's very much *not* an idea, though."

Sen knew that pensive tone better than anyone at the table. They put their liquor down, hands poised around it, and stared at her. Despite the people Valeska brought around often being fun to drink with, Sen long since figured it was best to be agreeable. Tonight, there was a massive, overdrunk sellsword and a slinking graveyard watchman to consider, as well as the Runt himself. They hoped Lon remained civil enough to prevent an outburst, from either herself or the men.

The graveyard watchman smiled that rancid smile, propping his chin on his fist to give an air of innocence. "How do you mean, sweetling?"

"Well, certainly you've heard of his… well…"

"His provocations?" The watchman tilted his head at her.

Lon set her shoulders back. Sen quietly applauded her stupidity as she met the stranger's eye without shrinking away. "Is that what you call an attempt to eradicate an entire group of people? An irksome little *provocation*?"

"Gods," the handsome one rolled his eyes, dropping his arm from Lon's shoulders. "Another champion for the dirt-footed Kahun. Why can't women just be pretty? They all have opinions nowadays."

Sen's eyebrows rose to their hairline. With an inquisitive glance at Valeska that said *where did you find this one*, their friend simply shrugged. It seemed odd that a man living in a country where revered matriarchs spearheaded families—and had been for centuries—carried such a sentiment. While the Isles sat under the eye of a governing council that often voted men into positions of power, women were not barred from competing. Many of what the Gilded Isles possessed in the modern age came from the scrupulously detailed minds of matriarchal leaders.

"He's earned his throne," the handsome one continued, his face turning into the awkward, disproportionate features of a troll the longer he talked. As if under a spell, every word made the glimmer of his looks fall away to reveal the pestilence underneath. "He's a gods-damned king, after all! He should get to do what he wants."

Valeska remained silent, disinterested in offering an opinion as he observed the back and forth with hungry, patient eyes. Lon responded with astoundingly willful strength as she tampered down the anger in her shaking fists.

Placing her hands on the table, she gave the watchman a soft onceover. Perhaps the men thought her complacent, or that their remarks somehow won her over, since none of the strangers assumed Lon intended to squeeze out their intolerant remarks like juice for breakfast.

"It makes sense, I suppose, that *you* admire him. After all, he represents everything a man is." Lon relented, eyes wide as she nodded lightly. She waited until the other men were nodding with her before clarifying: "He's a boorish, murderous, cold-hearted, *pathetic* end to a raging bloodline that's only caused the greatest economic decline in Esmar since the Age of Brutality—"

Tension boiling over, the watchman jumped up so quickly that his chair flew back to hit the man across the aisle. Sen did not see him draw the short dagger, but it glinted in his steady, weathered hand. Aimed directly at Lon, who stood the instant the other man leapt from the table, the dagger's point glinted.

"You want to kill the second in line to the YeSara Clan?" Lon's voice boomed louder than Sen ever heard. She opened her arms, silk-covered chest exposed to the threat on her life.

Upon mention of her surname, most of the tavern's conversations petered out into bated stillness. Everyone now turned to the watchman, and the young woman.

Lon's voice steady, she wore the vulnerability like armor. Sen had no doubts about her ability to knock the dagger from the man's grasp, but she was outnumbered. Lon had no intention of striking first.

Rising from his seat at a leisurely pace, the sellsword dropped his massive hand on the watchman's sword arm. Fury jumped in the man's gaze, all the more heightened by the reflection of the fire in his dark eyes. For a quick moment, Lon's gaze jumped to Sen, who blinked with the realization that she was trying to get them to leave. Meanwhile, the sellsword managed to convince his companion to put away the weapon, lest the wrath of not only the innkeeper but the Matriarch of the YeSaras befall him.

"Quite the company you keep, Demont." Lon said once the watchmen and the sellsword both fled the dingy tavern. Only the waif-like man remained, his beady eyes unsteady from drinking.

Her gaze slid accusingly to their guide for the evening, but Valeska only shrugged in indifference. "If you think our highborn associates aren't as interesting, *sweetling*, then you're painfully ignorant." He said before drowning the last of his drink.

"Right." Lon sounded unmoved by the obscure statement and looked to Sen. "Can we go now? I feel myself catching all sorts of diseases just standing here."

Sen's intention for the night was to make Lon uncomfortable enough that she would beg Naseria to revoke her punishment, yet their sister carried herself surprisingly well. While facing off with a dagger might not have been entirely ruled out for the evening, the surprise still left Sen's heart beating. If anything happened, they realized with a start, they were in no position to stop it.

While Sen found her trailing behind them embarrassing for more than one reason, they truly did not wish to put her in any serious danger.

The door to the tavern opened, though no wind stirred through the threshold. Sen only noted the approaching woman for a moment, thinking how odd her dower robes were, before taking another sip of their drink.

"Alright." Sen rose, wobbly on their feet. As they lifted, the world seemed to shrink away. What they thought had been the listlessness of alcohol turned heavy and foreboding in their stomach.

They blinked hard. *Maybe we should go now*.

Their hands, pressed firmly on the tabletop, doubled. In their mouth, their tongue felt leaden. Words failed Sen as the solemnly dressed woman drew closer. Was it a trick of the light or the drink that stretched her shadow tall behind her?

Lon's face dropped, quicky noting the change in Sen's faculties. The woman, her midnight robes stretching high towards the ceiling, appeared behind her, a warped version of Lon's own shadow.

"Sen?" She jumped forward to try and catch them as they teetered. "Sen!"

Their sister went blurry, a smear of rain in their vision. As the tavern slanted, Sen fell into a world of blue-black nothing.

CHAPTER TWELVE

Dice squeezed her fist, her heartbeat throbbing across her palm. The curved bone of her knuckles pushed against the taunt skin, the barrier between them and the open air so thin. A long teal vein webbed across the back of her scarred and dirty hand, branches of smaller lines disappearing into the thicker parts of her fingers. Releasing the desperate grip in her hand, red crescent moons brightened along her palm. She swiped the tiny cuts from her nails with her other thumb, eyes blankly following the smear of red.

Rest kept its distance since that night. After what she saw, after the fear dissipated and left behind a thick wave of confusion that choked every easy breath in her chest, she tried to find Evangeline. Despite the obvious distance between them now, no one else stood to comfort her. But that long night concealed Evangeline, and Dice grew more delirious with each passing moment she lingered in the darkness, trying to make sense of the blood, the knucklebones, the skinned man—

A hand, it mattered not to whom it belonged, dropped another flagon on the tabletop before her. Dice paid ahead with the last of her coin, not able to shake the change in the wind. *The Far Sailor* sealed every crack at the start of the season, yet a biting chill stabbed through her, and only bad ale shirked the frozen sensation climbing up her spine long enough for Dice to think on what to do next.

She lost the little income that she got as a peacekeeper for the inn the first night she blacked out. Apparently, in her attempt to blot out the image of pink, glistening intestines pinned to a stone wall, she got in a fistfight. It explained the crackling feeling in her knee, and the bruises that still lingered after healing for a few weeks. Otherwise, no one asked about her blood-soaked clothing, and she found fine enough threads on a corpse on the lower platform. She managed a stolen knife from the kitchen for protection, lamenting her dagger in the meantime.

Ale hit the back of her throat with a burning punch. Dice took half the drink in a single gulp, slinging the flagon down on the wood table. At the other end, a few fellows played Cheat. Some hours passed since they asked her to join, getting only a hearty *go smoke a pipe* in response. Each member of the card game shot her a nasty, narrow-eyed grimace before loudly slapping down their cards.

News of the nobleman's death hit the boardwalks the morning after. Dice remembered a body standing in the fog before she blacked out, and that seemed to be the only hazy piece that returned to her over the weeks.

A witness to her crime, or the killer themself?

Her shaky hands gripped the handle of her flagon. Leonora's connection to him made less sense the more Dice thought on it. Had she sold Evangeline to pay off a debt? But Evangeline also said that she got a better offer than what she had at the *Roses*.

None of it made sense. Nails bitten to the quick, she lifted a thumb to chew on its rough, short edge. So far, the Watch managed to keep what they thought happened a secret even from their own lackies. Dice thought she may hear more details, or if there was to be an actual investigation into his death, as she drank away the horror. Murders happened frequently, but this one was *interesting*. A noble, safe in his bed, decapitated and gored? Never mind the elderly woman shoved over the railing of a platform during high tide, or the knotted ball of displaced families from the mainland underneath Stormshale who froze to death. All of the attention directed at a rich fellow meeting such a frightening demise carried more weight than a few dirty sailors. It gave folk a story to bite into with gnashing, ravenous teeth, the poor hoping it might happen again.

Though details of the murder evaded everyone except Dice, gossip about the man himself hummed through every dimly lit drinking hole in Stormshale. Parts of the story itched at the wall of her mind, raking a broken nail over the grainy surface of her memories. He married someone below his station—Evangeline—but as the rumor went, needed *her* money. Considering the man's home harbored only shadows when Dice was there, not a servant or guard present to witness his death or see her leaving, this made sense. Yet it seemed the only gear in her mind to click into place, solving the least important mystery.

Had she done it? If not, what prompted the man to welcome her into his home? And why did she stay to drink with him?

Dice went to finish her ale, blinking stupidly at the empty mug as she raised it to her lips. Lucid thoughts drifted around her as she lowered it, resting it on the table in a daze. She wanted more.

She wanted to forget.

Music lingered in the air, settling on the heavy cloud of smoke from long pipes. The only fireplace in the tavern glowed orange, more ember than flame, dowsing the lingering bodies in auburn shadows. Dice's eyes roved across the shapes, hatches of light revealing wrinkles, broken noses, sinewy arms, stained teeth. All of the pieces created a patchwork person, and the patchwork person sat splintered in the belly of a tavern on the edge of the world. The kitchen closed hours ago but the smell of broiled fish and bread still clung to the walls, to the insides of her nose. Dice's limbs drooped in her chair, which she somehow managed to recline in despite its unforgiving wooden back.

In the murmuring stillness, she closed her eyes. For once, the mutilated body of the nobleman did not flash from the blackness and make her leap from her chair. Instead, across her mind's eye hissed the spray of a crashing wave. The ocean stopped its singing after that night, calling out to her in only its most natural language. She imagined what she heard was not the muttering of the *Sailor's* patrons, but the tide as it drew back away from the sands.

Dice missed the ocean. A shiver that pieced her heart at the thought led her to believe it missed her, too.

The bard plucked the wrong note in their song, ripping Dice out of the quietest moment since discovering the body. Rage ripped through her, eviscerating an already wavering peace. Sitting on a ruddy stool near the fireplace, the woman adjusting the large four-stringed instrument over her lap swore as she fiddled with something hidden. Long fingers, the kind perfect for thievery and sex, plucked at the strings a few more times. Each sound mimicked a tormented cat, the pitch so sharp it made Dice cringe. After another moment of fidgeting, the bard began to play a warble of a ballad about their ailing monarch.

Most of Stormshale felt indifferent when someone mentioned King Einar. The barren island sat far enough to be forgotten by the rest of the country, and in some ways this proved best for its inhabitants. Stormshale did not feel burdened by the king's tax, and as such the extra money vanished into the bulging pockets of the Watch and Stormshale's governor. But if someone stole from *those* cheats, it was the Watch alone that had to catch the thief. No authority on the mainland cared to take a three day boat ride to settle petty crimes.

Patrons gave little attention to the bard as she sang, her voice pretty but lacking passion. Dice watched in a drunken stupor, interested in the inky marks hiding past the wrists of the woman's sleeves. Tendrils peeked out as her hand moved up and down the neck of her instrument, dancing fingers strumming a tune that made Dice think of a storm. No words accompanied the melody, its low pitch rising into the wailing cry of a broken heart before drowning in the tremor of crashing waves. It was a song of loss, that much was certain, and Dice's heart began to ache for something she never possessed.

Moving her head to the music, the collar of the bard's thick coat revealed another tangled mesh of black ink. It looked the same as the lines at her wrist, and Dice fantasized about the hidden pieces underneath the woman's shirt.

"Do you like what you hear, pirate?"

The woman stared back at Dice. Mind staggering, the latter dropped her feet from the edge of the stone fireplace, resting them uneasily on the floor's wooden planks. Moments ago, she was sitting at the far end of a table, slouching in her chair until her head rested on its back, captivated by the twang of music and the methodic slap of cards.

A clawing, aching sensation spiraled upwards from the pit of her stomach when she tried to remember at what point she drew closer to the bard, or when she took the chair just on the other edge of the fire. Was drunkenness responsible for this gap in her mind, or madness?

"Do you have a request?" The bard's voice shifted, eliciting a memory of chasing a butterfly Dice forgot until that moment.

Evander shouting at her from a dock. The Jolly Marksmen is beached, the tide too far out to do anything more than wait on its return. An island vacation, the captain says, but there isn't enough food. White butterflies take interest in the strangers on their beaches, fluttering down from the canopy of palm fronds. Dice never saw one before. There were only gulls and fish at sea, and the strange meat they had to eat when the tide stayed out and the stores ran dry.

Words slipped from Dice's mouth before she chanced catching them. "*Seafarer's Woe.*"

The bard snickered. "You really are a pirate, then. All right, *pirate.*" Dice enjoyed the way the woman's mouth shaped that word, lips puckered slightly. She fiddled with the instrument, retuning it with three little knobs on the end of its neck.

On the inside of her wrist glowed a symbol in the darkness. Its bottom half still concealed by the shirtsleeve, it reminded Dice of a broken plate. Sharp edges drew together in what must be a word from a language she did not know. Swirling lines spanned outward from it, similar enough to the spiraling of the nobleman's intestines that Dice had to quickly look away.

A sick, twisting feeling knotted in her stomach. Eventually, the bard plucked the first notes of the song, lacking the typically jaunty tune. Dice meant to correct the woman when she parted her mouth to sing.

"*Turn your face to the moon, the moon. Raise your flagon hi-igh.*"

Shadows darkened, narrowing until only the bard sat illuminated by the fire. Her voice pitched high and dropped down in a mournful, shivering note that sent a feeling of desire into Dice's chest.

"*Drink heartily for the friends we've lost, for we may see them soon.*"

Dice's fingers prickled, shards of ice climbing up her arms. The bard continued, stripping the misleading joy from the shanty until the white bone of its pain remained. Many sailor's tunes hid their burdens behind stomping beats or a banging drum. This one was a mourning bell on a wedding day.

"*Turn your face from the sea, from the sea, lest he remember yo-ou. Sing heartily, for we're lost, dear friend. Remember me at the end.*"

"That's not how it goes."

Strumming the tune without looking at her fingers, the bard smiled at Dice. "Isn't it?"

Opening her mouth, then shutting it when she felt unsure, Dice leaned back in her chair again. Apprehension prickled at the base of her spine, though no one seemed eager to fight, lest of all the bard. Conversation throughout the room fell into a calmed, hushed silence as the woman lifted her voice.

"*I know the end is near, my friend. Raise our last flag high. Remember me as I'm lost, dear friend, lost on the edge of time.*"

Dice's fingers locked down on the edge of her armrests. Dryness stuck her tongue to the roof of her mouth. Shadows on the edge of her world pressed closer, weighing on the sliver of auburn on the edges of the firelight. The inky mark on the bard's wrists slithered, vines climbing across the back of her hand and down her fingers, staining her nails black. Those fingers no longer plucked at the instrument, despite the music in Dice's mind growing until it blotted out any thought, any instinct. Spinning in the middle of the chorus echoed a single word, rebounding off the curve of her mind to slam into itself—*hark, hark, hark.*

"*Hark.*"

Dice looked up. She and the bard stood before the fire, the opposite halves of their faces concealed in shadows. They were two parts of a mask, empty without something to give them a purpose, an identity. Staring into the woman's eyes as they blackened, the inky tendrils of her neck reaching up to touch the corners of her eyes and mouth, Dice tried to focus on her heaving breath.

Nothing sat at the edges of their world, only a silent, watchful darkness.

"*Hark,*" echoed the lighted half of the woman's mouth. Her black eyes reflected Dice's sweating forehead.

A familiar quiet drank all sound from the room. Popping in the fireplace was snuffed to death like an ember doused in water. Dice felt the rise and fall of her chest, felt the blood rushing through her fisted hands as she willed herself to look away from the woman. Yet no matter how badly she strained the muscle in her neck, her half-darkened face remained trapped in the woman's gaze.

"*Hark*, for the Duathi awakens." The bard raised her shadowed hand, and Dice saw that the palm was as black as regret.

She pressed it next to Dice's heart, right on the solid curve of her breastbone. Ice rushed down from the woman's hands, startling as the warmth seeped from Dice's body. Pain ruptured through her as she stumbled back into the shadows clambering forward, eager to sink her to their depths. Whispers lapped at her, thick waves of regret and fury, jealousy and sadness, wrapping their harbored lamentations around her arms, her torso, her chest, yanking her fervently underneath the black surface of their waters. Dice screamed out, her voice ripped from her throat in silent horror as shadows filled her mouth. She felt them staining the insides of her body as she stared up at the bard, begging with her eyes.

Looking on, the bard reached a hand into the encroaching darkness. Her own body dissolved into the shadows, stripping skin from sinew from bone until nothing remained. Firelight winked out as the shadows stretched over Dice's eyes.

With a shudder, her heart stopped.

CHAPTER THIRTEEN

When they were young, yet to be publicly introduced as the heir to the YeSara Clan, a woman abducted Sen out from under the very noses of their entourage. Why the woman chose them, Sen never knew, and their mother grew frustrated with every mention of the story that they eventually stopped asking. It might have been a woman bold enough to assume that with the abduction of a YeSara child came more gold than she would ever see.

In the fray of confusion, the woman managed to hide in a crowd that gathered close to the Upper Courtyard. A celebration unfolded in the streets, a wedding or a funeral, the bodies packed together to bid their farewells or whisper their blessings. Attempting to shirk judgement, the woman, cornered on a bridge, lifted Sen overhead. There must have been an arrow shot, for suddenly her grip went slack and Sen was falling into the water below.

This world felt like that moment, elongated and frayed like a nightmare. The sensation of falling sliced through their body as they plummeted from a great height. Nothing rushed to meet them as they flailed, a voice in their mind wondering if they were meant to fall forever when all at once a floor of moss and ivy appeared so close to their nose that Sen jerked to cover their face.

The impact never came, and slowly they uncovered their eyes to find themselves standing upright. Sen clearly remembered being in the tavern moments ago, and the look on Lon's face as they collapsed, and the taste of something more acrid that spoiled liquor on their tongue.

"*Bitterthorn. It is a fool's tool, dealt to you by a foolish hand. People are not so careful in their company anymore.*"

A feminine voice pitched low like the caves within mountains slipped out of the darkness. Sen turned, but beyond the cushions of moss stood a world aching in its emptiness.

"*Emptiness?*" The voice sounded impatient, a thread of disappointment cutting through the single word. "*What are you born from? What divides the worlds and the worlds between worlds? To what lands do you go when you sleep, or die? Emptiness is never empty. It is always the beginning, and the end.*"

Sen faced the direction from which they thought the voice came, but still there balked only darkness. A light shined from above them, spilling out from no direct source, cascading gently to caress the spindly moss and dirt, and their tired, confused face.

They were accustomed to drinking interesting things in order to fade into a hazy echo of the real world, so they took in a steady breath, feeling their heartbeat patter slowly in their chest. But bitterthorn was used for poisonings, not dazed journeys, and each inhale in the fabricated world scorched their lungs.

"I've never had dreams like this before," they murmured to themself, a wary palm on their chest. Each padded step across the moss felt vibrant, the green seeping up through their bones to soothe the ache of poison in their blood. Even the thick darkness around them ushered the heady scents of jasmine and everbloom roses.

Sen paused, taking in the smell of the dank flower that did not grow within the Gilded Isles. Its bloodred petals sought crags and rock paths. No memory accompanied the perfume, and they wondered if it was possible to dream of something they had never experienced.

"*I am no dream.*"

Moss withered, vines and ivy shrinking into themselves as their veiny leaves transformed into molten gray spots of decay. The voice bled out of the rot, washing down from the light that came from the world of darkness. Sen stumbled as the earth shook, rocking back onto their heels as the pieces of solid ground fell away. Clods of dirt broke off from the edges of the island, falling into oblivion.

"*I am sleeping. I am here in death and in dreams. Bodiless, voiceless without my herald.*"

Anger not their own ricocheted through Sen's body. Fury rushed upwards from their feet, hot and wild. The voice bellowed the echoes of a violent passion centuries old, smelling of dusty tombs and the sweet honey-wine breath of lovers. A confluence of emotions spilled out of the world beyond the patch of island and slammed into the voyager, forcing the careful breath out of Sen's lungs in a fiery dreg.

It *needed* to be felt, and Sen's body vibrated with the eagerness, the shame, the rage until their teeth were chattering.

"*But even the Godharker fails me. She is waning, eclipsed by the death of magic.*" Pain drifted into the feminine voice, the sorrow of futility cloaking the island in a blanket of regret. "*I am waning. I cannot influence the world without a body to walk in it, and even with my blessings my herald succumbs to time. Let my Godharker find you, child of Stone, of Salt, of River, of the ever-kindling flame in the lantern of the Traveler. Yield to me...*"

The earth shifted again, slanting as the sprays of dirt hit Sen's ankles. Too startled by the shape of the dream to speak, and too afraid of the aching burn of bitterthorn in their lungs, Sen gaped as their fingers dug into the remaining clumps of earth. Their feet dangled over the vast emptiness, the darkness surging with raw power unlike anything Sen felt before.

Inside of the terror came the whispering desire to let go of their safety and fall into that power. May it eviscerate them so long as it lingered in their bones.

"*Yield to me,*" the voice whispered, gentle as sin, "*and my power is yours*."

The island turned to ash in Sen's fists, and once more they were falling, the desire to be consumed by the nothing as fleeting as time. At first their body tumbled down, the light from above vanishing to plunge them into an inky, blank world. With a start, a great gale from nowhere slammed into Sen's stomach, shoving them upwards, and Sen felt their body drop, anchoring in the physical once more.

Air fled their lungs, the weight on their chest so heavy that for a moment they believed the death gods called to them. The world still looked like ink stretching and curling in a cup of water, but they were aware of a hand grasping tightly to their forearm. The bleariness dissipated once Sen forced themselves to blink away the troubled feeling in their chest, yet the sensation of being cut from their body remained.

"Great Ma'Ceste," Lon praised in a huff of air. She all but collapsed back into the chair that sat pulled up to the bedside. "I would've killed you, should you have died."

Died?

Their slow response made their sister chuckle, only a small bit of humor in the laugh. "Now I know how unwell you are, my sibling. You never miss a chance at correction. *How could I possibly have died when I knew you'd go through my things*."

Sen wished to scowl at the mocking tone, but even their face seemed dislodged from their will. Sen tried to relax back into the pillows, managing a raspy breath that forced out the words, "What—in the name of every damnable god—happened?"

With the strangeness of their dream wearing off, fading like dreams did, the events leading up to their unconsciousness flooded in to fill the silence. Unsure of how long they slept, or if their excursion to the mainland was the night before or a week ago, Sen clutched the fabric of their bedding.

Being back in their room meant they were carried from *The Dovetail.*

They remembered Valeska, the weaselly man opposite, and the watcher who threatened Lon with a blade.

In a surge of protectiveness usually foreign to them, Sen asked, "Are you alright?"

Lon did not hide her astonishment. "Me? You're asking *me* if I'm all right?"

"What—" A fit of coughing interrupted their next question. Without a moment's thought, their sister slipped one hand at their back to help them lean forward, grabbing an awaiting glass of water with the other. Lon helped them drink, the parental care and attention sending a bolt of awkwardness through Sen.

As Sen drank, they avoided the surprisingly tender gaze in their sister's eyes. Lon rarely looked at them with anything other than displeasure, so to not only witness her tenderness but see it in her gaze made them feel...*childish*, but something else warmer, and not at all unpleasant.

Sen tried again once they drained half the water pitcher. "That man, the watcher—"

"Ah," sighed their sister. Lon leaned away, confident Sen was lucid enough now to sit up on their own. "Right. Well, firstly, you've been asleep for almost an entire day, and your dog-shite of a friend left *The Dovetail* the moment you collapsed."

Though Sen might have been surprised if Valeska stayed, the complete disregard pricked like a thorn.

"And that mother's-milk sucking, goat-rutting *pig* of a watchman was waiting for us outside. If the barmaid hadn't called over a guard the moment that watchman brandished a knife, I'm sure he would've followed us home—or at least as close to home as possible. But he didn't, and you'll be glad to know that Naseria did, in fact, have someone tailing us the whole night. That's how you ended up back here. The woman doesn't trust either of us, it seems."

Lon rolled her eyes, but Sen felt the flush of gratefulness in her hasty words. Lon was an excellent swordsman, but fighting the reckless type of brigand that frequented *The Dovetail* while keeping Sen safe was beyond her trade.

Trickling like a forgotten pipe, they realized something pestered them about the recounted events. *A barmaid called over a guard*, Lon said. But Sen did not remember a barmaid, only the sellsword, and a woman in a strange cloak whose face was lost to them.

"She doesn't trust *Valeska*," Sen clarified, surprised that they were defending their mother. A prick in their chest urged them not to press Lon about why she lied, and, for once, they decided not to pester their sister.

"And after what's happened, she doesn't trust me. She just worries about *you*."

"She worries for us both. For all her kin." Lon snapped, as if it were a shock for Sen to think differently.

The scion of the YeSara Clan did not try to argue with their sister, which made Lon quirk her brow in disbelief. A vast part of Sen's relationship to Naseria existed on the basis of spite and disapproval, so it seemed ridiculous for them to believe that their mother desired anything other than a clan lead by the last elemental mage in their bloodline. Being groomed for that position left Sen thinking that their mother cared for structing power around the YeSara Clan more than she cared for the family itself.

But what would their Clan be without her, and the leaders before her, who carried what remained of their bloodline to the little island where they now reside? Was it fair of Sen to ask their mother for more when she already gave so much?

These questions never reached the edges of Sen's conscience before, and their feather-like touches startled them.

Lon dazed off through the open window. Evening light colored their room in golds and reds, throwing them in the middle of a blazing hearth. Wind hushed through the foliage to create a still song, and the breeze carried with it the smell of the cookfire. When Sen gazed at their sister, who pretended not to notice their staring, they felt a new sort of warmth growing at the base of their ribcage.

Lon's gaze was off, a memory playing behind her eyes.

With more carefulness in their voice than they ever used to speak towards their sister, Sen repeated their earlier question: "Are you alright?"

Their sister huffed, making a sound through her nose. Not a hair was ruffled, not a thread of silk crushed or rumpled. Yet Sen *knew* discomfort, knew the ache of layering a façade meant to please Naseria and the crowd of people waiting for them to fail.

Lon even gave Sen the same smile they reserved for lying or cheating as she replied, "It's nothing that YeSara coffers can't fix."

A fake laugh sat in the back of her throat, hollow to Sen's ears. Whatever sort of paternal doting influenced her earlier was gone, replaced with that stony distance that Lon built up the moment Sen came into their power. With the cold between them once more, Sen's stomach knotted into a fist of sorrow. Years of sibling rivalry moved behind their vision like a banner in the wind, some moments soft but the majority of them cracking in a violent gale.

Was *The Dovetail* really the type of place that bothered with calling the guards when *one* man brandished his knife? Perhaps Lon told the truth, but if that were the case, then what was she hiding?

"If you're going to kill Valeska," Sen started, catching a raised eyebrow from their sister, "then make sure you do it somewhere his brothers might see. Gods, they might even reward you for culling the runt."

"Such strong words for your *good friend*." Lon snickered. Then, with a genuine smile, she added, "Alright. I promise to any god listening to make his death public and gruesome."

As if bearing witness to the oath, a gust of wind shot through the open window—briefly, it reminded Sen of the air rushing past them in their strange dream.

Placing a hand to their chest, they thought back to Lon's shocked, half-joking words.

I would have killed you, should you have died.

"Gods, Sen," their sister's voice pulled them from their wondering. "I won't actually kill him! Naseria has people for that."

She laughed, but the glint in their sister's eyes spoke of daydreams when she *was* the one to the swipe the last breath from the noble runt. Sen could not name the feeling they got when they bore witness to that darkened spark, Lon's humorless chuckle echoing in their blazing, gilded room.

Not for the first time, Sen was glad for the fact they were not Valeska Demont.

CHAPTER FOURTEEN

Dice shot out of the darkness, briny saltwater in the back of her mouth. An animalistic sound scraped out of her throat, a shocked gasp mutilated by a cry of exhaustion. Her nails clawed at the fabric of her tunic, half expecting to find a gaping hole in the middle of her chest but colliding with the flesh of her breast, the bone underneath. Ice grasped her stuttering heart, persistent as it dragged itself out of the stillness of death. Pink tinged the sky, a red dawn fast approaching on a rare morning that sat untainted by storm clouds or rain. Grief dragged down her spine, left over from the solid feeling of loss that permeated her strange dream.

Cheated, the hands of the death gods sank back into the stone beneath her. Dice pulled her knees to her chest, body convulsing as she sobbed into the dirt and grime on her trouser legs. Hands cupping her elbows, she made herself small, hoping to vanish into the overwhelming sensation of frustrated sorrow.

Slowly, Dice lifted her head. It took a moment for the cold of the stone to bring her back to her tingling body, her spirit still filling its vessel of skin and bone. Blinking her eyes open, she pushed the swirling disorder in her mind back down until only a hushed silence remained.

Hunger gnawed at her backbone. Surrounding her rose great slabs of shalestone, jagged rotten teeth in the red of the dawn. They glinted in the morning light, sparkles of moisture winking in the sunshine. She must be on the edge of the city, past the boardwalks and fish market, though how she managed not to freeze to death overnight was another question to add to her growing sense of uncertainty.

Dice recalled little of the last few hours, shivering at her memories of the bard and the drinking, but the woman must have been another vivid dream. Perhaps someone gave her a tainted drink, or the delirium of her sleepless nights finally whittled away at any remaining sanity.

Whatever happened, it was not real.

So what did that say for the state of her mind?

With these new questions, Dice barely had the energy to push herself to standing. Uncertainty pressed down on her shoulders, locking them into tense, tight fists at the base of her skull. Her hair, shaggy and long enough now to tickle the nape of her neck, clung in sweaty ringlets to her forehead. As she turned to face the rocky, sloping decline towards the shore, a wave crashed into the shalestone. It kissed the edges of her boots, drawing her eye as it pulled back out to sea.

A wide, long platform of shalestone stretched out with the tide, and she realized where she stood. Half a day's walk east of Stormshale was an archaic remainder of a bridge that once connected the islet to the mainland centuries ago. Years of drifting and erosion long since destroyed the bridge, but slabs of its masonry lingered. On either side were pillars that marked the start of the bridge, only as tall as herself now after weathering hundreds of storms, but still thick as a horse. Underfoot, the shalestone was chipped but level, unnaturally smooth. Far out in front of her continued a stacked pattern of shalestone intermittently struck through with fat cracks that spiderwebbed out across the otherwise flat surface. The path endured a little further, disappearing into the thrashing waves.

An orange sun climbed over the horizon. Dice squinted at its painfully joyous light, bright and golden. She frowned at the red sky peppered with dark clouds drifting away from Stormshale, promising to return on a darker morning. In her flimsy, stolen clothes she crossed her arms to brace against the cold air. The chill made Dice alert, and she was glad for its unforgiving bite as she considered how long it would take her to walk back to the city.

While her mind tried to force her to look at the questions that swam within its depths, she ignored the rumbling to stare for a moment longer at the waking ocean, the rising sun. Only a short while ago, a view like this struck honor into Dice's heart. The sea her home since birth, its sunrises always carried with them a tenor of respect.

Thank you for sailing me, for understanding my cruelty and my kindness.

Dice felt nothing as she stared out across the blooming ocean. Waiting, hoping that it changed, the moments passed by with itchy discomfort. After what seemed like long enough, she let out a frustrated breath before turning, disheartened, on her heel.

Finding a footpath through the stone kept Dice's body occupied enough to tamper down the whirlpool of thoughts. Step after step, her boot found its foothold, but only a handful of moments lapsed before she became embarrassingly winded. Weeks had passed since her last climb, and Dice would be unable to hold herself up now due to sleepless exhaustion and the tremors in her hands from fear and drink.

Eventually the path evened out as she neared the pebbled coastline. Smooth, gray rocks crunched underfoot, the spray of small waves darkening the edge of her trouser leg as she walked. Dice relished the cold, focusing on the cool mist in order to remain awake. This kind of frozenness reminded her of nights on the open water where there stood little more than clouds on the horizon. A vast, empty world of ocean, of creatures beneath it stirring and thriving. No matter how many times her boots walked on solid land, she forgot that anything other than the wide expanses of unforgiving water existed when she was out at sea.

On her right climbed the mighty mountains, their cliff face a harrowing drop that no one she knew dared to explore. The shalestone gleamed purple in the red of the morning, and as the questions darting around Dice's mind rose in volume she tried instead to pick apart the details of the craggy rocks, the salt on the air, the *scrunch, scrunch* of the pebbles. Her own breathing grew ragged, her once frozen limbs warming from the exertion, a line of sweat dotting her upper lip despite the chill.

She braced against a sudden gull, the swipe of air knocking aside her distraction.

Had she died?

Dice certainly felt like death, her hand worrying over where the bard touched her in the dream. Nothing seemed unusual; beneath her coarse hand thrummed a fistful of meaty life, the warmth of her chest bleeding into her cold, achy fingers.

Thinking about it for too long felt like stepping to the edge of a cliff. Below her tossed the violent images of the gored man as though he were inviting her.

Join the dead—it's not so bad once the thrashing is over.

Dice shoved the ache away until it sat at the end of her fingertips. It may grab her once more, in vulnerable moments, but she knew how to keep it at bay.

Rounding a particularly nasty slope of shalestone interrupting the coastline, Dice trudged on, sloshing into the shallow water. While her boots where high and kept her feet dry, the icy sensation prickled at her toes. Breath sucked through her teeth instinctively as she braced for the next few steps, sighing in relief once her feet found the pebbles again.

Freezing and disheartened, Dice folded into herself to try and save her body heat. A distant part of her mind replayed the last few weeks like recalling a melodrama that a powder-faced man in a skirt might perform at one of the dock town theaters. Pretending it was not real kept the bile in Dice's stomach from climbing up her throat, but it did nothing to ease the shivering pain that murmured through the hollow of her chest. Every muscle in her body felt wound so tightly around her bones that she may crack, splintering to be gobbled up by the frigid sea.

The song in the waves sounded off, a tenor too solid to be the hush of water crashing against pebbles. When Dice ripped her gaze back into focus, she noted the weathered platform ahead that marked Stormshale's borders. The Watch boasted its fresh catches, naked bodies hanging by ropes, parading the deaths of their victims. Further on, she saw the fish markets, empty of buyers so early in the morning. Merchants were setting up their stalls, the cookfires carrying the smell of char on the wind. Dice's stomach growled, having drank all her coin, and as she drew closer to the hanging bodies that were meant to be a testament to the Watch's unchecked authority, she averted her gaze. Often, those swinging committed petty thefts, or *failed to comply*—the Watch's favorite and overused excuse for murder. Any person in Stormshale unwilling to obey risked a long drop and a sudden stop.

Dice preferred not to walk out this way since the morning she went for a swim and returned to find a child of no more than seven swinging naked in the breeze. She did not like to dwell on what they did with the body, or why it was bare.

Hark.

The little warmth from the exercise vanished. Water frothing like a rabid beast hit Dice's boot as she stood before the platform of drifting bodies. Wotag froze them neatly with only the barest smell of rot wisping down from the bright, pale skin of empty husks.

In the corner of her eye, they looked as though they were dancing.

Her heart galloped madly in her chest. Wind clapped around her head, gales roaring over the sea. Slicing up the pebbled shoreline, the water rushed towards her in a chaotic hum as she pushed herself to face the hangman's ropes, forcing herself to *look* so that she may prove to her addled mind that the bodies were dead and had not spoken out of that same dark pit from which she only just returned.

Evangeline gazed down at her, the black of her beautiful eyes illuminated by the golden sun. Wetness stuck her long hair, its ringlets heavy with water, to the slope of her lifeless shoulders. Twined around her gossamer neck, the skin red and irritated, the knot of the noose burrowed into the hollow under her ear like a kiss. Fresh bruises decorated her skin, some as small as fingertips, and each one Dice felt on her own body.

She felt the sting of a dagger on her hips, her forearms, until the sharp slash of pain across her navel dropped her body down onto the pebbles. The rocks dug into the flesh of her knees as she gaze upwards, face lifted in horrified praise to the empty woman before her. Beneath Evangeline's breast shined the birthmark Dice once kissed so fervently. Seeing the blot speared her, every emotion bleeding out of the wound and onto the shore, eagerly consumed by rumbling waves. The sun lit up the stone behind Evangeline, a gilded tableau for a lifeless body. Her deathly pale skin went luminescent in the sunlight, and unlike the gored horror, Dice did not want to look away. Evangeline's glowing body caught fire in the sun, burning itself into Dice's mind until there stood no love, no envy, no hate, only a black well of twisting, writhing shadows.

And, suddenly, a spark.

The sound of bellowing, a guttural tone from the belly of some great monster, ripping apart Dice's mind as the images flashed in angry, bright colors.

There had been a body in the fog, once indiscernible until the mist of her memories cleared away to reveal that it was the gored man on the mantlepiece, whole and utterly confused at Dice's presence on his doorstep. His words were lost on the breeze, the man smiling as she spoke to alleviate his worries.

"We have a common friend. I have a gift for you, from our dear Evangeline."

He brought her inside to drink, to talk, yet the rest frayed like tattered garments. Dice was still unsure whether she dismembered the stranger, or if there stood another in the recesses of her blank memories, lingering in oblivion. Each passing moment, the latter felt less and less like a possibility, and more like a lie she told herself to kept the edges of her reality from ripping apart completely.

The old song of the ocean warbled a corrupted tune as it pounded the shoreline, the spray hitting Dice's back at she felt her limbs grow numb in the cold.

Evangeline.

She gażed up at the body of the only woman that gave Dice the tiniest sliver of warmth in the hollow town. Gossip said there were no leads on her husband's death, but that was because the Watch considered *her* the best suspect. They had no care, time, or money to investigate like the peacekeepers of the mainland territories. People of the Watch wanted things like strange deaths to be done and over with so that they may return to their drinking and thievery.

Pain cracked inside her chest, breaking apart a rib to stab its boney point into her heart.

This was all her fault.

If she had not been drunk, or mad—if she stayed at *The Far Sailor* and ignored Evangeline's petty jabs of superiority, then maybe the young woman would not be hanging from the end of a rope.

Thrown in the midst of a cyclone, everything ripped away from Dice's vision. Her body lifted out of its confines to linger in some space between the solid world, and the proverbial Other. Like in her dream about the bard, Dice felt the shade of night stain her until the bowels of her body ran as dark as grief. A handful of thoughts, the pieces of their words slamming together to create awkward, half-legible statements clattered around in her mind.

Leave.

Hide.

...hark.

She closed her eyes against Evangeline's glowing body, the last word ringing around her head in the bard's harmonious voice. Behind her, the low tremor of the ocean's mournful chorus rumbled, beckoning.

CHAPTER FIFTEEN

"Am I supposed to marry *her*?"

Pelagios squinted against the early morning sunlight. Amidst the thick wheat fields glowed the king in his green and brackish-gray robes, a circlet of beaten iron glinting in the sun as he turned his head to speak to a man who emphasized his statements with an arching sweep of his hand. By his side, hands folded at her back, stood his wife. She listened intently to their conversation, chin bobbing in affirmatives. Crow marks defined her eyes, her sun-worked skin proof that despite holding a noble title, her small farm required her to work alongside her servants.

Their bodies rose as banners amongst the nodding heads of furry wheat. A gentle gust of wind pushed the wheat forward, a sea of gold rippling in the breeze. The king put out a hand to catch one of the heads of wheat as if to show his companions its vitality.

Shimmers of rainbows blinked around them, refracting the light, changing the scene into a vision of scattered radiance. In an odd way, Pelagios felt the shimmering light might conceal a figure standing directly behind it, that something or someone stood further beyond the colors.

The general smirked, looking down at the prince as he thought of how terrifying it must be to consider marrying a woman who may be old enough to be his grandmother. The dancing streams of light vanished as he turned to gaze at the young boy.

"Fortunately for you, Sire, *that* is the girl's mother."

Einar let out a sigh of deep relief. Beneath him, the speckled pony flicked her mane side to side. Flies landed on her neck, and the prince batted them away in annoyance. Pelagios held fast to the reigns of King Mycin's horse, his own steed padded with the riding leathers of a nobleman despite never officially earning a title in court. Mycin's horse shifted on its feet, kicking up the rich smell of earth wet from that morning's rain. Sunlight, white in color, spilled out to touch the rolling green and gold of the hills. If Pelagios squinted and focused hard enough, he spied the rocky peak of Carn-Duhl on the horizon, five day's ride away.

The journey to Marspik made the general nervous. Only a morning's ride south was the border separating Esmar and Sovil, the Crossing a bubbling bridge city connecting the two. While Mycin refused to seek war council in the presence of his youngest son, Pelagios understood how tenuous the relationship between the two countries remained after the royal family restored their place on Esmar's throne. Matriarchal pods formed an established monarchy during their absence, organized very differently compared to what Mycin's people knew, and the dismantling of their system resulted in refuting treaties made with Sovil. The southern country's queendom did not take kindly to the amended declarations, so for the last few decades, communication in general was sparse. This effected Esmar greatly, for Sovil brought them great iron from their mines, and threads good for weaving. Pelagios was unsure as to whether or not Mycin intended to fix this weakened alliance during his reign, for the ailing king seemed more intent on finding his remaining sons suitable pairings.

In Marspik, a singular noble family remained from a plague that miraculously left the wheat fields unblighted. Mycin took this as a sign of blessing from the Mother and Father. Of the noble family's seven children, two sons and a healthy daughter remained. Mycin spent the better part of the morning discussing the arrangement with her parents, leaving his boisterous entourage back at their manicured but small estate and bringing only Pelagios as his guard. Einar forced his father to take him along, refusing to stay behind and be left to suffer through the rustic entertainment the small manor prepared.

By the drooping look on Einar's face, he might regret joining them. Little ones struggled to take interest in things like how beautiful the wheat fields were, and the warmth of the sun on their necks. Pelagios meant to enjoy the stillness for as long as possible. The constant search for suitable proposals, and Mycin's deteriorating awareness, kept him alert for much of the last season. So he closed his eyes for the briefest of moments, taking in the warmth on his arms until he filled up with the smell of rich earth and wheat.

Sweat trickled down Pelagios' neck, leaving an icy trail. Breath tickled his ear, a woman's voice speaking in a tongue that made him think of stone and ivy, of fur clotted with blood. Despite sitting on a horse high off of the ground, the voice appeared next to his ear. No matter how desperately he tried, he could not open his eyes to take note of the speaker, or move his lips to warn the king.

This is the moment where death is decided: in the stillness of peace.

"If Tally's wife is prettier than mine, I shall have to kill him."

Pelagios opened his eyes, raising a brow at the round-cheeked boy. Fear at some unknown thing evaporated, no memory of the voice tainting the world surrounding him.

Einar picked at the leather horn of his saddle, dismayed.

Pelagios sighed. "You'll be king much faster then, since he's the elder."

The prince scowled. "I will take my sword and run him through. I'm better than him, anyways, even if he's bigger than me. And true kings have pretty wives. Maybe I will take his wife, if she's *very* pretty."

Pelagios crossed his arms on the horn of his saddle. He dipped his chin until the prince raised his gaze to meet the old man's. "If you want to kill a man bigger than you, you cannot fight him. Rest easy, prince, for there are other ways."

He calmed the boy, whose face went red in denial. Einar boasted the shortest temper of all his siblings, though as the youngest of the boys it did him well when the others tried to fight him. He became a mad wolf when cornered, and Pelagios knew that with the proper training Einar may be one of the greatest swordsmen of Esmar.

"You can try poison, or hiring someone else to do it for you."

"That's *cheating*."

"So, your father wins his wars by cheating since he has an army?"

Einar shifted in his saddle. "Well. No. He's the king. King's get to do whatever they want. It's not cheating when *he* does it."

"Hm." Pelagios knew better than to try and contradict a child with a temper, and returned his gaze to Mycin. The noble couple bowed, a bell of laughter ringing out from the woman's decorated throat.

Bruises dot her skin, finger prints, rot spiderwebbing out of blue-green veins and climbing her eyes. Dead, a week after her daughter married the king. Strangled in her bed, her husband taking a new wife before the mourning rites were finished. Aletta did not rise from bed for months.

"I should be the crowned prince." Einar, resolute, straightened his posture in his saddle. When the older man gazed down at him, he was surprised by the fury in his small eyes. "Not Talbin."

"Your brother…" Pelagios searched for the right words that would not outright support the young prince's bloodlust, or shame him for his desires. "The Crowned Prince may not be as suited to rule, Sire, but there are other ways to dethrone him that don't required his death."

"But Pelagios," Einar's gaze swiveled up, blank and uncaring. It chilled the older man despite the heat of the sun on his neck. "I *want* him to die. Aldar and Isbin, too. My father has too many sons.

"Do you have a son, Pelagios?"

The wind stilled, bobs of wheat lifting their heads up high in the calm as if draw upward by an unseen force. Mycin's voice drifted as but a murmur. Sweat beaded at the nape of Pelagios' neck, a chilliness trailing across his hairline. Far beyond the peak of Carn-Duhl, and plummeting south towards the Erewildes, lived a woman who might have been his wife, and a son that may be his own.

His hands tightened on the reigns, his gaze steady on that distant point, when he answered.

This is the moment your fate is sealed. Wax on a letter, sap to bond the cut.

"No," came his unwavering lie, and he smiled down at the young prince to keep the guilt away.

Satisfied, Einar nodded and looked back to his father. "That is good, then. Less people who want to kill you."

Pelagios palled, baffled at the overwhelming carelessness in the prince's voice. Mycin lifted a hand, calling out to them joyously, but Einar's gaze was unfocused. With an aching pain in his belly, the general realized Einar's murderous fantasy did not stall at the death of *just* his brothers.

"I hope you die alone, Pelagios." The prince's voice was genuine in its sentiment. "It's easier than thinking of all the people who might be left without you."

The wet of the marshland squelched between Pelagios' toes. Blinking away the dreamy memory, his eyes drifted, unfocused, until they settled on the pink sunrise. Black mud clung to his legs up to the knee, the smell briny and thick with rot. A chill sharper than iron ran through him, whipping at the white locks of his hair. Sprigs of scraggly weeds, not the gold heads of wheat, reached out to grasp at him as a gale knocked him sideways. Unfolding before him were the marshes of the encroaching ocean, small rocks and thick mud sucking at his legs as he walked, startled at his disarray, back to the solid banks of a roadway. Dressed in only his long pants and a tunic, Pelagios felt the bite of the winter season like the angry gnaw of a mad dog.

Do you have a son, Pelagios?

No.

Shaking the memory from his mind, the guilt stuck behind, a parasite clinging to the leathery folds of his skin. It stung tears into his eyes, tears he batted away in shame as he walked the short way down the dirt road towards the city of Farstone. Its shadowy maw opened to welcome him as he ran, stumbling, hoping that no one witnessed his humiliated confusion. He wished nothing more than to be enveloped by the gloom of Carn-Duhl, hidden from the curious eyes which followed him from behind half-shuttered windows.

"I've considered you unfriendly, General, but never a reclusive man," was Damalis' greeting once Pelagios finally arrived at the southern balcony. "I never suspected I would need to send a message if I ever cared to see you outside of proper court."

Proper court. Pelagios wanted to scoff, but kept up the surely image the advisor placed on him as he lowered into the seat opposite. Gaps of reasoning still stood in the places between his options of betraying the king's loyalty, or Damalis', and Pelagios feared that his discouragement was apparent.

After his sleepwalking episode that morning, the general scraped himself raw in a hot bath. The frustration did not ease from him afterwards, so he called upon a favorite maid of his. Whatever her name, she bore the most resemblance to the young—*deceased*—queen. It took little handling and thrusting for Pelagios to be satisfied, the guilt and disgust paling the thread of anxiety hounding him since his visions.

He offered the bath to her as they dressed, but she fled the bedchamber before she finished retying her apron. Only a moment later did Damalis' pretty errand boy arrive with the advisor's request to join him for the noonday meal.

A tinge of bitterness settled between the general's ribcage as he motioned to the servant to pour his drink. Weeks ago, Kana told the general that they would call upon him to specify what exactly they needed, yet the advisors remained cautiously distant. This noonday meal with Damalis was the first private meeting the general took with any of the advisors since the night of his treachery.

Wine sloshed into the cup, so deliciously rich it poured black, the thick smell of mulberries wafting upwards.

Snatching the bottle from the servant's hands, Pelagios sniffed it, frowning.

Damalis grinned, letting out a small laugh. "If I had any intention to poison you, it would not be with witnesses."

"This is from the reign of Elbert." Mycin's father enjoyed his drink more than his women, and had ordered one of the old wings to be remade as his own winery. Only a certain amount of bottles were left from that maddening experience, for when Mycin killed his father to take the throne, he made sure the wine was the first thing to burn. He threw his mother into its flames as some sort of attempt at poeticism, marking the start of his rule with violence against his own kin. Pelagios had only just been knighted, and recalled the cindered rooms and charred bodies vividly, punctuated by the sickening aroma of mulberry wine.

Had Damalis chosen the bottle for that very reason?

"I find that there happens to be fewer and fewer moments to enjoy a distinguished wine on a chilly but surprisingly bright day." The man's voice grated on. "I've decided that I will welcome them, however rare, however small."

Pelagios clunked the bottle down on the short table between them with little care for its contents, Damalis flinching at the sound. Clouds rolled in thick sheets overhead, unthreatening but carrying with them the first snowfalls of the cold season. But what sunshine pressed through was indeed bright and warm, shining down on the vast southern balcony that overlooked an abandoned courtyard.

This side of the public grounds was neglected by most of the court since it sat in the shadow of the mountain, leaning towards miserable on even the warmest of days. Damalis sat with a fur throw over his lap while Pelagios wore only a long coat over his day clothes. Unlike the advisor, he was chastened against painful weather. Even during their hunt for the Kahun throughout Esmar, Damalis was not far from his throws and blankets.

The meaning of the advisor's words did not go unnoticed. Leaning back in his chair, he noted food neither decorated the table, nor sat waiting in the hands of the servants. Apparently, he planned only to gorge himself on stolen wine.

"You have something to celebrate, then?"

Damalis beamed, the inside of his lips black from the wine. "There is good news, yes, but I wanted to inquire as to how you're feeling, Pelagios? It's hard for me to believe a man of your loyalty is at ease with the decisions you face."

The older man shifted in his seat, as his kind often did when confronted with personal questions. His walking dream left him unsettled in the strangest way, a part of his mind whispering that *this* was the dreaming world—but then, what would be in the waking one? It stripped a half of Pelagios' soul from his body, making him feel like an ambling corpse. Violence still surged in his heart towards the king every time he thought about Aletta's decay, how she must have been alone in those last moments.

Recalling the dead flowers littering her blankets to try and mask the smell, Pelagios gritted his teeth. All of these things, and with treason settled neatly on top, made his focus soft as rotten fruit.

"A delicate question, I see. Well," Damalis cleared his throat, which seemed a signal for his servants. They moved away from the men's seat alongside the balcony, pressing themselves against the wall by the door but not leaving. With a smile, Damalis added in a low voice, "Seeing the queen like that would shake even the most sullen of warriors."

"*You knew?*" Pelagios' voice shot out at a half-whisper, spittle hitting Damalis' chin. His fingers gripped the armrest until he remembered the servants.

After struggling for a moment, Pelagios managed to relax his shoulders enough to lean back into the chair in a strained, faux leisure.

Damalis, still smiling with his eyes as blank as a raven's, nodded. "Of course. Einar cared little for the advice of his physician, so I oversaw the little he allowed *me* to control. I did my best to instruct him, but we all know the state of his mind even before we left to hunt his fabricated adversaries."

"She was alive when we left?"

His voice was soft. Weak. Pelagios assumed as much, but the events of the past week brought into question everything he thought he knew. Damalis having known of the queen's state made the general even more wary of trusting him. Did the others know as well, simply keeping the fact of the queen's death quiet, or were he and Damalis the only ones privy to the truth? Beyond the physician and the chambermaids, who were no doubt too afraid to speak and thus carried no cause for worry, it seemed the other members of the court operated under the idea that their queen still lived. But Pelagios doubted Aletta rotting in her bedchamber laid beyond the imaginings of the court.

"Hm," the advisor hummed, then clarified. "I believe she died some time during our journey. Do you remember Gaelis? Stupid enough to get his head smashed in on our first day back home?"

Only managing a pert nod, not trusting that he had complete control over his faculties yet, Pelagios waited for the advisor to elaborate.

After a hefty sip of his stolen wine, the man wiped the corners of his mouth with his thumb. The general knew that Damalis chose this long, seemingly thoughtful pause with intention, not just from his experience dealing with other warring generals but with the court. Damalis may think himself the smarter man, but every noble on every continent wanted the attention of an audience, however small. Because of this, Pelagios figured the man wanted to bask in this moment of *whatever* justified the wine and this meeting.

"I'm rarely patient in my old age, Damalis."

The advisor noted the clench of Pelagios' fist atop the armrest. "Very well, Sir General. You won't need to beat an answer out of me. Riven and Kana have found a mage."

"I thought the other one was in charge of that?" Pelagios did not bother to recall the name of the woman who first suggested the idea all those nights ago. If advisors and counselors did not fall like mayflies in Einar's presence, he may have remembered it.

Shifting in his seat, trying to string his thoughts together, he added with a note of petulance, "Did we not decide on a different path?"

Damalis quirked a brow, confirming that the council members met without informing Pelagios. Whatever flame of annoyance and panic sparked inside him was snuffed out quietly, quelled for a moment when there were not so many eyes upon him. The council did not yet trust Pelagios to be allowed in *every* discussion, just as he did not fully trust them. If he wanted to protect Einar and Theon from any plot on their lives, that needed to change.

"Lanet made the suggestion, but if one wants things done *outside* of the eyes of the King, then Riven and Kana are the better choices."

Pelagios reached for his cup. The advisor's gaze rested heavily upon him, tracking the smallest twitch of muscle. "Do you know when the mage arrives?"

Damalis sucked his teeth, wearing an amicable grin as he poured himself fresh wine. "I'm afraid I know little of the mage, or his whereabouts. Riven seems to have been the one to find him, but the bastard only wants to speak with Kana. But even she has sent letters only to get no response… thus far."

Letters meant there was a place to receive them. Pelagios had enough coin to hire a runner smart enough to follow Kana's message, so perhaps he might be able to find the mage after all. However, this meant little to the general if the members of council suspected him of betraying them to the king, and were prepared for such an event. To learn more about the mage and what threat he may have over the king, he needed to speak with the councilmembers who found him.

Rusted gears in the old man's head began to turn. He sipped his wine casually, feigning ease as he mulled over this news. "How do we know this man is truly a mage unless we see his power?"

A light glinted in Damalis' eyes. "I considered this when the correspondence first began. I'd still hold that wariness if the mage had not been the one to send the letter first."

Pelagios frequently sensed the eyes of strangers in the dark watching him as he paced about Carn-Duhl. Oftentimes, the dreadful sense of being observed followed him to his rooms. Blood rushed to his ears, every sinew urging him to prepare for an unseen guest, but when nothing stirred in the shadows or behind the curtains he brushed it away. Out on the balcony, the general felt that very same wariness rush down his spine. Eyes belonging to servants watched him and Damalis without truly seeing them, as good servants did. There were no other guards, but up from some distant hallway flittered the sound of laughing courtesans.

Good eyes went unnoticed. Pelagios considered how they were being watched, wondering by whom, when he next spoke. "How is that possible? Who else knows of this outside of the council?"

"Only yourself, Sir General. Hopefully."

Pelagios grimaced at the lazy answer.

"I only mean," continued the advisor, "that it's hardly in anyone else's favor to risk saying the wrong thing to the wrong person. As we've established, there are still zealots within the court who may be excited at the chance to turn on one another to honor their king. The Council knows this."

"Let me see the letter." Pelagios did not intend for his voice to sound so irritable as he proffered his hand, but the lingering sensation of being watched caused his skin to prickle in discomfort. He wanted to disappear inside the cavernous halls, allowing the embrace of the darkness between the torches to cover him.

Damalis flitted a hand. "I don't have it. Kana wanted to observe it."

"Observe a *piece of paper?* Is this what the king's men do, then?"

A muscle under Damalis' eyes jumped. The advisor, an expert in courtly appearances, expertly swiped away any other sign that the comment irked him. A man who stood only two steps below the king was likely to have the same ego, though Pelagios long guessed Damalis was simply better at its concealment.

"We are not the *king's* men anymore, General, as much as you are no longer your mother's son. While we are a part of that which created us, circumstance has ushered us into new being." His eyes, storm clouds on the horizon, flicked over the older man in distaste. "I'm beginning to wonder whether you would truly save Esmar if it meant betraying your king. Tell me, Pelagios; is one man worth the lives of one hundred? More? A whole country? No," he laughed dryly, turning his cup to look at the droplets of wine left behind. "We are not for the king anymore. The moment you understand this—and why we chose this, with heavy hearts—will be the moment I permit Kana to give you the letter."

"*You are not my authority!*"

Pelagios stood over the small table, a wave of querulous anger surging through his veins. Wine ran over the tabletop, the bottle tipped on its side from his jarring movement. How dare a man who has never truly bloodied his hands in war assume any position of power of *him*?

Looking up at him from those mesmerizing droplets in his cup, Damalis let out an easy sigh. Unfazed by the old man's outburst, the advisor simply nodded. "Does that mean, then, that you are *my* authority? Is that the position you've given yourself in all of this? You know nothing, Pelagios."

Damalis stood, setting the cup down easily on the table sodden with undrinkable wine. Checking the cuff of his sleeve for any stains, the advisor turned. "For the time being, I think it's best to keep it that way."

And with a short bow, Damalis drifted out of the balcony, taking any chance of Pelagios figuring the secrets of the Council with him. Leaving Pelagios to rage without an audience, the advisor seemed to forget *he* was the one who asked for the general's help, not the reverse.

It embarrassed him, being belittled even in front of servants, but Pelagios tampered down the frustration long enough to even his breathing.

Sitting back down in the chair, he stared at the shallow pool of wine before him. Dripping off the edges of the table, *tap, tap, tapping* on the stone with each drop, it called to memories of blood pooling in the foot prints on a battlefield.

Is one man worth one hundred?

The haughty question made the old man sneer. What is a king if not a man worth more than that?

But what was a king without a country to fight for him?

Pelagios grimaced. For now, he must set aside these inclinations put into his head by the silver-tongued advisor. Damalis might not be interested in informing the general about the mage for a while now, but he gave Pelagios enough to start his own scheming. Managing a runner to follow Kana's letters was a start, no matter if the councilmembers figure out his man. Pelagios wanted to have his own eyes to command, and the sooner he found out the mage on his own, the better.

Damn any soft-bellied advisor who tried to get in his way.

CHAPTER SIXTEEN

Kairdwillo-Nhan. Mother's Rock, in the Old Tongue. Neoma spied the white-blue sheen of her family's stoney home far down the path long before any of her relatives noticed her approach. The walls facing the ocean were smoothed out by temperamental storms, erosion weathering the rounded structure of the main house while those facing the tiny village Neoma docked in were still rough as a mountainside. The structure was built long and wide, the child of an ancestor's dream of a sprawling family that might still live as a singular unit. Neoma was certainly not the first to break away from the family home, nor would she be the last, but there was a certain pleasure in knowing a room awaited her return.

Chimneys puffed out dark cooking smoke that wisped away on the wind, the fishy smell of *spinksammon* drifting over Neoma. From her spot on the crest of the hill, she saw her family in the shallows of the beach carrying buckets on their shoulders. In their own turn, they waded out into the water to catch the waves as they crashed into the sand until the buckets shaped like hollow turtle shells were full. Walking up to the beach, they swayed back and forth, waddling along the shoreline to deposit the saltwater across the dark, packed-together sand that left behind clumps of salt when the seawater dried. Further down the shore, relatives raked up a harvest, the crystal granules glowing white under the sunlight as they scooped their pans to filter out the sand. The shoreline by the house ran white with salt, thick clumps collecting against rocks sitting just beyond the shallows, but the right flavor was brought out after it baked in the sun for three days, mellow and briny.

Someone must have seen her, for a bellowing call of laughter went up. It was echoed down the shoreline until Neoma's family stood, their tasks forgotten for the moment as they raised their palms in ecstatic waves. Voices crying out like joyous gulls rippled down the beach until Neoma dropped her sack from her shoulder, lifting both her hands to swing them wildly overhead.

Her first real smile in weeks strained her cheeks. There was no joy like homecoming, even when her world felt so dark.

Neoma's nose did not lead her astray on the *spinksammon*. Once the overjoyed welcome from her family settled into gentle laughter, and those assigned to work that day returned to their duties along the shoreline, Neoma was conveniently pulled into the cook room to help prepare that evening's meal. Despite it being the part of the season where all hands were needed to harvest the salt, Calily and Roland had been called away to visit one of their sellers in Linlocke. Neoma missed them by a handful of hours, and their ferries may have even hushed by one another as she journeyed to Kairdwillo-Nahn.

In the hot cook room, she beat a roll of dough flat with the heel of her palm hard enough that sweat began to dot her upper lip. Two of her cousins took turns flipping the pink length of fish on the flat iron sheet that rested atop the fire, one of them tossing seasonings of every color onto its crisping skin as the other made sure each side browned nicely. An uncle sat over a large bowl of water, shedding potatoes of their thin skin and dropping the naked lumps into the basin of saltwater to soak. The skins went into a separate bucket, where they would later be oiled, fried, and salted. All around Neoma danced the smells of peppercorn, ash, heady oil and the tang of drying, bitter roots. The family kitchen made her own bundles of herbs look limp as she recalled how they hung over her counter. Here, shelves were carved into the dome of the walls, each one harboring vials of oils and covered containers of spices, some jars as wide as her torso. Down the hall, the voices of those in charge of smoking flavor into the freshly harvested salts ordered *more cayenne, less parsley, this batch needs to wait until we clean up because it's going to be sweeter—we can't ruin the flavor*.

Over her shoulder, the oil on the flat pan made a loud, crackling *pop*. One of the cousins jumped back, the seashell beads in her finger-thin dreadlocks clattering in the way that mimicked the snapping of a crab's claw. Inara laughed at herself, the pierced hoop in her bottom lip stretching with her smile.

The hoop came from an older tradition of marriage Neoma chose not to acknowledge, more for fear of the needle than shame of it. On Inara's face, it shined as a proclamation, and made her heart swell with the gladness that her family was able to practice such a tradition at all. Neoma remembered the day her cousin sat under their old grandmother's wrinkled hands, the needle steady in her grasp as the cooking for Inara's wedding left the room smelling like spicy rice and fish. Afterwards, with her swollen lip and shining wedding jewelry, Inara told Neoma it made her feel whole.

Neoma felt so lost within herself that she feared jewelry, even done in honor of the women before her, might fail at putting those pieces together.

"I'm surprised you caught spink this late into the season." Neoma pressed the dough out in a flat, rough square before she began folding it corner to corner. The dough was light and already incredibly thin, and her mouth watered thinking about the next steps of quickly frying it in oil and sprinkling it with sugar. As a small treat, it would be served before the actual meal, but Neoma knew her and her cousins would sample the dish before it made its way to the long table outside.

The cousin opposite Inara snorted in place of a laugh. Sulien stood a full head taller than Neoma or Inara, leaning a little over the stove so that her head did not brush the hanging herbs. The stick in her hand moved like water around a rock, fluidly turning the crisping fish without splattering oil anywhere.

"You should've seen them," she rolled her eyes, flicking one hand towards the ocean beyond the cooking room's walls. "So many of them out there in the shallows, jumping and harking. They're lucky they didn't scare the thing away!"

Inara nodded. "Spinks are so shy. I'm surprised it was that close to the shallows at all."

"Mm." Neoma lost herself in imagining her excited family members running over one another to try and capture the fish, grinning.

Once the bread sat in a neatly folded square in front of her, Neoma turned to face her cousins. Her blood ran warm, sweat beading her neck, so when she looked at them she was surprised to note their faces. Inara fixed hers carefully, a small smile on her lips despite her sad eyes. They searched Neoma's face for any sigh of weariness or grief, prodding gently.

Moving the fish off the pan and onto a bed of salted kelp before it burned, Sulien dusted off her hands before pointedly staring at her younger cousin. Even her uncle, who had been minding his fingers as he peeled, stalled to look up at Neoma. Their watchful eyes made the grief sharpen in her chest. The deep breath Neoma took was a salt rake slicing down her spine. Despite the ache, Neoma did not mind it as much as she stood in the warmth of the kitchen.

She found herself asking, in a tone mixed with humor and exhaustion, "What is it now?"

"Well," Inara started, and the uncle began slicing potatoes once more. "We just think its so kind of Ocean. There's a spink swimming along the shoreline this morning, and suddenly you're here, without a letter preceding you!"

Neoma, not expecting those particular words, only smiled kindly at her cousin. A heavy, angry spot in her heart wanted to argue with Inara that it was *the ocean* that took her son, but she knew those words might land harder than intended.

Worshipping Ocean seemed like a game of playing pretend. After Koa's death, rising to great the morning waves unfolded like another chore she had to suffer through. But some peace came to her in the days when she and Koa would swim along the shoreline, *those* moments drawing Neoma closer to a sensation of connectedness for which she had no name.

Calily did her best to show her daughter what was left of the worship and practice, though pieces of it fell short for Neoma. The practice had no name, no expansive mythology like some of the mainland religions, only pushed for an ever-growing relationship with the sea. It made sense considering her family, and her family's family and so on, were salt farmers. Neoma appreciated the lessons in being mindful of the sea that the practice gave her, and would be lying if she said she did not find comfort in the prayers that were passed down through the ages. Yet, it all seemed distant to her, and after being reminded of the sea's quickly changing habits, Neoma felt that her connection to the salt waters were severed in a way she alone could not mend.

Sulien huffed, resting her fists on her hips. "I told you not to say something so silly—"

"No, it's alright." Neoma, in an attempt to prove that the statement was no bother, went on with preparing the sweet appetizer. The pan over the fire was still hot, so she simply took a wet rag to it to wipe away the fishy oils and burning seasonings. "I understand what you mean, Inara, but I just find it to be a happy coincidence."

Her cousin nodded, crestfallen. Disappointment lingered in the air for only a moment, the scent of unspoken words underneath, before Inara walked around the cook fire to take up the bucket of potato skins.

"I'll take these out to wash." She hid her face as she whisked out of the cook room.

Neoma glanced at the basin of water filled on the counter opposite of Sulien, noting Inara's desire to quickly be rid of their company. She sighed, continuing to prepare the treat by throwing fresh seed oil on the flat top. Sulien's eyes watched her for a moment, pupils like needles on her skin as her cousin searched her face.

Ever since they were young, Sulien weighed her words against the possible impact they might have on their listener. Eight years Neoma's elder, Sulien helped her mother, Calily's sister by marriage, with running the family estate while Calily healed from birth. Everyone told stories about how Sulien guarded the fresh babe from dirty hands and bad smells alike. Under supervision, Sulien even walked up and down the beach with Neoma in her arms. It was a respite for Calily, and with every fresh cousin Sulien adopted the same steadfast protection. Neoma, though, was the first, and something about that bond tightened around her heart as she saw the consideration in Sulien's eyes.

With one quick glance from Sulien, the uncle stood from his squat stool. He gave them both a kiss on the temple, complimented them on how good the fish smelled, and left them in privacy. With only the cookfire to witness them, the words in Sulien's throat unknotted.

"Inara thinks the fish was a sign from Koa. She believes he was letting us know you were on your way home."

Neoma flicked her gaze to the fish on the counter. A sickness punctured her stomach, making the glorious scent of oil turn rancid. To busy her hands, she flipped the bread on the pan over and searched for the sugar. Sulien grabbed the jar on the counter, holding it out until Neoma took it with a small nod.

"I don't know how I feel about those stories, personally." Sulien loosened a small breath in her chest. "I liked the ones about our ancestors walking out of the Sea well enough, as any child does, but the tales about our people turning into fish when they died?" She waved a hand, as though batting at a fly. "Comforting tales of an afterlife where we return to nature. That's how I see them, at least."

Flipping the bread, Neoma sprinkled the other side with a pinch of sugar. The thin dough crisped under the seed oil, and the sweet smell rose into the air. She wanted to admit her confusion over Koa's death. She wanted to cry about how she did not see the signs. He walked into the water, into the high tide, in front of Urias. What made him do such a thing?

"I liked the one about the moon the most," she murmured, recalling small pieces of the fae tale. *Doused by the light of a candle, she saw her mother's face; younger, bright with love and the glow of new motherhood. She leaned over little Neoma to whisper the story of fated love and jealousy.*

"You never heard me say this, for my mother would flay me like that fish," she nodded to the spink, "but I think people need stories more than they need something to worship. It brings comfort and… unity, in a strange way. People need people. But people also want to believe in something bigger, like the tales of the Moon and the Ocean falling in love and birthing little babies that, ages ago, were our ancestors. And," Sulien pressed her lips together, sucking in a breath as though bracing for icy water, "I think, in times of grief, people who believe in those stories can only make sense of that pain by saying a fish is a sign for a guest's arrival."

Neoma took up the flaking bread from the stove, and Sulien moved out of the way like she had not spoken. Adjusting the sweet dish on a long wood tray already dressed with accompanying fruit, Neoma breathed in her cousin's words.

After a moment, she nodded. "I know Inara's only trying to help. I know she's probably not the only one who believe the fish was from… was a sign." Her voice choked on Koa's name, and she cleared her throat. Sulien's hand came to rest gently on her upper arm, and Neoma's heart blossomed under its warmth.

"I also believe," Sulien murmured kindly, "that in times of grief, stories can help us feel connected again. You don't have to believe them, Neoma, but the tales and the hope for signs all came from some older knowledge. That knowledge is in your bones, like it's in mine. If you don't want to listen to Ocean, then listen to *that*.

"Now." Sulien lifted the tray of fish off of the counter. "Let's get these out there before people start complaining, hm?"

Traditions often came from accidents—this is how dinners with the last spink of the season began in Neoma's family. No set date marked the moment where the workers gathered sunbaked driftwood to make a looming triangle of a bonfire. With the changing currents, it was near impossible to keep the dinners a yearly festivity, but somehow one long, slender fish always managed to be left behind during migration. Even if each person was only allowed a single forkful off the thin backbone, it was reason enough to gather.

Spink scales glinted pink under the water, but once it broke the surface they dinged to a sparkling gray. Neoma once sat through a long speech from one of her more educated cousins on how this had something to do with the way the sun broke apart beneath the water—but that was where her interest ended. The most important part of the spink was not its scales, but whether it tasted good.

While the fish sat in the place of honor in the middle of the hand-hewn table, encircling it sat platters of accompanying side dishes. Deep bowls of fried kelp and boiled, salty bird's eggs sat near the spink, with bowls of cut fruit accompanying. Loafs of plain bread sat nestled against long saucers of cheeses, honey butter, and savory pastes. The sugar-crusted sweet bread was engulfed by other pastries filled with mashed red berries that caught the light of the climbing fire.

Shallow wooden plates were doled out as the children ran to the table, those too small to reach the sweets waggling their fingers and gazing sadly up at their parents. Laughter sprung up like blossoms, the heads of thick natural hair or twisted curls of intricate designs bobbing in the night like bundles of ivy come to life. Everywhere sang the clacking of seashell beads, gold lip rings catching the firelight as faces smiled and talked. The orange blaze kissed their black skin with gold, the deep hues of night unfurling into shimmering bronze and streaking their tufts of hair or long braids or thick twists with glowing washes of red and yellow. The elders, with their white or graying heads, wore crowns of star bursts as the sunlight fully vanished and doused the supper in the cool beginnings of night.

A particular topic did not cloud the gathering, heads bowed in their own conversations or chins lifted to shout an opinion across the fire. Neoma sat between her mother and Sulien when the somber dregs of something half forgotten settled beneath her breast.

With a jolt that almost sent her plate sliding to the ground, she realized that for the first time in over a month Koa was not occupying every spot in her mind.

Calily's warm hand rested on Neoma's forearm, an unspoken understanding flushing through her. All at once, Neoma sensed the grief stirring in her belly, tossing the fish and bread until a wave of nausea made her set her plate carefully on the ground. *This would have been a beautiful farewell ceremony*, she thought as the tears made the world around her hazy.

Quite suddenly, though with the grace that seemed to befall the elders, Calily stood. Roland gazed at his wife from across the fire, his conversation with one of Calily's brothers falling short as she drew his respectful attention.

While there stood no singular matriarch in the family, Kairdwillo-Nan had been given to Calily on the anniversary of her mother's death. Despite having three brothers, she was the eldest, and so the responsibility fell in large portion to her. Such responsibility always came with it a manner of respect or title, however unspoken.

"I couldn't ask for more beautiful faces to gather with me around the fire."

Beaming smiles were shared in the warm light. Calily's loving gaze did not leave Roland's, and while this would make some children uncomfortable, Neoma heart gladdened in the presence of love between them.

"However," Calily tittered, "there is something we women do at these things, when we are happy with wine and have full bellies and are under starlight. So I'll ask kindly for everyone else to leave."

The men and those who did not consider themselves women made harmless sounds of protest despite the grins deepening their faces. Those who married into the family readily stood without a sound of annoyance, knowing that while they were always welcomed, they had no room to argue with Calily. Each kissed their partner before swooping up their allotted child, bidding the rest of the family a good night. Uncles and cousins eventually followed, making a show of how unfair it was that the women should stay around the fire and the food while they were sent back to the homestead only a few steps beyond.

"Away, away!" the women around the fire ordered with laughter coloring their voices, their seashell beads emphasizing the word as they shook their heads. A cousin of Neoma's had shaved her beard and wove her own seashell beads into her hair, and she waved away her grinning brothers in excitement. Talaya's face blazed with its own light as she anticipated her first firelight gathering since changing her name.

Once the tittering died down, Calily called the women's attention again with, "Now that the distractions are taken care of..." Smiles and laughter roared, a wave from Calily stalling any more bantering. "I love Roland, I do, but sometimes he simply doesn't understand why we need this."

The laughter turned into grateful, knowing nods. A chorus of beads rang in the air. Neoma sensed the next words on her skin, the connection between herself and her mother like a rope around her heart. When Calily's arms encircled her shoulders, Neoma leaned into her mother's welcoming embrace.

"While birthing a child does not make a person a woman, there is still a connection between earth and the seed. There is no true severance of that, not even in death." Calily's breath, spiced with wine and fruit, warmed Neoma's temple. She closed her eyes against her mother's words not to block them out, but to feel them completely. "And tonight we celebrate a seed that only had little time to grow and bloom. Tonight, we eat as we should've eaten, and we celebrate Koa's life as it should've been celebrated—under the stars, around family, and with full stomachs."

"This reminds me of a story." Yor, Neoma's great-grandmother who buried her own daughter some years ago, interrupted. Calily nodded to older woman, keeping her arms tight around Neoma as she planted a kiss on the top of her head.

"Ages ago, we came from the Sea. Well," Yor chuckled, "the Sea and its union with the Moon."

Yor shifted in her seat to draw everyone's gaze out to the lapping waves behind them. With a cloudless sky, the stars reflected their twinkling light across the quiet, dark waters. In accordance with Yor's tale, the full moon above cast its silver glow across the land.

The old woman sighed contentedly, a sound Neoma herself had not made in what seemed like a year. "Hasild-Neht built for Herself out of pure desire an ocean to watch over, to mold. From that desire, she, the First Night, created then Her love, the Sea. Kai-Dua spilled out of the foam of the raging waves and calmed what agitated His lover, and when the full moon touched the horizon is when our Ancestors were born. In us lives a love like no other—through us, that love goes on. My sweet girl."

Neoma opened her drooping eyelids to find her great-grandmother regarding at her with misty eyes. A sweet, gentle love that Neoma often felt in Calily reached for her across the fire. It swaddled both Neoma and her mother in an affection that spanned decades, settling into her skin like the scent of lavender.

"I know you don't much care for the stories of Hasild-Neht and Kai-Dua, but Their love made my mother, and my mother before her, until it trickled down to make *you*. It made Koa," Yor's breath hitched slightly, a great mourning beneath the sound of his name, "and it welcomed him back with the open arms of a *spectacular* homecoming."

Weeping danced around the sounds of popping firewood, those gathered around the flames crying with Neoma, and for the cousins or nephews or grandsons lost to the waves. Koa did not mark himself the first child in their family to be lost to misfortune, and Neoma felt solidarity as she turned to her cousins and half-sisters who mourned their own children.

Gazing at them brought along a realization that Neoma foolishly missed on that rainy day weeks ago; that grief was not meant to be experienced alone.

She did not know at what point she collapsed into Calily's lap, only that she grew deeply aware of the comforting circles her mother drew on her back as she cried. Sulien clutched one of her hands tightly, and even though their palms grew sweaty her cousin did not let go. As she wiped Neoma's tears with the back of her free hand, others came to crouch next to Calily's feet so that they could rest their heads on Neoma's hip, her shoulder, her knees. Yor did not rise, but placed a hand over her heart before extending it to the tangle of dark arms and twists of hair, welcoming her gods to the fireside.

Love encircled Neoma with a resounding note that echoed within her. It did not shake away the grief, but sat next to that aching pit in her chest to comfort it. But Yor was right—she did not know how much she believed about the stories and Koa's homecoming, or why Ocean would do such a thing. But a little voice begged with deepest sincerity to set that aside, if only for however long her mother's arms encircled her.

Surrounded by her family, some knowing the sensation of dread and loss that she carried, Neoma felt validated in her decision to leave Urias. Yet that thread of pity, and perhaps what was left of her own love for him, made her pray to gods she only partly believed in: *Let him find a peace like this.*

CHAPTER SEVENTEEN

When water grew too cold, it turned black—at least, that was Dice's explanation for the pitch colored waves that crashed along the shoreline. Temperatures next to the sea felt like being plunged in a barrel of ice, naked as birth. Shivering, she wrapped her tense arms over her torso, bracing against the winter wind that blew across the sea. Frosty gales carried the weight of a giant's fist when it blew into her. Every other gust threatened to knock her tired, drunken body over.

She never recalled being so unsteady in her life, even out at sea. At some point during the sleepless nights she spent pacing the dock, too scared to go back into the town proper, the whispers of her mind turned to something darker. But it was not the mindless darkness she saw flickering in the eyes of her fellow ingrates of Stormshale. This writhing, sharp-edged shadow trembled with intention, consuming her mind to the point that even awake, Dice's body belonged to a foreign creature.

On her right, the waves crashed. She imagined the decaying body of Evangeline some miles behind her, her wide death-gaze tracking each step. For the last few days, ever since she looked up upon Evangeline's bruised and naked body, the ocean carried a single low, harmonious note. A tremor cascaded down Dice's spine when she focused too long on the sound of the water, having no beginning or end, so she did her best to ignore it.

During the colder months, the tides rose and remained impassibly high. Entire sections of the beach disappeared, but this reliable drowning did not prevent some fishermen from building huts along the shoreline. These one roomed features were held together by silverwood sap and thus tended to remain upright, but no one in Stormshale—no fisherman, at least—was rich enough to afford silverwood logs being shipped this far out from Menthis. When the tide receded, the shack might still be upright, but the wood needed to be replaced or shelled of barnacles. She intended to find one of these, keeping the hope that it had a dinghy, preferably one large enough for a sail so she could ride off to the mainland.

Capsizing at this time in the season grew likelier with every passing day, but Dice shoved that bit of knowledge to the back of her mind.

Ideas of death presented itself as she walked, shaking without her good coat. If she did not find a fisherman's hut soon she may never get the chance to leave this place. Dying in Stormshale—dying anywhere other than out at sea—felt so wrong that her gut recoiled at the thought.

Coming around the bend she saw a hut nestled up against the shoreline. The sea was already climbing, but Dice managed to keep that panic at bay when she noted the dinghy pitched next to the structure. Her feet carried her swiftly, the threat of death kept away for another moment, and she checked the hull for any signs of damage. To her dismay, it had no sail, only nets gathered in the bottom that she shoved away to check for holes or rot. The oars were sturdy, if a hazard for splinters.

Satisfied after her inspection, she turned her drowsy gaze to the hut. A ring of water damage lined the outside walls. From her waist down, the wood appeared dark with rot, yet somehow it remained standing. Dice passed a finger over the rough grain, hardly wincing at the splinter that caught the skin, walking around the structure until she came to the open door. Stepping inside, the useless floor squelched under her boots with every movement. Water came up from the soggy floorboards, but the dense shoreline of pebbles offered stability as Dice turned about the small room.

A cot was strung on a riser and did not seem moldy, meaning the owner brought it in at the start of the warmer fishing seasons and simply forgot to fetch it. One window, cloudy with grime, pointed outward towards the ocean, and a second pointed towards the way she had come. No decoration or sign of personality identified anything about the shack's owner, the piles of nets in the corner and a disturbingly large hook hanging from the wall the only other signs of occupancy.

Dice glanced over a low bench that ran the length of the wall facing the ocean. Atop it sat a stack of oddly dry papers next to an inkwell and leatherbound journal. Nothing more than curiosity and an urge to further encroach on this stranger's life made her walk towards the ensemble. Thinking it a diary or log, she picked up the journal first and thumbed through the pages. Each passing sheet of parchment made her more confused, the language within not being one spoken in Stormshale or written at any dock town she visited before.

In the back of her mind, the darkness whispered. Heart racing, she dared to think that the murmuring voices sounded like the words on the page, but that made no sense. Dice never read this language before, never heard it spoken.

And yet, the curling lines interrupted by slashes and dots felt like looking into a mirror.

Dropping the book, Dice flexed her hands. Lingering on her palms drifted hundreds of invisible needles. Her skin seemed to protest the detachment, which urged Dice to cast another look over the writing station.

Humming gently, the notebook echoed the song of the ocean.

"I'm losing my mind." The waves outside crashed in response. With every hissing spray, a thought rose higher in her mind until it stood before her so solidly that she felt its walls rise up around her. *How much longer can I go on like this? Would it be better to end it now?*

People often lost their minds at sea. When water became scarce, some turned to the briny currents beneath even though it meant dehydration. Voyages thrown off the trail due to storms or bad sailing resulted in people being trapped for months with nothing but blue on the horizon. Who knew what happened to *those* ships, whether they docked or landed on an island or sank to the pits of the water, but every sailor knew that madness set quickly. Dice witnessed Evander turn away people who wanted to board but had lost enough of themself that they resembled animals more than they did people. They survived death at sea only to be landed for the remainder of their lives, unwelcomed by any crew. Only desperate captains took on a person lost to themselves, or they were sold as food to the Revkyn beasts.

Dice saw the beginning of madness in Evander's previous second-mate. She must have only been nine or so, with little trust in strangers thanks to her guardian's upbringing. Olan was not a stranger at the start, but when he began to look at her without that beam of recognition Dice learned to be wary. Evander put it off for as long as he could, until they docked in a place that might treat Olan better than if they returned to Esmar.

The man tried to kill Dice then, but he was feeble, and she still little enough to squirm out of a person's grasp. He called her a rat, and said that rats are bad for the ship, and at that early age Dice came to the decision that she would rather toss herself into the ocean if the alternative was losing her mind.

That day seemed to be approaching faster than she liked.

Whoever lived in the shack took all their food with them. After wrapping herself in the blanket she stole off the cot, cutting out a hole for her head and fashioning it around her waist with a bit of rope, Dice took one of the smaller nets out into the shallows. Despite her boots keeping her feet dry, she only managed standing against the waves for a few moments at a time—hardly long enough to cast a net and wait patiently for anything stupid enough to swim into it. If she braced herself, Dice might be able to search wade pools for crab, but *that* was being optimistic.

No matter her desperation, or the hunger gnawing at her backbone, returning to Stormshale was impossible. Merely thinking about having to pass in front of Evangeline's body caused Dice's stomach to tighten with nausea.

She could not return. She *would* not.

"Gods *damn* it all to the Aether!" The netting slopped onto the rocks at her feet as she tossed it, the chilly slips of rope leaving red lines across her palms. Dice swore everything to that infernal netherworld in which she did not believe just so that the crashing waves and the ocean's call were not the only things breaking the hungry silence. Her voice climbed as she shouted at the water, at the fat thunder clouds on the horizon. Lightning streaked between their gray bellies, the storm still far enough that thunder rolled over the beach in only a gentle murmur.

The skin inside her throat felt raw once her voice dipped out, breaking under the strain of her shouts. Despite the pain, the animalistic yelling loosened a fixture within her chest. Dice breathed a little easier, and her shoulders fell from their knotted position under her ears. For a moment she sat between the frayed edges of peace and calamity, relishing the pause where nothing was real to her except the aching in her throat. She closed her eyes only long enough to take a salty inhale, but when she released it and spied out towards the horizon she noted a ship that had not been there before. Perhaps it was hidden in the gloom, but there it sat on the edge of the world, little more than a needle-prick in the gray.

Dice hated crying. She liked screaming and slamming her fists against solid things, breaking the world to reflect how broken she felt inside. Crying was a waste of water, so the crew of the *Marksmen* often chided, but even recalling her distaste for it did not stop the tears from gathering along her lashes.

She cried for a lot of different things then, some without a name.

Evangeline, her glowing body permeating Dice's mind, struck her almost breathless with agony. For the last few days, Dice had not wished to consider the actions of the Watch when they levied their decision, yet she forced herself to stand in the frosty water, forced herself to acknowledge her part in Evangeline's death.

Remembering the glistening dread of the flayed man caused the heat of terror to warm her face, but she refused to look away from those flashing red memories either. It was *all* her fault, every skinned muscles and broken knucklebone. Dice might as well have tied the noose around Evangeline's neck, and bruised her soft skin in death.

At that moment, Dice believed herself no better than the Watch. Even if she killed Evangeline's husband in some blackout, even if she would not dare to do such a thing sober, his flaying and Evangeline's hanging were *her* fault. Now, she did not dare return to Stormshale out of cowardice. Leonora was no fool, either, and knew Dice's feelings for Evangeline. With Dice having witnessed the strange alliance between Leonora and the flayed man, perhaps the madam sought to cover her own tail.

Would she tell the Watch to look for Dice? Would they even care to find her? Some men grew hard at the thought of killing a woman, and some of *those* men acted under the authority of the Watch. If they found Dice, she may wish for death before they were finished having their way.

Gazing out over the roiling ocean, so blue it was almost black, a foreign peace came over Dice. Underneath the rumbling of the encroaching thunder sang the oceanic tune which haunted her every moment, but right then it sounded beckoning. Loving, even. Its strangeness hushed over her body in the way a lover murmurs against the soft shell of her ear.

I could finish it here, now. No more seeing those... She squeezed her eyes shut against the memories of blood pooling around her boots. They flashed open when Evangeline's blank, white face appeared. *I don't want to see her like that anymore. I don't want to remember her that way.*

A beautiful streak of lightning sliced across the nearing storm. Dice felt a chill hit her shins, rising up to her knees. Around her, the ocean pressed its lips against the shape of her calves, clawed at the fabric of her pants that separated her from its grasp.

What a waste of water.

Evander's voice sounded distant, the faint memory weak against the gore that pervaded Dice's mind. Even so, it proved enough to shake the haze out of her vision. Shock shot up her legs as the icy grasp of the ocean made her suck in a breath. Looking back, she saw just how far from the shoreline she walked, the water licked at her hips. With every step, the ocean seemed to suck at her, draw her backwards. Her heart slammed in her throat as the music in her head climbed a little louder.

Freezing, Dice ignored the fixation of a drowning death and made her way back to the hut. Folding in on herself kept what little heat her body possessed, the fear lodged in her throat chilled her past the bone.

Had the ocean wanted to drown her? Was the music she heard a siren's call?

Weariness hung so heavily over her shoulders that Dice had little room to consider any more questions. She needed to get out of her damp clothes before she froze to death. Braced against the wind, she eventually rounded the hunk of rock only for her hopes of shelter to be dashed when she noticed a candle in the window facing the shore.

Dice crouched, squinting against the frosty gales to try and see anyone beyond the flame. Tiredness made her vision waver, and the hunger in her gut protested a fight. Like a newborn idiot, she left her small knife in the shack, so her options were limited. Perhaps if the fisherman returned to gather the last of his things, she might reason with him to let her stay there for the night. There seemed no need to let him know she planned on stealing his boat.

Drenched in icy water, sitting in the way of a storm, Dice figured she needed to decided quickly *before* she caught her death.

Easy footfalls over the pebbles, keeping out of view of the window for as long as possible—this was easy to do, even in her less than operative state. But as she drew nearer to the shack, it quickly became clear that whoever stood inside was not the owner. Beyond the shabby walls, the person flung about the room, their swears low and deep in their throat.

She pressed up against the spot by the window. Craning her neck, she peered carefully over the rotten sill.

A man much taller than herself with luminous silver hair paced the small area, his steps squelching loudly. Overturned and pressed against the wall opposite was the cot, its matching shabby pillow soaking up saltwater on the floor. The man stepped on it unceremoniously, his back to Dice as he raised his hands to run his fingers through his hair. Along the side of his neck that she could see were three white scars as thick as her little finger, glowing like silver moonbeams.

Eyes narrowing on the scars, a needle of familiarity pressed underneath her skin. Feeling as though every drop of blood within her leaned towards the window, towards the stranger, Dice felt the nausea rising in her throat.

She shook her head, confused. *It's no more than a scar. I've seen plenty before. I've seen worse.* Someone likely tried to kill him in the past, and if that man survived *three* solid swipes to his throat, Dice needed to move with caution. She ignored the sensation of forgetting something and trying desperately to remember it, her palms sweating under the task. The shack offered no place to hide, and the stranger was growing angrier the longer he went without finding his prize.

He stalked over to the little bench that boasted the journal and loose papers. To her surprise, he flipped the pages intently before pausing on a diagram that resembled a conch shell with those strange symbols wrapping around its edges. Trailing a finger across the page, the man's lips moved quickly, reading to himself. Dice leaned forward a bit more, peering through the window to try and see what exactly he read, when the glass pane groaned against her shoulder.

Breath stilled in her chest—she ducked the moment the man's jaw twitched at the sound. Dice kept her face turned towards the edge of the wall, waiting for him to saunter out of the shack to come around for a look.

A beat passed.

Another.

Dice swallowed back her breath, rising so slowly that her knees shivered with the exertion. Pressing one boot down, then the other, she walked so carefully that the pebbles only barely shifted underfoot. Her hand came down to her hip, and she swore when she remembered again that she left her dagger behind.

Rounding the edge of the wall, she bared her teeth, fingers flexing into a fist as she swung around—

—to see an empty room.

Turning to face the open door, she leaned her head out of the shack. Whoever the stranger might be, he left no trace other than the overturned cot and scattered notes.

Curiosity brushed her temple. Dice faced the journal and the notes, wondering again what language inked its pages. The leatherbound volume sat open where the man left it, the strange conch shell spiraling over most of the entry. One of her fingers landed on the symbols like the man's did, mimicking his movement across the page. The trail brought her to one of the dozens of lines bursting outward from the middle of the shell. Each line had a note upon it—at least, she *thought* they were notes, harried but intentional.

Dragging her finger further down the line, she followed the spiral curve of the drawing until the end. A shimmering sensation climbed up her arm, the spark of recognition coming on so suddenly that Dice recoiled from the drawing.

"What, in the name of the gods…?"

Pebbles clattered behind her. Whipping around, the silver-haired man barred the door. Without the window pane separating them, she saw how his skin glistened, as though sprayed by water. But it was his *skin*, the textured bumps giving the appearance of dampness. His clothing looked pilfered, the trousers fitting him at the waist but stopping a handsbreadth above his ankles, and his feet were bare in the cold. The coat stopped just below his hips like a child who outgrew his clothing during the night.

His gaze jumped to the journal behind Dice. A sneer pulled at his rosy mouth, which stood out oddly against the silver sheen of his skin. When his eyes fully settled on her, they carried a hard flicker that Dice once saw in a hangman before he dropped the level.

"Your gods are dead, landfarer." He took a step forward. "Now, leave."

Many colorful insults had been slung at Dice over the years, but *landfarer* was a first. It jabbed at her pride, the years of pulling rope and sailing prickling her memory. Nerves rushed through her body, prepared for a fight, but she knew that with hunger and exhaustion sitting in her chest it would be a short one.

"Listen," she started, cautiously taking a step forward with her hands raised. "I could leave, but you've got to move first. You are barring the door."

"And *you* are trespassing." He sneered, fists clenching and unclenching.

Dice quirked a brow, glancing about the messy room. "Apparently, so are you."

The man launched himself at her, deciding quite suddenly that he refused to take any answer that was not submissive. In the little room, she barely sidestepped him, eyes half-wandering for her dagger while trying to note his next move. In the tiny shack, he could have her in an instant.

She needed to get through the door.

Pivoting on his heel, the man whipped around to bash a fist against her ribcage. The wind flew out of her lungs as Dice overcorrected, stumbling forward. Two slender hands caught the back of her damp shirt, fingers curling into the fabric of the makeshift tunic as they yanked her backwards. Her fingers found the rope around her waist that kept her tied to the blanket and she slid free from the cloth, and his grasp. Dice relished his aggravation as he look down at the limp blanket in his hands. On her knees, Dice kept her hands raised, begging any god that listened for a sign of her dagger. The man tossed the blanket aside, his whole lanky body blocking the door once more.

In a morbid answer to her silent praying, the man lifted her dagger from his coat pocket. The sheath of metal glinted in his hands as he raised its narrow point at her.

Words fell from his sneering lips, landing deafly on her ears. Whispers slid out from behind her as the pages of the journal rustled without wind to shake them—then a gale blew into the shack, startling Dice as it kicked up the loose pages and sent them sailing through the air. As they slid past her vision, the man took advantage of her confusion and leapt forward with an arm shooting through the tornado of papers. The hand not holding the blade lifted her by the collar, the knife narrowly missing the soft flesh between Dice's ribcage as she pushed her arm out to block it.

Pain hissed over her forearm, and as the man pulled the dagger out of her flesh he dragged her out of the cottage. To her shock, instead of ending her life right there the man tossed her onto the rocks. Blood slicked Dice's hand as she clamped down on the puncture. Her eyes trained on the man but the tinge of iron in the air threw her back into the blood soaked room.

The stranger's face warped, twisting into a macabre version of the severed head. Bile rose in her throat as she kicked at the pebbles, scooting away from the approaching knife-bearer when, in an act she did not understand, he tossed the dagger into the water.

Her eyes followed it into the oncoming wave. Foam and water hungrily devoured the weapon before receding back into the ocean.

"Where I come from, we do not kill by blade."

Hot anger rushed over Dice's chest as she raised her bloodied forearm. "I take it this is cheating then?"

He rushed forward with teeth bared, the hangman's gaze returning. Brine and the scent of fish enveloped Dice as he lifted her easily off the ground. In a mere flash of seconds, she noted a second set of white scars on the other side of his neck. She hardly had the time to consider them when the man shook her violently. Without another word, no doubt tired of her retorts, he dragged her towards the shallows.

Dice's heart leapt into her throat. *He plans to drown me. I'll get a pirate's death yet*. As much as she struggled, exhaustion wore down each movement. The man was taller than her, stronger than her, and bore all the signs of an excellent killer. Each smack of her fist against his chest turned desperate, no longer landing with intention as she flailed against his grip. Water splashed up his legs as he walked, drenching her shins in ice as she kicked harder, only managing to let out a scream right before he plunged her head into the next wave.

A cold like nothing she felt before knocked away what little breath remained. Climbing into her spine, the feeling of the rocks and pebbles disappeared as her skin went numb from the chill. Fingers clamped neatly down on her shoulders, her thrashing quickly losing its ferocity under their grasp. Dice's frozen hands tried to peel away the man's fingers. Failing that, she clawed broken nails along the skin of his forearms, ripping small lines into his rigid flesh. Another wave crashed down, and he lifted his hands up to take hold of her neck as streaks of blue-green blood dotted his arms.

The world went black around the edges. Weight that both pushed her into the pebbles and ripped open her chest from the inside strained within her torso. Along her wounded forearm, she no longer felt the sting of saltwater in the bloody flesh.

Her hands drifted down, floating in the water, landing softly on the pebbles.

A sharp piece of something drifted over the back of her hand, the edge making a fresh cut. In the faded space that stood between her and unconsciousness, the memory of fighting made her fingers twitch against the steel. Not caring for the hilt, or taking the time to make a proper grip, Dice grasped the dagger by its blade before raking it across the man's wrists.

Breaking free of the ocean, of the man's grasp, air rushing into her lungs, Dice clamored forward out of the water with a raggedy gasp. Her body shook as it scrambled away from death's edge, her head dizzy as she regained her breath. Behind her, the man shouted in frustration, a hand clamping down on her ankle. A wave of irritation slapped into Dice as she turned to kick a heel into the man's nose.

"Leave me *alone!*" She screeched with a broken, raspy voice.

When he stumbled backwards, a beast took over her body. It felt violent in its fury, hungry for reparation. Leaping, she shoved him down into the water, standing on his chest to keep him pinned beneath the waves. His hands came up to grab her leg but the man did not struggle under her boot or thrash like she had.

His hands curled around her ankle. Dice barely had a moment to realize what he was doing when the *pop* reverberated up her leg. She screeched, jerking backwards into the water and landing heavily on the dislocated foot. As the man rose out of the water, Dice crawled backwards, her brief strength fleeing as pain ruptured her body. Saltwater sloshed into her mouth as she tried to make it back to the shore. She gazed up at the stranger, at his damp silver hair, at the scars along the side of his neck as they opened and flexed like a fish's gills.

Dua-Nythi. The Sea's Children.

A myth taken flesh.

Eyes wide, she gaped at the pink lining of his skin, watching in disbelief as they closed to settle like scars against his neck once more.

With fear dropping in her belly, Dice raised her dagger up shakily. The man laughed at her tremoring hand, and so taken aback by his strangeness was she that Dice could only shout as he ripped the dagger from her.

The bone in her thigh broke under its edge as he stabbed into the water. Blood rose up, black in the dark blue waves, turning the foam a bright pink as every nerve lit on fire. Dice's mind went hazy, narrowing on the pain as the song of the ocean turned from its solemn hum to a screaming cacophony of gulls, of splintering wood. The ocean pulled at her blood, dragged it out of her body like a tidal wave rearing back from the shore.

Give it back, give it back, give it back.

A hundred voices shrieked up from the bloody water. Dice was only partly aware of the man stumbling away from her, trying not to let the red stain him.

"Give it back—" A voice not belonging to her hissed out of her throat. Her blood in the water changed the song in her head. Underneath the shrieking, beyond the crying of angry gulls, it turned malicious. Anger centuries old unfurled behind her heart, making her blackened insides rot under its touch.

Insurmountable pain flooded through her body as she stood, mouth dropping to scream the order echoing out from her very marrow. *"Give it back-give it back-give it back—"*

Dice reached down, fingers twisting around the hilt of the dagger. She did not feel the steel slide out of her bone, passing her broken flesh as it unsheathed from her body. Unlike Evangeline's home, where the world went black only to deposit her into fear and uncertainty, Dice *saw* this. It felt like she was cast backwards in her mind, her limbs jerky as they moved through the water towards the man.

Her ankle throbbed with every step, but her mind did not care. The man fell to his knees in the water, his palms raised as he begged her with words she did not understand at first.

They slid together in her mind, symbols reshaping themselves into something familiar. *We do not kill by a blade*, he said over and over again.

She leveled the weapon at him. "*You* don't."

His eyes went wide. Defeated, he dropped his shaking hands, not even bracing himself against the waves that peltered them in the shallows.

Dice never stood for ceremony, even in the altered state she drifted between as she towered above him. Grabbing the back of the man's hair, she yanked his head away to expose the gleaming underneath of his neck. There was a moment when her mind screamed out to wait but the ocean reminded her that letting him go meant dying.

With a start, she realized she did *not* want to die, not by his hand or anyone's but the ocean's.

The dagger was not strong enough to sever his head from his shoulders, but she dragged a deep smile from gill to gill. The man accepted this, neither begging for his life nor struggling once the blade touched his skin. Blue-green blood pumped out of the wound, gushing down over the front of his stolen clothing. He did nothing but make gurgling sounds of pain, keeping his wavering gaze on Dice's face up until the moment he collapsed forward into the water.

Waves slipped past her legs to crash in muted whispers along the shoreline. The man's body drifted face down, arms splayed. He rocked side to side as the tide pulled out and Dice spared him only the smallest glance before the creature within her steered her onto the pebbled beach. Agony sat on the edges of her awareness as she walked, her throbbing ankle searing. On the beach, she stood for a moment to take in the weight of the dagger before sheathing it in the leather sleeve at her hip.

All the world narrowed as she moved in a fevered state towards the dinghy.

The shape of the pebbles and the slant of the mountains sharpened in painful clarity. Rain began at a sprinkle, dusting her cold face and slicking her curling hair to the nape of her neck. Gazing up at the clouds that finally found anchorage along the beach, Dice watched the lightning jump across the gray.

It seemed to dance. It seemed to be *happy*.

Underneath her fingers, the dinghy groaned as it hushed over the pebbles and slapped into the water. Hunger stabbed her belly, but all Dice truly felt was the fatigue shaking her limbs. The oars were heavy when she lifted them, barely managing to slot them into their notches. Waves protested her movement at first, the cut in her hand where she grabbed the dagger stinging with every weak turn of the oars. Eventually, she made it past the shack.

Dice glimpsed the stranger's body floating in a cloud of black before the mixture of exhaustion, pain, and hunger sent her reeling towards the belly of the boat.

CHAPTER EIGHTEEN

Sen happened upon the private meeting between their mother and Lon as they turned down one of the dozens of paths sprawling out from the homestead. Waist high stone figures of women in calcified robes dancing under curls of ribbon littered the way, the eyes of the statues like smiles on their round faces. The greenery bowed towards the scion in flicks and shivers when they passed underneath the shaded archways; the tips of their fingers hummed with a magic that sat on the edge of their physical body.

No one understood how frustrating it was, knowing wild magic existed in one's bloodline but all that remained was a shift of air, a burst of wildfire, a storm cloud no larger than a pet dog. Every matriarch before Naseria held close the stories of great magicians who brought the YeSara Clan their fame and fortune, and there remained a particular type of anger at it being ripped from their bodies. As each generation passed, they were hollowed out by the receding magic like a fishmonger gutting their catches. Perhaps others within the Clan sensed that removal of magic on the edges of their being like Sen did, not truly comprehending it.

Sen felt misplaced among of a world of people who were not like them, increasingly angry at every passing year where their ancestors and the magic belonging to them felt further and further out of reach.

Stumbling upon this intimate meeting between their closest relatives felt like Sen was pushed back yet another step, the separation driving the wedge further between themself and their family. Shame briefly flicked across their conscience as they stilled, bating their breath to see whether or not either party noticed them.

The humming whispers continued, interjected by the scraping sounds of leaves against one another in the salty ocean breeze. It was a particularly warm evening that promised a season of dampness for Lesser Syvon, and sweat accumulated on the nape of Sen's neck as they drifted along the edge of the clearing that sheltered Lon and Naseria.

Gold glittered on the crown of Naseria's head, her hair stacked like a tower. Twisted and folded, the plaits resembled water as they wove in and out of the grand crescent structure that curved from the top of her head downwards. Crystals hanging off the ends of the downturned crescent moon shined in shades of green, the jade pearls singing as the wind moved them. The rest of her hair fell freely down the back of her emerald robe which melded into the greenery. Rising from the hem were hundreds of leaping swordfish embroidered in gold and red thread; it was the most extravagant of Naseria's robes, but what drew Sen's gaze was their mother's bare face. When she wore such finery, it was painted white with only dots of rouge on the highest points, but in the dense garden, in the robes of a great leader, her naked gaze observed Lon with a look that never before passed over the heir: *concern.*

Lon wore her typical but no less fine threads, though her dark hair sat over her shoulder in a lazy plait. Sen knew she was talking by the way Naseria's head gently bobbed in acknowledgement. As they drew closer, a fiery bit of resentment forging in their belly, they hid behind a large statue of a swordfish rising on a wave.

"…wouldn't bring it to you if it wasn't important." Lon finished. Tears hitched her voice, the words clogged with emotion.

Their mother took a moment to respond. Sen twisted their neck to get a look around the edge of the statue. Lon's back was to them, and their mother practically glowed as the sunlight leapt from the gold on her headpiece. If Sen actually believed in the stories where the gods came to the earth, they might have said she resembled one.

Concern turned to fury, though not for the reason Sen expected. Instead of chiding Lon for wasting her time as she prepared for an obviously important meeting, Naseria spat on the earth. Sen gazed alarmingly at the wet spot on the ground, shocked at seeing their mother act so undignified.

"I should order that entire House flayed, sickly father and all. We are too good for them. And now they dare to make a leap for power by—"

The crime that the mysterious House committed too vile to announce, Naseria turned on her heel with a sneer of disgust. Her headpiece jangled with the sudden action, tinkering jewels singing. Sen expected her to pace, but their mother walked only a few steps before facing Lon once more with a warring expression.

"This… was a grab for *power?*" Lon sounded so tired that her voice struggled to leave her throat. "Do you think Jora would order such a thing? Are we not on better terms with them since saving their estate?"

Saving their estate? Confusion filtered through their body, but Sen could not recall anything about House Demont being so poorly funded that even their familial homestead was at risk. Valeska never mentioned anything either, but pride kept him from sporting something other than a highborn attitude.

Did his mother really ask the YeSaras for money? If the YeSara Clan financed the Demonts, it came with stipulations. Owing any Clan, especially for the rescue of a generational home, meant shame of the highest kind if anyone found out. Were the Demonts so destitute as to risk that kind of embarrassment?

"How long has it been since you bled, my darling?"

The softness in Naseria's tone made Sen's heart ache. Never had she spoken to them in such a gentle, unpracticed way.

Wondering at the question, Sen gazed at their sister from around the statue. Lon stood rigid, her shoulders hiked up next to her ears. Moments passed, and those defined muscles started shaking with tears. Naseria's hands cupped Lon's face as though she held a precious glass lantern.

Sen's heart withered in their chest as they turned their misting eyes to the ground. They were unsure whether they cried for the limited affection Naseria showed them over the years, obvious now in the way she held Lon, or something else. Guilt pressed at their heart, urging them to turn away from the conversation that should not be overheard, but Sen *wanted* to hear Lon's answer.

Sex, a natural expression of desire, was never shamed in their household, and so long as those falling under the YeSara name practiced safety and consent, there hardly stood room for fear. But this conversation felt different, dense with a writhing darkness under the surface of Lon's tears.

"Long enough to know, mother." Fell her quivering response.

Naseria took in a small breath, bracing herself. "And… do you know which one did it? Or do you believe only Valeska to be responsible?"

"It was him." Lon's voice, despite the tears, was resolute. "I feel it just as I feel his wretched parasite growing within me. It was Valeska."

Sen palled, their hands growing sweaty in their balled fists. *No.*

"You will be sent to the summer homes. One of the aunts will go with you, as well as her entourage." Naseria's tone was serious but no less kind, the instructions quick. "The aunt will fetch a doctor. He has pocketed so much of our coin, he will take our secrets into his grave. You are not so far along that it is impossible to flush out this disease. No YeSara child will ever be born under a forced conception, least of all to a dog like Valeska. If you don't want this—"

"I don't—" Lon hiccupped, a sob racking her shoulders.

"Hush." Naseria pulled her into her chest. Her massive sleeves covered Lon's shoulders like a robe. "Hush. It is settled, then."

Terrible stories often filtered through the gossip of party-goers. Events were filled with wine and things more often found in the backwater vales of Esmar. Sen never placed themselves into such a crowd as that, not publicly at least, but they relished hearing those awful stories of people waking without their clothing in the bed of a stranger—or worse, a *friend.* As the heir, these risks never found Sen. Even without a guard, no one dared to shame the scion of the YeSara Clan in such a way. Such terror was displaced from Sen's life, and so they sought after it in the idle, careless words that fell on indifferent ears.

But to know this happened to Lon—to understand in the core of their being that it happened after the events at *The Dovetail*—felt too close to reality for Sen's comfort. She lied about what happened that night; Sen saw it on her face the moment they awoke from their strange dream, yet they did not care to ask further.

To acknowledge this any more meant shining light on their part in it, however small. Looking upon such a reflection made Sen's knees weak with regret. They told themselves as they crouched behind the statue, Naseria and Lon's words muted as Sen grappled with the guilt, that they were not responsible for *Valeska's* actions. Did they vouch for him in times where his behavior was questionable? Yes, but just as all friends spoke confidently of each other. It was not *their* fault what Valeska did or did not do. *They* were drugged, a fact they so quickly brushed away before it festered in their consciousness. What happened next was not *their* responsibility.

But all of that sounded like a pitiful excuse, even in Sen's ears.

Before Sen gleaned any more from their conversation—before the widening pit in their stomach swallowed them whole—they slipped back out onto the path they came down. Once they made it far enough away from the private alcove, they ran all the way back to their rooms, but no matter how much distance they placed between themselves and Lon the sickening remorse continued to fracture their selfish veneer.

Soon enough, they would be forced to look at what lay beneath.

Dinners in the evening were something of an event despite only including members of the immediate family and Naseria's siblings, but only silence greeted the young heir that night. Entering the room stripped with dark wood and silk screens, no music from a bard sang from the corner, and not a whiff of steamed dumplings tinged the air. Dressed in a rather fine robe of pale blue, Sen huffed at the fact that there was no one to greet or flatter them. They patted the low slung knot of hair at the nape of their neck as they looking about the room with a frown.

At their feet, the shining, low wood table bounced back their annoyed reflection. The longer they stared at themselves, the sharper the conversation they overheard echoed in their memory.

Do you know which one did it?

Sen swallowed hard, lingering by their place at the top of the table before they snapped their gaze away from the polished wood.

After some time, the clatter of beads from beyond a silk partition announced the arrival of the matriarch. Another beat passed, and a kneeling servant glided back the screen to reveal Naseria in the same garb as earlier. Only, a pale painted face met Sen's gaze, rouge touching her cheeks and her bottom lip painted red to match. She reeked of incense, and heavy around her was the ancient feeling of the ancestors. Naseria did not possess magic, but the world recognized her regardless.

Energy, thick as lightning before it strikes the grounds, hit the air and made the palms of Sen's hands tingle. Their mother did not step into the eating room, remaining in the darkened hall beyond. Her hands, concealed by the voluminous sleeves, laid across her stomach in detached professionalism.

Naseria did not don the air of a mother joining her family for a meal but of a matriarch setting forth a new rule for the House.

They were flung backwards in time to the moment they returned home, Naseria standing in her house robes as the incense curled around them. Distaste for their behavior, disappointment in their fleeing the

Amalak, had strained her features then. In the present, Naseria wore an indominable mask.

The silence engulfing the room became agitating. It burned Sen's ears, and they wished more than anything for the griping of their sister or the candid laughter of their father. They wished for anything that might pull their mother's hollow gaze from their face.

Swallowing back their discomfort, Sen kept their hands plainly by their side. But they could not stand the quiet, the disapproval, for too long before words tumbled out of their throat.

"Is everyone eating at the pavilion tonight?"

Naseria's chest lifted in a deep breath, not unlike how she braced herself to ask Lon those intimate questions earlier. Sen felt the gooseflesh rise on their skin, wondering why their mother needed to steel herself.

With a tip of her head, the silence broke. Her guard, invisible until that moment, slid around her from the hall beyond and filled the room. People gazed on in a mixture of steely distance and practiced focus. Behind the scion, more of the guard filtered in; they surrounded Sen to block off every exit.

"I'm sure I've not curried any favor recently," Sen admitted, trying to speak past the knot in their throat, "but, mother, isn't this a bit dramatic?"

Their attempt at comedy fell on deaf ears. Naseria's vacant, distant gaze did not waver when she leveled her voice to Sen.

"Sen Ilet YeSara, Heir and Seram to the YeSara Clan, hear the proclamation of your Matriarch."

A claw coiled around Sen's gut. They felt, very suddenly, like they were being dropped from a great height.

"Lest this family suffer duress under your impudent behavior and selfishness, you have been stripped of your heirdom. Before the spirits of the Matriarchs who carried this family before me, *I reject you as my successor.*"

Naseria's voice broke, but only barely. She smoothed it over, quickly continuing her proclamation as Sen's mouth fell open in shock. "Whatever reason I gave you to preform honorably and in favor of the Clan has been met with spite. Whatever correction I instigated in an attempt to amend the path you chose has been met with defiance. You have given me no reason to trust you with the continuation and protection of our bloodline when you placed your own blood in the way of harm and disgrace. As such, you will be relieved of the title, protection, and coin of the family you so despise. You are banished from this island and shall not be permitted to return unless directly invited by myself or your sister, who shall be declared the new scion this season.

"May you find peace," Naseria's voice dropped low, escaping her practiced tone, "since you could not find it within all your luxuries."

Swords left their scabbards in a ringing of steel. Long, thin blades leveled towards Sen as they were now deemed an uninvited guest in the household. The swords were intimidating, so clean that the metal reflected Sen's astonishment.

Naseria's commandments slammed the air out of their lungs. Its force sent them stumbling backwards away from the Matriarch, right into the awaiting hands of two guards. Fingers clamped down on each shoulder, the opposite hands grabbing their wrists and pinning them behind Sen's back. The twinge of discomfort snapped them out of their shock for just long enough for them to gape at their mother.

"You can't. You *can't*." Sen's voice came out in a pitched whine. Betrayal stung their eyes as the world went misty. With a soundless order, the guards began hauling them out of the room.

"You can't!" Sen jerked their arms, wincing as the guard's grip held true. A throbbing began in their shoulder, and as they struggled to find footing in their soft slippers against the gleaming wood floor, they cried out to Naseria.

A flash of pain crossed her face—the only sign that she was still Sen's mother, the only evidence that hearing them cry out brought a stab of agony through her chest—and then it was gone.

Everything they knew blurred around Sen as the guards unabashedly dragged them through the main building. Figures moved behind silk screens. Were they servants, or their family listening in on Sen's shame?

Sen's voice cracked as they called out to those flickering shapes. "It's not fair! She can't do this, I'm the heir! I'm the scion of this Clan! I'm your *family—Let me go!*"

Behind their silken barriers, the figures moved away from the hall and vanished. Sen felt their heels thump down two steps before dragging across pebbled gravel. They lost a slipper, its blue silk glaring back at them, refusing to continue any further. One of the courtyards breezed past the edges of their vision, figures looking down from the windows in the rich wood balcony that ran the perimeter. Sen shouted the absurdity of the order, screaming at the injustice of being handled in such a way as they were dragged through the public areas of the house.

The richness around them became smears of teardrops as Sen went from shouting to begging. The docks drew nearer, the smell of the ocean tinging their nostrils and making them feel sick with dread.

A boat sat prepared at the end of the dock. Ferris looked on as the seram tried to order him to leave the boat, to not row out to the docks at Dunhet just beyond.

Ferris glared, the wrinkles in his faces knitting together. "You sent me home, and I was not paid for my work." Tears rimmed his eyes. "My wife died because I could not afford her medicine in time. And here I am, unable to take another day to mourn her."

The scraggly old man turned his back on them. It was a slap in the face that stalled Sen's attempts at freedom as they stared at the man's drooped shoulders.

Four guards stepped into the boat, surrounding Sen as the old man pushed off and headed towards a twinkling city. Sen tried to call up fire to burn down the boat—to burn them all—but their hands ached with a painful dullness. The magic seemed to withdraw from the surface of their skin. In the shock of being dismissed from the family completely, it hid somewhere deep within their being.

Dunhet glittered with lanternlight, the bardic tunes of flutes and drums rising up from the street performers beyond the docks. For the first time in their life, Sen ignored the city, turning in their seat to gaze at the YeSara island behind them. Slopped roofs lined with gold shimmering in the moonlight made it shiver like a mirage.

This is a dream, Sen tried to convince themself as the opposite docks drew close. But they did not wake as the guards shoved Sen out of the boat. Their eyes did not blink open as they stood on the pier and screamed curses at the old man and their mother's servants. Even when the light chill of the night touched the toes of their bare foot and the gravel scraped at their soft heel as they turned away from the water in defeat, Sen remained in the nightmare alone.

CHAPTER NINETEEN

Pelagios received correspondence from his man all the way out to Neighweather before the crows stopped returning. Either Kana's runner noticed they were being trailed and carried out orders to deal with their tagalong, or the mage himself dealt with the unwelcomed follower. Perhaps the general's man simply took his coin and disappeared over the border to Thantis. Whatever the reason for the letters ending, it meant that Pelagios needed to do the rest of the work himself.

He was no stranger to this, but even so, a thimble of anxiousness pitted his stomach.

Most of the councilors lived on the same level as himself and other stately, recognizable members of the court. Pelagios walked the long, slightly curved hall with the last of the letters curling around his knobby finger. The tiny slip of parchment carried a few glyphs to conceal the message: *The runner waits at a hole in the ground like a badger's den.*

Befuddled at its meaning, the old man was left to his imaginings as he walked. Every now and then he was required to incline his head at the odd couple who swished by in their traditional Esmarin garb, but the hall was otherwise undisturbed.

Snow fell that morning, powdery and light. Pelagios only bothered to gaze at it for a moment from an upper balcony before the cold seeped into his fingers, causing them to stiffen terribly. He left behind the laughing courtiers and servants, ignoring how immaculate the dank country looked when he peered across the land over his shoulder. Nothing so lovely remained that way, not in Esmar, and now the cold stained the stone so deeply even the torches lighting the hall provided little warmth.

Pelagios slipped the parchment into his vest before raising his hands to the fire. Yellow light tinged his palms; he saw it glow through the underneath of his fingers, turning his nails orange. The flames popped, a spark hitting the heel of his hand, and behind him came a great sigh.

The hall remained empty. No doors scraped open with rusting hinges to announce any oncoming persons. Not even the scuttling of a rat broke the silence. Pitch drenched the stonework, the tapestries which hung on the wall turning black where the shadows touched them. From just beyond the light, Pelagios sensed the gaze of something waiting impatiently for him to turn around. It almost begged for him to put his back to the shadows, to dismiss its presence just as he dismissed all other vile and wicked things that happened within Carn-Duhl.

This is the moment your fate is sealed, wax on a letter, sap to bond the cut.

Pelagios turned his face around, gazing down the other length of the hall. It was not his voice that spoke, but it seemed too distant for it to have come from anywhere other than his imagination.

Without meaning to, he thought of Aletta. More than once since *that day* he wondered if she was doomed to walk the halls of the fortress. At least natural light touched her face as she died, whether moon or sun. To die in utter darkness, to vanish into these halls and fall down in a forgotten corner, was a fate only good enough for vermin.

"Sir General."

Riven stood in the hallway, materializing out of the shadows that were no longer so deep, so still. He stood in his simple clothes, the robe stating his position on the Council slung over his shoulders. The same gold beads sat in his ruddy beard, yet while he had been a fearsome picture all those nights ago his crinkled face appeared kindly in the torchlight.

Dropping his hands from around the torch fire, Pelagios flexed his fingers. Damalis bothered to include the general in *this* secret meeting, though gods knew how many went on while keeping the old man at a distance. Thankfully, the invitation was not a trick, and Riven's presence eased the general's mind.

"How fares our great king?"

Noting the less than cordial tone, Pelagios struggled to figure the hidden meaning. After Damalis, it was best for him to assume all members of the Council sought their own agenda. However, this was a question that put off the general for a moment, since he was then avoiding Einar's summons. Any other member of court would have been beheaded, but Pelagios told the king's messengers to let Einar know that his general sought a lead in the chase for the remaining Kahun. Such an answer tended to be enough for Pelagios to be left alone as he paced his rooms. He gave only enough to Einar for the king to assume treachery was afoot, but never enough to point towards his own Council—not yet, at least.

"He rules with a guiding hand." Pelagios' response was sharp.

Riven observed him in the way a mother might her child after they shattered a prized clay vase. "May the Great Lantern light his way. Hail the King."

"Hail the King," the general echoed.

...hail the king...

Pelagios did not give the whispering shadows any acknowledgement. He walked alongside Riven the rest of the way to Damalis' rooms, trying to find some manner of polite conversation during their short walk.

"I didn't know you were a *Lightbearer*."

Riven quirked a brow at the distasteful undertone. "How would you? You have your great Mother and great Father, and that's enough. All thoughts of a person believing differently in this court fled your mind the moment Einar established the Path as Esmar's practice—and thusly justified his condemnation of the Kahun as a righteous proclamation."

The general caught himself from saying that Riven's statement was treason when he remembered where they were headed. Instead, he simply said, "I follow what feels correct."

Even in his own ears, it sounded like a lie.

Favoring to keep things as amicable as possible, the general did not attempt another topic. They walked in silence the last few paces to Damalis' door, which opened to greet them suddenly.

Kana stood in the doorway, her hair affixed in three heavy twists that cascaded over her shoulders and down her back. Her councilors robe sat neatly on her shoulders, and her dark gaze slid over Pelagios with a touch of irritation.

They entered the room, Pelagios once again noting how much larger it was than his own and now doubt the other council members' all the while avoiding Kana's duplicitous gaze. Riven easily took the seat he held many nights ago, the lingering shadows of that memory whispering across the general's mind. He touched the back of the chair he himself once took, hours after the bludgeoning of Gaelis. That same chill of *knowing* lingered, the sense of something beyond himself about to be revealed.

The more he considered that night, and the span of nights between, he realized the absence of the council members. At first they simply kept their distance from Pelagios, but as he stood behind one of the chairs at the massive table he was startled to realize they vanished from his sight altogether.

He glanced to Kana as she took her own seat. "Where are the others?" He began just as Damalis entered from the bathing room.

It was the head advisor who answered. "This meeting will involve only the four of us, per the request of our mage-finder." He nodded towards Kana.

"That isn't what I meant."

Damalis took his seat at the head of the table. No refreshments or wine littered the top, no show of his station. The candles were lit, and that was that. Damalis seemed unprepared for the meeting just as Pelagios was surprised to be invited.

Instead of answering further, the advisor motioned for Pelagios to sit. Once he did, Kana took hold of the conversation. "Our mage is quite precise with how he wishes to be discussed. He requested that no more than four know of these letters."

It seemed to be the only explanation Pelagios would get, so he nodded. The thrill of learning more about this mage hushed over the base of his ribcage, tightening in his chest. A sense of finality closed around him, as though this meeting might end the constant back and forth with himself.

Kana retrieved a letter from the sleeve of her gown, along with a short letter opener. Resting it on the table with the interior facing up, the candlelight revealed a blank page. Pelagios opened his mouth to state the obvious when, with a quick slash, Kana cut her index finger with the letter opener. Hovering her bleeding finger over the parchment, they all watched as the droplet of blood elongated in the air, turning into a red thread of magic as it was drawn down onto the page. The thread unfurled when it touched the letter, spiderwebbing across the parchment to fill out the hidden words. Once every symbol darkened the page, Kana popped her finger into her mouth.

"It took me a moment to figure that out," she said, rubbing her thumb over the sliver in her skin.

Damalis leaned forward, his chin lifted as he gazed at the letter down his nose. He seemed to mutter to himself, "Do you think any blood reveals the message, like another person, or a bird? Or is it only yours that uncovers the message?"

"Mine," she sighed, suggesting she had tried the blood of some unfortunate creature already, and likely an unwilling servant's.

"Well, if we had any doubt about his magic…" Riven inclined his head to the page.

Damalis hummed. "This isn't simply magic—it's *power*. And it's been a long while since Esmar saw power like this."

The chief advisor's gaze looked hungry. Each of them took a moment, considering the letter and the binding magic within. What did this mean for a country, for a *world*, whose magic was lost long before the Common Age? Did this prove that the fabric resting between the physical and the mysterious never closed, but only came down like a curtain over certain people? The old Clans of Lesser Syvon liked to boast that they were the only casters left on this side of the Nameless Seas, and until now Pelagios believed that true. It shook his resolve, this little sheaf of parchment with its words written in Kana's blood. How did this happen?

And why had they not heard of this mage before?

Pelagios glanced around the table, noting the sensation of awe and dread on the face of his companions. Perhaps they were asking themselves the same questions. Riven appeared speculative, a hand paused in the middle of stroking his beard. What was he thinking?

Kana broke the stupor by taking up the letter. Her eyes scanned the page, brow knitting together as she read. Having scoured the letter during her attempts to see what blood worked best, she consumed the note as if for the first time.

"He stills refuses to give his name. *Names have an authority all their own and should never be shared for the first time through a page instead of one's breath*, he says." She chuckled absently to herself, a joke lost on the others.

Damalis grew more impatient with every moment. He pinched the bridge of his nose and sighed. "This is your third letter from him, yes? Why is this one suddenly so important that you must address it now?"

"Because," Kana's tone bit through the annoyed air surrounding Damalis, "it was not *my* man who brought the letter back."

For a moment, the general's heart dropped. He desperately wanted to ask for a cup of something to save his parched throat, to busy his hands. In his vest pocket, his last correspondence burned against his breast. *The runner waits at a hole in the ground like a badger's den.*

No one spoke, ingesting this revelation, and then Riven asked, "Then who brought this letter to Carn-Duhl?"

"My runner vanished, and the… *person*… who brought the mage's response was someone I'd never seen before." A sliver of discomfort passed over her gaze as she recalled the memory. "It—they—I don't know.

They felt *wrong*. They stood before me in the garb of a human, with the face of a person, but their limbs… the air around them…"

Inside the chamber, the flames of the candles twitched. Riven leaned away from them, eyes wide and affixed to the flames. The four observers gazed as the fire stretched high and thin before bending towards the letter in Kana's hands. It followed with their pointed, flickering tendrils as she placed it back down with a gasp on the tabletop. When her hand pulled away, the candles returned to their normal, upright wavering.

The shadows thickened, as though a person stood in the spaces between the darkness and the stone wall. Pelagios felt the chill in the air rise out of the stonework; when he breathed, a cloud of mist passed his lips.

"Yes." Kana nodded to no one, gazing around her. "Yes, it felt like this. Are we certain we want to continue on this path?" Her eyes locked with each of them before settling on Damalis. "Are we certain of ourselves, of these choices? If we invite a mage within these walls, it will no longer be under the guise of distracting the king—if it ever had been to start. Something rests here, waiting, and we know nothing of this man who so readily affixes the shadows without standing in their presence. What happens when—"

"Kana, it appears you've taken council with Einar for a hair too long." Damalis straightened in his chair. His gaze, despite watching an inexplicable feat of magic, was unwavering as it bore his insult into the other councilor. "Finding a mage was always meant to give us the upper hand with Einar, whether that means healing this supposed curse on his head or distracting him from running the country into the ground. We cannot kill him, as we don't have the manpower to fight off an uprising, so we do *this*.

"As for your earlier question, Pelagios: The others have been spread like seeds across Esmar to attempt some sort of foothold. Einar spent too long chasing after the Kahun to bother with maintaining any real control over his country. They shall return at the end of Hattash, hopefully with news of grain or cattle."

The general nodded, finding it hard to focus with his back turned towards the darkness. He thought the meeting might continue for longer, but after Damalis instructed Kana to write to the mage of when they should expect him, they were dismissed. Kana swore to herself as she stood, arguing with no one in particular how she might send a letter to a secretive mage, and Riven bent forward to whisper something in Damalis' ear. Pelagios found himself leaving the meeting with more questions than before, the doubt still nestled in his belly.

Explaining this to Einar was impossible. He might claim they were all mages conspiring to bring down his lineage, and no amount of past valor would save Pelagios then.

He needed to prepare for when the mage arrived.

As he passed, a candle snuffed out. He would have thought it the breeze of his movement if he had not seen something beyond the shadows flicker.

Pelagios felt the worry rise from his bones as he considered what may happen when Einar was confronted with the very magic he swore to hunt.

Once the door closed behind Pelagios, Kana remained standing but placed her hands on the back of her seat. Her finger still throbbed from the cut, her heartsong pounding in her head as she felt the shadows in the room grow lighter. Neither of her compatriots seemed to note the difference. Damalis, his gaze impatient, pressed into her skin like needles.

When she requested that Pelagios be included in this meeting, the chief advisor took some convincing. She promised half her entourage to him as spies, keeping the better ones for herself of course, but annoyance still churned beneath the surface of her skin at the loss. It was not hard to see that Damalis, like many others on the Council, felt inclined to take advantage of Esmar as it teetered on the edge of a blade. He put out a decent façade most days, but the state of the country, and of the court itself, wore him thin.

Councilors were out in the country, but who sought to learn more about the marsh sickness that risked submerging Farstone within the next turn of the seasons? Should they not work on relocating not only the villagers, but the seat of the throne itself? What did it matter if Carn-Duhl was the oldest monument within Esmar's borders—a king could not rule from the bottom of the sea.

"I hope our friend shows his gratitude for how dutifully you follow his orders, Kana." Damalis griped. "After all, what does it matter that Pelagios is undecided in his loyalties if a stranger requests his presence?"

"By name."

Damalis' narrow gaze slid from Kana's aggravated features to Riven's, who spoke. The boar-like councilor kept his massive hands folded on the tabletop but Damalis knew from which region Riven came. His people were of giant's blood, so the story went, and while Damalis did not believe in giants or the Old Gods he did recognize brute strength. One of Riven's hand could easily encircle Damalis' throat.

"The mage asked for Pelagios *by name*." Surprise tinged Riven's otherwise placid tone. "That alone is a feat, yet he proved himself from miles away by the candleflame."

"That is not *proof*."

Riven prepared to argue, but Kana interrupted him. "Damalis is right, in a way. Asking for Pelagios specifically is not a sign of magic, but it *is* the sign of a good spy. Does he know that Pelagios is a part of this, or did he ask for his presence for another reason? We know our people," she nodded to them both, "and we know who we employ. Pelagios has been at a king's side since the reign of Mycin. He might not be as important anymore, but he's a fixture of this court. Could this have been a lucky guess?"

Damalis scoffed at that, yet did not debate the statement. He seemed a bit more relaxed after Kana agreed with him.

She let out a tight breath as she remembered the strange messenger. Gooseflesh bristled on her skin as she recollected their pallid features and toadlike eyes. Their skin sat on their bones like a wet cloak, and if Kana had not watched them amble down the road she would have assumed it no more than a skeleton playacting its life once again.

"*But* to ask for him at all is strange." She inclined her head to Riven, who seemed the more interested of her audience. "There is something else going on here, and it would be foolish to think ourselves in total control. Invite the mage, bring him to court... but we mustn't, not for a moment, assume he doesn't have plans of his own."

Obvious though the statement was, Kana knew it served as a reminder. Damalis crafted his own desires in the background of this task, and while she had no clue what he may do with this mage, or how it worked in his favor, she knew a man's hunger for power. Her time as a mayor in Centrust was her first stepping stone into the realities of selfishness within the hierarchical societies of Esmar. While *she* did not always reject an extra coin or two, she had no desire to overtake an entire kingdom. But taking coin to turn her gaze was different from letting one person—Damalis, or whoever else—take a bleeding, broken country by exploiting its open wounds.

"It seems you have your mind set." Damalis slapped his hands lazily onto the table as he stood. "Very well, Kana. Consider your words heeded."

Riven stood as well. Their host was at the end of his patience, so they bid one another goodbye and left the advisor to his flickering candles.

Still feeling as though the severity of her tone went ignored, Kana walked the length of the hall back to her room in deep thought. She did not notice when Riven vanished to do his own secret crafts, or when the silence filled the hall so deeply that even the flicker of the torchlight was a murmur.

She quickly disappeared into her rooms as the gooseflesh pimpled her skin, as if the wooden door might actually keep out the watchful eyes in the dark.

CHAPTER TWENTY

"All right, time to talk." Calily stood in the shallows with her trouser legs rolled up to the knees. A wide straw hat sat on her head, tied down over her braids with a ribbon twined beneath her chin. With her hands resting on her hips, her posture threw Neoma back into the days when she was a child about to be scolded. However, worry marred Calily's features, not anger or disappointment.

Neoma corrected her awkward leaning, adjusting the yoke carrying saltwater on her shoulders as she ambled back to the shoreline. "What of?"

Calily *tsked*. "Oh, I'll have none of that."

The days at Kairdwillo-Nhan passed with near oblivion. Neoma felt useful as she worked the tension in her heart out through the labor her family did for decades before her. An addition was being constructed on the north end of the homestead, one that would become a playroom for the smaller children, so her hands were needed as those adept at carpentry set the structure.

And, in truth, the work kept Neoma from having the very conversation her mother pressed for now.

Pacing the shoreline, Neoma convinced her mother to at least let her finish readying the saltwater. Expecting her daughter to vanish, like she tended to do as a teenager when the promise of a tough conversation seemed too much, Calily waited on the sand dunes with arms crossed.

The water reminded Neoma of being embraced. Despite her distance towards Ocean, and her struggle to find comfort in the old prayers, she could not deny the softness of its touch as she worked. In a macabre way, she even felt thankful that it held her son when she could not.

Calily watched Neoma swing the buckets, and approached her when the yoke finally dropped from her shoulders. Neoma's entire body was sore in a way that brought her joy. She was glad to be able to come home to a life like this, where riches sat for the entire family to enjoy but all were expected to be a part of adding to the bounty. It kept her hands busy, but without the yoke she felt naked under Calily's serious gaze.

"Out with it then." Neoma braced her heart, feeling the grief there shiver. It was less potent since the dinner some nights ago, as though the embraces from her family mushed the pieces of herself together again.

One of the many things Neoma loved about her mother was how she wasted no time in getting to the topic at hand. With a heavy breath, she said with no joy, "We should talk about you and your husband. Meaning… *is* he still your husband?"

Was he? Had Neoma meant it to be final when she placed her marriage token on the table? No one pressed about Urias or why Neoma suddenly came home, for which she was grateful, yet her family failed at averting their prodding gazes. Roland tried to pry a detail or two out of her in that solemn, careful way of his, but each attempt evaporated as his daughter found one thing or another to distract them. It was foolish of her to think that Calily meant to ignore discussing Urias at all when she had simply been waiting to get Neoma alone.

She was honest—to be anything other in front of Calily resulted in chastising. "I don't know. Everything feels like it's shifted. One moment, I was standing there, next to him, and all of a sudden it feels like I'm… well, still next to him, but… not. I don't know." Neoma huffed, the right words illusive. In all her summers, she never felt anything similar to the weary distance in her chest.

"It wasn't all of a sudden, flower." Calily murmured. She cast her gaze out over the ocean, likely recalling the moments she admitted her distrust of Urias over the years. Neoma had ignored it all until it became truth. Then, out of embarrassment, she avoided looking at the truth entirely.

"You always loved broken things," her mother continued with a small, sad grin. "When you found a crab missing its claw as a child, you watched over it for nights on end. You wouldn't believe us when we told you it grows back. No, you had to keep it safe. My flower, you are not meant to keep *grown men* safe."

"Mother—"

"If you don't mind." Calily raised a hand, stopping any further argument. "I've been wanting to say this since you wed him. I promise, though, that if you go back to Urias I will embrace your choice because it's yours to make."

After a pained moment, Neoma sat down on the slope of the dune next to them. Her mother followed, nestling as close as the noonday heat allowed. The ocean shined slate blue, the clouds wispy in the sky. Warmth surged up from the sands, comforting the slight pang in Neoma's tailbone, and she thought of that beauty she observed on her first trip to Linlocke after Koa's death. Closing her eyes, she lifted her face to the sun.

Calily was gentle in her admonishment. "You're my only daughter. Kairdwillo-Nhan will be yours if Sulien decides not to keep it. As much as I love you, you put others too far ahead of yourself. That man—Urias—he saw this, just as I see it, but even if love came of your union, it began all wrong. I thank him for my grandson," her voice was serious, soft, "and I thank him for the roof over your head. We embraced your courtship because he seemed to make you happy, but after Koa was born he brought you nothing but worry. A man should not make you so uncomfortable in your own life, Neoma, especially one who claims to love you."

It feels wrong now to be loved by him… by any man.

This, Neoma kept herself. She did not yet understand why such a thought occurred to her, or what it meant.

Or why Monty and her beaming smile came to mind.

She wrapped her arms around her knees, a hunger like no other settling in her stomach. Silence lapsed, the murmur of the sea along the shoreline softening the quiet. The gentle *pick, pick, pick* hammers on nails echoed from behind them.

After letting the gentle sounds hold them for a while, Calily bowed her head, forcing Neoma to meet her gaze. "Will you consider my words, at least?"

Neoma smiled at the tone in her mother's voice. "Of course."

"Good, because that was probably my *best* motherly speech to this day."

Laughing, Neoma threw her head back to the sky. Calily went on to say that she rehearsed it with Roland that morning, urging another shake of laughter from her daughter. Eventually, Calily released Neoma, allowing her to take up the yoke once more but not before another word of advice.

"If you have the chance to make something new of yourself, then take it. It's never too late to shape your life."

Neoma titled her head, her earlier laughter still lifting her mouth. "Did you rehearse that with Roland, too?"

"No, no, that one was in the moment, but no less serious."

They parted for the evening, the words lingering in the air around Neoma as she scooped up more buckets of water. The methodic swinging of the saltwater, the slap as it hit the packed sand, eased away the rest of the noise in her mind.

Sulien was determined and willful—if she took charge of Kairdwillo-Nhan, the family business might expand to Greater Syvon, even as far as Thantis. As Sulien was the first child to be born from Calily's siblings, it made sense the estate should fall to her. Neoma thought of no one better as she finished her tasks for the day, the sun dipping lower into the sky and ushering in a chilly wind that cooled the sweat on her dark skin. Let Sulien have the family name and business, and let Neoma be strong enough to embrace what this world had left to offer.

That was all she could ask for.

CHAPTER TWENTY-ONE

Standing at the threshold of the room, a figure of no discernable gender paused in a flowing peach colored robe. Their dark eyes scanned the display of flesh dutifully, the corner of their nose crinkling at the explosions of silk sheets and flower petals littering the floor and bed. Wine stains pooled in various locations, undoubtedly ruining the plush rugs and staining the wood floor.

Rich, dark hair sat piled in defiant braids, and a strand came loose as they swung their head around to take in the damaged headboard, the linen room divider with a puncture through it, the pile of clothing that only grew since they last checked in on the guest.

They flicked the strand aside with a huff, the gold bracelets climbing up to the elbow jangling. A dozen men, women, and other companions slept wherever they dropped from exhaustion, bare asses and gleaming breasts shimmering with love bites and bruises. Omalia knew this sort of extravagant painting well, as their House reigned over every established, high-end brothel in Dunhet.

Their weathered patience hung over the room, diminishing the pleasant tableau the longer they scowled at it. Omalia refused to step any further into the room, as if waiting for either an invitation or a chance to turn and run. Their client laid sprawled on the bed, one woman's head laying across their crotch in a way that suggested she fell asleep mid-pleasure. A man nestled into the client's side, his tousled hair concealing the client's face.

Lifting their hands wide, Omalia slammed their palms together. The clap resounded throughout the room, a roll of condemning thunder. Every naked body jerked awake in a gasp, bemoaning the pounding in their heads as they sat up from their awkward positions on the floor or the lounge chairs. One figure lifted himself out of the pile of clothes, earning a confused grimace from Omalia as he ambled naked out of the room with the others. Only the client and their two companions remained, which meant the pristine manager of *The Silver Lantern* had to risk crossing the stained, soggy, reeking-of-various-odors threshold after all.

Approaching the bed, Omalia slapped a lazy hand down on the bare rump of the sprawled man. They did not desire physical pleasure, which is what made them such an expert manager of their family's property, so it was more in annoyance than anything sexual.

Groggy with sleep, the man peeled himself off of the client once he recognized Omalia.

"Sir," he bobbed his head. As he rose, the woman across the client's hips roused.

"Ah, madam," she murmured to Omalia.

Dannette was one of their favorites. Instead of smacking her, Omalia flittered their hand to urge them both away, and the two remaining companions tittered out of the room like disturbed hens.

"Up." Omalia glared down at the sleeping nakedness of the disgraced YeSara. When Sen did not immediately rise, they reared back and kicked the already slanted mattress. Feathers puffed upwards, and the mattress barely moved, but it was enough to agitate Sen.

"While you're here, get us more wine." Sen rolled onto the stain next to them, making Omalia shiver with disgust. They could never image sleeping on anything other than freshly laundered sheets.

"Us?" Omalia scoffed. They flung their hands around the now empty room. "There is no *us*—and there shan't be anymore! Your credit has expired, just like my patience. Get out."

When the former heir arrived at *The Silver Lanter*, their family's line of credit was still open, with Sen's name yet to be removed. Sen stole weeks of companions' time, and Omalia may never see any of that coin.

The poor excuse for a mage might have kept up the ruse if Omalia had not woken to a letter that morning from one of the many accountants employed by the YeSaras. In it was a copy of the receipt Omalia sent out to any family with open lines of credit, and beneath it a gentle scrawl that explicitly stated how there would be no money sent to pay off Sen's numerous fines and expenses. When the realization struck Omalia, pure fury surged through them, as well as embarrassment. They needed to tell their own familial accountant about the lost funds now.

Sen was mindful enough to look ashamed. Their dark eyes gaze up at Omalia, filling with tears.

Omalia's family, though wealthy, never reached a high enough status to be considered as honorable as the YeSaras. Even though more than enough of their ancient coin disappeared under the roofs governed by Omalia's family, recognition evaded House Trulan. For that, Omalia reserved a certain type of venom for their egotistical counterpart.

Sen's voice was hardly above a whisper. "I've nowhere to go."

Once, Omalia might have cared. As a child, they related to Sen, finding a confidant in them as they each grew to realize neither fit the confines of their sex. Omalia never cared for what people called them—man, woman, to them it mattered not as long as the soul within their body found joy. They respected Sen's similar yet opposite blossoming, but the moment Sen was announced as the heir everything changed. No compassion softened their gaze at Omalia, no lingering sense of comradeship remained.

As an adult, they worried little for the plights of those who bought House Trulan's business while looking down their noses at the same time.

Omalia's voice was firm, unwavering. "If you do not leave," they said, leaning in across the bed to hover over Sen, "then I will feed you to my dogs. Maybe then your misery will have meaning."

The biting words cut through Sen's misty tears. Rising from the bed, they shouted one profanity after the other, throwing pillows down at Omalia as they screeched. Omalia, disgusted at the childlike behavior, dodged every plush item before summoning the guard that followed them from the main foyer. The sight of the giant gave Sen a moment's pause, allowing Omalia to speak.

"I will throw you out, naked as they day you were born, if you don't take your stolen things and leave. *Now*."

Sen's gaze flickered to them. A fierce anger glinted in their eyes as the soft underside of their palms went orange.

But Omalia laughed. "What will you do—start a Clan war because your sex wasn't satisfied? I know you have nothing more than a spark there, Sen. Put it out, and leave with whatever dignity a disgraced *former* heir might have."

Sen's ego shattered under the disregard for their magic. The pillow dropped from their hands with a gentle *thunk* onto the mattress, the fight leaving them quickly. Omalia stopped the guard from stepping forward with a lifted hand, watching as Sen rummaged about the room to find their clothing.

Good riddance, Omalia thought as Sen, fully dressed, shuffled out of the room with their chin held high and no more than a backwards glance.

A current of resentment moved up from Omalia's gut and spilled out of their throat. "Every reputable establishment in Dunhet knows your shame now, Sen. It'll be better to stay with a friend for a time, if you have one."

While Sen kept walking without so much as a slant to their step, Omalia grinned at the deflated fall of their shoulders.

Being displaced from the life they knew changed the very scent upon the air. Before, Sen remembered catching the notes of floral colognes wafting from the necks of beautiful highborns, or from the stalls of the perfumers who offered up the handblown glass bottles. The stone smelt like copper and salt after it rained, and the food stalls positioned throughout the better parts of Dunhet dragged the smells of frying meat and butter over the throngs of people who went about their way.

Now, walking alone in the disappearing light of the sun, Sen noticed the rankness of emptied chamber pots in the canal ditches in secluded alleyways, running water sloshing the waste out to the sea. Sen walked with no sense of where they were going as the ruinous stench filled their lungs.

Their wandering provided ample ground for bitter anger to take root. Shame roiled in their gut, having been dismissed from their haven. When their family's credit was not immediately rejected at *The Silver Lantern,* they thought they managed a foothold in keeping up appearances. Of course they should have expected it all to shatter in an instant, but they spent those days flouncing and bedding beautiful people and being *exactly* the sort of person Naseria expected.

Sen realized how stupid they were to think someone they once shamed would not take the opportunity to do the same.

Walking through the city without an entourage felt like parading the streets naked. People glanced at Sen, some openly staring at their threads as they passed, and they realized with painful clarity how weak they truly were. Omalia pointed out their failures by laughing at whatever magic remained in their bloodline, and now even the wind seemed disheartened as it brushed across Sen's face.

They had no coin to pay their way into any establishment. Sen owned no properties, their names being wiped from entry into any YeSara assets. For the last few weeks, they avoided looking out across the water whenever they crested a hill or gazed out of the *Lantern's* window, but now they turned to face their old life.

Expecting it to shimmer like a mirage, Sen balked at how small the island seemed, while at the same time so grand. Lights twinkled from behind waving palm fronds, though in the fading light it was a mash of greens and deep grays. The matriarch's rooms and inner courtyard could not be seen from Dunhet, but Sen traced with their minds eye the path they took when they returned from the Amalak.

Did Naseria mean to keep them away forever? Surely they were not the first YeSara to embarrass a matriarch. Their severe punishment had not been delved out to anyone else in the family—to their knowledge, at least, but perhaps that was the point. If someone years ago was revoked of the YeSara namesake, they were forgotten completely.

The thought of being erased so thoroughly made Sen ill. Guilt sat behind their breastbone at the action which led to this consequence, but it still seemed unfair. Did Lon agree with Naseria's proclamation? Even if she did not, what power did she have to speak out against her mother and matriarch?

Did Sen even deserve grace if Lon disagreed with Naseria?

Sen was poor, broken, and hungry. They thought of only one other place to go that might accept them. Even as their feet turned towards *The Dovetail*, Sen became overwhelmed with the urge to run in the opposite direction. But that would simply take them back to the docks, where they would stare longingly out at a life that so willfully abandoned them. It might be better to be miserable around others in their new station than to keep pretending they belonged to the old one.

Considering only for a moment that without Valeska's protection they may be seen as an item to pawn, Sen made their way to the squat structure. By the time the horizon swallowed the sun, a few lanterns were the only thing to distinguish the buildings from the shadows. No one gave more than a glance when Sen pushed the heavy door wide, and no one but the barkeep noted the single coin they laid on the counter. It was enough for a drink, but not enough for the stupor they wished to drown in.

Despite it being early in the evening, most of the tables were filled with brawny seafarers and scraggily people of no obvious profession. These people drank their breakfast, midday meal, and dinner; they were not ignorant of the way Sen stood out in the crowd.

A card game went on by their elbow. Sen needed to squeeze in between two people to get a seat at all, but it was hard to confine themselves to the little space they made. The man on their right seemed ready to howl at them for being too close when the chair across became free.

Sliding into it before another took the spot, Sen blinked at a strangely familiar, weasel-like face. They almost dropped their drink when the recognition struck. The man who accompanied Valeska that fateful night took a sip from his shallow saucer, placing a bottle of the rice liquor between them with a smile.

Sen's gut churned when they recalled Naseria's words. *Which one did it.*

Had they each taken a turn?

"I didn't expect you back, young scion." The unwelcomed stranger's voice grated out of his throat. "How fares the life of the highborns?"

"You should know." Sen hated how shaky their voice sounded, how weak.

The little man chuckled. "Yea. I should. I'm surprised you're not out celebrating with Valeska." He snorted. "There's a highborn not worth his station. You, though, were made for all that. Can't say I'm displeased at seeing you—"

"Celebrating what?" Sen did not have the patience after the events of the last few days to suffer through the man's monologuing. They had been tampering down their guilt with sex, and pretending not to wonder if Lon made it to the summer homes, and if she was healing well. "Where is he?"

A glint appeared in the man's eyes, sharp and wicked. He sipped his drink slowly, relishing Sen's attention before saying, "Where he usually is when he desires company. There's a brothel some doors down, and a turn. It caters to his vices."

Sickness rooted in Sen's chest, aching. Too many thoughts slammed into them at once but the fear of having ignored Valeska's true self came to the surface first. Did their so-called friend spend his time enjoying defenseless women? Is that where his coin always went, and why Sen always paid for their outings despite the runt of the House Demont boasting of his allowances?

The spit of a man wasted no time in directing Sen to this brothel, explaining it had nothing to mark it but a wooden sign with some drawings. Sen left their drink, too sick to their stomach to finish it, parting from the smoky din of *The Dovetail* with a sallow warning in their chest.

Every shadow from the tavern to the mysterious building made them leap in discomfort. They gave any passers-by a wide berth, crossing their arms over their chest to warm the chill radiating through their heart. Upon a nondescript door sat the wooden sign the man mentioned, the drawings actually being words in the Common Tongue.

Vices and diverging flavors. Public and private seating.

Sen's eyes grazed the statement, confused at its meaning, before pushing open the door. An odd smell hung in the air, rough with the scent of body odor and something sharper underneath. Every muscle in Sen's shoulders tightened as they took in the low slung ceiling and bare room, save for the woman sitting on a stool by the only other door. They liked the woman even less than the empty room, her wild blonde hair glowing in the light of the single candle in a sconce by her feet. Sen squinted as they approached, only to find that her features were expertly hidden behind painted marks around her eyes and mouth. She appeared a skull in the darkness, her broken, stained teeth sitting crooked in her dark smile.

"Public, or private?"

It took a moment for Sen to recall the sign. Heart pounding in their throat, they struggled to say, "Private."

The woman nodded, as if she knew the answer already. "Private is not required to pay upfront, but if you want to keep your face hidden, deary, I'll require a coin now."

"Hidden?"

Frowning, the woman's gaze turned skeptical. "I've seen you in your garb and all, bare faced and bold. I'm *extorting* you."

Sen balked. They were not stupid—if this place required the guard to extort anyone who passed, then something wicked happened beyond the darkened doorway. An urge to turn away assailed them for a moment, sharp in their chest, before they tampered it down. In a strange way, Sen felt like this would make things right with Lon. They did not want to face the pain they put their sister through, but as their old life quickly slipped from their grasp they understood that hiding did not change reality. With understanding who Valeska was, and what he did in the shadows, Sen felt they might finally grasp Lon's distaste for him, and the severity of his behaviors. Anything less, and Sen feared they might excuse Valeska, treating Lon's pain as unimportant and proving Naseria right.

"Will you take this as payment?" Sen rested a hand on the fine outer coat they wore. Silk pressed against their palm, soft and luxurious. They knew the woman never owned such an item when her eyes sparkled in their black paint.

"My, that's lovely." She ran a dirty finger down the sleeve, pinching the embellishments on the cuff. Snapping her gaze to them, she spit, "Hand it over."

As soon as the coat left their shoulders, the woman donned it over her threadbare dress. This seemed to mark the end of Sen's richness as they watched her run her hands down, smoothing out the front. Their bare arms pimpled with gooseflesh when she finally opened the door and a dank, chilly breeze hit them. The odor from before wafted thickly out from the dimly lit hall, and they swallowed against the unease rising in their throat.

The woman jerked her chin. "Private is down there, and to your right. I'd tell you not to swindle me by going the other way, but you look too fresh. Have fun." She winked, though there was malice behind the gesture.

Too scared to disobey, Sen followed the directions. The hall was short, and they quickly came upon the door on the right and threw it open to reveal a room a little longer than their old closet. One of the four walls was a panel of wooden slats, the space between them barely wide enough for a finger. What little light spilled into the room came from another beyond. Sen shuffled awkwardly to the solitary bench that sat rather close to the slats, the sickening feeling in their stomach growing when they understood that while some came to enact abuse, others enjoyed watching it.

Beyond the slats, a few men chuckled together, low notes in their throats. Sen braced themself, preparing to hear the sound of screaming or fighting or worse, the sound of a fist hitting flesh.

After some time, the noise of an opening door interrupted the murmurs of conversation.

Everything fell silent.

There was the sound of something being dragged into the room, followed by the heavy thunk of it being laid properly on a table.

Valeska's voice, a voice Sen knew well, asked if the gentlemen minded if he went first. He said, with a haughty tone, that he had just secured his place in the world. The men laughed, congratulating him, and urged him to have the honor.

Pressed up against the slats, Sen felt the cold reaching down into their bones. Air pulsed around them, a sensation flooding up from their feet that begged them to turn away.

But they pressed their face further, narrowing their eye between the gap of the slats to see Valeska in a gilded mask unbuttoning his trousers.

Sen glanced to the wood table at a lifeless, naked body, the bruises around a slender neck shining The woman's gaze met theirs, empty.

Broken.

Bile surged into their throat as they scrambled away, horrified. The frigid air—air that reeked of the staleness of a tomb—iced over the sweat on the back of their neck. Vomit hit their tongue and they leaned over, retching onto the stone floor.

"Someone sounds fresh," one of the men beyond the slats laughed.

But the sound was not enough to cover Valeska's passionate grunting, or his deep moan of satisfaction at the coolness of the body.

The hall rushed around Sen as they fled, stumbling past the woman who shouted that she would not return the coat. Tripping over the threshold and into the night, Sen did not care for coats or for anything other than ridding themselves of what they witnessed.

Everything in their stomach heaved onto the patchwork stone of the road. The few sips of alcohol from earlier burned as it hit the ground, splattering and reeking sharply. Someone walked by them, laughing at their plight as tears filled Sen's vision. Nothing else was left in their stomach but the convulsing did not stop, not until they were sobbing over the putrid vomit, their shoulders aching from exertion.

Remorse slammed its iron fist into Sen's belly. Lon suffered under a man who took pleasure in defiling *corpses*. There were diseases that lived inside the people who did such things, but most of those stories came out of Esmar. As it sank, that foreign country wanted to draw everything else down into the darkness, too.

Did that mean their sister carried more than a parasitic child?

Sen hoped not. For all their shame in the world, they begged to whatever god listened for Lon to be all right. *Let it only be dealt with by tonic, and nothing more. Don't let her be ill. It's my fault.*

"My fault," they sobbed, a dribbled of spit falling out of their mouth.

Behind them, the air stirred. They waited for the jaunty laughter of another late night roamer as Sen sat back on their knees, wiping the spit on the chin with the back of their hand.

Valeska's voice cut through the dark, brittle and breathless. "Oh, friend, don't tell me you tried drinking alone."

I'm not your friend, Sen wanted to yell. Rawness in their throat made them only grunt up at a maskless Valeska as he made his way down the path to them. Nothing about his features or the way he carried himself revealed his sickening vice, proving to Sen that he had always been the better liar.

Crouching down next to them, Valeska even feigned worry over their disheveled features. "Where's your sister? Or your guard, for that matter."

He looked around, a hand coming down carefully to pat Sen's shoulder. A violent shiver went through them as they recoiled. Valeska's head whipped around, his eyes beady. In the dark, shadows cut into his features. His stark white hair made him a lantern in the night, a violent, otherworldly being so removed from Sen that they felt they might be hallucinating.

"Don't touch me," they spat, stomach clenching. "Don't you *ever* touch me again."

Valeska opened his mouth, either to quip or to argue, when his eyes followed Sen's anxious flick to the door beyond.

A dense wariness filled the space between them as Sen watched their old friend weigh his options. Nothing the man said would sway them—this, Valeska realized quickly.

To Sen's shock, he smiled. Crouching on the road, Valeska rested an elbow on his knee, cocking his chin in his hand. "I suppose this may make things odd between us, especially when I wed your sister. Don't worry," he lifted his other hand as if swearing an oath, "I shan't bring Lon into these things. She won't have the time with the child, anyways, and a man needs his own thrills separate from his wife. Besides, it's all the rage in Esmar. I hear that there are port cities with whole buildings dedicated to it."

The audacious tone in his voice made Sen bark a single empty note of laughter. Right in that moment, they understood everything about Valeska and the extent of his desire for power. He meant to take it from anyone, even the soulless husk of a person who could not fight against him.

Neither of them were ever friends, only pawns in one another's games. Sen used Valeska to spite Naseria and seem interesting to their highborn counterparts while Valeska schemed with his mother. He not only threatened to shame the YeSaras with an unsanctioned child, but by marrying into the family, too.

Blinking down at them, Sen noted that Valeska was waiting for them to do… what? Call a carriage to take them both to the docks and return to the island?

"You don't know." This made Sen laugh in honest, the sound hollow in their chest. "You don't—*ha!*"

Furrowing his brow, Valeska watched them as they threw their head back. The taste of vomit still on their tongue, Sen had a little pleasure in the fact that no matter how Valeska or his mother tried, they were still too low for the other highborns to even gossip with.

Sen threw their arms open, delirious. "I've been cut off because of *you!*"

In the middle of their mad chuckling, a muscle under Valeska's eye twitched. He attempted to regain control of their conversation by saying, "Our friendship might be a strain on your sister, then. I think it best that our journey ends here."

His earnestness made Sen laugh harder. The shaking hurt their sore shoulders and stomach, but Valeska's foolishness was comical.

"Do you honestly think," they gasped between breaths of glee, "that *my* mother, the Matriarch of one of the oldest Clans on the continent, would let my sister carry your poisoned seed?"

Valeska's face drained of all emotion. Shifting so quickly from amused superiority to calloused emptiness sent prickles down Sen's back.

"What do you mean?" His voice was sharp in warning.

"I *mean* that you're not the first fool to try and sleep his way into power. My mother works quickly. If the Old Gods are real, then Lon already dumped your clot of blood into a river. And, since my mother works so quickly, she might even have a bounty on your head." Sen grinned at the blankness on Valeska's face.

It felt good to have even a morsel of their power back.

Pain shot across Sen's cheek. White spots dotted their vision as they slipped backwards, landing in their own vomit. Giving them no time to raise a hand in defense, Valeska's boney fist cracked into Sen's other cheekbone, then their jaw. Each hit landed with a shout as Valeska screamed at how Sen ruined everything, that his chance at being more than a runt was lost. The confirmation of his vicious plan would have made Sen sick again if they had anything else in their stomach.

They tried to raise a hand but Valeska leapt atop them, pinning their arms to their sides with his thighs as he slammed his fists into Sen's jaw, their chest. Rearing back his hand, Valeska drove it into the side of their temple, and the world tilted, their face pounding with their heartbeat. Dropping their cheek into the puddle of vomit, Sen coughed, spitting up blood onto the bare feet of a stranger.

A figure stood above Valeska, who took no notice as he screamed down at them. She wore a long cloak of blues and ashen grays, no embroidery or bobbles upon the heavy fabrics. In the darkness, her familiar eyes born down into Sen. The line where her lips met was stained a deep blue, almost black in the night, and it spiderwebbed out into the veins of her chin and cheeks.

Sen opened their mouth, gurgling a weak, "P-please…"

"I'll kill you!" Valeska shouted, still unaware of the woman. "You ruined *everything*—"

Tears thickened his screaming; the villain dared to be upset that his plan of raping Lon did not end as he desired.

The woman standing above Sen bent lower. Her hair was tied underneath a veil wrapped to cover most of her neck, but they saw symbols painted into her skin as she drew close. Speaking without moving her blackened mouth, a voice echoed out of the cracks of the stone road.

Swear.

Were they dying? Sen's face went numb, one of their eyes swollen so tightly that the world darkened. They tried to speak to this messenger of death but blood and spittle choked them. Valeska shouted as the spray hit his tunic even though his knuckles were already shining red.

Her eyes searched Sen's broken features. In them sat a boundless darkness that drew them deeper. A memory surfaced as Sen laid there, numb with pain, of a dream where they were falling.

Swear.

An echo of the word settled like a feather on their chest. Valeska stood, huffing with exertion, and his body slipped through the mirage of the woman, her body wavering slightly at the disturbance.

Sen felt the word being pulled from their bowels. Scraping upward, it spilled out of their mouth with a shaky breath. Their mind struggled, screaming in protest.

To what were they swearing?

To whom?

The words filtered out, a hopeless plea for safety. "I swear."

The woman's stained mouth stretched into a grin. However gruesome it looked, warmth cascaded over Sen's body. Euphoria rushed through them as they laid on the stone road, aching and broken. They felt death creep forward slowly, and perhaps the woman came to ferry them off. Relief followed the blissful hum, their muscles loosening from their aching tenseness.

Screaming cut through the moment of quiet. Snapping open their good eye, Sen watched the robed woman pass her hand over Sen before raising it to Valeska.

Gaping, Sen scrambled to their knees, neck craned upward. Floating in the air above the city, Valeska thrashed against tendrils of magic. All around him shivered an orb of light; Sen noticed, too, that it covered themself and the robed woman. Her outstretched hand bore dark symbols of a language they did not recognize, the palm inked with a glowing circle with two parallel lines through it.

In his hovering orb, Valeska's screams were stripped of their broken echo. Sen did not know where to look—upon the woman gazing adoringly up into the sky, or to Valeska as he writhed, weightless, against the starlight?

Valeska's unwinding began with the threads of his clothing, and Sen's body froze in awe. Each thread unwove itself from its fixture as his shirt, his trousers, his small clothes. Even the leather of his shoes broke apart, dissipating into shimmers of nothingness until Valeska hovered above the world completely naked. His bare chest gleamed in the moonlight, his gaping mouth shaping noiseless shrieks as the tips of his arms were forced out to either side by an invisible hand.

Curling away like ribbon on the wind, the skin along his fingers and toes loosened, pulling away from the sinewy muscle underneath. Valeska's eyes went wide, his body struggling against the unraveling as his arms and legs became nothing more than bloody limbs in the moonlight. It continued up his torso, the ribbons of skin vanishing into dust, and Sen watched, mouth agape, as Valeska's shining white-blonde hair grew red with blood. His scalp peeled away, revealing the pink that covered his skull.

Whispering under her breath, the woman bent her wrist as though offering her hand for a kiss. Sen watched her mouth shape a single word before flicking her hand palm-up.

Inside the orb, the strands of Valeska's muscles untethered themselves from the binding of his bones. He shivered, still alive as his body was stripped layer by layer. Sen could not pull their gaze away from the horror, even as Valeska's intestines slipped out from under his ribcage and hit the invisible barrier of his spherical prison before turning to ash.

Only when his bones remained did the woman release her hold. Sen watched what was left of Valeska plummet to the earth, melding and taking a new form as it fell. Not a single bone hit the stone in a clatter, the skeleton hushing together silently to form a leatherbound volume as unassuming as the books of the Amalak.

When it struck the stone before the woman, she bent down to retrieve it. The pages glared white as she thumbed through them, inspecting the lining and texture of the parchment. Satisfied, she turned her gaze on Sen. Pressing the book against her chest, it disappeared inside herself with only a twitch of her robes. The disgraced heir felt another world press in closer as she took a careful steps towards them, one that smelt of the incense of their family shrine, and carried the pressure of unspoken burdens. Once more she stood over them, once more she gaze at them with a look of care mixed with impatience.

Sen opened their mouth. *Who are you? What's happening?* The questions perched on their tongue begged for answers, but the woman swiped her thumb across Sen's bloody forehead.

"Hark." The woman's voice slipped out of forgotten graves, unfurled from the flicking bodies of writhing earthworms. "Hark. *Hark*, for the Sleeping One awakens."

A twitch of pain shot through them from the point of her touch. Sen's soul dropped out of their body, disappearing into the stone below.

CHAPTER TWENTY-TWO

Agony in every movement, every breath. Dice's insides congealed, calcified, liquified, thickened again in her gut. Roaring pain sliced down from her knee to her ankle, a dancing heartbeat pounding in her thigh. The bone felt wrong, splinters in her muscle that shredded the meat when she twitched in feverish sleep.

Faces peered at her from the edges of half-consciousness, figures standing cloaked in shadows about the edges of the dim room. Evangeline stood among them, naked and rotting, her pale skin pitted where the decay grew most rancid.

At some point during her tossing, the specter walked over to stand above Dice. Evangeline's putrid mouth leaned down and kissed her slowly, the foulness depositing thick, tarlike darkness into Dice's sputtering mouth.

Evangeline meant to haunt her now, and Dice was unsure whether she hated the thought.

Vision fading back into the dim of fever, Evangeline's blurry figure receded. Dice felt the turning in her stomach, leaning over the side of the bed to vomit. A hand touched her back, familiar in its heaviness. Patting her shoulder, it helped her as Dice collapsed into the bed and drifted in the world between wakefulness and sleep. The figures watched over her in a parental way, their forms neither menacing nor angry. Even Evangeline's deathly white eyes looked on with a type of pity as Dice hallucinated Leonora pacing about the length of the cabin, her gray whisps of hair floating, caught on the wind. The edges of the woman spilled into the world, her figure hazy as she told Dice that the people of Stormshale might be broken, but at least they knew who they were.

"Unlike you," the woman muttered, voice shattering like fine glass as Leonora broke apart in the air.

Dice's throat, sticky with Evangeline's kiss, forced out the words, "You killed her."

"No." The woman frowned. "*You* did."

She saw many people who died by her hand waiting on the borders of shadows behind Evangeline. Shimmering with his strange blue-black blood, the silver-haired man whispered to one of the shades on the edges of her vision. The gills shined and flexed along the sides of his neck. When he stepped back into the darkness, the figure he spoke to remained, the scrawling symbols on their bare arms ringing with a song that had plagued Dice since birth.

Hark, the symbols echoed across the cabin. *Hark.*

"Hark." The word fell from Dice's lips like a lover's gasp. Rising out of the world of eerie medially, reality took solid form. The figures vanished, Evangeline's dead eyes the last thing to disappear as Dice rose from the sweat-drenched bedding.

Familiar maps hung on the wall opposite, the scrawl of Evander's handwriting marking which ports carried what, and who in those port cities owed him money. A desk sat under the haphazard display of parchment and notes, facing the rest of the cabin with the chair's back against the wall. An unlit lantern weighed down more sheafs of parchment, though the captain was missing from his usual brooding posture over them. Evander's cabin otherwise remained the same since she last saw it—since they last argued—with his shelf of books locked behind their wooden covers for when the water grew reckless.

Dice felt the evenness of the sea as she leaned forward, intending to move out of the bed when pain cut through her left thigh.

Wincing, she removed the damp blanket from its tangled mesh around her body. Someone, hopefully Evander, changed her out of the dregs she last remembered wearing. Leaving her in only a long tunic that hung from her starving frame, Dice pulled back the hem that was speckled with blood to reveal a massive bandage around her thigh. She remembered the silver man and his angry blade, stomach clenching as she considered the wrappings.

Uncovering the layers exposed a crusted but healing wound as long as her finger, red from discomfort but with no signs of infection. She prodded the swollen skin, hissing at the pain, when the memory of a knife sliding through her bone cut into her thoughts.

"You might not walk right again, but you'll live."

Evander stood at the open door, illuminated by the gray-blue light of the morning. Despite it being only a few turns of the season since she last laid eyes upon her adoptive father, the captain looked older, more weather-beaten and bent.

Dice figured she did not look much better as she covered the wound once more. Silent awkwardness pressed into the space, but Evander let out a breath of relief that shattered it. He stepped into the room like a man trying to feed a starving dog on the street.

Did he expect Dice to bite him as thanks for saving her life?

His tightly knit braid hung over his shoulder, the wrinkles set into his forehead knotting together as he leaned on the edge of his desk. It felt strange to be back in the room with him, back on the *Marksmen*. Lingering in the wood of the ship were the words of their last argument, and they floated around Dice like a mist.

"That fever almost took you," he started.

"I'm sorry," Dice muttered at the same time.

Evander's brows shot into his hairline. "That's… unexpected."

She frowned at him. "Well, all right. Don't get dramatic about it."

Opening his mouth, Evander then thought better of his words. Perhaps he simply took pity on her in her weak state.

With the haze of fever gone, Dice properly felt the stiffness in her limbs. Replaying in her mind, the events leading up to the darkness offered little: finding the strange man in the shack, the knife in her thigh, the sound of the ocean rising so loudly as she spilled his blood in the water.

His *blood*, which was not red with life but blue-green with something else, something more.

And a journal of symbols that shaped strange words in her mind.

Dice glanced up at Evander, whose gaze stayed on her since he stepped in the room. Recalling a gentle hand on her shoulder when she was sick, she figured the captain had split his time between commanding his ship and taking care of her.

Would he have done as much if he knew what happened in Stormshale?

"Wait a moment," Dice pinched the bridge of her nose. "How am I here? What happened?"

"I was hoping you'd tell me. That's a nasty wound." Evander nodded to her thigh. Crossing his arms, his voice thickened with worry. "I meant what I said about walking, Dice. If you can manage to get out of that bed, it won't be without a cane."

"*Grand.*" She tiffed sarcastically. "How'd you find me?"

Contrition brushed over her heart when she noted the exhaustion in his eyes. There the man stood after who knew how many nights of making sure a fever did not kill her, and Dice snapped at him.

He held his tongue again for a moment before answering. "We've been picking up a quick job or two as a ferry for questionable Esmarin nobles. Things've been getting worse on the mainland, so now anyone who can afford to is leaving for Sovil, Thantis, the Isles. I heard some've even booked passage to the Erewildes, though why any fool would go to that wilderness is beyond me." He shrugged. "We were crossing into the Port of Mann when we spied a dinghy. Then, behold, there you were muttering about a book with a hole in your leg. Which I hope you plan to explain?"

"The Port of Mann?" Dice's gaze flicked to the map behind Evander. That was a week of sailing from Stormshale. How had she *not* died before the *Marksmen* found her?

She shook her head, reeling. "Wait. A book?"

Evander lifted a shoulder. "You weren't making sense, Dice. I was worried there, for a good while."

Emotion tinted his voice. Evander did not like getting sentimental, but Dice was his kin in everything but blood. He liked his crew, even cared for those who had been with the ship since Dice's childhood, but in all the world the only family they had was each other.

"I'm sorry you left." Evander said lowly.

Dice picked at the edges of the blanket, feeling small under his gaze. A hand gripped her heart when she met his eyes, then quickly looked away. After all he did to help her, she was going to disappoint him again.

"As am I. But I meant what I said." A breath loosened in her chest. "I can't take the *Marksmen.* I can't take a crew that came on to follow you, and expect them to trust me just because I'm your kin."

Pursing his lips, Evander looked away. The heat of their argument pressed against her skin. Though it happened what seemed like an age ago, it was still tender to the touch.

Before, Evander said he did not trust anyone else with *The Jolly Marksmen.* He expected no one else to keep its name or its treaties with other ships. And after what Dice went through alone in Stormshale, and what was happening to her failing mind, she thought she was even less deserving of such an important legacy.

"I'll help whoever you want," she offered, as she had all those months ago. "I know how to talk with your partners, and I'll show them the ports. But I can't lead, Evander. I'm not a captain, I'm… not fit for it."

That part was true, at least.

Instead of arguing, her father simply bobbed his chin once. Peeling away from the desk, he averted his gaze all the way to the door to his cabin.

"I'll fetch your clothes, and a cane for you." A small smile tugged at his mouth when he finally met her eyes. "Rest up—I've had to keep Brutis and the others from barreling down the door. They've got quite the evening planned, if you're up for it."

Dice knew that the celebrating was more for the crew, and despite still feeling like she had been pummeled by a Sovilian berserker, she nodded. It was better than telling Evander the truth, or letting the rottenness of her guilt seep any further into their conversation.

Upon *The Jolly Marksmen* stomped, danced, and drank the only group of men Dice trusted. Each boasted his follies, yet none of them put her at risk since the moment Evander found her in the belly of the ship. From a babe, Evander's closest and oldest companions helped the floundering captain raise her, the stories of putrid cloth diapers and losing her on the supplies level more than they cared to admit flowing freely with her homecoming. Dice no longer felt embarrassed by them despite brightening red with shame as a young girl, instead adding her own memories. Recalling the time Crest brought her all the way up to the crow's nest just to forget her there moments later made everyone whoop with laughter.

During their tasks as ferrymen, Evander hired extra hands. Unfamiliar faces took the offered ale, listening to the stories with wide grins, and twins who were little more than skeletons played the pipe together as they stomped out jaunty beats for the evening. These people with their unfamiliar posture and distant gazes she watched from the corner of her eye, especially as she clacked defenselessly around the deck with her cane.

One of the new hands, a man who caught her quick glance and returned it with a lift of his chin in a dare, made her blood sing.

It felt like a tide being drawn back into the ocean.

It felt like the same prickle of inexplicable familiarity that coursed through her when first laying eyes upon the sullen creature in the shack.

On the side of his neck were scars like the man she killed—not scars, *gills*, she reminded herself. Disbelief clung to those memories, hope that it was all a delusion vanishing in her chest. Paranoia and confusion took its place, stringing along questions.

Did the new crewmate know the one she killed? Did he find her and join up as a hired hand while she was reeling from fever? What seemed the most puzzling was that, besides the scars along his neck, the man looked like any other seafarer. His skin was not prickled, nor his features palled and sickly. So, what was the difference between himself and the man in Stormshale?

Dua-Nythi. The Sea's Children. A myth to her right up until one of them stabbed a knife through her leg. Pieces of her old self refused to believe it, but after the gaps in time, and the goring of Evangeline's husband, Dice found her body harbored little energy to explain away the existence of an underwater race.

Evander would not believe her. The captain had an air permeated by his own superstitions, but people who breathed water and lived in cities beneath the ocean never made it to the table. Dice doubted there was any world out there where he listened when she told him one of those very creatures was aboard his ship.

As if knowing her thoughts, a small grin played at the Dua-Nythi's lips. Dice grimaced, planning at once to keep an eye on the fellow when someone swooped in from behind, stealing up her cane in gleeful pestering but catching her by the hip before she stumbled down onto her bad leg.

The first-mate had the decency to look regretful when she snapped a vicious look at him.

"Ass." She spat on the boards at his feet.

"Yellow-belly." Brutis set her down, proffering the cane. She snatched it back, the grimace not lasting long as her heart began to soften.

Brutis stood as tall as Evander but twice his width, his biceps the size of barrels. Dice's childhood was filled with stories about how he came from giant's blood, which she readily believed since as a toddler the man blocked out the sun. While Evander struggled to carve out a path as a father and a pirate, Brutis was there to hold her hand along the way.

"What sort of pirate jumps ship after being *offered* the damned thing?"

Dice hesitated, adjusting her grip on the cane. The affixture would take Dice a while to get used to, but needing assistance was common on a pirate ship. Her fellow brigands shined hooked hands and oiled peg legs made of silverwood, and they all laughed with her when she hobbled out of the cabin. Now, she was a *real* pirate, they said.

It also gave her something to do as she tried to think of a way to edge around Brutis's hurt tone. Brutis took on an air of severity when on deck, but his giant's blood danced through a soft heart.

"Usually, you bother with an angry note before you disappear." He said, bald head gleaming in the last burst of daylight.

Despite the laughter and drinking, the lighting of lanterns as the sun set and the music in the air, they crew glanced in her direction with hurt in their eyes. Leaving suddenly happened a lot with pirates, and more than once she ran off when Evander pressed her into a mold she did not fit, but this was the longest she ever stayed away. The men never planned to admit as much, but they missed her—and surrounded by the drunken comradery now, she realized how much *she* missed *them*.

"He pushed a little too hard this time. I didn't know what else to do."

The apology was invisible, but Brutis nodded understandingly. If Evander was Dice's father, this mountain of was her more lackadaisical uncle. Brutis seemed to feel things deeper than Evander, which made him easy to pick at but nonetheless a good friend.

A shiver of guilt tremored up her spine.

"I forgot something," she muttered, and swung around before he could see the tears in her eyes.

It was a perfect evening for a celebration, the crisp air growing warmer the further they got from the Esmarin coastline. Fat sails filled with wind groaned overhead, the sound a blanket of comfort as Dice clacked her way across the deck. Even the sea cascaded outwards like a mirror, blessedly flat and reflecting the spotted clouds so perfectly on its surface that the lone *Marksmen* appeared trapped between the skies of two worlds.

It was all *too* lovely. Rich wood beams underfoot, balusters, ropes, and lanterns swinging their orange light overhead, laughter mingling with the groan of the ship as it surged onward. Warm salt on the air, in her aching lungs. It pinpointed the blight within Dice, calling forth the strange dream where a darkness filled her to the brim. Maybe it was the lingering effects of the fever that made her uncomfortable, or perhaps the beauty of sailing was lost on her for good.

Avoiding Evander as he turned to watch her hobble into his cabin, Dice shut out the happy world behind her. Deep in her belly woke a painful stirring that cramped her gut. Her heartsong slammed against her chest, daring to break open her ribcage at any moment. She placed her palm flat against the thumping spot, hoping to stop its escape, but it just reminded her of the bard in her dream.

Breathing deeply through her nose, Dice felt the world press in. When her eyes flashed open, she hallucinated the entrails of the gored man tangling around her feet, the blood slick on her hands.

Filled with helpless rage, she threw the cane down and squeezed her eyes shut.

Pulsing up from the floorboards hummed the song of the ocean. Dice forced her eyes open, fingers curling in her hair in an attempt to soothe the panic in her throat. Her eyes dragged over to Evander's desk but she knew what waited there before she saw it resting on the corner, stacked atop a pile of letters.

The journal the Dua-Nythi wanted so badly that he tried to kill her to keep it secret, its pages of strange symbols and words without voices that spilled out of its pages, emerged from her memories into the solid world. Like a horrid, strange gift it sat there, waiting to be touched, to be opened. She thought of her fevered vision where he spoke into the shadows. Had the veil thinned enough for him to pass the strange thing off to her?

Dice limped over to the desk, not feeling the pain in her leg from the shock of the journal's materialization. A thrill of excitement mingled with worry sang in her chest as she stood over its plain leather cover. Fingers stroking its rough edges proved it true, solid. Slipping a hand in to open the book to a random page, the pad of her finger moved over the ridges in the parchment, the smoother lines of ink.

It *followed* her.

Picking it up, the journal weighed more than a regular volume, almost as though it once had a life of its own. A new note collided with the ocean's song in her mind, changing the singular humming to a sound like the ringing of steel as it was freed from its scabbard. Energy climbed up Dice's forearms, an eager trill bringing an unassuming smile to her lips.

As she flicked through the pages, the tinkering song growing louder, a headache started to throb upwards from the base of her neck. She rubbed it absentmindedly. The heaviness of the journal was hard to manage with her one hand, her grip slacking awkwardly, and the sudden throat-clearing behind her almost caused it to tumble from her hands.

"You're missing the revelry."

Just as she knew the journal waited for her on the edge of Evander's desk, she felt the Dua-Nythi's gaze settle on her back. Dice turned to him slowly, bracing herself on the desk as she glanced across the floor at her cane. At the same moment, she snapped the journal shut. It sat in her hand like a canon ball, but she refused to free it from her grasp as the stranger leaned against the open doorway. For his part, he did not walk further into the room, but his coal gaze prodded her still.

He wore a slack vest without a shirt, and billowing trousers held up by a long ruby sash. A gold band encircled his left bicep—Sovilian merchants wore similar jewelry as a way to mark their station. Those with bronze or silver cuffs were lower in the caste and remained along the docks or poorer areas of the city to sell their wares. Any person decorated with the gold ones, some encrusted with refined obsidian and emeralds, pitched their stalls within the actual markets, or even sold directly to their Queen.

Dice thought he peacocked a bit too much to be a pirate. He was too pretty, with thick dark lashes and kohl eyeliner to help protect against the glare of the sun. She did not like the way he stared, his lowered lids observing her like a sweet dessert set down before him after a rich meal.

With a lazy smile, his dark eyes observed the journal. Though he tried to hide the flicker of recognition, Dice watched the muscles in his shoulders tighten.

"You must be *fresh*," she bit, "since you think you can just walk into the captain's cabin."

"Yes." He smiled, his incisors sharper than expected. "It's been a while since I've been on a ship. I forget the rules."

Lilting his voice was an accent Dice could not place—certainly not one local to Sovil, which made her question his threads.

Opening her mouth, ready to make another snide comment, he cut her off.

"I'm not good at pretending like you, Dice. I don't like all your people's rules, and I can't block out the sea's music. Then again," he sighed, disappointment lingering there, "I don't *want* to. Perhaps you'll come to understand why you shouldn't. Perhaps then you'll make it up to me for killing my friend."

Dice palled, her breath shallow. *Like me?*

No, that was not possible. Was she still in the depths of fever? Nothing else made sense, for how else did he know about the song in her mind? Dice told no one, not even Evangeline, about the music that followed her since she was a child. Somehow, Dice always knew it needed to remain a secret, yet there stood the proof of myths, gills shining along his neck and his egotistical smile rupturing the last of her crumbling foundation.

"How did—" She shook her head, blinking at him stupidly. Then, the question that made her heart rumbled: "You hear it, too?"

A beat of uncertainty passed over his features. Something about the way she voice the question surprised him, which lead Dice to believe that he did not have a cacophony of low, mournful humming but something softer.

His gaze, though, was sharp as he said, "As loud as your blood, and my friend's."

Before Dice could gather herself enough to make sense of his response, he continued with a swarthy, mocking grin. "Welcome back to the *Marksmen*, Dice. I look forward to learning more about you."

Swears rang out in Dice's mind but none of them managed to get past her lips. Gaping, she only managed to blink stupidly at the Dua-Nythi as he nodded once more before taking his leave. He even shut the door behind him, giving Dice privacy as she lost her grip on the journal. A heavy *thunk* rang out as it hit the floor but she barely managed leaning against the desk before she followed suit.

She thought that the Revkyn were the strangest part of this world. What was worse than living a life where one must survive off the blood of others, unable to bask in the sun? If Revkyn did not exist, Dice figured it would have been near impossible to believe in the Dua-Nythi.

Even so, all her assumptions came down, a tower crumbling around her. It was too much, too fast: the gored man and the horn from the deep, the stripping of her faculties bit by gruesome bit, the journal with its otherworldly music, and now a Child of the Sea, aggravated that she killed his friend.

But…

Dice looked to the closed door, heartbeat finally leveling out. For the first time since Stormshale, there was a possibility of answers. Even if new questions peeked out of the darkness, she had an opportunity to find a compass through the dark.

She bent down slowly, careful with her bad leg as she grabbed the heavy journal. It was difficult, but she tried not to think of the flicker of hope, for if he heard the music of the ocean and proved it did not affect him, then maybe she was not lost.

The Dua-Nythi recognized the journal. He *knew* this book, so did that mean he understood its symbols? Was it possibly written in his own language?

It pulsed against her palm as if in answer. Reluctantly placing it on Evander's desk, Dice lowered herself into the highbacked chair. The pain in her leg helped to sharpen her focus, which was good. She needed to figure out a way to not only get the stranger to work with her on actually answering her myriad of questions, but do so in a way that avoided any suspicion from Evander, kept the journal private, and the crew safe.

The less people involved in the deterioration of her mind, the better.

CHAPTER TWENTY-THREE

Trilabold gleamed silver with late morning sunlight when Neoma docked at its harbor. A sickly-sweet perfume filled her lungs as she stepped off the ferry, turning in a full circle to admire the woodwork of the docks. Great beams of silverwood curved into archways at the end of each pier, the carvings of wood nymphs and Dua-Nythi dancing in waves so detailed that they might leap from the fixtures at any moment. One nymph stood as tall as Neoma, supporting the base of a carved beam with hands raised in laughter and hair spilling out in a curling ripples around her head. Leaves with impossibly small veins hung from her hair, and Neoma's hand stretched out to stroke the marksmanship in awe. Following the arch upwards, a fat, smiling face sat at the highest point. She noted the same jolly carving decorating the archways next to the pier like wards against misfortune.

Talaya settled the payment with the ferryman, getting their tickets marked for their return at the end of the day before she followed. "This is the only place to go if you want to find the fabrics they sell in the Market in Dunhet for half the price," Talaya said. Slung over her shoulders was a satchel prepared to carry her eclectic finds. "Even a highborn can't spot the difference."

"What's that smell?" Neoma's excitement mirrored a child's as she faced the city. The docks immediately deposited ferries into the throng of long, tall buildings that, though made mostly of silverwood, were painted dazzling colors of blues and greens. Bronze fixtures caught the morning light and glowed like fire stolen away by metal.

She wished more than anything that Koa had been able to see it.

"I'll assume you're talking about the sap, if not the food." Talaya grabbed Neoma's hand, her warm palm keeping the chilly thought of grief at bay as she guided them into the city. "It lingers after they fell the trees. Did you know, the woodspeople have to wear special gloves and practically oil themselves up before moving any lumber? *That's* how sticky the sap is! Absolutely ruinous. Two, please."

Talaya drew them up to a stall that smelt of fried sugar. The man behind took Talaya's money with a smile before passing over two sticks towered high with balls of dough sprinkled with flakes of sea salt. Neoma bit into hers, surprised at the softness inside despite the crunchy, sugary shell.

Relishing the treat, she was content to listen to her cousin's rendition of Trilabold's lumber practices. Talaya's voice lilted with the crowd, her hand grasping fast to Neoma's so as to not lose her.

Every doorway, whether to a merchant's storefront, a home, or a bank, showed off extensive woodwork made from deft hands. Molded like clay into odd, twisting shapes, the fixtures climbed up the side of the homes or peered at them from windowsills.

A massive wood carving of ivy drew Neoma up short with a gasp. She studied every leaf as it climbed up the side of a building otherwise made of sandstone, swearing the fixture even twitched in the breeze. Another building made of mahogany planks advertised its wares with a twining dragon hanging above the entryway. A bronze sign hung from its open maw that read *Diverse Assortments: Sovilian Rarities and Trade* in three languages underneath the Common Tongue.

Peeking in, Neoma gazed at the stalls of people with skin as varied as her family's, but with finer black hair. One woman nearby gave a demonstration on how to properly string up a paper contraption that flew on the wind, its ribbon tail flapping above her head. Talaya urged them onward, saying that if Neoma found those carvings and merchants along the dockside of the city to be beautiful, wait until Seawake's Circle.

For the first time in what felt like an age, Neoma thought of Koa in a way that did not immediately shroud her in sadness. Looking at the brightly painted woodwork of Trilabold *did* cause her to feel regret at not having brought him to its shores, and the life teeming around her made Neoma think of how short his was cut. Even so, the joy seeping out of the faces of the children awed by the demonstrations of toys, as well as the laughter of women as they sat at little tables outside of tea houses, wove a pattern of delight into the tapestry hanging from her shoulders.

It could be that knowing how quickly joy might be cut short made Neoma relish Talaya's hand in hers, not balk in anger at the birds who whistled their happy tunes. Some private moments might be harder to carry, but her burden felt lighter when she knew a cousin or aunt or grandmother might be around the corner, ready to offer conversation or communal silence to share space with her pain.

She resigned herself some nights ago to the understanding that her days may shift evermore between *good* and *bad*. That morning she woke from a dream where she saw Koa grown and walking the shoreline towards her. She felt her heart cracking in her chest like ice underfoot when she rose with the foreboding sense that something was wrong, that he was a child again and calling out to her in the night. Talaya found her in the early dawn making tea with eyes rimmed red with tears.

Her cousin's invitation for Neoma to join her on her quest to Trilabold was easy to accept. Talaya walked the streets as a local. With her dreaded hair stacked beneath a floral bolt of silk, and her brazen open-faced dress belted with studded leather, she appeared to have grown up in the colorful streets of Trilabold instead of Saltshore's harsher beaches. With her transitioning into the bolder clothing that feminine people wore, she wrapped her true self in vibrantly stained fabrics that made her happiness shine outward. It touched the face of the busker even as she shoed him out of their path, and the perfumer who tried to offer richly scented oils that Talaya called overpriced. Both of them only waved and smiled, Talaya's confidence spilling out to make the world brighter. It even urged Neoma to walk with more of a sway in her step, her plain canvas shoes dancing across clouds instead of cobblestones.

"You seem happier." Neoma remarked suddenly. Memories of a younger version of her cousin, awkward in her limbs as the stubble came in and her voice changed pitch, seemed pale compared to the woman before her now.

Talaya squeezed her hand, beaming. "I am."

In the center of the only city on the island of Menthis stood an altar to Khiro, the local deity of the sea. While Neoma's family called them Ocean, the deity went by hundreds of names. Some of the stories wove Khiro and the Duathi together, since the ancient deity's holy animal was a tentacled beast as large as a ship. In the stories, Khiro hitched the beast to their ship without sails and steered it through the Seas.

Neoma marveled at how different cities told varying stories of what might be the same entity as she read the bronze inscription mounted to the basin encircling the altar. Glistening in the water were trinkets, and prayers sealed to little stones with wax. While she felt undecided as to whether or not she worshipped one of the faces of a singular sea god, or if they were completely different entities altogether, a warmth passed through her as she tossed a coin into the basin.

Khiro's ambiguous stone features honored her little gift, even if she was not their child. One of their stone hands lifted out to the sea with the palm up, marvelously carved water spilling over, as if anointing whoever stood beneath.

Seawake's Circle bustled with people *intent* on spending their coin. Only food stalls took up the walkways while merchants pitched their booths under covered awnings. The buildings were set back away from the Circle to allow more space for the market and the ebbing throng of people.

Neoma followed her cousin easily now that the crowd did not push or shove at her. She kept pace with Talaya's longer stride as they wove through the covered market, picking up bright fruit to smell their ripeness or running gentle fingers over gorgeous bolts of cloth. With their stomachs growling, and Talaya complaining of needing to rest her shoulder, they found a food stall that had seating next to its bowl-sized cookfire.

Setting her bag down in her lap, Talaya rubbed her shoulder. Her eye roved for anyone who might try to swipe it, but Neoma doubted any thief wanted the burgundy fabric and cheap trinkets that her cousin bought for their looks, not their usefulness.

The owner of the food stall brought over a tray of fried fish on a bed of sea kelp, handing them each a wood bowl once Talaya gave him the proper coin.

"It's not the best, and it could do with salt," Talaya warned. She wrapped a piece of the fish in a long strand of kelp before popping it in her mouth. A look of complete satisfaction wafted over her face. "But the fish is cooked to *perfection*."

Neoma grinned, eating with a full heart. They both sat in silence for a while as they stuffed their bellies, waving down a person who walked the length of the Circle holding a tray of dried sugar-dusted peaches when their fish disappeared.

"So." Talaya chewed one of her slices thoughtfully. "How are you, really?"

Hattash nearly over, Neoma's family rightly assumed that she was not leaving. During most of the month, Calily or Sulien were her fast advisors for those weepier nights. The others respectfully kept their questions to themselves, even though they were undoubtedly the same as Neoma's. *Why was a boy so young so desperate to end his life? Were there any signs that Neoma missed, or people who drove him to doing such a thing? He was only twelve, so what darkness made its home in Koa so quickly?*

Things might have been different if Urias talked to her, but the day of Koa's drowning he stood in another world, unreachable. With every pass of the sun Neoma felt the answers drawing further away. She expected a letter to arrive at Kairdwillo eventually, yet Urias seemed to accept her departure in all its permanence. Sooner than she wanted, the scalding heat of her grief became a singeing ember, a healing sore tender enough to ache when her clothing brushed it. It had not festered, and to that she credited her family, yet another sensation rested beneath the wound.

Koa's name stirred her resolve, only barely shrouded by the pain of loss, a part of her refusing to believe him dead. Her spirit still resisted its new reality, urging her to keep her eyes on the sea in case Ocean presented to her the resolution for which she prayed.

"It feels strange." Neoma turned to the people who rushed by them or walked leisurely, enjoying the bustle of the market. "I keep thinking that when I go home, I'll have to tell Koa to bathe before dinner. Then, I remember."

Talaya nodded, not in understanding but in a way that meant she was *listening*.

Neoma focused on the tartness of the dried peace, the crystals of sugar melting on her tongue. "There's a piece of myself I'll never have returned to me. That's how I feel it is to give birth. I made him—Urias did what he did, but I *made* Koa from my bones, my blood. Sea, to me."

"Sea, to thee." Talaya murmured the phrase under her breath. The blessing fell over pregnancies and births, but was for any great physical change in one's life. Neoma recalled giving such blessings to Talaya as she began the journey of consuming the root that grew her breasts.

"I know I'll be alright," she admitted with a shock of guilt, "but it hurts to know one day I won't remember his face, or his laugh. All I'll have within me is the love left over for him."

"Not for Urias?"

Neoma shook her head. Picking at the leftover slices of her peach, she felt her dismissal of him under her ribcage. Beastly and stiff, it pushed against the softness of her heart, willing that she voiced its existence.

"I don't think I've ever loved Urias in the way I should've."

Talaya launched a peach slice at Neoma, hitting her squarely on the forehead. With another slice in hand, prepared for assault, Talaya pointed at her cousin. "There is no such thing as *should have*. You're just making more space for other peoples' opinions. You loved him to the best of your abilities."

"Did I?"

Neoma wondered if there stood a path somewhere in the past that she might have taken, instead of one out of the hundreds she chose to walk. She let Urias court her after their drunken romp, she accepted his marriage token because it seemed right. Not just *right*, but her cousins were marrying or starting their families; she felt like the family expected her to settle down, too. All of those things were tinged with the scent of regret, but was it really regretful if it gave her Koa?

Another thought pricked at her mind, one of a smiling laundress who beamed like the sun.

Talaya was already looking at Neoma when she lifted her gaze, sensing another question there. Her cousin lifted her chin, propping it on her folded hands.

"How… did you know something was different?" Neoma's voice was swallowed up by the market, but Talaya heard her perfectly clear.

Her cousin glanced almost mournfully down at the forgotten dessert. "I knew before I *understood*. I knew that my body didn't fit my spirit, but I didn't have any idea that it could be different. Our family is accepting, that's not what I'm saying, it's just… so hard to accept such a violent correction of yourself. I can have all the support in the world, but changing the way I viewed my body, my identity? That can only ever be *my* responsibility.

"When I knew I wasn't a man, I had to figure out what being a woman meant for *me*. So, cousin," Talaya reached across the small table to take Neoma's sugary fingers in hers. "What is it you're really trying to ask me?"

"I… don't know."

Desire pushed up from a cool, quiet part of her heart. Under its surface whispered a reality Neoma was not sure she felt prepared to face.

Not yet.

Talaya noted this with a small grin. She kissed her cousins fingers before releasing them. "I know what you need—to get out."

Neoma balked, waving her hands at the crowd around them. The movement also dissipated their serious tones from before. "What's this, then?"

"No, no. I don't mean a place you can just go to on the ferry, returning whenever you feel homesick or bored. I mean out, like to… Who knows, maybe Sovil?"

"Sovil? Really." Neoma tried to imagine her in the throngs of beautiful, talented people who boasted lineages derived from warlords and goddesses.

"Well," Talaya looked remise, "certainly not *Esmar*."

Thinking about being an ocean away in any direction made Neoma's stomach cramp. She must have looked ill, because Talaya made a face like she smelt something sour.

"Alright, not Sovil."

Together, they finished another round of candied peaches as they walked the rest of the Circle, fantasizing about the many countries neither of them ever saw before. They talked about the fights in the Sovilian queendom, where champions lived like royals, and the unmarried men and women and elected eunuchs in Thantis who wove the finest sheets high up in their mountain villages. Talaya found another strip of fabric sold at a discount because of its fraying edges, voicing her plans to make her mother a new headscarf as a nameday gift.

Though she did not intend to buy anything while in Trilabold, Neoma convinced herself to part with her coin over a thin silver bracelet. It shined like starlight against her black skin, and stamped across its surface were the tiniest etchings of waves. She might have gotten another to match it, but then Talaya grabbed her arm, ashen with fear.

"We're going to miss our ferry!"

Scrambling through the crowd, apologizing to every person they bumped or pushed through, the women screeched with laughter as they became not bodies but dark streams of color and midnight skin, jangles of seashell beads and bracelets. Neoma's heart felt light as they tumbled up the plank and dropped messily onto the deck of the ferry, earning themselves a disgruntled frown from the ferryman. Their cackling, breathless glee was the music for their departure as the sweet, sappy smell on the air mingled with the briny salt of the ocean.

The boat ride home did not stop consistently like it did that morning, the islands surrounding the edges of Lesser Syvon moving past in vacant sandbanks and blurs of dune colored homesteads. Con-Quary whisked by on their right and every dockmaster, captain, sailor, and thief seemed to be shouting orders. The women leaned against the railing of the ship, the spray of the waves far enough to be only a gentle kiss of salt against their faces as they moved along the coast.

A long ship made of ashy white wood caught the breath in Neoma's lungs, the flag drifting lazily in the breeze confirming her shock.

Revkyn only docked in the cities when absolutely necessary. Nowhere, not even Lesser Syvon, suffered the blood-eaters for exceedingly long. She heard a rumor out of Con-Quary that once a governor was late to overseeing the docking of a Revkyn boat, and as a result multiple dockhands went missing before his arrival. Each boat carried a different crew indifferent to continent or king, but their ships were required by the Confluence to bear the same flag. This order came from the governing heads of Greater and Lesser Syvon Ages ago, yet no Revkyn ship dared to be without the maroon flag hanging from its mast when they made port.

"I think you should buy a ticket on one of them, or see if they need a cook."

At first Neoma thought Talaya meant the bone colored ship before realizing her cousin gazed out over the rest of the dockyard. She sighed heavily, pressing her stomach against the railing to look at her reflection. The waves broke apart her features, giving her a crown of seafoam.

"I'm starting to think you hate me," she teased.

Talaya smacked her arm. "How dare you. I *love* you. That's why I'm telling you to leave."

Neoma groaned, feeling helpless under her cousin's beseeching stare. But she would be a liar if she argued that the thought of exploring the world did not fill her with the thrill of anticipation.

"You don't have to go now. I'm only saying," she waved her hand out towards the sea, "there are other horizons."

The sun beamed, a faraway candle in the sky. She wondered what magic caused it to rise in the morning and fall at night, thinking how the same power must course through the ocean as the water swallowed up the golden coin every evening.

What stood beyond that white-blue line splitting the sky and the sea? Was there a point at which they met?

Talaya's words planted something in the soft soil left over from her other life. A new world stood at her feet, one where she carried the remainder of motherhood on her shoulders. Hidden were her next steps, still her heart pulled her forward, drawn by that unmistakable thread of hope. Something hooked itself in the soft flesh, tugging painfully, begging her not to draw so deeply into the comfort of her family that she forgot to live.

She looked at Talaya. Her cousin smiled, sensing the shift of realization, and placed a hand on Neoma's upper back. Warmth spread through her shoulder blades as they gazed out over the sparkling ocean.

CHAPTER TWENTY-FOUR

She smelt of the fragrant blue lilies bobbing their starburst petals along the beaches of his youth. Such small, frail things surrounded by the prickling stems that protected them from gulls, facing off against the onslaught of crackling waves. Ballads of long dead champions told tale of how the flowers sprouted where lovers died in each other's arms, their blood washed blue as the waves consumed their decaying embrace.

She smelt of these flowers as he kissed her, the scent of petals, of lingering death, fraying the ends of his unwilling senses, and when her hand lifted to his face his every muscle recoiled from the frozen touch.

"*You shy away from your lover?*"

Aletta's voice split, a deeper one underneath that shaped her cracking, blackened mouth. The second voice spoke a heart's beat quicker, a slow dance, a ribbon in the wind.

Wrapping her soft hand firmly around his wrist, Aletta forced Pelagios into a submissive posture on the bed. Darkness pervaded the room, the stench of gutted fish, of petals left to become blackened stems, clogging his every pore. Long tendrils of hair wisped over his face, writhing snakes that covered his mouth. Aletta hovered above him without touching his body, suspended in the darkness as her fragile nails bit into his wrists and broke under the pressure. Her open maw dropped unnaturally low, the muscles in her jaw unable to support the bone.

Aletta pressed herself out of the darkness above Pelagios, who struggled against her grip as she kept his arms pinned above his head. Foulness wafted from her sullied mouth, the scent of retribution.

His own voice barked down from that rotten gullet, Aletta's mournful screaming rising underneath. "*Don't pretend to be coy, whore! You have begged me to take you!*"

The screeching roused him, the sound fracturing the dream and ringing into the bleary reality around Pelagios. Blinking against something wet that spilled out of his hairline, he shivered violently. Dread pulsed up from the base of his spine, weakening the muscles in his legs when he looked around him at the soft firelit glow of the king's chambers.

Resting next to Aletta's rotting corpse was Einar. His long, brown hair spilled across his pillow, his sleeping shirt bunched underneath his armpits. One muscular arm rested on his exposed stomach, the other drawn protectively underneath Aletta's bruised, veiny head. Locks of her hair were missing, and her half-lidded eyes snapped open to gaze up at Pelagios.

Stumbling backwards, the old man dropped the knife poised in his hands overhead. When it landed safely on the rug, his now free hand reached out to brace against the bedpost.

Aletta's eyes remained closed. If not for the pitted spots where the decay already sank the tissue of her skin, she could be asleep. The smell reminded him of gutted piglets, but Pelagios knew it a hundreds times over from his years of stepping over splayed bodies and intestines curling in the mud.

He braced himself, a slippery hand over his chest.

Surprised by his nakedness, Pelagios looked down as his wiry body. Slicked with blood, the dark, fresh stuff glistened in the low light of the fire. His hands scoured his body, heart galloping as his prodding fingers searched for the telltale signs of impalement. He touched his head, looking for a gruesome cut, but he came away unmarred.

Terror stabbed into his heart as he shuffled away from the king's bedside, the shock of what he was about to do making a crater in his chest. Pelagios bent down, lifting the knife from where it fell, his feet slipping on the flagstone as he moved. His body did not fall far, but his bare hip screamed out in pain as it thumped against the floor.

On the bed, Einar stirred.

Pelagios knew what it looked like, his bloodied body and wildness. How might he convince Einar that he was *not* going to stab a knife through the stomach of Esmar's king?

After a long draw of silence, the old man felt confident that Einar remained deep asleep. He rose, quickly scurrying out of the king's bedchamber with fear sinching ever tighter around his throat. Pelagios ran all the way to his rooms, shoeless steps coming down hard on the stone as he careened through the shadowed portions of the hall. It must be deep into the night or early into the morning, for only the torches along the main halls were lit.

He sensed another presence in the darkness behind him, walking with the easy gait of a predator that knew its prey had no chance of escape. Even when he slammed the door to his rooms shut behind him, tossing the knife into his ashen fireplace, Pelagios felt the concealed monster pacing the length of the room.

Shaking, his muscles tensing fiercely, Pelagios entered the small washroom after swiveling his head to make sure no one lurked in the threshold beyond. He bathed his face in the shallow basin, throwing the water against his chest to try and rid himself of the crusting blood.

Blood never startled him or made him uneasy, but the uncertainty of *whose* blood gave him pause. His nightmarish vision filled him with the rhythm of unease, heart pounding in his throat. The water turned a brackish pink as he attempted to clear away an unnamable sin, his broken reflection scolding him before his fists broke it apart in the water.

The stranger arrived on horseback. Cowled in a long robe of crushed blue velvet, its emblems of fish stamped in silver embroidery, they glowed against the harsh murkiness of dirty snow piles. Knights sat at the top of the battlements next to archers who drew their bows, each awaiting a call that either meant assault, or admittance. Beneath the unexpected guest patiently stood a mare with glowing caramel hair saddled in maroon leather. Even from the slitted archer's windows one noted the richness of the visitor's ensemble, and together the horse and rider created a tableau of spring against the wastes of snow behind them.

When the herald instructed the bedecked stranger to announce themselves, they only responded by lifting their arm out of the circle of their cloak. Their risen hand boasted a glistening cobalt diamond on its middle finger, and a note.

"I have been summoned by a member of court..." Lifting his gaze, the stranger revealed the weathered but handsome features of a cleanshaven face. "I am here to take council with your king."

After a startled pause, the herald about to state that no such command passed to him, there was a shuffling of iron. One of the counselors was announced, and Kana rushed out of the throng of curiously awaiting knights and archers. Dressed in deer skin and furs, Kana braced her gloved hands against the icy stone banister.

"Let him in," she ordered once her eyes landed on the folded parchment in the stranger's hands. When there was pause, she shouted the order with wide-eyed authority.

Tucking his hand back underneath his cloak, the stranger watched the drawbridge lower before him, unimpressed but smiling politely at its massive structure. Kana scrambled down the steps of the tower, slipping on the gathering ice and barely catching herself as she fled to met the stranger in the mosaic courtyard.

He was already dismounted when she arrived, his hands fast to the reigns of his horse despite the stableboy trying to shelter the beast. When Kana scuffled into the chamber, his sea green eyes slid carefully to observe her heavy breath and flurried cloak. His polite smile held despite obviously finding the stableboy irksome, but something akin to interest—or *hunger*, she was never certain as a woman in Einar's court—made it shudder.

"Go." Kana ordered the boy, who eventually slinked off but not without a backwards glance at the stranger.

The man inclined his head. Curls black as Kana's skin tapered off just below his plain jaw, flecks of snow melting into their darkness. His cloak fanned out around him, long enough to drag on the floor like a king's, and his winter trousers were tucked into boots swaddled in gray furs. His body was lit from beneath the skin, turning him the bronze color of a low fire's shadows.

Kana had not expected the corresponding mage to be so impeccably dressed, or so handsome, taking a moment to shake away her previous imaginings. She thought him a creature of dank and darkness since the descriptions from her man *before* he vanished spoke of a cavern in the ground. As such, she did not trust this mage, however attractive, since her runner was still missing. Yet, Kana knew working alongside the stranger might justify the loss.

"I apologize." The stranger gave a short bow. "I gave no inclination of my arrival other than a vague statement. I hope this didn't disrupt the court too much."

The councilwoman shook her head. Flicking aside a tiny braid that came loose from her rushed topknot, Kana returned his politeness with a tilt of her head. "It's alright, there was no—"

“My proclivities align with honesty, Councilwoman.” The mage lifted a hand to gently pat the neck of his steed. “I work best when the knowledge I’m given is right and true.”

Kana frowned. Dealing with enough interruption from her fellow council members as well as the king, she flexed her gloved hands at the disregard. She understood his meaning though, choosing to keep her tone cool as she replied.

“Yes, it *was* a problem. We’ve not yet figured how to tell His Majesty that a mage was arriving. You’ve rushed us. Now, it’s... dangerous.”

He gave her a true smile this time. Reaching his eyes, it crinkled their corners. *It wasn’t before?* his smile inquired, but his mouth shaped other words.

“I’m mindful of this, Councilwoman. If it’s easier to tell them that I’ve made an unprompted appearance, I promise to handle the weight of whatever the decision may be.”

Doubtful. Kana wanted to argue, but worry-laden anticipation pressed against her ribcage. Gaelis being bludgeoned to death simply because he could not command the queen to be well still sat in the forefront of her mind. Nights whisked her to sleep to the sound of Einar’s fist cracking his skull with his gauntleted hands. Moving in the court felt to her like a dance where the stone around her was littered with bear traps. One improper move and she became immobile, ruined. *Dead.*

Whatever happened inside the throne room determined the Council’s next steps. If Einar did not blame his counselors and kill them for treason, then they might actually be able to save Esmar.

Everything hinged on how their king received the mage.

“We’ll need to announce you.”

The mage’s gaze, which never left her, sparkled with a thread of pleasure.

Kana swallowed, feeling that he watched the motion in her throat. “There are no letters between us now to dimmish your name, after all.”

A bark of a laugh escape him, luminous. “Quite right, Councilwoman. I am Avenir of the Silverfish.”

“Well,” she grinned, “that explains your robe. You’re free to call me Kana in private. Titles—”

“Protect us.”

The odd statement brushed away her annoyance at being interrupted. Looking over Avenir, she watched as the deep of his eyes turned stormy in warning. The violence hidden in his gaze did not seem directed at her, but at the gathering shade. Sunlight hid behind gray clouds, its descent noted by the deep purple of night that climbed up from the cracks in the stone. Servants arrived to begin lighting the torches on the walls around the mosaic, dowsing them in golden light tinged with purple. The shade behind Avenir did not seem as crowded, or threatening. In fact, simply standing across from him made the thickness which pervaded Carn-Duhl wait along the edges of light.

Avenir broke the observant moment with gentle seriousness. "I don't mean to offend you by using only your title. In small words, it's a superstition of mine."

As if drawn forward by a glamour, Kana took a step closer. A wide space still remained between them, but even so, she felt the shadows slip further away.

The mage must have seen the questions in her gaze, the curiosity dancing there, for he then brought on the politely smiling façade. "Now, toward destiny."

"What of your horse?"

Kana rushed to fall in step beside the mage as he suddenly turned towards the maw of the entrance—as though he knew where they needed to be.

He glanced at his mare over his shoulder, indifferent. "She'll find her way, soon enough."

As they plunged into the bowels of Carn-Duhl, the councilwoman felt the depth of night part around them. For the first time in years, ease settled over her heart, releasing the tension in her shoulders. It would be all right.

It *had* to be all right.

CHAPTER TWENTY-FIVE

Whatever pressed in along the twilight of shadow and torchlight shivered in restlessness. Pelagios sensed his unfamiliar victim peering out from beyond, enshrouded, waiting. He knew that the body may never turn up, for the marshlands concealed numerous victims. Since the sea's reclamation of the land, it proved a favorable way to dispose of one's problems.

Knowing his own skill with the blade, Pelagios felt uncertain about the amount of blood on him the previous night. There must be a corner in the mountain hiding away the massacre, withering away to feed tittering vermin.

Still, this peering seemed different, the intention hidden by a pervasive edge. Pelagios intuited the force of the shadows but as he walked the long hall that deposited him in the antechamber of the throne room, they parted easier than before. They did not blacken out the doorways or the spaces between the torches, nor did disembodied whispers thicken the air.

Something within the shadows *changed*. Concealed hands unwove the darkness, restitching the hems of night to cloak Carn-Duhl in a robe no less foreboding but quieter as it swished along the stone floor. Pelagios arrived before the massive doors of the throne room, surprised to find Riven standing in his court finery. The slate councilor's robe was pinned neatly across his shoulders by an iron ring, his House's pin of a silver halfmoon underneath. His tangled beard finally met a comb, the braids and charms woven into it shining brightly against the ruddy tendrils.

He looked over the old man in a manner of dissatisfaction. "Is that any way to meet a mage?"

The general faltered, righting himself quickly. *A mage?*

Their armor groaning, the knights by the door gave one another a suspicious look. As if in answer to the wordless questions, Kana and a well-dressed stranger pierced the veil of darkness. Pelagios' eyes settled on the handsome but plain features, sea green eyes snapping to meet his own inquisitive stare.

"Gentlemen," Kana beamed, though a feverish doubt touched her eyes. "This is Avenir of the Silverfish."

She appeared relieved, but cautious. Her outdoor cloak fell from her shoulders as she folded it neatly over her forearm. Avenir smiled at them both, crows feet in the edges of his startling gaze.

Vines of hesitation reached up from Pelagios' tailbone, twining around his spine. The stranger made his proper bows towards the general and the other advisor, but the old man knew the air of a performer when he stood amongst one. However lighter the air seemed, this Avenir was too elegantly dressed to be a mage living in what his runner called a *badger's den.*

"Where is Damalis?"

Riven, after observing the surprise guest for a moment, answered Kana. "He got your summons before myself, and went to prepare Einar for the arrival of a guest. However, he didn't specify if he'd be sharing with the king exactly what *kind* of visitor we're having. We're lucky we have a moment to prepare at all."

Avenir placed a hand over his chest in apology. "This is my mistake alone. I was vague in telling the Councilwoman when I'd be arriving, only that my arrival was imminent."

Trying not to be frustrated at once more being left out of communication, Pelagios glanced between Kana and Riven. When neither seemed interested in making introductions, he inclined his head. "I'm Lord General Pelagios Yan of the Fishmen Gales."

"Riven Stormblot of His Majesty's Council."

Pelagios watched Kana's eyes settle curiously onto Avenir as he said, "Sir Councilman. Lord Pelagios."

Something narrowed in the councilwoman's gaze as, introductions finalized, the mage turned to face the guard. Kana moved to his side, Riven to the other, leaving Pelagios to stand and observe their small parade from behind.

On Riven's command the doors opened, revealing the throne room doused in the light of a fire in the massive hearth. Heat sweltered throughout the room but all within preferred it to the frost beyond. The king sat in his grand throne, the iron branches like fingers reaching out in search of something to grasp. Einar wore a modest version of his courtly attire though the cloak itself sat as a tapestry on his broad shoulders. The sharp smell of olibanum bathed the room, wafting from the crackling fire that cast Einar in a shadow.

Pelagios watched the edges of Avenir's dark hair grow bright with the glow of the distant fire, the silver fish on his own majestic robe shivering in their velvet ocean. Courtiers gazed in awe mixed with trepidation as the council members escorted the new arrival to the foot of the dais.

Theon was not in the chair placed next to the king, the cushioned miniature throne taken up only by the iron circlet intended for the prince. It was best that the prince was abed, and that he would not witness whatever might happen.

Pelagios, distracted by this, came to an abrupt stop behind Avenir. Nearly running into the mage, he peeled away from the group to stand along the edges of the room with the rest of the guard. Damalis stood by the king's elbow, a step down from the dais. His robes shined with the riches allotted to him as chief advisor; with a flourishing extension of his arm, he bade the company to step forward.

Kana and Riven bowed, and when she rose Kana began the introductions. "My King, a thousand blessings from the Mother and Father and all Their Children. We have—"

"We've sought long and hard for answers that may bring Esmar peace, Your Majesty." Damalis' gaze cut away from Kana, disregarding the momentary shock on her face. "As I explained before, what plagues us may be a matter of forces beyond our understanding. I've tasked your Council to search for answers—this, too, I explained."

Einar made a noise of acknowledgment in his throat, his eyes not having left Avenir's face since the doors opened. Whatever Damalis told him in the moments before their arrival had not swayed his full opinion on magic. Pelagios considered this, a hand present on his blade's hilt in a manner that was more comfort than preparedness. Still, it was not outside the realm of possibility that Einar might ask his most trusted general to slay the chief advisor.

Nor was it something Pelagios minded.

"I'm brought no joy in enlisting the help of a *mage*—"

The court's voices tittered, birds caught high in the treetops. Avenir glanced around at the fluttering, a small grin on his lips.

A mage? Here, in Esmar? But true magic fled the world Ages ago!

"—yet dire circumstances call for peculiar solutions. Yes, I have found a mage, and I am confident that he will rid us of this blight."

Silence fell over the room. Kana managed to reserve her anger, but Pelagios knew that murderous glint in her eyes. The rest of the counselors watching Damalis' blatantly inflated ego from the opposite side of the room waited, observant and fearful in their rigid posturing. Lanet frowned, her gaze moving steadily between Kana and Damalis as another council member leaned forward to whisper something against her ear. While the Council might argue that decisions were made as a group, and thus attributed to the group as a whole, Damalis seemed more interested in either taking the potential blame, or all the glory and admiration.

Einar's gruff voice cut off the chattering. "Is this true?"

Avenir bowed at the unspoken order to speak for himself. Hinging fully at the waist with an arm out to his side, the ring on his finger shimmered. It matched the one on his other hand's middle finger, but was a blood red gemstone instead of another cobalt diamond.

"I introduce myself as Avenir, Sir King, of the Silverfish. I am indeed here to end a great blight on this country."

Relief touched the edges of tension in the room, but Einar, still shaded by his throne, raised a hand to silence the murmurs of interest. Splinters of firelight made their way around the odd shapes of the throne, shards of light across his iron crown and broad shoulders. When the hall fell obediently silent, their king leaned forward to rest his elbows on his knees. The casual posture made him appear at ease but the foreboding edge in his gaze cut away any idea of gullibility.

"Your title—Silverfish? It's not one I've seen record of before."

The air stirred as every head turned upon the mage.

Avenir kept his body inclined in a docile way, his green eyes remaining level on the king. "It's a humble surname, Sir King, for farmers who became fishermen and were blessed by an ancestor of yours. Before, we were Kuligan. Then, during the Withered Stalks in the Age of Plights, we were given the title Silverfish by King Lornetif Ulgret as thanks for our work in feeding the lesser villages. I am the last of my line to carry the name."

"This was after my ancestors retook the land." Einar brightened, sitting forward like a child being told a story.

The mage bowed in reply. "I'm gladdened to see that you—"

"I've made no decision, Silverfish." Einar interrupted, and Avenir respectfully fell silent.

Fingers tightening around the hilt of his blade, Pelagios glanced once more to the advisors. Lanet met his gaze, her lips pursing in thought. When she returned her focus to the exchange, Pelagios moved his own to Damalis. The advisor smiled down at the mage, but it did not reach his eyes. Standing next to the king, Damalis glowed with the firelight, a ghoulish figure of orange and gray.

Only a buffoon thought Einar was in charge at all, or that any of the counsel members besides Damalis had a final say. Within Pelagios swelled a final understanding that made his jaw cinch tightly with fury. Was Damalis eager for them to contact the mage to begin with, only feigning discourse to conceal his own plans?

Einar interrupted his musing with an order. "How do we know you aren't a charlatan? Good magic hasn't been seen in these lands since the before the Plights." Implying that the power any Kahun possessed was filthy, Einar sneered at the mention of inexplicable forces. "There were people who spoke to trees and ordered whole forests to move. Oceans turned solid underfoot, allowing spellcasters to walk all the way to the Erewildes—but there are more than enough tales of kings being cheated by tricksters who could no more control these forces than a fish can climb a tree. So, Avenir of the Silverfish, prove to me you aren't an impostor here to make me out a fool."

Before the king finished speaking, Avenir straightened his posture. Pelagios recalled the night of bending candleflames, of Kana's blood spiraling to craft words upon a page. His own eyes witnessed an inexplicable feat, and this was done *without* Avenir in the room. What power did the man command while he stood in their presence?

He saw the same thoughts glinting across the faces of Riven and Kana, but Damalis kept his own features placid.

Avenir's voice reminded Pelagios of his nightmare. When the mage spoke, the general's mind itched, trying to recognize the tone beneath. "You worry about a curse, Sir King, which hides in the shadows of your mind."

The court fell into an uneasy silence. It reminded Pelagios of mornings when he walked a field after the battle was won, his eyes searching for life but finding only death's blank gaze staring up into the sky. Every heart strained against the fear, the *thrill*, of waiting to see if Einar took the mage's statement as insult.

Einar's bearded chin lifted in defiance. The king leaned back into his throne, pulling himself to a severe posture, a bear rearing up on its legs. In a deep voice that resonated across the stone, he said with a narrow gaze, "It pervades these *halls*. It blights my *country*. It is a curse not just on my mind, but in my *blood* and the blood of this land, where my ancestors are buried and their rivals, felled. What make you of this?"

The court let out a breath, some looking disappointed.

Avenir lifted his gaze to the dark ceiling high above them, his face both forlorn and awestruck. "It's an old magic, older than the foundations of this cavern. I feel it reverberating in the mountain. I know not it's name, or who first cast it, but I know I can uncover such answers and bring about a long sought-after peace."

Despite the discomfort he felt in the presence of the mage, Pelagios admired his unwillingness to cower before Einar. His answers were fluid in the manner of one accustomed to direct questions, the honor threading his tone a practiced cantor.

Above this, Pelagios felt the urgency in the mage's voice. Avenir believed the shadows of Carn-Duhl might be tamed. He believed Einar might be saved. For the first time in a long time, Pelagios allowed himself to consider that peace might be attainable. Not for him or his twisted soul, those things were long rotten, but for Esmar and its future.

"Then," a glow filled the king's gaze, "such a mage won't mind proving that he can manage such a thing?"

"Not at all, Sir King." Avenir lowered his face, a smile of pleasure stretching across his burnished lips. "Not at all."

Pelagios assumed nothing other than another show of fire and blood like before. Damalis stepped away from the king's side by only a few paces, just as Kana and Riven turned to their seats along the edge of the throne room. The introductions over, the air shifted into a manner more fervent. Every person in court adjusted their posture, hands wringing in excitement as every nervous eye bore into the mage. Einar, however, did not show any spark of anticipation. He sat on the throne as a judge, not a spectator, and stroked the length of his spiderwebbed beard.

Avenir surprised the court by saying, "I've heard tell of your queen's beauty. She cannot grace us with her presence?"

"No."

The mage grinned. Pelagios turned to glance over his shoulder at the stone wall, feeling suddenly a presence behind him. On his either side, the knights remained faced front. When he focused on the mage once more, his hand clutching desperately to his blade, Avenir stretched his arm to the crowd of onlookers.

Frowning, Pelagios watched as the mage approached the maid of a noblewoman. After being ushered by her mistress to take Avenir's hand, she kept her gaze on the floor as he led her to the center of the room.

Avenir's hand did not clutch or pull, only kept the young woman's fingers softly enclosed in his own. He walked as though guiding a feather, the maid drifting to stop beside him. His mouth moved, too low for anyone to hear, but his words caused the maid to snap her eyes to his. Her brow furrowed, a new terror tightening her shoulders, but she nodded.

Slowly, she removed her fanned cap. Her dark hair was braided like a crown so that it remained hidden beneath the linen. Air tinged with intimacy, she fingered her locks until her dull hair flowed over her boney shoulders. Damalis watched this with boredom, but Einar studied the odd instructions with twinkling curiosity. When the maid stood before the room with her hair free, hands clasped before her like a pious servant, Avenir slipped a finger under her chin. A tinge of red blushed her cheekbones, but her demureness faded with the humming tenor of his voice.

"Lift your gaze, my dear," he murmured, now loud enough for all to hear "For you are a *queen*."

The word left his mouth in an echo cascading down from the dark ceiling. Nothing moved, but Pelagios felt his mind shake. A sickness swelled in his stomach as he watched others within the throne room grip their armrests in discomfort.

As Avenir stepped back from the maid, his hand drifting to his side, the air around her began to glimmer. Pelagios squinted as the edges of her shape turned blurry, ink bleeding into water. Bright spots stabbed his vision as though he had been gazing up at the sun, and when the mirage of light cleared, he felt his heart stall in his chest. There were no drums, no whispers, no darkness closing in, but the earth had shifted, and there stood his heart's greatest desire.

Einar rose slowly from his throne, mouth agape. Not a rustle of silk or a sigh of breath escaped the throng of onlookers as they stared, horrified, where the maid once stood.

"*Impossible*." Damalis' voice shook with breathless terror. His authoritative haughtiness vanished beneath the shroud of disbelief, his hands shaking as his side.

Pelagios dropped his fingers from the hilt of his sword. The air fled his lungs, a swell of love and absolute fear pounding through his body.

"Aletta." Einar took a cautious step off the dais towards his bride. "*My love*."

The queen stood before her court, dressed not in the simple robes of a noblewoman's maid but draped in the fine linen of a sleeping gown. Her scalp was not riddled with hairless, blackened patches of decay but flowed over her shoulders, the rich locks the color of sweet-smelling hay. Her twinkling eyes settled on Einar as he approached her, a hand outstretched but shaking, afraid to touch the vision lest it break apart. A light from within cast Aletta in an otherworldly glow, a star trapped inside her chest. She reached out to grasp Einar's hand, bringing it slowly to cup the roundness of her cheek.

A painful sound scraped out of the king's throat. Every eye saw the wetness in his gaze as he brought his other hand to hold the queen's face. Aletta pressed her cheek into his palm, closing her eyes to relish its warmth.

Her affection towards the man who let her body rot in her chamber made Pelagios shiver with fury. Looking around, he saw the awestruck and terrified gazes of a few counselors, while others gazed in confusion, shaking their heads and refusing to bear witness to the miracle. Those who were horrified, Pelagios realized with a bite of surprise, had known the queen was dead.

An arm blocked his path. The general did not realize he stepped towards the embracing couple until his head snapped to the side. Avenir stood next to him, green eyes glowing—but that must have been a trick of the mirage, too. Pelagios felt the venom in the man's gaze alongside the magic, a writhing energy that called to mind the marshes hidden beneath the snow.

As much as he wished to shove Avenir to the ground, a sharp warning reminded him of his place. It was not by Aletta's side, or even the king's. It was on the edges of *their* world, not important enough to encroach upon the tender moment but too useful to vanish entirely from the king's life. The rawness of Pelagios' wants and desires belonged to them in diverse ways, each with their own brand stamped on his heart.

"Stop this."

Einar's voice trembled. Aletta's face turned up to him, her soft brow coming down in confusion. Her fingers lifted from his hands to touch the path of the tears on his cheeks. The king's eyes fell shut in mourning, and sorrow-filled love.

"*Stop this madness—*"

The king jumped away, his wife's touch suddenly burning him. He raised his hand back, eager to strike Aletta's face when suddenly Avenir commanded the magic to dissipate with a wave of his hand. The cobalt diamond flickered abnormally, causing the earlier parade of lights to shimmer about the room once more.

The king's hand remained poised, even when the maid dropped to the floor in shock. Her dark hair made a curtain around her face, and every member of court held their breath as she lifted her chin. But the queen vanished, and all that remained was the same plain maid from before.

Avenir approached the shaking woman gingerly, his gaze moving smoothly between her and the king. Einar forced his hand down, wiping furiously at the dampness on his cheeks.

His gaze fell onto the mage as the stranger helped the young woman stand. Avenir placed her linen cap into her shivering fingers, the motion releasing her. As she scrambled back to the side of the noblewoman, the mistress, transfixed, grasped the sleeve of her maid's dress.

Einar's breathing came in painful gasps that shuddered around the room. Pelagios watched the trembling rise and fall of his chest, waiting for the call to slay the mage, for this was not the action of a man eager to prove himself useful but one intent on assertion. They had not only witnessed the mage's power, but his calloused and treacherous subversiveness.

"You'll be given a room and a servant. Nothing more."

Avenir bowed low as the king turned in a flurry of shattered power. The general gaped, fingers stalled over his blade. The entire court scrambled to their feet as Einar left, voices halted in their throats until their king and his entourage of guards vanished into the rooms beyond.

Once the door shut behind Einar, the court's voice rose in collective screeches of shock, horror, and fascination. A few nobles approached the mage as one would a hungry wolf, keeping their distance but slinging their questions and praise in harried tones. The Council remained in their seats, their own discussions thickening the cacophony as councilmembers antagonized in harsh whispers those who knew of the queen's *worsening ailment*.

In the onslaught of noise, Damalis took a step toward Pelagios. The advisor went ashen the moment Aletta's visage shined before them, and the color remained drained from his sickly features. Pelagios did not wish to hear the man's musing, but the shock radiating in his bones prevented him from vanishing after the king.

Damalis finally spoke after a moment, his hand lighting on the general's elbow. "Was it truly our queen we saw," he murmured, "or a glamour?"

Both general and advisor knew the truth of the queen's condition—and both feared what the answer may be.

CHAPTER TWENTY-SIX

When snow fell on the ocean, it caused a great mist to stir up out of the warm water. *The Jolly Marksmen* saw the fat clouds shaking off their thick storms as they left Esmar's shores; by then, the ship's deck sparkled with all the salt Cook could spare, and the three sails were tucked neatly into their rigging. No one wanted to be blow around during a snowstorm, least of all Dice. Since managing a few steps without any assistance, she knew slipping on ice would not only shatter her pride but cause more pain to her damaged leg.

She hated that Evander was right. More than a week passed since her rescue, and despite the wound healing nicely, the pain refused to dissipate. The captain, knowing as much, refused to let her do any crew work that required climbing the nets or scurrying to the crow's nest, nor did he allow her to lift anything too heavy. So, with nearly every task barred from Dice per the captain's orders, she was stuck salting the deck, checking the men's lifelines, and making sure Bella, the ship's honorable mice murderer, was doing *her* part. Once the snow finally hit, Dice was allowed to help the men scrape it overboard, but only just.

Leaning on the staff of the shovel for support, Dice caught her breath. It misted in the air, a little cloud of white. Her crewmates looked ready to force her to sit down, so the respite lasted only as long as an inhale before she barred her teeth against the ache in her left high. It persisted, throbbing with each heartbeat, causing her knee to stiffen painfully as she bore down and shuffled the snow overboard.

Dice refused to let anyone see how much it bothered her as she scraped the deck, the limp scarf around her neck *thwapping* in the wind.

Evander's old jacket fit her well enough, but when a call went up that the deck was clear enough she stuck her bare fingers under her armpits. How Brutis walked around with just a sealskin vest and thick fur trousers made her both annoyed, and impressed. Perhaps there really was giant's blood in those veins.

The first-mate ambled over to her once his checking of the deck was complete. Snow still fell, but only at a small dusting, melting as soon as it hit the deck thanks to the fresh dredging of salt. Brutis, however, turned up his nose at the mist surrounding them.

"Thicker than Esmarin pig-pudding." He scowled as if ready to fight the weather. "We'll have to drop anchor if it doesn't clear soon."

Dice wiped a dribble of snot with the back of her hand. "And our heading would be…?"

Brutis clicked his tongue. Crossing his arms over his massive chest, he considered her for a moment.

"The captain doesn't give the crew headings anymore?" Dice challenged, fully relaxing now on the staff of the shovel. She tried not to favor her bad leg, but an inadvertent wince escaped anyway.

For his part, Brutis did not draw attention to it. "Sovil. But first, Con-Quary to resupply and get payment for delivering goods to the Port of Mann."

"Good to know I still don't have to twist your arm." Dice chuckled, though the location pressed curiosity into the back of her mind. "Are we picking up something? A job?"

Brutis gave her a smile that mothers often reserved for their pestering children. "You don't ask these questions of your father, the captain?"

"Right. Well."

Dice refused to tell him outright that she was avoiding Evander since being deposited back into her bunk below deck, though Brutis noticed as much easily enough. No longer pampered in the captain's cabin, mostly because she hated the idea of being treated any better than the crew, it provided her enough distance to wrap her mind around the events in Stormshale. Evander was able to read the emotion on her face easily, so she did not want him to see how *wrong* she felt.

The *book* she kept tucked inside the hem of her trousers as she slept, but working on the deck meant finding a proper hiding place from the stranger.

It called to Dice, just like the sea. Music layered over the waves, silver on water, adding to the mystery of its symbols and magic. Even thinking on it urged tendrils around her mind, so she gave Brutis an uncharacteristically cool dismissal before limping off to put the shovel back below deck.

She might risk a moment to gaze at the tome, but it was a risk she needed to take. The book called to her bones, to something itchy and deep inside her gut.

As she locked the shovel away, she checked over her shoulder. No one came down the steps, and no one came up from the storage level. Ambling over to her bunk, which was little more than a hammock and a trunk tied to a post so it would not slip during a storm, she flipped open the lid to find her iron file. She liked it for picking locks, but it had others uses. Dice knew none of the regular crew dared to go through her things, but she hated the thought of being predictable to the Dua-Nythi. He already seemed to know her, know the music in her head, and while she despised the stranger for his knowledge it also made her more curious.

Getting down the steps to the storage room was harder than the ones to the bunk. She gripped the rope guidelines with stiff iron fingers. Somewhere in the dark, Bella yowled at a tittering rat—and, according the sound of leaping and crunching, she caught her dinner easily.

Dice kept one hand brushing against the stack of barrels as she made her way down the narrow path cutting through trunk and crates. The pungent smell of rum wafted from nearby barrels, mingling with the dampness hanging over the room.

Slipping off the path, she approached a barrel filled with rice, using the file to pry open its lid. Digging into its grains, she searched until her fingers brushed the leather edges of the book. Then, fearing someone might see her, she only let the feeling of its papers ease her breath before slamming the lid back down on the barrel.

"It's hard for you, letting go of things."

A shock of alarm punched through Dice's chest. Keeping her hands on the rim of the barrel, her throat tightened. Breath quickening in her ribcage, she turned to look over her shoulder. The wood of the barrel was a lifeline as Dice braced herself for the rotten image.

Evangeline stood across the aisle, the cut of light falling from the stairway washing her gray. The young woman's body wavered between the rotten structure that remained hanging along Stormshale's coast, pecked-at skeleton and threads of hair, and the rich beauty she wore that fateful night.

Dice said nothing. Be it ghost or illusion, speaking to it only made the pain in her heart worsen. Such a vivid hallucination made itself comfortable on the ship the last week, proving it was not the heat of fever but Dice's shattering mind. Evangeline would be standing behind Evander as he steered the ship, or hovering patiently above the surface of the water when Dice looked out towards the horizon. It sat in the shadows, stood next to her hammock as she tried to fall asleep, only vanishing once it finished what it came to say.

She never tried to fight it, but it refused to be ignored.

"You don't look well." Evangeline's mouth slipped from rosebud lips to yellowed, lipless teeth. *Mirage in a waterfall, the blurred vision of a drunkard.* "You should rest."

Still glaring at the illusion, Dice snickered. "You should let me."

Helpless. Hopeful. *Stupid.*

Evangeline's eyes sharpened. "Why? You didn't let *me*."

Dice snapped her gaze back down to the barrel when the mirage dropped its gorgeous silks and gems, but she saw the flick of the eyeless skull, the stringy hair, the bits of meat the birds had not yet gnawed away.

"Look at me."

Dice's nails cracked against the wood.

"Look at me, Dice."

A step closer on the wood of the deck. Another. The air parted to make way for the vision, the ice of Evangeline's wrath striking the back of her neck.

"*I said look at me!*"

The boney hand landed on Dice's shoulder, solid and smelling of rotten cartilage. Panic rose in Dice's chest as the sharp fingerbones gripped the fabric of her collar, pulling her around to face nothing but empty, gray-lit air. Dust motes floated where the vision once stood. Dice's breathing clawed raggedly up her throat, panic sinching until she was gasping for air.

She was real. The creature was *real.*

A call pierced the air from above—a ship spotted in the mist.

Dice scrambled up the steps to the crew's cabin, not daring to look back at the book, her feet coming down hard on the wood planks as she ran away from her stabbing guilt. Up on deck, the men were gathering around the starboard banister, swords in their scabbards but faces bright with interest. She caught the eye of the Dua-Nythi as he climbed down the netting, his gaze at first annoyed when it landed on her face.

Then, a strange softness despite the hard line of his mouth.

She noticed the wetness on her cheeks, and angrily swiped the tears away.

The stranger moved closer to her, but every step she matched by taking one further away until she stood next to Evander. Brutis had the wheel, and the captain was eager to see what approached. The Dua-Nythi, if he had anything to say, would not utter a word next to their captain.

Bearing out of the mist drifted a ship without sails, groaning wood calling out to them mournfully as it floated. No flag hung from it's nest, and no crew save a figure tied to the mast could be seen. An eerie pall hushed over the crew of the *Marksmen* as they watched it slink across the water. Brutis maneuvered the ship out a little ways before the smaller one risked puncturing the hull, but it still drifted close enough for them to peer across its deck.

Surrounding the tied figure were eight bushels of spoiled fruit, and a speared boar facing the bow. Dozens of gifts sat littered on the planks, from scrolls sealed with glimmering wax to lanterns filled with parchment slivers covered with unreadable words. Gilded coins littered the deck, and resting upon them were eight swords. They were evenly spaced around the mast, their points aimed at the figure bound and gagged with a fabric token in their mouth. The person was blindfolded, their wet, greasy hair falling over their bare breasts.

Gazing down at the ghoulish procession, Dice saw the figure stir. "They're alive. Evander—"

The captain paled. His grip on the banister made his knuckles bulge against the skin, and he did not acknowledge that Dice said anything.

"That's a lot of gold," someone else murmured. Another crewmate uttered an unenthusiastic sound of agreement.

"We touch nothing." Evander finally said, his voice even despite the strain in his jaw. "These offerings don't belong to *our* gods. We touch *nothing*."

Dice's gazed jumped back to the ship. The figure yanked weakly against the mast at their voices, the ropes holding them upright as their feet dangled. They hung weakly, shoulders jerking as they tried to cry out past the token in their mouth.

Slowly, the crew dispersed from the banister, unable to watch. Dice could not pull herself away from the ship's edge, even when the Dua-Nythi took Evander's place beside her. They watched silently, a morsel of respect in the quiet as the ship was once more consumed by the mist.

"You know what's happening." *To me*. That part fell silently out of her mouth. When the Dua-Nythi broke his gaze away from the last of the ship, she kept hers trained on the mist.

He leaned against the banister, forearms bracing his body. He wore only a fitted tunic underneath his vest, and fur straps around his ankles for warmth.

"Wilder things are waking up. I need to know why. I need to know why *you.*"

She met his gaze then. Things were making less and less sense to her as the days passed, but Dice knew she had to stop ignoring the change. Could it be that something wild out in the world was doing this to her?

What had she done to deserve such sentencing?

"Do you know me?"

He shook his head slowly, dark hair stirring in the wind. "Not in ways that'll help."

"But you can read the book."

"Don't." He straightened, glancing around at the crew. Some were gathered in a circle, chattering about what the ship meant and who might have sent it out. Evander vanished into his cabin with Brutis, and the second-mate gazed out over the mist at the wheel.

Dice pursed her lips. She crossed her arms, hooking a hip to the banister as her gaze dropped to the dark water. The world around them felt cut off, and a part of her mind wondered if they were not sailing through the mist but through a channel to another world, or perhaps the end of the map.

While his gaze wandered the deck, she said, "It's mine. But I… I hear it, but I don't know how to read it."

"It's yours just as the sea is yours." He sneered, the corner of his mouth twitching. His nose, curving down like a hook, reminded Dice of violent cliffsides and winding roads.

"It found me." She had no energy to argue with him, not after the interaction with Evangeline's haunting. "That means something. So, you'll tell me about it, and how to read it."

"Why should I help the woman who killed my friend?"

Dice let out a breath. The Dua-Nythi's eyes slipped to meet hers when she did, troubled.

It bothered her, the way he moved between arrogance and pity.

"Listen," she bit, exhausted from the music in her mind, from the way everything unraveled around her. "I could threaten to kill you, too, but we've already gotten off on a bad foot. You're sitting here saying that you need to figure some gods-damned things out, acting like *I* have something to do with it. Well," she stepped forward, lifting her chin so that her nose nearly brushed his. "I need to figure out why I'm losing my mind *before* it's gone. Understood?"

Looking down his nose at her, the Dua-Nythi tensed his jaw. This close, Dice clearly saw the silver notches along his neck. The scent of him was strange, too. Most crewmembers ended up reeking of odor and sweat after a week on a ship, but he only smelt of brine.

Distracted, she quickly stepped out of the closeness. A thread of amusement pierced his serious gaze, but only for a moment.

"Fine. *Fine.*" He repeated when she scowled up at him. "I'll tell you what I know, later. But I can't promise it'll be enough."

"Fine." She parroted.

He held out his hand, the palm riddled with little scars. Working hands, not soft and weak like she wanted to believe.

"For the sake of our alliance, I'll even tell you my name. It's Saltraroran."

Dice took his offered palm awkwardly. "Rory, then."

He *tsked.* "I knew my name might be too hard for a pirate."

The Dua-Nythi winced as Dice's grip cinched around his fingers. Pulling him down to her level, she said very slowly, "Insult my intelligence again, and not only will I burn that book but I'll cut off your—"

"Dice."

Brutis stood over the pair, his amused gaze jumping between them. She immediately dropped Rory's hand, finding a more casual stance as she crossed her arms and leaned against the banister once more. Rory simply grinned, locking his hands behind him as he took a step back respectfully. In his fleeting time aboard the *Marksmen*, Dice felt him watching her interaction with Brutis and Evander. No doubt he noticed the depth of their relationships, not just the quips from old stories but the respect—and protectiveness—between them.

"Watch the lifelines. The mist is clearing, and we want to drop the sails before too long."

She cleared her throat. "Right."

Brutis, after relaxing his authoritative stance, winked at her as he walked away. Everyone on the ship knew Dice's proclivities swung whichever way the wind blew, even if she did not get involved with the crew. Brutis, however, always urged her to get with a person of like-mindedness every time he tried to shove his opinion in.

As Dice shook even the *idea* of the possibility out of her head, she started towards the lifelines. Behind her, Rory chuckled audaciously.

"I'd like to hear the rest of that some time, Dice. Perhaps later tonight?"

If anyone else overheard such an offer, then it would be impossible for Dice to squash any rumors. Evander might even pull her aside to give her a good talking-to about keeping things professional despite being twenty-seven years on a ship and never mixing with a crewmember before.

Instead of bothering to look at her new bedfellow, Dice lifted a hand in acknowledgement. The moment might have been light if Evangeline was not standing by the mast when Dice looked up.

It smiled, its silken gown a hush of dove's feathers as it turned and vanished behind the wooden pillar. Dice sensed the air press in, a foreboding premonition that argued against her decision to enlist Rory's help. To ignore it, she worked the knots of the lifelines until her fingers went pink with blood.

Night fell quickly. No other sign of snow clouds hung on the horizon, some of the crew even pausing to watch the decline of that golden orb into the sea. Lanterns, a mismatched set of boxy ones from Esmar and beautiful round globes from the Gilded Isles, were lit before the darkness took over the ship. The air grew warmer as they sailed, though a gentle chill on the breeze made some keep their longer sleeves. Evander only met the crew for the dinner hour, his face no longer pallid, a superstitious air about him. Around his neck hung a new fixture since that evening; a jawbone Dice knew had been gifted to him by a Kahun woman. She was fleeing Esmar at the start of the Mad King's hunt, passing it along to Evander as thanks for refusing her meager payment. Dice did not care for such trinkets, but was glad that it brought her kin peace.

The ship felt the disturbance left over from the odd sighting, even when Gallan took up a flute and Lindle following by slapped his hands on the table. The twins attempted to distract from the melancholy feeling. Dice hardly paid attention to anyone as she ate, spooning the under-salted broth into her mouth. Evander clapped her on the shoulder as he passed, the only sort of goodnight he gave her since she was hip-high, before vanishing up the steps leading to the deck. Everyone else seemed interested in their private conversations, the seasoned crew of the *Marksmen* finally warming up to the hired hands. Voices flittered, speaking of their stop in Con-Quarry, and how eager they were for the sunshine and sweetmeats that were sold along the dock. With the groaning of the ship, their voices mingled to create a solemn tune that reminded Dice of popping fires in a hearth.

Dice was unsure whether she preferred the gruesome memory of the flayed merchant to Evangeline's lingering ghost, but she was exhausted enough not to care. Her life felt out of control, but with Rory's help she may get a foothold onto something tangible.

Looking across the tightly packed room, Dice watched the strange person laughing at something the quartermaster, Julian, said. The lanternlight made the bronze of his skin glow, a man with sunlight trapped inside. He turned suddenly to her, holding on to the laughter but meeting her gaze with a wordless question. As if in response to his gaze, the book tucked neatly into the waistband at her back hummed in familiarity.

Her stomach tightened. Did she really want to learn more? What happened if she found out it was worse than her reality? What if their conversation only provided more questions, a twining, knotting ball of yarn that tangled every time she tried to pull at it? The thing was, Dice knew enough about strangers to assume anything out of Rory's mouth might be a lie. Though the Dua-Nythi seemed intent on figuring out his own mysteries, it was safe to believe he cared more about finding *his* answers than answering *her* questions.

Dice drained the last of the broth and took the bowl to Cook. He dumped it in a barrel of saltwater before turning to order the swabbie to stop wasting time. The scrawny man circled the stone pit in the middle of the room, carrying with him a long rod to open the grate above that let out the smoke. Other crew members took this as a sign to leave or get smoked out by the dead fire.

Rory stood with them, his eyes trained on Dice as she left the room and returned to the deck. The sailing master stood at the wheel, his hands lazy around the pegs. Drooped sails were doing most of the guiding at this point, the sea calm enough for Dice to walk evenly with her cane. She resigned herself to the fact that she might have a limp for the rest of her life, but that was better than dying.

A lookout scrambled up the ropes to get to the crow's nest, but the others filtered into the cabins below. Evander's door was shut tight, the glow of candlelight spilling out from the crack beneath. Brutis passed her with a wiggle of his eyebrows, and she barely had the heart to smile in response.

Let him think she planned to knock boots with Rory. It was better than the heartache of one day needing to tell him to kill her if she tried doing anything like in Stormshale.

Dice faced the sea, feeling suddenly nauseous. The thought occurred to her earlier about what might need to be done should that pitch inside of her take control again. It meant needing to tell Evander and Brutis the truth, but she must understand *before* that conversation. Telling them to kill her without actual proof that Dice might be a problem would only make them tense. Evander might take it seriously for a moment—madness often happened on a ship—but she knew he had no desire to make promises unless Dice told him exactly *why* they needed to be made at all.

It was strange, planning one's own death. Who did she want to brace her as she fell on the sword? What song should accompany her body when they tossed it overboard?

Against the skin of her back, the book grew heavy. It felt as though it was absorbing into her skin, trying to meld itself to her spine.

"I thought Cook's food was bad *before* we used up all the salt." Rory stepped forward, materializing from the wood. Dice just looked at him, taking a moment to peel herself out of her macabre line of thought.

"Imagine twenty-seven years of that." She finally quipped. Let the thoughts of death be stalled for a breath.

Rory chuckled. He leaned forward to match her posture, reclining with his elbows on the banister. "I'm surprised you're not shaking with malnourishment."

"Hm. There were moments."

"I'm sure."

They fell quiet. Their individual questions lingered under the surface of the silence, but Dice felt them both take a moment to observe the black slate of the ocean. Stars hung brightly overhead, the constellations ingrained in Dice's mind. The Mother's Arrow pointed the way north, the bow a line of three bright stars, and the arrow a string of faraway clouds that never moved, never dulled. Littering the night like coins, the lights twinkled, untouched by the maladies of their observers. Dice liked to think how, despite the chaos turning in this world, the stars remained consistent. Pirates and sailors and ferrymen alike traveled under their guidance. Their driving glimmers never led them astray, never squashed out their hope for landfall.

Rory stared down into the dark sea. She watched his eyes flick away from the echo of her face, the rippling waves breaking apart their features as the ship drifted. Neither of them broke the silence for a time, mostly because Dice had no idea where to start. She thought she might want to learn about the music in her mind, which had quieted when gazing at the stars but now lifted in a murmur of notes.

Glancing back at the sailing master, she brought her gaze down to her white-knuckled hands.

"It's a history, of sorts."

Rory's voice sounded lamenting. His nails picked at the varnish of the banister, something Evander despised. The sailor droved his thumbnail under the chip, flicking the freed piece into the ocean absentmindedly.

It's yours like the sea is yours. His words from earlier clicked together, gears in her mind. Did that mean the symbols belonged to the Dua-Nythi, but the history may talk about more than their cities under the ocean?

That early sense of something shifting prickled at her neck. Blessedly, the ghost of Evangeline did not meet her when she glanced over her shoulder. It was only Bella sauntering across the deck, doing her nightly rounds of rat-catching.

"If it's your history, that means you can read it." She looked over his profile, but Rory kept his gaze on the water. Did homesickness cast his features down?

Dice wondered what that might be like, walking the floor of the ocean, breathing the sea water like air. What sort of creatures did he see? Did they have their own version of lanterns, or did they live in darkness?

It sounded peaceful. Nothing like her life now.

"If it's what I think it is, no. I can't read it." Rory met her disappointment with an apologetic, empty smile. "We've been here longer than you landfarers. Our languages were created, lost, reshaped, remolded… We have something like your Common Tongue now, something that connects us all, but," he shrugged, "we still have our differences. Those tomes are one of the few similarities that connects us to a time when we were one."

Guilt hung over Dice, different than how it felt with Evangeline. It was shameful, scolding her for latching on to something so important to the Dua-Nythi.

Yet that pitch in her gut stuck. It clung to the edges of her skin, sinking into the covers of the book.

Dice slipped her hand under her shirt, untucking it from her waistband. The leather cover was warm from her skin, and she felt a strange sense of vulnerability in passing it to Rory. He took it with a pause of doubt, his eyes finally drinking in the leather when she did not move to take it back.

Even with it in his hands, standing there next to her, Dice felt the cold distance like a stab wound. She swallowed that pain down, driving it deep into her chest until it curled like twine behind her heart. Watching, his fingers draped over the edges of the volume with admiration for the stitching. When he opened the pages, Dice felt her heart surge forward towards the spiraling, inky marks. The song of steel became one of hushing wheat in the breeze, as soft crashing in her mind, when his fingers traced the dark line of what looked like a breeching whale.

Voices murmured from it the longer he stared at the page, pressure tightening at the base of Dice's neck. The headache climbed upwards, encircling her scalp—Rory's lips moved, talking to her, but the world grew dark, her pinprick vision narrowing on the pages.

Everything slammed backwards, the pressure rushing outside of her body. Dice's cheeks felt wet, her chest strained like she had been holding her breath. Rory grasped the closed book in one hand, the other rising to her cheek.

"By the Aether!" She griped, jumping out of his reach. "What are you doing?"

"Your eyes." Rory's brow was furrowed, his hand stilled in the air between them. His gaze searched her face, thick with worry.

Dice lifted her own hand, touching tears along her cheek. Her fingers came away slick with blood, bright and tanging the air with iron. She met his worry, heart thumping in her palms as she looked between the glistening red of her heartblood and his tense gaze.

Rory briefly glanced at the sailing master, who did not seem interested in their conversation. His voice was low, careful. "Has this happened before?"

Dice shook her head. Panic settled, heady and ripe, as she rubbed the last of the blood from her vision. She was a fool for thinking that talking to Rory would make things any better.

"We should stop," Rory began, the knot in his throat bobbing. "We don't know what it might—"

"No." Dice cut him off, dropping her bloodied sleeve. The word came out broken and haggard, but she pressed on. "*No*. We can't. I can't. Just… don't open it again."

Rory seemed prepared to argue, then slowly closed his mouth. With a single nod, he acknowledged both Dice's own fear, and her desire to comprehend it.

"You said it's like a history book." She surged on, trying to move past the bloody tears despite the rush in her head. *This isn't a good sign. This isn't a good sign at all.*

"Only a little." Rory tried to step back into a normal tone, but his gaze locked on her face. "In our stories, these tomes were sacred texts.

Some of them told stories about how the Dua-Nythi came to be, but most were magical."

Magic explained how it affected her. It had to be old, outdating the beginning of the Syvons. But real magic of legends and ballads had fled the world Ages ago, so why now? And why her?

"We think there are others, but they're lost to us. When we started evolving to look more like you, some of the Dua-Nythi took to land. Never far, never leaving the edges of the sea, but they walked both worlds. Perhaps some of the volumes are lost on land. Now, we may never know."

Dice thought about the fisherman's shack. "Your friend… was he…"

Rory twinged at the mention of him, the knowledge of Dice ending his life burning against his skin. He did not answer.

"Is that why he looked different than you?"

He glanced up, nodding. "Once, our people walked the worlds easily. Land and Sea. Now, if we stay too long above, we grow ill. Talamondin—the man you killed—had his troubles. He wanted to be like you landfarers."

Dice snickered, heating with shame under Rory's knife-sharp eyes. She prevented herself from griping about how Talamondin should have picked a better city than Stormshale considering *she* also landed there to escape.

Dice was the last person to judge anyone for their vices.

"He told me he wanted to find the rest of these." Rory passed a hand over the book. Dice felt that same familiar thrum of magic hush out of the pages, welcoming his touch. A shiver of delight brushed her skin, and she was thankful for the darkness that hid the blush in her cheeks.

"I told him they must be in Adelhart if we haven't found them yet."

"You mean the Historian?" She balked at the ridiculous notion. "That's a fantasy. We've sailed past those islands dozens of times. There's *nothing* out there."

The way Rory stared at her made Dice feel more foolish than ever. It was worse than the look Evander gave her as a child when she forgot to mind her tasks.

"Some of these contain the language of the Duathi. Some are said to unlock portals between here and the Godrealm. I would remind you, Dice," he said lowly, "that we have more pressing matters than arguing the existence of a magical library. *You were just crying blood—*"

"I know." Dice hissed. Mentioning the Duathi stirred a distant dream up from the darkness.

Hark, hark, hark. The song in the ocean took on the shape of the word. She tried not to focus on the echoing command.

"You *don't*." His own voice was venom now, never mind the curious looks from the sailing master. "You seem thrilled with the idea of drawing closer to your own death. This book will give that to you all right, but you shouldn't be able to even understand it enough to have this reaction.

"These tomes, they *mean* something." Rory stepped back from her, and for a moment Dice worried he was ending the conversation. He gave her a look that said *not yet*, but that if she pressed any more then he would walk away, taking the book with him.

Rory continued after Dice raised her hands in defeat. It was an apology, or at least the best she could manage.

"You call your casters, mages. We called them Godharkers, or Heralds. It varies in our texts, but my people believe some of these tomes were their visions. They all have the same story of the origins of the Dua-Nythi. *Before our bones were felled in twine, our tails turned stems of flesh, we drank the blood of—*"

"I admire the history lesson," Dice grunted, exhaustion slamming into her bones as she fought the word in her mind. *Hark, hark, hark.* "But get to the point in the story where you come aboard my ship."

Rory stopped. His lips went tight, refusing to let the words fall.

"Damn it to the Aether. Fine." Dice pushed away from the banister, from the balmy night and the possibility of answers. Every step away from the book made it feel like a piece of herself was carved out with a butcher's knife—still, she limped sullenly away from the only peace she felt in months. Blood pounded in her ears, and she barely heard Rory's words against the groaning of the ship and the gentle hush of the parting water.

Dice turned, facing him slowly. She walked a step closer, thigh cinching in pain. Drawing near, her whisper held turmoil and wonder. "What?"

A muscle in his jaw twitched. "I heard your blood when it mixed in the water. Not Talamondin's—*yours*."

She stepped closer, mind reeling. "I thought you heard the sea? It's music?"

"I do. But after tonight, I think we're listening to vastly different tunes."

Dice could not agree more. He hardly seemed mad, or distracted. If they were not listening to the same ocean's song, then what riddled her mind?

His next words shattered a piece of her resolve. "I don't understand how a human can hear it. Unless you have the blood of the Duathi, yet that's impossible. We can't breed with you landfarers."

"You can't?" Genuine surprise lilted her voice, not that she planned to have his children. Rory looked like any other person, besides the scars hiding his gills, so she had simply assumed the Dua-Nythi were a version of average people, like the Revkyn.

"It must be magic," he continued thoughtfully, "or a curse. But why now?"

"Well, that's the gods' fault then." She rested against the banister, thigh aching. She massaged it absentmindedly, the senseless world heavy on her back. Bitterness tinged her voice. "I'm hardly someone deserving of magic."

"Agreed."

Rory shrugged when her gaze swiped to him, but her response died in her throat. What he told her both did and did not make sense. The journal affected her, yes, but she was unable to read its markings. Something in the deep rang out, and Rory confirmed that it was not uncommon, at least for the Dua-Nythi. Yet their songs were different, hers a warped version of the pure tunes within *him*.

What irked her the most was the sudden thought of her mother, whom Evander believed to be a stowaway searching for a better life. She had not thought about her in years—the ship was home, Evander and the crew her family. But she started thinking once again of a life cut short, for when Dice was found in bloodied rags in the hold there was no trace of the woman who bore her.

Dice did not have gills or magic, yet Rory believed something about her was different. Finding out *what* might be able to explain not only her fractured mind, but her own lineage.

"I'm tired of wondering." She sighed. "I'm tired of worrying. I'm *tired*."

Her companion let out a sound of agreement.

"I came to the surface to find my friend. Instead, I hear a song of blood that was loudest on a strange ship, and find a tome lost to my people. Trust me when I say that *you're* not the only one reeling."

Earnest annoyance flicked in his eyes. When the world came down around a person, it felt impossible to see that same thing happening to their neighbor. In that, at least, Dice was not alone.

Crossing her arms, she looked down into the water. Rory's gaze fell, sullen in the mourning of his friend and in the fact that neither of them learned much more about their circumstances.

When she met his eye in their reflection, neither of them looked away. It seemed easier to talk to a mirrored image of him than to face him directly.

"I'm sorry about Talamondin." Dice pursed her lips, her reflection morose.

Blinking at her, Rory gave her a small dip of his chin. "Me, too. I know he hurt you. I know it was in defense."

But I'm worried you might do the same to me. Dice felt those words on the wind. Instead of responding, she lifted her gaze to the glimmering sky. They made an odd pair, but they still shared the night in peace. Answers would come, Dice believed this with all that was left within her black heart.

Even if they were not the ones she wanted, they would come.

CHAPTER TWENTY-SEVEN

"I can't believe you—"

"Believe it!"

"This is too sudden. You made this choice for me, and I'm not sure it's one I want." Neoma stood at the bottom of the boardwalk, hands fisted not out of anger but fear. Talaya held one heavy trunk in front of her while Calily and Sulien protected the bags of *Neoma's* things slung over their shoulders. Even though her words were biting, their canter shook with uncertainty, the threat lost.

Her mother gripped the strap of the bag but did not relinquish it to her daughter. Instead, she took a large step behind Sulien, comedically looking around the taller woman's shoulder. Her cousin stood with arms and legs braced for attack, as if Neoma had ever been the type of person to do such a thing.

"You want it," Sulien said firmly. "You're just too scared to take it."

"So you ambush me?"

Inara, who held a note meant for Neoma in her grasp, rolled her eyes. "We hardly *ambushed* you…"

Neoma wished she possessed the energy to argue. If she knew that morning they planned to turn dinner in Con-Quary into boarding a ship *leaving* the docks, she might never have agreed. To her, that felt very much like an ambush.

Releasing her fisted hands, Neoma leaned against one of the posts along the dock. Behind her, *The Countess* bobbed in the water. It was a beautiful vessel made of rich cherry-colored wood, a carving of a sea goddess situated on the bow. Taupe sails with golden edges were cinched, nestled in their rigging. The whole ship wafted with the rich smell of incense, sweet and sharp. The hull was narrower than the ships on either side of the dock; *The Countess* itself was not a massive vessel, but it loomed over Neoma decidedly.

The letter in Inara's hand boasted fine penmanship that happily welcomed Neoma aboard *The Countess* as their hired cook. During a meeting with friends at a teahouse, Talaya found the advertisement on a local news board nearby. With the thoughts in her head about her last trip with Neoma, she wrote to the captain on her cousin's behalf. Talaya made sure to mention their family name—Cardea, which Neoma readily took once the reality of her broken marriage set in—and all her familiarity with cooking and preparing salts. The letter, according to her family's romantic retelling of the story, arrived yesterday morning, urging Neoma to bring her things. There was a dock number listed, along with the time *The Countess* planned to set sail.

Neoma glared at her mother as the others waited to hear what she might say. They would not *force* her to get on the ship, not if she wanted to return to Kairdwillo, but something stalled her voice.

"I can't believe you're trying to get me on a ship you know nothing about."

Talaya guffawed, dropping the trunk to put her hands on her hips. "I know *The Countess* docks here at the turn of the season, and has for the last two years. I see it all the time!"

The turn of the season was no so far away, should Neoma climb the boardwalk. She paused, thumb pressing into her other palm in nervousness. "Alright. Well, I know nothing about the crew—"

"It's all women, *captained* by a woman."

Neoma blinked at Talaya.

Her cousin quirked a brow, daring her to ask another question.

Sulien moved to stand between them, bending to look Neoma in the eye. Her eyes were kind but no less assertive. "Cousin, you love the sea, and it's always loved us back. It'll protect you."

"I thought you didn't believe in those stories."

"I believe in them for you."

"You'll always have a home here, you know that." Inara smiled, the ring in her lip sparkling. She placed the letter in Neoma's hands, the weight of its meaning sending energy up Neoma's arm. "But you deserve to see if something else fits."

Talaya wrapped an arm around Neoma and Calily. "I love you, but you deserve your own tales to tell. You can't keep hanging on the edges of mine."

The women laughed, their notes of joy tinged with the sadness of farewell. Dockhands and merchants shouted in every direction, but the family kept their circle close. Any shouting not their own went unheard as they teased one another, jabbing as Talaya admitted she thought herself the more interesting.

These were not people who ever lead her to a choice for which she did not eventually thank them.

"All right." Neoma's voice at first was too quiet; Sulien wagged her fingers at Inara, who apparently said something in defense of Talaya. Only Calily noticed, her arm tightening around Neoma's shoulder.

With tears in her throat, she said again, "All right. I'll go."

Their heads snapped to her, silence falling over their little group. All at once, they crowded Neoma, kissing her cheek and muttering blessings as she tried to spread her arms wide enough to embrace them all. She hated that Roland was not there for her farewell, but she knew that if she saw the tears in her father's eyes she would not board *The Countess*.

"Neoma Cardea, I take it." Sighed an unfamiliar voice from above.

Straining to look around her cousins' heads, she gaze up the boardwalk to the person sauntering towards them. The woman stood a little taller than Sulien with rich black hair tied in loops at the nape of her neck. She looked over their happy foolishness with crescent eyes as she squinted against the sun. While her attire was plain, strapped to either hip hung a sword and a short dagger. She said Neoma's name again, uncertain of who in the throng of smiling, teary faces the new cook may be.

"Yes," she said, standing out of her family's embrace. Her skin felt cool without their touch, a farewell in itself. "That's me."

The woman's eyes affixed on her, quickly perusing the simple tunic, trousers, and calfskin boots. She did not bother giving the same judgmental look to the others before turning on her heel. Calling over her shoulder, she shouted, "We raise anchor soon."

Continuing up the boardwalk, she left Neoma to her farewells. Sulien and Calily dropped the strap of their bags over her head as though gifting her medallions. With a heave, she lifted her trunk from the ground before giving her mother one long, tight hug. That thread around her heart shivered, knowing the distance between them would soon be at its widest.

Talaya grabbed her hand, pulling her back for a moment off the boardwalk. Her eyes sought Neoma's with love; a proper amount of sadness was there, too. "The ship is all women."

She blinked at her cousin, waiting for the rest of the sentence. "Yes… you told me. That does make it easier, I suppose."

Talaya gave her a soft look of understanding, but was not finished. Leaning in so the others heard nothing, she whispered, "I understand what it feels like, not knowing who you love."

Neoma tilted away, heat climbing up into her cheeks. An argument did not find purchase on her throat, but a grasping sense of excitement. Talaya only patted Neoma's arm gently, and released her once more.

"Go," Calily urged, tears falling from her bright amber eyes. It seemed that any moment, she might beg Neoma to stay. The woman had cried tears filled with many distinct kinds of grief, but one the docks of Con-Quary she knew that the Ocean would not take from her another child. "Go, my child, and *live*."

Her mother's words the blessing her heart desired, Neoma turned her back on the largest city she knew. Before her, the wood climbed upward, disappearing at the opening that brought her to the ship's deck. Standing there patiently was the woman from before, her arm raised to block out the setting sunlight.

"All right," Neoma echoed to no one. But the sea listened, the lurch of the waves slapping against the ship's hull. "All right."

Steeling her breath, she climbed up the boardwalk. She did not turned to face her cousins or her mother, every step threatening to be her last before she turned and ran into the arms of her mother. The woman above studied Neoma, one hand on the railing, and when she grew closer she noticed the gilded decals painted in a dark red along the beams of the railing.

This is a fine ship, she thought, thanking Talaya in her heart as she stepped onto the deck of her new life. Only then did Neoma gaze down the boardwalk to see her cousins with their fists clutching their chests, keeping their own hearts from calling out for her to stay. Calily hugged Inara tightly, and the woman swiped tears from her cheeks. Sulian and Talaya held hands, Talaya's arm encircling Calily. The four stood as a wall, not to keep Neoma out but to remind her that the path backwards was closed.

It was only forward from now on.

The woman gave her another apprehensive once-over, narrow eyes dark and observant. She had the same long, round features of the older families in the Gilded Isles, her almond eyes sharpened with lines of kohl to block out the sun's glare. Neoma felt embarrassed for it being the first time aboard a ship that was not a ferry or fishing boat, and smiled nervously. The tears in her eyes did not help, and she struggled to breath against the sad, excited tightness in her chest.

"Everyone is paid six-coin a week." The woman said, plain-faced.

"Oh." Neoma was not sure if that was a fair wage for the cook of a ship, but nodded. Even though talk of payment was normal, it felt strange to have such an indifferent conversation after saying goodbye to the only life she knew.

Despite the haze drifting over her body, she tried to focus as the woman ushered Neoma towards a dark entryway. "*The Countess* provides a meal at dawn, high noon, and sunset. No one is allowed into the stores between those times. You'll be given a key, understand?"

Neoma nodded even though the woman's back was to her. She struggled to keep up, her trunk hitting her shin with each step. But it was enough to distract her from the pain of her goodbyes, and for that she was grateful.

"This is where we gather; there, in the back, is the cook's station." She nodded across the packed tables, the bolts that fastened them to the floor gleaming. Beyond sat a low counter, an iron pot on top, with a tall stone circle that must be the cook fire set just beyond. Sunlight gleamed down from the grate above, turning the gray ash white. Neoma did not think it an exceptionally large kitchen, but *The Countess* was not a huge vessel anyhow.

The woman eventually introduced herself as Viorel Duhane, the master boatswain and close friend to the captain of *The Countess*. She led Neoma through the belly of the vessel, clarifying that the lower decks were for the cargo that they moved between the Syvons. When Neoma asked what specifically they traded in, Viorel did not answer. Instead, she motioned to the bunk that would be Neoma's when they stepped down into the crew's quarters. It was a tall cubby built into the wall, long enough for a mattress of hay and plenty wide for comfort, with even a lip along the edge of the bed to keep her from rolling out during restless sailing. There were little shelves for person items, and Viorel lifted the mattress to show the storage beneath.

"Put your things here, and I'll show you the rest of the ship. I can't stand how long this is taking."

Neoma bristled, but listened. Shoving her trunk in the compartment, she tidied the mattress under Viorel's intense gaze. The entire perimeter of this level had the same bunks fixed into the walls; Neoma counted thirty in total.

Viorel spoke with a brisk lilt in her voice, the accent an amalgamation of local tenors. Muscles wrapped around her wiry frame, attesting to the strength of her slight body. Neoma could not help but look at the dual weaponry on the woman's hips, thinking how long it might take to learn such a skill.

They returned to the eating room after the master boatswain showed Neoma the lavatory and, separately, the supply room for the meals. A strange scent hit the back of her throat when Viorel opened the door, but the woman assured her the supplies was just brought in from Con-Quarry, and that nothing was spoiled.

During the tour, Neoma expected to run into her new bunkmates, but it was just her and Viorel walking about the ship. Each step echoed loudly, a testament to their solitude. The captain's cabin across the way kept its door closed, not that Neoma expected to meet her right away. However, it was odd that no one else accompanied them during Viorel's lecture about the hierarchy, and what was expected of Neoma as the cook.

Pacing behind the counter, Neoma found the drawers with other pots and cutlery. Other than that, the cook station seemed painfully understocked. There were serving bowls, but little else. It looked like she was about to get remarkably familiar with different soup recipes.

Viorel looked over her shoulder as though she expected someone to walk down the steps. Neoma waited in the patient silence until the woman turned back around to face her.

"The crew is finishing gathering supplies. Some also send off letters when we dock."

Feeling an eerie chill that seemed like Viorel peered into her mind, Neoma shrugged. "Should I start now, then, or…?"

"Gods, no." Viorel snickered. "You'll set us on fire at cast-off. Wait until we're out of the harbor, then you can start dinner. Here, before I forget." She laid the key to the storeroom down on the counter, but did not take her fingers off it for a moment. Looking at Neoma, she instructed with a serious tone, "Let me know when supplies drop to two of each. Rice will last a while—so will the salted meats and dried fruit. But I don't care if the crew is starving, you *don't* make a thing if you get down to the crates in the very back. Am I clear?"

"Starve the crew." Neoma nodded. "Yes. Got it."

For the first time since their meeting, the corner of the woman's mouth lifted. It was not a strong smile, but it was enough to make Neoma feel she was, in some part, in Viorel's good graces.

"Welcomed aboard *The Countess* then, Neoma. I hope it surpasses your expectations."

The groaning of the ship would take some getting used to, as well as the swaying underfoot. According to Viorel, Neoma was in charge of not only cooking but the menu, and the latter was a struggle to figure out at first. Some of the meat was too dry to eat alone, so her earlier fixation on stews seemed to be the best option. As she managed to get the ingredients together, she found herself leaning with the tilt of the boat as she stirred. She worried about what it would mean for the cookfire, remembering Viorel's words about possibly setting *The Countess* aflame if she started too soon.

When a call went up to raise the anchor, she found herself scrambling up the stairs to watch. On deck, more people appeared but not as many as she expected. They pulled the lines, readying the sails as Viorel and a few others pushed a heavy mechanism that drew the anchor back into the ship. Everything, even the groaning wood, came to life as the crew jumped into their positions. All hands pulled, tied, swung, or signaled, the seafarer's language flying around Neoma as *The Countess* lifted off from the docks.

With a surge of sudden homesickness, she ran to the banister and there, hands clutching her chest, was Calily. Neoma lifted both her hands, waving them madly as tears rushed to her eyes. Her mother jumped too, throwing her arms overhead in their last farewell. Neoma stayed at the railing for a long while, even though she could no longer see her mother as Con-Quarry pulled away from them. *The Countess* took to the sea with the grace of her name, and the swaying was not so bad once they hit open water.

"Cook!" Viorel's dour expression matched her sharp voice. "I'd hate to toss you over before we leave port!"

"Aye!" Neoma shouted back, the woman next to her shaking with laughter.

Talaya was correct, though Neoma was afraid to hope that a whole ship might be crewed by women. They walked in tandem, every shape as different as their hair color, currents cutting through the water. As Neoma made her way back to the eatery's steps, she marveled at their strength as they pulled the sails free from their rigging. One woman, lithe as a cat, scurried up the netting around the mast to swing herself into the lookout high above them.

"Cook!" Viorel screeched, sending her scurrying down into the kitchen.

Neoma fetched fresh water from one of the many barrels, bringing it to boil over the cookfire. Once the bubbles rose to the surface, she threw in great handfuls of rice. As those cooked, she chopped up a variety of the dried vegetables, lamenting her family's jars of spices as she doused the mix in salt and pepper. For flavor, she let some of the dry meat soak in the heavy pot before pulling it out to chop it up into finer pieces. Neoma was not entirely sure what animal it came from, as the length of it was cut thick like pork, but when she tasted the stew it had full flavor.

The light streaming down the stairway turned a balmy red. She worked some of the flour into dough when the lanterns were lit, the darkness pulling in closely. A deckhand ambled down the steps to light a few of the lanterns hanging over the tables, but the cookfire threw warm flickers across most of the room. Sweat bead on her forehead, and she swiped, replacing it with a line of flour. When the crew started filtering in for dinnertime, Neoma already prepared the stack of bowls for people to take up.

Everyone thanked her with a nod as she dolled out a ladle and a half of the soup, surprised at the sliver of bread she cut out as well. Though they kept their voices low when they reached their tables, they seemed please enough with the new crewmate. Neoma figured they were tired as dogs as she scooped up her own bowl of dinner, dunking the slice of bread into the stew she thickened with sprinkles of flour.

She sat on a stool behind the counter, uncertain as to whether or not she was even allowed to eat with the others. Her family had no rules when it came to dinner—you sat wherever you wanted—but she knew things may be different.

Viorel, the last to arrive, nodded her thanks as Neoma dished out the stew. "You'll have the Fifth Day off," she said, scooping one of the bits of meat up with her bread. "The crew knows that day will be someone else's turn to cook. With how well you made our first dinner, expect them to ask for seconds on the night of the Fourth. Everyone hates when I cook. But you won't just be cooking—we've all to earn our keep. Have you manned a ship before?"

"Only small vessels with a single sail." Neoma went out to sea plenty of times growing up. Roland taught her complex knots as their small dinghy bobbed in the water, Brite's sun kissing their dark skin. They always cooled off at the end of the lesson with a long swim.

Neoma smiled, weariness making her a poor conversationalist. One question did present itself in her mind, however. "So, this is a cargo ship, yes?"

Spooning the dinner into her mouth, Viorel nodded.

"What's our heading?"

The master boatswain took her time chewing. Neoma thought the look in her eyes was similar to when Koa decided whether or not he told the truth.

"Past the Nameless Seas," Viorel said finally, spooning the broth down while Neoma balked at the information.

Talaya mentioned the ship docked at Con-Quarry at the turn of every season for the last two years. She wished she could knock some sense into her cousin's head for not asking a single soul about the voyage. Floating across the Nameless Seas would take three seasons at least, depending on their destination.

"Well done. Thank you." Viorel placed the empty bowl back down on the counter. "You can leave the dishes. The night crew cleans them."

"Night crew?" Still wondering if she should press about their voyage, Neoma blinked out over the small gathering. It made sense there were others, but during the tour Viorel did not show any extra sleeping quarters.

"You'll meet them when you wake at dawn to start breakfast. Some of them, at least."

"Will I meet the captain soon, too?"

"Listen." Viorel's voice cooled. Bracing her palms flat on the counter, she leaned in with the air of someone not used to having to repeat themselves of clarify orders. "Captain Arlowe rarely leaves her cabin to speak to *me*—and that's all for the better. You will, however, meet her first-mate and quartermaster. Other than the captain, *they're* the people you really want to impress."

"You said there's a night crew. Does that mean there's a night cook?"

"Goodnight, Neoma. Thank you again for the meal." Viorel gave her a pointed looked before moving through the tables towards the stairs. She vanished, intentionally leaving Neoma with more questions than answers.

She sensed no malice in the woman, only a harried energy akin to worrisome rabbits in the springtime. Viorel had a ship to manage, and no time to watch a grown woman do her chores.

As dinner wound down, the crew rose, leaving behind their dishes and nodding their thanks to Neoma. After making sure three separate times that the embers in the cookfire were out completely, she did her best to tidy her work area. Even though Viorel said the night crew did the cleaning, it seemed unfair to leave everything so messy.

By the time she got it to an organized mess that looked neither planned nor cluttered, Neoma had not seen a soul for an hour. Her journey across the deck to the stairs leading to the bunks was quiet, her steps punctuated by the creaking of the ship. Gentle waves lapped at the hull, and the stars winked happily down at her.

Hope blossomed in her chest, real and heartier than the day it was crushed. When Neoma paused to look out over the water, body aching in a way not dissimilar to when she harvested salt, she did not curse at it's waves or shake her fists at Ocean in anger. In fact, it felt like her son stood next to her, looking out at the blue-black world side by side. He felt closer to her than ever as *The Countess* drifted, the water drinking in his soul to spread it out across the Seas.

At some point, she peeled herself away from the beautiful tableau of the flat blue where the stars reflected perfectly on the ocean's surface, slowly making her way to her bunk. A single lantern hung in the middle of the room, the bodies of the women in their beds rising and falling with deep sleep. By the time she dressed down to her small clothes, her body was happily warm with exertion. The night moved quickly, ushering her into her new life with quiet words and a warm work fire. Neoma's head landed on the pillow with a grateful *thud*, and she was consumed by her deepest sleep in months.

CHAPTER TWENTY-EIGHT

For the first time since his death, Koa *spoke* to her in a dream. The flashes of him Neoma chased since returning to Kairdwillo had lost their aching permanence, only an echo of grief touching the edges of his face in the visions of him walking along the white of the salt beaches, but she had been furious that she was forgetting his voice with every sunset. Sometimes her mind allowed her hands to cup the mirage of his face, soundless laughter spilling out of her chest in the glory of feeling his warmth on her palms. The image of him often wavered between the adult he will never be and the child that was taken by the sea, but both figures fell happily into her arms. Neoma's mind even mimicked the fragrant oils she used to shape the kinkiness of his hair.

Those dreams where every sense tricked her into believing he was alive were the hardest. In this vision, though, there was a new strangeness not tinge by grief. The light was too sharp, harshly refracting across the flat blue of the ocean. Like before, he appeared as a young man, solid features and the dark eyes of his grandfather smiling at her, but a new energy pulsed beneath. When he approached her, walking out of the shimmering light that hung over the sea, a glorious fear hit her stomach.

He walks out of the sea, blessed and figured now, a creature of only spirit no longer. Solid and fractured from his Blessed, he mourns his permanence, and leaps with glee for the impermanent skin which holds him. Kai-Dua, may Ocean always carry him, and may he bless the Currents of the world.

"You seek Ocean now, mother, without realizing it."

Neoma felt the sand underfoot, the old fable humming out of the light around her. She looked up into the eyes of her grown son, feeling that she knew his eyes but not his face. She spoke his name with a soundless voice, questions fading away into the hum of the dream. Koa's large hands settled on her shoulders, a parental care that Neoma once used. His voice kind and deep, the beauty in his gaze contained a world Neoma might not be a part of for some time.

Not until she was ready to follow him into the endless seas of the next realms.

Her son wrapped his arms around her. Into the seashell beads of her hair he murmured words of a language that was familiar to Neoma's bones, but they shaped confusion in her mind.

"Hark," Koa's grown voice murmured in a sound that reverberated with awe. "Hark, mother of mine. Hark, for Great Ocean awakens, and in Its arms shall we be carried into a new Age."

Neoma's eyes flickered open. They searched the cherry wood of the boards overhead for any flecks in the grain that might remain of the vision. Warmth glazed her heart, the tears falling from her eyes ones of an unnamable joy. Koa's words rang in her mind like a wave drawing back from the beaches, and as she rose with the dawn her weary bones surged with a new energy.

Her heart ached for Koa to be in her arms but she found herself silently praising Ocean for granting her such a beautiful dream.

Bodies stirred in their bunks as she rose. The single lantern in the middle of the room swung, lightly creaking like a snore. Neoma dressed in her plain clothing, fastening the ties of her boots with deft precision in the low light. More than familiar with early mornings, she felt a trill of excitement in waking on a ship out at sea. It was her first dawn on *The Countess*, and the dream of her son promised it to be a meaningful one.

"Ah, good. I came to wake you."

The high voice came from the steps leading to the deck. A silhouette stood against the blue-gray light of a rising sun, hardly enough of a beam to see the woman's shape. Neoma straightened, quietly dancing across the boards. Drawing closer to the woman, the soft tinge of gunpowder touched her nose, making it crinkle in surprise. Perhaps the night crew spent their time readying the canons of the ship, and manned them during the hours where pirates tried to catch them unaware.

Making room for Neoma to pass on the steps, the woman kept her head turned towards the cut of shadow that the growing morning light did not touch. Hanging from the sash tied around her forehead were tokens and what Neoma supposed were good luck charms, and when the nameless woman titled her chin for her to walk on, they jangled beautifully.

"Everyone's cleared out now. You'll have the deck to yourself, save for Viorel." The woman spoke lowly, her voice dipping in odd places. She did not seem familiar with the shape of the Common Tongue. "She wanted to speak with you about something before you began. She's above, talking to the quartermaster."

"All right—thank you."

The woman simply nodded, following Neoma up the steps and onto the deck. No one else was seen, and the woman moved around Neoma with the ease of silk on the wind. She wisped across the boards, offering her a good morning over her shoulder in place of a farewell. Neoma wanted to ask where the rest of the bunks were, but simply watched as she slipped down a narrow stairwell hidden on the other side of the captain's cabin.

"Good morning."

Viorel looked down at Neoma from the upper deck. Behind her stood the quartermaster, her hands steady on the wheel as she glanced over Neoma. Settled on her head was a wide-brimmed cap, and a long auburn braid hung over the shoulder of a thick brown vest. Rolled up to the elbows, the sleeves of her jewel blue tunic billowed in the easy morning breeze. Viorel ushered Neoma up one of the double staircases that led to the upper vestibule, waiting until she stood before them to make official introductions.

"Cyra Veles, meet my new cook. Neoma, this is our quartermaster."

Neoma bobbed her chin. "Pleased, ma'am."

The quartermaster smiled at the pleasantry, mouth crinkling. Cyra looked quite plain, yet the air swirling around her was more studious than Viorel.

Other than the smile of acknowledgement, she said nothing. Glancing at Viorel, she simply nodded and relinquished the wheel to the master boatswain. She gave the new cook one more observant look, the color of her eyes hidden in the slant of shadow her hat cast across her features. Only when her back was turned to them did she bid them a good day, voice crisp as apples, not turning to acknowledge either person when they did the same.

The quartermaster knocked twice on the captain's door. Neoma strained her neck around the mast in a vain attempt to peer into the cabin as it opened, and Cyra hushed inside.

Viorel let out a deep sigh as she took her position at the wheel. "I have to apologize for Cyra. There was a skirmish on deck that she spent most of the night settling. Long nights with a rambunctious crew make for bad introductions."

She scratched at a spot on her neck, absently staring out across the deck towards the captain's cabin. Viorel seemed disconnected from the moment, and in the handful of hours Neoma had known her, it was strange to already see a crack in the façade.

"You'll give the crew gruel this morning." Viorel snipped, as though Neoma interrupted her thinking by simply standing there. "Your stew was delicious, but it used more meat than we prefer. The bread was lovely, too, but the captain didn't take too kindly to whole loaves being made on the first night out."

Neoma pursed her lips, folding her hands at her back. Viorel did not sound chastising, though the embarrassment at already being reprimanded heated her cheeks.

Viorel, for her part, gave the woman a softer look. "You've not had to portion as strictly for a crew before, I take it? I know your family's name, and their business. It is good that you can feed them well." She nodded, the tinge in her eyes softening the reprimand in her tone. "In all honesty, it could've been worse. *But* a ship isn't the place for feasts—or egos. It'll get bruised, eventually. Wait until you're a month at sea, looking at the same faces morning, noon, and night." She snickered, shaking her head. "It'll make you rethink your love for the sea, that's for certain."

Neoma wanted to tell her she already doubted that love, but pressed her lips together. The bruise on her heart did not want to be seen so clearly by a stranger, not yet.

Sun cut over the ocean, beams of gold brightening the yellow of Viorel's skin. The master boatswain glowed with memories as she thought about life at sea. Neoma tried to imagine the woman in other livelihoods, and even though she just met her, she could not place Viorel anywhere other than *The Countess*. There were those who might be successful in every endeavor—Inara and Talaya could step in cow dung and walk away smelling light as roses—and there were people who excelled beyond understanding at only one. Viorel expressed a divine solemness, one of a fixated patience that came with years of trials.

The Countess was her home, her perfect endeavor. That mysterious captain might be in charge, but Neoma believed that Viorel knew the seam in every creaking board.

"Dawn's coming." The woman's voice cut through Neoma's thoughts, and she met her daydreaming gaze. "The crew will be up soon, and hungry."

Neoma nodded, turning away with a sense of pride as she took the steps down to the main deck. She took a moment to watch the sun rise, thinking back to those restless nights where she mourned Koa in the depths of darkness. Viorel seemed to feel the severity in the air, and did not disturb Neoma as she watched that golden coin pull itself into a pink morning sky.

It was the same sun, the same ocean she gazed over when her heart shattered in her chest with every beat. Now, the pain was not so visceral. Neoma thought of her mother at the edges of Con-Quarry, and felt the thread connecting her and Calily sing with love. She knew her mother felt that same twinge, and laid her palm tenderly over the soft beating of her chest.

Whatever the night crew prepared for their meals still clung to the boards of the room. Neoma felt her nose crinkle at the thick scent, neither unpleasant nor sharp but simply strange. No spice that she knew of left behind the heady smell, but she knew there was a majestic world out there with foods and flavors and life that she could never imagine. She began her preparation for that morning's meal with a smile while thinking of that, wondering what new experiences *The Countess* might usher in.

I understand what it feels like, not knowing who you love.

Neoma's hands stilled, the cool flintstones warming against her palms. Her cousin's words sat gently on the top of her mind, though she felt it would not be much longer before her heart followed.

Striking the flintstone angrily, uncertain where the fury came from, Neoma blew a deep breath into the embers. So what if she cared for women, *if* she did? Attraction came in many different forms, and was acceptable in even rigorous places like Esmar. The shame that bore into Neoma when she thought about kissing another woman made no sense. Why did it feel wrong to imagine doing with a woman what she did while married to Urias?

And why did it cause the recesses of herself to coil away when she envisioned another woman's physical embrace?

Trying not to focus too hard on all the questions, their answers certainly life-altering and heavier than choosing to board a ship, Neoma brushed aside a few crumbs. Her fingers came away slick, the coarse pads shining with a thin, reddish liquid. Bringing it to her nose, she sniffed the notes of cranberry and wine. Viorel mentioned offhandedly during their turnabout that the captain collected a few bottles that she brought out to share during longer excursions. Perhaps they celebrated casting off, though Neoma thought it unfair to reserve the wine for only the night workers.

Her tongue darted out, tasting the liquid. A bitter tang of berries and iron, a strange combination, filled her mouth. It tasted as though she bit a hole in her tongue. Neoma *tsked*, never having liked wine all that much anyways, but still annoyed that it disappointed her.

"Well, that doesn't bode well for breakfast."

Standing at the base of the steps was the most beautiful woman Neoma ever saw—but not in the way of fine ladies in Con-Quarry, even if the air about her was regal. The woman's umber skin rivaled that of a perfect doll's face, not a blemish or sunspot to be seen. A long coat of heavy fabric stopped at her knees, the boots a gorgeous leather stained crimson with the most intricate pattern of flowers up the sides. Her simple blouse cut deep to reveal the shining black tattoo of a crow in flight on her sternum. Closely cropped hair flicked out from underneath the sash tied around her head, a single teardrop emerald gleaming in her left ear.

Smiling, her piercing silver eyes crinkled at Neoma's awkward silence. Before, Neoma thought Calily to have to most startling gaze, but staring into captured moonlight enticed a shiver from her core. In tandem came the sensation of being desired, both as prey and lover.

Captain Arlowe.

Just as Neoma knew the palm of her mother's hand, she knew the woman standing before her commanded *The Countess*. Where else might someone get such swagger as when she walked deeper into the room, and closer to Neoma?

"Though, most people don't taste random streaks of mysterious liquids," the captain chuckled. She hooked her thumbs in the loops of her trousers. At her hip, a golden hilt to an imposing longsword sparkled. "Pardon the interruption. I'm Captain Armonia Arlowe. I wanted to meet our new cook myself, and apologize that I couldn't walk with you and Viorel."

Neoma spoke without thinking, flustered by the woman's materialization just as much as her startling features. "After my son spent a month throwing anything he could grab, I'm used to mysterious liquids in my mouth." She said, her cheeks darkening with a blush.

Armonia came up short, blinking like Neoma struck her. She suddenly let out a glorious laugh, a bell in the wintertime.

"Gods, Above and Below, remind me to never have a child. How old is he now?" She leaned in, and Neoma did not remember the captain having been close enough to lean against the counter.

Neoma knew the question was of genuine curiosity. It jarred her still, the realization of how quickly his nameday approached giving her pause. It would pass while they were still out at sea, the golden sun dipping into the sea, the moon and stars rising to highlight to moment Koa was born after hours of labor. Her water broke while walking the beach, but he did not slip from that spiritual realm and into her arms until a full moon brightened the bedroom.

She had thought she would celebrate the day with her family. It was the first without him, after all.

A small twitch of disappointment struck her heart.

"He would've been thirteen." Unshed emotion sat in her throat, but she smiled down at the captain to assure her no harm was done in the question. Neoma considered how, before this, no one other than her family was privy to her grief. Was it uncouth to share so much with the captain?

Armonia straightened her posture respectfully. Neoma waited for the usual comforting words, bracing herself for their blandness. Everyone meant well by them, but she could only take so many *I'll think of yous* before she screamed at someone to just bring her back her son.

"You must be the bravest woman among us, then," Armonia surprised her by saying, "for I can't think of anything more frightening than suffering a grief which might shatter me completely, then sailing off to the middle of nowhere to face it."

The emotion she barely managed to hide slipped out in a tear. The captain watched it move gently down her cheek before Neoma swiped it away with her thumb, nervous under the earnest gaze.

She had no idea what to say other than a quiet, "Thank you."

Neoma thought carefully about the captain's words, feeling a piece of herself locking them away to savor them. Her mother called her brave for leaving Urias. Sulien made sure to call her a fool before giving any sort of compliment on starting her life over at her age. But in all their loving embrace, she did not recall anyone in her family saying she was brave for simply *feeling* her grief.

Not knowing how to tell the captain the importance of her words without sounding overbearing, Neoma busied her hands with preparing breakfast. "I'm really sorry, captain, but I—"

"Quiet alright." Armonia nodded, already stepping away from the counter. "I didn't mean to keep you from your duties, although I might steal you away on your first off-day. I doubt Viorel went through the documentation with you?"

Neoma hesitated. "Erm… documentation?"

"Ah. Well," Armonia winked, "between you and me, Viorel can only read a compass but I wouldn't have anyone else manage the crew—but yes. Everyone on board receives a proper contract outlining their tasks, payment, and how long they'll be under the command of *The Countess*. We also take note of names and lineage in case any ports have a question regarding who I've employed. I'll send Cyra after you. You've met her, yes?"

Neoma almost poured salt into the porridge instead of a handful of sugar. Overcorrecting herself, the salt spilled across the counter. "Gods, damn it all to the Aether—Yes. I'm sorry. Just this morning."

When she peered up through her lashes, cheeks darkening with embarrassment, the captain gazed at her with that look from before. Armonia seemed both a hunter and a doting friend in that moment, a sharpness Neoma did not dare name in her eyes.

"Breathe, Neoma."

Caught off guard by the instruction, she became acutely aware of the rise and fall of her chest.

Armonia smiled gently. "There. It's only salt. Your tears'll be more of a waste. I'll fetch you on the Fifth Day."

The captain bobbed her head, sealing the arrangement, the emerald earring sparking in the cookfire. Neoma watched her turn and walk up the stairs, heart in her throat, the quick interaction leaving a burning in her chest that was no unpleasant.

At the top of the steps, someone spoke briskly to the captain as she left the eatery. Their words were hushed, but Armonia carried the whining tone of a younger sibling complaining to their elder.

It was nice to have met the captain before too long—Neoma's daydreaming was getting the best of her—but the interaction made her feel raw for some reason. Was it Armonia's dualistic gaze as it observed her, or the swagger that cloaked the captain's every movement that made her heart thrum? Urias, or any suitor, had never been as bold to walk the room like a royal, and Neoma did not know how to behave when such attention fell completely to *her*.

Perhaps the captain was sizing up the crew's newest member, using paperwork as an excuse to judge the woman without the distraction of the crew. Either way, Neoma thought she passed whatever the secretive judgement was, though something about Armonia's solid, dazzling presence made her skin prickle with apprehension.

CHAPTER TWENTY-NINE

They woke in a land between lands to a song shaped by tongues whose countries were long dead. Voices of stone and water, campfires in the deep wood and towers that touched the clouds, murmured wisdom that coveted to be heard but that Sen did not possess the ability to translate.

Languages fractured over their slowly waking eyes. These shapeless memories glowed a symphony of blues, their forms moving like squid across the ocean floor. From above Sen's head the memories pulled away, acknowledging Sen's wakefulness before sinking into the stone of the walls and ceiling.

Water reflected against the room, shivering seams of white, but when Sen turned their head they saw no pool. They laid in a narrow stone room large enough for the simple bed they rested upon, the gaping doorway in the wall revealing only more flickering stone.

Valeska's withering body flashed across their memory, the gore making their stomach turn. Sen touched their face, bracing for the pain of their prodding fingers as they recalled his wailing fists—and his uncovered sin.

No splintered bone ached under their skin. Along their forehead was a simple bandage, but when they tore it from their scalp it was barely crusted with blood.

Around them, the air parted. Sen felt their gaze pull towards the middle of the small room, drawn but a hum they did not hear but felt in their blood. Their eyes struggled to focus on a shimmering aura as it wavered, splitting like a cut on the skin, and from that fractured space the robed woman slipped into reality. **

She materialized before Sen with an undercurrent of power that sent the hair on their arms on edge. Unlike before, her mouth was not dark and veiny with sickness, nor were her robes dull in hue. The strange woman, vibrant with healthy warm skin and deep brown eyes, seemed the better twin of the creature who flayed a highborn with magic.

Magic.

Sen felt their blood sing. It was not the itch beneath their skin when the wind turned, or the tingle in their palms when they called up a flame. What surged through them, pulsed up from the rocks underfoot, was the magic that their ancestors once called upon as easily as breathing.

Questions tripped over one another in their mind. Sen gazed at the woman, her navy blue attire struck through with reams of silver starlight. As soon as they opened their mouth to ask their first question, the answer filled their tongue.

"This… is the Godrealm." It felt like a delicate hand placed the sweet round cherry of the answer on their tongue. Sen's mouth filled with the magic of *knowing*, though understanding was still beyond their reach.

The woman smiled. It shined, a beam of sunlight. Sen thought of that same warmth that cascaded over them as they laid, aching and broken, on the street.

"It has many names." Under her voice were a thousand others, soft and careful, toes dancing on glass. "But in your time, most know it as the Godrealm."

Just as before, answers bubbled up from a deep well within Sen. *Cherries, and slices of candied peaches. A taste of peace after grief. Sweetness after the bitter aroma of mourning.*

Sen tasted this memory that did not belong to them, waiting for the trill of interest to fade before they spoke. "Time works differently here."

"Yes. And you will grow accustomed to this feeling flowing through you now, of the ancestors speaking with your tongue."

Sen pulled themselves up on the small bed slowly. Waves of power shivered around them, some of the currents like sharp pierces of lighting while others moved across the surface of their face like water. They looked down, seeing they wore robes similar to the woman's, their bare toes flexing after a long sleep.

A strong feeling pulled in their gut. It railed against all that Sen once believed. Their body did not fully belong to them in the Godrealm, but Sen was not afraid of whatever lingered in their blood.

No—whatever was *awakening* inside them.

She sleeps… Ma'Ceste.

Even though they had not spoken, the woman's eyes brightened. The excitement in them did not settle the queasiness in Sen's gut. Power covered their head, bearing down with the mention of the ancient goddess' name. Whoever the voice belonged to, it did not slink away from the power but leaned towards it, almost pulling Sen's body off of the stone bed.

The gods... are real?

They thought of every holiday that went without an honorable fast, every death anniversary when they did not stand long enough at the altar to their ancestors.

Shame—and a fiery tendril of exhilaration—burned through them.

"Yes, child, yes." The woman's voice ripped them from their stupor. "Rise, and come with me. There are other things awakening, and you are not meant to dwell here."

Sen obeyed, tilting as they stood. Their feet hit the solid stone but their mind rose to the sky. Their stomach dropped, but with a gentle placement of her hand against their back, the woman sent a gentle wave through them. Sen felt their mind drift slowly back into their body, the planes evening out until the nausea was gone.

"You will get used to it." She grinned. "Your body and spirit are unaccustomed to walking in the Between places. Give it time—you will learn."

The woman said so with a disturbing attitude of certainty.

Sen pressed their palm flat against their chest. They *seemed* real and solid. The stone that hushed underfoot scraped against their bare feet. But this must be a dream, like the one when they were in the throughs of bitterthorn. Had Valeska actually killed them, and now their mind was making up a story in its lucidness?

"No," the woman said carefully. Then, "With me, young heir."

She led the dazed Sen out of the room. It sat on the edge of a larger chamber, the smell of brine thick. The entire room was doused in blue, mystical and deep. Eyes drawn upward by the light, Sen balked, and drew up short. Above them glistening the belly of the ocean, the sun a pinprick of light overhead. Shards of light danced along the walls, interrupted by the bodies of massive sea creatures lazily drifting through the scene. A school of fish danced high above them and Sen watched their glittering scales, mesmerized.

They were *underneath* the ocean.

They wanted to stay longer, to spy what other creatures might drift along the ocean's current, but the woman urged them to cross the threshold to an opposite hallway. She did not seem as fascinated with the scene.

"I have no name now, which is why your ancestors cannot recall it." The woman did not seem remiss, adding, "I am Her Godharker. I was called an Age ago to be her Vessel during the great Apathesis, when men once regarded one another as only contracts and not siblings, part of a greater whole. But She has been sleeping since before the Plights."

Let my Godharker find you, you child of Stone, of Salt, of River, of the ever-kindling Flame in the lantern of the Traveler.

When the voice lifted from their mind, pulled from the depths of their memory, the Godharker paused. Raising the hand not guiding Sen, she murmured, "Praise to the Sleeping One, Ma'Ceste. May Her slumber end soon. May Her wakefulness guide us into a new Age."

A shiver of pridefulness drifted over them, and the Godharker continued on down the narrow stone hall.

Chambers in the deep, mirrors of the Goddess when she was wakeful, walking, watchful.

"Yes," hummed the Godharker in reverence, talking to the voices in Sen's mind.

The hall was plain stone, unassuming in its nature. Sen let their hand drift over it, relishing the cool feeling under their fingertips. Was this truly the place where the ancestors of their family once dwelled? Sen wondered if this world beneath the waves once thrived like the ocean that concealed it. Perhaps there were even vines of seaweed climbing up the stone that withered once the goddess shut her eyes.

A new question surged forward, one that made their skin heat with interest. Is the sleeping goddess the reason their family's magic has nearly vanished?

The Godharker gave them a look that said she heard Sen's musing clearly, even when their voice remained trapped in their throat. Whatever moved through them to deposit the answers on their tongue fell silent during their slow walk down the hall, the murmurs stalled as the Godharker led them to a room with a serene, crystalline pool in the middle. Its water shivered at their entrance, ripples breaking away from the edges of the stone, their steps a disturbance. Sen felt the magic wafting off the pool, walking against a heavy tapestry. While the magic did not reject them, its very essence resented their disturbance. From the water lifted the scent of lilac and smoky wood fires; the Godharker did not pause at the threshold but brought Sen to the very edge of the pool.

Gently, she placed her fingers beneath Sen's chin to guide their gaze to the pool's foundation. Far below the surface of the water rested a statue of a woman, her eyes shut against the blue light. Folded over her stomach were two sets of arms, one with its hands in a position where the fingers stretched up towards them. Sand rested across her body like a blanket, sea kelp dancing against the stone of her hair.

A small bubble drifted out of the nose of the statue. Sen's gaze widened as it rose up and up and up until it finally broke the surface of the water.

It was not a statue at the bottom of the ocean, *but a goddess.*

Stumbling away from the edge of the pool, Sen's stomach flipped as the splitting feeling returned. All at once, the power of their surroundings hit like an iron fist to their gut. Gasping, they wrapped their arms around their torso, struggling to hold themself in one piece. The Godharker watched them carefully as they caught their breath, shivering under the weight of looking upon the face of Ma'Ceste, of their family's goddess, as she laid trapped in stone.

"You feel the magic in the air."

It was not a question. The Godharker raised her hands, attempting to catch the reflection of the water against her skin. "It's so strong, even as She sleeps! Imagine how She will change the world once that slumber ends."

"What's happening to me?" Violent disruption surged through Sen's body. It was not simply the splitting feeling from before, but a great wave of panic. The Godharker said something about their ancestors—was this a warning in their blood?

"What did you do?"

"I only did what he wanted to do to others." The Godharker lowered her hands, narrowing her gaze onto Sen when they realized she spoke of Valeska. "And he desired much worse than flaying. It was grace that ended him swiftly. His bones are perfect to hold the curses for my enemies." She patted her chest, where the volume disappeared that night.

"What's happening to *me*?" Sen begged again. Blood rushed in their ears, the voices of their ancestors screaming from behind door that was suddenly impenetrable.

The Godharker stepped forward. "You have sworn to Ma'Ceste. She visited you where She exists now—in your dreams, on the brink of an illness from a poison fed to you by a friend. She came to you, and marked you so that I may appear in the world while I am still able."

Sen matched the woman by taking a step back. Thoughts swam in their mind, the pressure rising until it felt like their skull might split in half. *A great beast, unimaginable, wavering with the strength of a hundred godrealms, a horn bellowing from the deep. A woman, a son, a great and vast ocean that spans lifetimes, and a silver eye watching it all in the depths of the night. Sinking earth squelching underfoot, but a man lifts his hand in the dark to hold the hands of his ancestors.*

"You've sworn—"

Sen felt their stomach turn, bile churning against the proclamation: "*No.*"

The Godharker opened her arms, predatory eyes seeking its prey. Her voice boomed across the cavern, the millions beneath rising in a cacophony of screeching dominance.

"*You have sworn, and you will listen! By Fire you will be purged, by Water, renewed! The Earth shall eat your flesh and the Air shall pour the spirit into your lungs, and you shall be ready to take my place as Godharker.*"

Crumbling beneath the weight of the magic bearing down from every direction, Sen shook violently with fear and rage. They squeezed their eyes against the Godharker as she approached, no longer vibrating with the power of a thousand voices but still reeking of woodsmoke. The burning scent permeated the room, a sign of ancient power, of Ma'Ceste.

The Godharker bent to her knees, the robe of her sleeve draping down Sen's back when she put her arm around them carefully. Her forehead met theirs in an embrace that was more considerate than anything their mother ever did. Cupping their face, the Godharker's palm was cool, as frozen as winter.

"You will die unto yourself," her singular voice whispered gently. "You will be stripped of the confines of your blood that make your magic *weak*. You, Sen of the Sleeping One, Godharker Apparent, will share your body with divinity. What more can a person like us ask for?"

Like us?

Sen met the woman's close gaze only to see a familiar pain reflected there. Had the Godharker been forsaken by her family, too? Was she one of those ancient mages who were exiled from the YeSara Clan, erased from their family lineage?

But it was all wrong. Is not a person meant to come to a path of devotion willingly? Sen did not know why they were swearing, or for whom the oath was meant. Their whole life before being shamefully dismissed from their Clan was measured by their mother's legacy, the legacy of the Matriarchs before them. Naseria wanted an heir with magic so that she could strength her station. Now, at the lowest point of their life, yet another creature wanted to take Sen's freedom of will and mold it from their own desire because of the echo of magic in their veins.

"*No.*"

The Godharker's gaze narrowed.

"No." Sen broke away from her grasp and struggled to stand. They felt the weight of the ocean bearing down on them but managed to rise, looking at her. All their wrath shot out towards the Godharker, towards the sleeping goddess at the bottom of the pool. A chorus of vengeful joy sang out in their blood, and as the Godharker rose to standing, they pointed an accusing finger at her.

"This is *my* body," they spat, feeling the tremor in their arm against the pressure. "I won't be forced into the submission of a goddess who can't get her own followers without making them swear *unknowingly* to her."

"How dare you!" The woman screeched. Any kindness in her gaze vanished. Sen noticed the black, rotten flick of her tongue as she screamed at them. "Your body belongs to Ma'Ceste! She granted you your power, even when your blood is weak and tinged by the blight. You *will* be Her Herald! How dare you—*How dare you defy me!*"

A voice of thunder and freshly turned soil barreled out of the Godharker's mouth. The woman stumbled forward, catching herself before slamming against the stone floor. Behind her, the water in the pool churned and frothed against the edges of its confines, the stone shaking violently all around them.

"*Creatures wake in the depths of my ocean*," the resounding voice said, the Godharker's eyes darkening into something wild and beautiful. "*I must reclaim my place in the Aether before the Duathi rips apart the seams of this world and vomits his putrid filth with reckless abandon! I must find his Godharker—I must walk the earth! My Godharker*," the woman, her body controlled now by the goddess, pressed her hands lovingly against her own face. "*She has served me too long between the worlds*."

"Yes, well," Sen grimaced, "that sounds like a failure of foresight on your part."

The Godharker screeched, launching herself up from the stone floor with clawed fingers, scrambling for Sen's robes. They stumbled, careening out of the room and back into the long hall. Blood rushed into their head as their feet slammed down on the shivering stone, no clue where to go, only trusting the pull of their blood as they ran back into the chamber with the ocean as its ceiling. Water sprinkled down from overhead, threatening to burst and wash Sen into nothing.

Eyes jumping wildly around the room, they spied another hall that turned suddenly, concealing its path. Sen figured it was better than standing there, and scrambled across the floor when the Godharker condemned their insolence with a screech.

Sen met the face of their ancestral goddess *and spit in it*. Yet for some reason, the blood in their veins surged with the sense of freedom.

The hall deposited them into another room with pools sitting as mirrors on the wall. Despite the stone shaking with the anger of Ma'Ceste, the water remained flat, still. One showed a bright, white beach where a dark-skinned man with kinky hair stood, his face towards the sun. Another gazed down at a ship gliding across a dark ocean, the its sleek, cherry colored wood almost black in the moonlight. The one directly across from Sen revealed nothing but a black pit of swirling smoke, but they felt eyes gazing out from beyond daring them to keep staring.

They forced themself to look away from that one, a flash of those strange visions of a creature from before making their stomach hurt.

"The Tularin Baths are out of season."

Sen whipped around, heart in their throat, to face the man who stood on the glowing white beach. His smile was kind, dark eyes shining with friendliness, and his clothing was well-tailored but nondescript. Jerking his chin, the man motioned to the pool on the wall across from him that showed the picturesque lakeside bathhouse in the Gilded Isles. Sen faced it, glancing between the man and the curved shoreline of a large lake.

"That's where that pool leads—the Tularin Baths, in Lesser Syvon. Your friends won't be there because it's the off-season. Just step through."

Too many questions rambled in their mind, but their blood did not roil against the man, and the voices seemed pleased with his help. Despite the strangeness of it all, and the sickening roil of magic in their head, Sen felt they could trust him.

He smiled again, but there was urgency in his gaze. "The Godharker can only risk going into the physical world in short periods. She's exhausted what magic is left this day. If she followed you now, it would kill her."

Sen felt no shame in their relief at that. "Thank you."

The man nodded, turning his back to Sen, not bothering to watch them slip through the portal or explain any more about what he knew or who he was. He walked towards the water with an easy gait, peace radiating out of the mirage that softened the fear in Sen's chest.

Over his shoulder, the man added in a casual tone, "You mustn't hate her—either of them. The world's forgotten everything. That's a type of pain that never heals, being forgotten."

The stone shook, throwing Sen out of their daze and away from the man's words. A sleeping goddess, and angry herald, a man in the wall—what did it matter if they dove through a portal of water?

Holding their breath, for they did not understand how this magic worked, Sen leapt through the shimmering surface of the water-mirror. They felt the sharp nails of the Godharker rake the back of their neck before they were yanked upward towards a light, spun around like they were thrown down a steep hill. The vision of the Tularin Baths faded as murky gray-blue water rushed around their head, granules of sand and lake weeds slinking over their skin.

Sen's head broke the surface of a great lake with a deep gasp of shock.

Flailing, breathless, Sen cried out at the bright sun, the dollops of clouds. Situated on the banks of the lake were the gleaming pillars of the familiar bathhouse, string music flittering down as soft as butterfly wings. Covered gondolas split the water, cozying up to the docks as the end of the day approached and patrons returned to their rooms.

Leaning back, exhaustion hammering through their bones, Sen allowed the lazy pull of the lake to carry them. A bark of humorless laughter escaped them as they drifted, squinting against the bright evening sky, but beneath was a spark of unease.

Ma'Ceste, the goddess mythology stated was the ancestor of the YeSara Clan, was real. She slept in a realm beyond Sen's comprehension, solid as stone but as uncatchable as the wind. Stories made her out to be a divine, loving mother to their bloodline, but the power Sen felt in the strange world was not kind or gentle.

A mother, childless, whispered those voices, the sadness unmistakable. *A child forgotten by the sea. Blood spilled on sacred ground, tears from the gods rising up from the earth.*

Sen did not understand what the visions meant, letting them drift over their body just as their body drifted in the lake. All it left behind, mingling with the uncertainty, was a feeling of disconnectedness and grief.

They ignored the wish of a goddess and her ancient vassal, so they should be terrified. But the journey to another world reshaped the fabric of their inner being. Sen's blood *shifted* into something else entirely, and while there were no voices murmuring ancient whispers, the thrumming in their body sang like the most glorious battle cry. Inside, a part of themself was awakening. Even though the confusion surrounding it all meant they had no idea what exactly changed, it brought a strange peace over them as they floated.

With tears in their eyes, Sen realized they no longer felt *alone*. Even the strange visions tied a thread around their hearts, the other ends unknown but a welcomed heaviness. The Godrealm tore down a wall dividing Sen from their guiding, powerful ancestors.

Love—foreign, but not unwelcome—stirred in their heart, the embrace shielding them against the tenacious fear left behind as they wondered how long it may take for the Godharker to regain her strength.

She would find them. After all, they were *marked.*

Sen barely remembered that faded dream, and felt a fool for dismissing it. Paths twisting in every direction, and they had been forced down one for someone else's gain. Heroes in fables were tricked, like Sen was tricked, to carry out great feats in the name of some divine Being.

But that did not mean anyone deserved the right to claim to *their* body. Not even a goddess.

CHAPTER THIRTY

It was hard for goodness to stick in Dice's mind. In Stormshale, she dreamt of returning to the *Marksmen*, to her normal life aboard a ship. Clever work came from being under a flag with no loyalty to any country, as did certain freedoms, and she thought finding her way back to the sea meant healing the ache of shame and loss in her chest. Busier hands, the brine in the air—these things used to keep her darker thoughts at bay, thoughts that festered and clamored to the front while on land.

But the fear in her belly seemed palpable on the open ocean, as if an awful circumstance meant to fell the entire crew and sink the *Marksmen* to the depths of sunless sands. Rory offered something of a comfort, but Brutis teased her for it. It called back to a softer time, like when she was first taken with a dockhand as a young girl. Brutis did not stop calling her *lovebird* until she begged Evander to make him. Even then, the man laughed, not out of bitterness but out of the joy from watching her discover the beauty of infatuation.

Yet the teasing made her uncomfortable when she considered the real reason she came to depend on Rory's company, but Dice understood Brutis' watchful gaze. Evander made sure she stayed alive, but it was Brutis she went to when she first bled, and when she first thought about having sex with women as well as men.

Ever since returning to the *Marksmen*, her avoidance of those who were her family was a solid knot around her heart. Days passed since her return, and other than allowing Brutis a moment to ask about her limp and if the wound caused her pain, Dice kept their conversations short. She eventually hobbled away with a brief remark, busying herself with chores or disappearing into the decks below to search for the book.

Almost a week passed since Rory watched her cry blood, and thus decided to hide the book from her. It was his to do with, Dice knew this in her core just as she knew to respect the superstitious crowds in Sovil's docks as they blessed every ship that came into the harbor. It was not her culture, it was Rory's, so how did she explain to him that the more time she spent away from the book the more she more she wanted to peel off her skin?

One benefit of knowing the *Marksmen* better than Rory meant she knew its hiding places. Loosened floorboards, if not made by her, were used by the crew to disappear all types of paraphernalia, from gold to crude little booklets sold outside of whorehouses. Dice found plenty of those as she searched, pocketing one that boasted drawings of the women in *The Queen's Clam* in Trilabold.

What was strange about the haunting of Evangeline, other than the shift of its appearance that made Dice's stomach sink, was when it decided to emerge. Dice dug into the rice barrels at one point, wondering if Rory and her were of like minds, and suddenly there was Evangeline. It simply stared, offering no biting statements that called to the pitch colored guilt within Dice.

She closed the barrel, facing the apparition with a sick feeling in her chest.

Dice swallowed past the dryness in her throat. "You know where it is."

Evangaline smiled a rotten, toothless grin. It lowered its balding head in what seemed like a nod. Either the apparition fed off of Dice's knowledge of a decaying body, or it really was showing how much the rot set in.

Neither option made her feel more at peace.

The haunting turned before Dice said anything else, vanishing lower into the floor with every step until it disappeared.

Of course.

Dice had not given Rory proper credit. She wove through the supply room to the steps leading down into the dank, unlit hold of the ship. Iron creaked from the darkness, one of the gates swinging with every small dip in the water, ushering as her heavy boots *thumped* on the steps.

With a trembling hand, her fingers caught the cool metal and slid the grate back into place. It released an angry groan, but relented under her grasp. The only light came from the steps behind her, and she allowed her eyes to adjust to the depths.

All around her, the boards moaned against the pressure of the sea. Standing in the near darkness, Dice sensed the book, its fingers dancing across her skin tantalizingly. It yanked the heartstrings in her chest, making her scramble forward like a hungry dog into the darkness. Her fingers sought out the random barrels, nails scraping against the wood as she searched for any nooks that might conceal a journal. At one point, she dropped to her knees to pat her hands along the damp boards, fingers coming away smelling of mildew and rot.

The closed gate to the first cell creaked open behind her. Dice stared at it over her shoulder, watching as the iron swung open, then closed, then opened again. Evangeline's ghost had vanished, but Dice knew that something else was urging her to find the book just as she knew her hair was black.

Within the cell was a single bench meant to also be used as a bed. Nothing rested upon it or the floor, and as Dice stepped past the threshold she felt her skin pimple with unnatural cold. The hair on her arms rose, the painful guidance within her chest straining so tightly around her heart that she gasped.

Slamming closed, the grate locked itself shut. Dice whipped around when she heard the movement but only managed to catch it as the bolt connected. Fear rose in her belly as she shook the thing, shouting at the damnable iron before calling out for help. If anyone found her, they would have questions, and the strangeness would reach Evander before she could blink—but Dice did not care. The fear inside her turned visceral. She leaned away to kick with all her might against the grate, panic slickening her palms.

She felt the air split, knew that Evangline stood somewhere in the cell with her, but Dice needed to get *out*, needed to be free, needed to—

"Look."

Evangeline's voice carried the weight of the lives Dice stole.

Gripping the bars of the gate, she shook it in weak frustration. Tears clogged her throat. She took lives before, just as she was taught. Some were in self-defense, some were accidental, but none left her feeling a wound so deep that it bore a hole right through her.

"I don't know what happened." Dice sobbed the words against the gate. She pressed her forehead on the iron bars, fighting against the strain in her throat. The dead eyes of Evangeline's decapitated husband watched from behind her closed lids. "It can't have been me. It can't have been *me*."

She waited for that boney hand to take her, but it never came. Instead, something more wicked hushed over her limbs.

"Dice." The tender voice of her old lover almost made her turn, but Dice's gaze dropped to the floor in shame.

Evangeline sighed. "Dice… of course it wasn't *you.*"

The air stilled. Looking up, Dice saw the dust motes in the weak light of the stairwell hanging in the air, immobile. Beneath her feet the boards went still, not even creaking as she pulled away from the gate. Her hands shook as the words reverberated through the cell.

It was not you.

A voice from the bowels of the sea murmured, and the song of the ocean went completely silent.

Dice felt the grip of a hundred eyes turning to gaze upon her. Her gut dropped, sluggish in her belly as she, against her will, turned to face them.

Screams climbed in Dice's throat, eyes wide, but the emotion died in her mouth. The wall of the cell was gone, replaced with a swirling pool of vibrating darkness that pulled back in a way that made Dice's eyes struggle to focus. A world of violent purple storms extended beyond the faded boards of the ship, expanding across the horizon as a red sun set over an ocean of dark, churning blood.

Until, overcome with a panic that solidified in her bones, Dice realized it was not a sun at all but a creature so bright and powerful in its image that her mind refused to see it. Its body surged through the water; it drew upwards into the sky to create a wall of red. The thundering storm clouds drew close, obscuring everything other than the approaching monster. The smell of magic hit the back of her throat as Dice pressed herself against the bars of the gate, pressed herself away from the onslaught of pain that poured through her senses. Underfoot, the planks ripped away from the floor and disappeared into the swirling vortex with a crackling groan. She kicked back, standing on her toes until she was gripping the bars, or else fall into the purple, furious clouds below.

The glowing creature, its body moving like a flag caught in the wind, rose out of the bloody ocean. Rivers of carnage sloshed from its hide, landing into the sea with heavy drops that splashed Dice's trouser leg. Power radiated from it, the pressure so heavy against Dice's chest that she struggled to inhale. The iron smell of the world overpowered her, her body struggling between remaining upright over the swirling clouds, and simply letting go.

Letting go would be so easy.

Dice's eyes jumped away from the creature, knowing it influenced her sudden desire to drop into the horrors at her feet.

You fight against it, as though it's a shame you must carry. Do not.

She squeezed her eyes shut, and the wind cut across her body like slivers of glass. Her knuckles ached, grip on the iron so tight that her forearms shook with fatigue.

Evangeline. The innocent man who was gutted and killed by my hand.

"It *is* my shame." She choked out, fighting with the little will that still belonged to her. But it *hurt* to argue against it, and the insolence threatened to shatter her mind.

The creature despised her response. It reared back and poured from its throat the sound of death, of a mother who buried her child and a grief of disconnectedness. Howls of regret drenched Dice's mind, clouding out anything other than her need to *make it stop.*

Make it stop.

Dice opened her eyes. All that was left of her world was the gate she held on to like a lifeline. The creature vanished, leaving behind only the waves of purple clouds. Lightning jumped across their billowing surfaces, the wind swirling the haze into thick eddies.

It was horrific.

It was beautiful.

Rolling through her mind was a song she never heard before. The ballad drew up from the core of her being, humming together to meld with rolls of thunder. It was the darkest parts of herself, there before the pitch stained her insides, there before the moment of her birth. The darkness swam in her blood, just as she swam in her mother's stomach. It stained her long before Dice was a thought, long before her mother drank the blood of a beast under the deception of its followers.

Dice's vision wavered as a memory which was not hers stole the breath from her lungs. The world pulled back, leaving a sharp pain in her chest that dripped like wine into her stomach.

A woman with hair as dark as pitch, a man with a cowl that hid his face, a promise of fortune and a god's favor should the woman simply drink. A stomach swollen with love, left in anger, the child swimming in the water of the womb of a woman tired of lies. A hope that it will be better, that the god will bless her, that the god will kill those who shamed her. A smile as bitter as the poison the woman choked down. Fear, and instant regret, but it's done, it's done.

She felt the tears of blood on her cheeks, chest heaving as she dropped to the floor. Pain ripped through her, a scream so thick that it shook her being. Another sound broke through, the begging whispers of a familiar voice, hands holding fast to the blade of a dagger in her grasp, struggling to keep it from plunging into her own chest.

"*Stop, stop—please, stop.*" Rory's arms shook with exertion. His bare hands gripped the blade, Dice's fingers clawed tightly around the hilt. Eyes squeezed shut, his brow knit as he prayed, begging, dragging the blade away from Dice's chest even as his blue-black blood dripped down the length of his forearm.

The momentum from when she released the blade in shock, horrified at what she might have done, sent him falling backwards. Rory gaped, watching the awareness return to her gaze. Then he threw the blade into the darkness of the cell and grabbed her shaking hands, her bloody face. As their blood mingled, damp and hot with life and rich with the smell of iron and salt, Rory stared into Dice's eyes.

A violent wave of fury came over her, fury at his softness and his safety, and she shoved him back. The stranger caught himself but waited, eyes searching her face as though offering a lifeline.

"Why did you stop me?" She bit, chest heaving. "Why did you stop me? Why? It could be done! *It could be done.*"

Rory's bloody hand reached out for her, hanging in the space between them. A deep cut sliced across his palm, a blue smear on the soft skin. He said nothing, made no move to shout or show his discomfort.

His ease made her angry again.

"I wanted it."

"No." Rory shook his head sharply, not moving his gaze from her face.

"I did." Every sinew of her being strained to search for the book, for the knife, for anything that might relieve the discomfort that promised to rip her apart. "If I don't die, then what? I kill someone else?"

Rory's brow knit together. "Talamondin was ill. I regret his death, but—"

"I'm not talking about him!" She howled, scrambling further away, wishing to be consumed by the dark like in her dream with the bard.

The shining intestines sliding down the wall. Knucklebones on the mantle. Bodiless head gazing at her accusingly. Her dagger in his throat. Evangeline's body, shining, abused to the moment of her death, and then after.

Defeated, Dice pulled her knees to her chest. Her chest cracked, splintered mind weary with pretending. "I'm not talking about *your* friend."

There was the sound of shuffling. Rory settled at the threshold of the cell, his hand still reaching out, eyes still filled with worry. He kept the distance between them, but even so, Dice felt the heat radiating off him.

The word came before she could stop it: "*Why?*"

"You can't kill yourself, Dice."

"No," she cut him off sharply. "Why do you care? Why do you care enough to stay? You have your book." The venom in her tone made it obvious that she was still bitter about him hiding it. "What does it matter if I die, if—if—"

She had no words to describe the vision of the creature, or the strange world. But she knew now it was impossible to ignore the call, for it was not the song of the ocean in her mind but the summoning of the Duathi.

Its music had been calling to her since the moment her mother drank its blood.

The warmth of Rory's bleeding hand jolted her out of her limp acceptance of the truth. A creature she could not satisfy, a mother she did not know. What did it matter if Dice could not make sense of it, when death would call her soon enough?

He dared to lean closer when she did not pull away, scooting on his knees into the cell to sit across from her.

Slowly, he lifted a hand to her chest. He laid it over the wound there, the nick deep enough to sting when he pressed it. The weight steadied Dice's breathing, an odd comfort as his eyes roved over the bloody, frightened mess of her face.

"If this book can harm one, it can harm many."

Dice shook her head. "It's not the *book*. Not completely."

"Then you're someone in need of a friend."

"You don't want to be my friend."

Rory gave her a small grin. "That's probably true. But you don't get to decide that for me."

His kindness startled her, so still, she pressed. "I killed—no, I did worse than that. What if I do it again? What if I do it to *you?*"

"Then I'll haunt you like whatever haunts you now." He chuckled at her alarm, her mouth gaping but finding no defense. "Yes. I see you looking over your shoulder, I see you whispering to it. I don't know what you've done, Dice, other than kill a friend whom I loved but was no doubt lost to himself and to the world when you found him. This *book* did that to him. The *book* made him stay on land until it brought his death. *It* holds you in its grasp and urges you to kill, even if it means taking your own life. I don't know why the book hasn't influenced me yet," his breath caught, the fear there leaking into his words, "but I want to be prepared when it does.

"But all of that aside, I don't need a reason other than empathy to help someone who's hurting." Rory moved his hand from her chest, the print of his blue blood an emblem over the red of her wound. "If I left you like this now, the guilt might destroy me."

"I am *not* your burden." The tears broke free, the weight of his words and the gentleness in them too much for her heart to accept. She sobbed, catching the sound in her throat, angry at such weakness—angry that she was not stronger.

Rory frowned, his own eyes glistening with unshed tears. "You are a fool if you think kindness is a burden."

A great curtain of sadness fell over her. It weighed down her shoulders, muffled the sobs wracking through her chest as reality huddled to the front of her mind. Dice wanted to beg Rory to abandon the ship but the selfishness at hearing those words made the request die in her throat. She wanted to tell him it was not foolishness that rejected him but fear, for if she had it within herself to gut a complete stranger, then what stopped her from murdering him, or Evander, or anyone trapped on this ship with her?

He sealed the promise of his death as he took her slowly in his arms like one would a violent child, uncertain if they might fight or surrender to comfort.

She thought it better to die in Stormshale than to have Rory hold her, knowing that whatever happened next would be both their fault.

Rory smelt of the iron of his blood, and the salt of the sea. Inhaling, in the darkness of the *Marksmen*, in the arms of a friend who promised to her his death by staying, Dice felt the eyes of the Duathi find her. It wanted to know what she thought of her vision, of the story of a mother she never knew, of its child of the water that held her despite it all. It was strange to sense as much in her mind, the barrier dropping after her horrid vision.

Now, the connection spanning between them felt like a chord tying Dice to a boulder. At any moment, by simply its will, Dice would drown.

"Promise that you'll kill me if—"

The sound of heavy footsteps on the stairs behind them halted her request. Rory stared down at her, not bothering to look at the figured who appeared in the low light. But Dice knew his footsteps as well as her own heartbeat, and swiveled in Rory's grasp as Evander stepped into the shallow light of the brig.

His head jerked around the room, studying the blood on her face, the unnatural smear of blue on her tunic.

Evander's eyes slid, rich in fury, to Rory. Dice, already scrambling to her feet, moved into the space between the two men. Her limbs shook with exhaustion, and the weariness of her pace made her father draw his focus to her.

The look in his eyes softened, but only just.

"You," he said, voice low, "will tell me what's going on."

"Evander—"

"You'll tell me why you're screaming, why you are forgetting what you live and breathe." He took a step forward. "And you will tell me what *he* has to do with it. That's an order from your captain, which I still am by the way."

Rory stayed quiet, rising to his feet behind Dice. His wide eyes met hers, fear at being exposed sinking his features.

...you're someone in need of a friend.

She whipped around, suddenly resolute despite her fatigue. "He has nothing to do with it."

Evander scoffed. She avoided him for too long, now marking anything she said to him a lie, but lie she would.

"I'm riding him, Evander. Is that what you want to hear? That, yes, something is going on, but I'm distracting myself the best way I know how?"

As a pirate, this did not shock Evander. "Explain the blood, then, and all the ink." He motioned to Rory's blood on her shirt, on his hands.

Ink.

She rolled her eyes, trying to force a grin. "It's a nice Thantis trick I heard about in Stormshale." The lie came too easy. "You make a little nick right when you're about to finish. The screaming was just because he's so gods-damned good at—"

"Damn it all to the Aether, Dice." Evander relented with a scowl. "All right. Leave him out of it then, even if I don't believe you. However, *we* will talk—*now*."

If exhaustion did not settle in every fiber of her being, she might have laughed. Begging Evander to let her rest beforehand would only make him angrier, or leave Rory unprotected for relentless questioning. Despite the rage settling into pain in her bones, her bad thigh screaming with discomfort as she started to follow him up the stairs, she settled with the fact that respite might not come for hours.

Or for the rest of her life, however short.

Rory caught her hand briefly as her boot hit the first step. He glanced up at Evander, who was already starting up to the main deck quickly to avoid another angry outburst. He was not a man who relished screaming, as much as Dice believed she deserved it.

"I can't do what you ask," he murmured. "I won't."

She slipped her fingers from his grasp, annoyed at his earnestness. "Then what happens won't just be on me anymore. Clean that up," she nodded to his split palms, evidence of their troublesome friendship, before turning her back to him.

Nothing seemed real to Dice as she walked behind Evander through the supply room and up to the main deck. Moonlight hit her face, startling her enough to cause her feet to stumble. It was closer to midday when Dice followed Evangeline into the brig. How much time had passed?

When Evander turned back to frown at her, she overcorrected with an unnatural yawn. Stretching her arms overhead, she feigned the exhaustion came from her presumed *activities* with Rory. As such, Evander ignored her the rest of the way to the cabin.

As they walked, she noticed that not only was it strangely quiet, but the lanterns were unlit. "Did we spot a Revkyn cruiser?"

Evander paused. His long braid looked unkempt and dull in the moonlight. It whipped like a tail when he faced her, quick as the wind.

"Yes," he sneered. "And we were missing our lookout, so it's a good thing we blew out the lights in time."

Dice palled. She had nearly killed the crew already, and the realization made her mouth go dry. "I… I forgot it was my turn to watch."

"You seem to have forgotten a lot of things." Evander's voice dropped, the dejection there forcing Dice to lower her gaze in shame.

He held the door to the cabin open for her. Inside, the curtains were drawn over the porthole, and Brutis looked up at them from Evander's desk. The mountain of a man swallowed up the chair, but the worry in his gaze sized him down into a gentler creature. Dice did not look at either of them, feeling more like a child getting caught with something too sharp, or too sweet. In the light of a few lanterns which hung about the room or sat on the edge of Evander's desk, the strange unit avoided one another's glances for a beat. Dice expected one of them to begin the conversation, swiping awkwardly at the drying blood on her face until her sleeve no longer came back red.

Brutis watched her, mouth puckered like he ate a sour candy.

"It's for sex, apparently." Evander crossed his arms and sat down on his bed.

"I knew it."

"All right, *stop*." Dice raised her hands, silencing both of them before they got too far into discussing her bedding activities.

Evander scoffed. "I'd say we're only just starting, Ward."

Dice's eyes snapped to him. He hardly seemed ashamed at the harshness in his voice, though his gaze left her face for a flicker of a moment.

"That's right." Dice waved her hands, the laugh dying in her chest. "I forgot. I'm not your *kin*—I'm your ward."

In the candlelight, the shadows in her father's face deepened, and it struck her how old the man was now. Evander, like most seafarers, did not have an exact nameday but he guessed himself to be nearing his sixty-fifth turn of the seasons. Approaching her thirtieth in only a handful of years, Dice still felt small in his presence, and pitifully unremarkable. Here was a man who had his own ship by her age, and a crew to follow him willingly across the Nameless Seas.

Then he found a bloody child in the hold of his ship and decided to keep it.

And she cut him out of her life like a rotten limb.

"You're not acting like kin," Evander replied, sensing her thoughts. "Why should I treat you as such?"

"Enough." Brutis cut in. Years of weathering their fights made him the final voice in most matters. "That goes for the both of you. Sit down, Dice."

Dice scowled, arms crossed, but obeyed. Sitting in the chair on the other side of Evander's desk, she positioned herself between her two guardians.

Then, seeing how her posture mirrored Evander's, she straightened her back and uncrossed her arms.

Brutis pushed forward. He always ended up being the voice of reason, often marveling how Dice and Evander shared such a temper despite not being blood relations. "Anything we say here, we say because we care."

Keeping her gaze on the floor, Dice nodded after a pause.

"There's no easy way to go about this… Odessa?"

She lifted her eyes. Brutis wore a look of absolution, the heartbreak clear on his features. He never used her given name unless something was important to him. It never came out as a scold or insult, but a lighthouse to bring her back to the severity of his tone.

"What happened when you were gone?"

"It's Stormshale." She scoffed, pretending she did not see Evangeline appear over his shoulder. "I trolloped. I drank. I made merry."

"None of that." Evander griped. "None of those half-answers. We gave you your space. We thought it was something left over from the fever, or your leg."

"My leg is *fine*."

"You can barely stand for more than an hour, Ward." Evander hung on to the title, salt burrowing into a wound in her heart. He knew it pained her to be divided from him that way. "But nevertheless, we waited. You're lucky most of the crew reared you up from cloth nappies, or else we would've had men begging us to dump you at the next port for endangering the peace on this ship."

He was right. Every word rang true. Dice was too tired to do more than listen, the desire to argue weak as her limbs grew heavier by the moment.

Brutis chimed in, his gruff voice soft compared to Evander's. "What I think he's trying to say is… We *know* you, Dice. And if I'm wrong about this, then so be it, but the last time you were this distant was after Olan tried to kill you."

"That was ages ago."

"And you were a child." Brutis folded his hands, leaning on the desk. "You hid below deck for most of Sommet. You wouldn't even let Evander talk to you."

Rat.

Dice remembered the cold, the fear. She had no name for it then, the panic in her chest. Trauma wove into her body, and the memory of Olan's hands wrapping around her little throat made her touch her neck.

Rat.

But she could not tell either of them the whole truth, so what pieces might she give them? Rory's secret needed to remain safe, as well as the existence of the book. There was no telling what Evander, in all his superstition, might do with it. And Brutis loved her in the ways mother cats loved stray kittens. He would not let her leave the cabin without discovering that which divided Dice from the very thing she loved most.

Them.

Dice lifted her gaze to Evangeline's ghost, hoping it only seemed like she gazed off into the distance.

Evangeline tilted its chin. In the light, it donned the plumpness of life, filling out the beautiful silken dress Evangeline wore to *The Far Sailor*.

Bracing herself for the words, she took a deep breath and told them about the first time she fell in love.

It had only been a few days since landing in Stormshale. At the turn of the season, she remembered it being a little too warm but the air blew cooly up from the water. She was taking a walk, not yet certain what she might do in such a distant city so far from the mainland. Dice must have walked up and down the beach in front of the boardwalk a dozen times before someone broke away from the crowd and approached her.

You look awfully lost in thought, the young woman said, heavy lids gazing up at Dice through their thick lashes. *Want a distraction?*

Dice told her that company bought was company she could not afford, but she wore that sly grin she learned from her life on the ship. *But if* you *want a break from work,* she remembered saying to the woman, *then I'll be glad to waste a moment with you.*

Evangeline introduced herself after the first blissful evening of unencumbered lust, even thanking Dice for not being too judgmental of her performance. *It feels nice not having to pretend to enjoy myself*, she murmured into Dice's shoulder as she caught her breath. *I feel like I don't have to look pretty or thrash or make those awful faces, either.*

Faces? Dice laughed.

Oh, you know. Evangeline knitted her brows and crossed her eyes, making a face like a man in pain. It sent Dice howling as she imagined who wanted Evangeline to look that way during passions.

The feeling started then, with their laughter. Not with the lust, which hung over their heads for the remainder of the evening, but in those moments of soft sighs and quiet giggles that Dice coaxed out of Evangline. She spoke without words with every nibble of Evangeline's soft thigh, every kiss she placed on the birthmark underneath her breast.

Then, Dice told them of her anger. Of her debts, and Leonora's rightful banishment. She skipped over most of it, itching to rush past the details of her betrayal when she told them of Evangeline's marriage.

Brutis made a noise in his throat once she mentioned the ring, but Evander kept his arms crossed, his gaze steady on her.

"I killed her husband, and the Watch hung her for the crime."

Dice's voice echoed deadly, the tone flat despite the turmoil it conveyed. Of course, she could not tell them of the music, or of the horn or the outright terrible way she dismembered the man while in a trance. But they knew passion, and knew it well enough that they filled in the spaces she left in the tale. That was safest.

A heaviness hung in the air with the words outside of herself now. Standing above Brutis, the ghost of Evangeline took a careful step backwards into the woodwork. Nothing save for the creak of the ship and the gentle sounds of the water broke the silence. Anxiety and shame climbed up her spine as Dice waited for their judgement.

Evander leaned forward after a time, surprising them both with breaking the silence first. Placing his elbows on his knees, he pursed his lips in consideration.

Not looking at either of them, he said, "I never figured myself for a father. I don't love people the way you do. I never dreamt of a life on the land, marrying a person who I couldn't care for. I can't pretend to understand how you might feel, Dice, but I'm angered to know you thought you must feel it alone."

The use of her name meant he forgave her, but she did not voice her thanks. Neither of them seemed able to face one another, the rawness in his confrontation stinging. Knowing only part of the story, Dice worried that if he saw her face, Evander might guess she was withholding more.

Brutis shook his head, uncertain of what to say. He picked at the wood of the desk, his gaze lowered. Dice felt awful, but she needed to protect them from what may happen. If she asked them to throw her in the brig with a watch, they would press as to why. If she told them about Rory or the book, Evander might really drop her off the next port for the safety of the crew, even if Brutis fought him every step of the way.

If she told them the truth, there proved no guarantee they might believe it.

Dice felt utterly alone.

"Keep your head down until… until you can find some peace. Yea?" Brutis ran his gaze over her before passing it over Evander.

The captain nodded. In a gentler voice, Evander ordered, "Get some sleep."

Dice stood, acutely aware of the dried blood on her sleeve and the handprint across her chest. Rory's mark left little for the men to imagine, neither of them suspecting that the proposed ink was actually the blood of a Dua-Nythi.

She gave them her goodnights, fleeing the cabin like a child. The moon hung with its accusatory crescent smile bearing down on her head.

Footfalls slowing, Dice paused in the middle of the deck. A faraway dream resurfaced, the inky tendrils of a bard's markings writhing to life in her mind.

Laying her hand on her chest, she remembered the warmth of Rory's palm, and it mixed with the icy touch of the bard in her dream. A word rose from the depth of her body, an explanation that drifted just on the edge of her awareness.

Godharker.

CHAPTER THIRTY-ONE

Gazing at the sea from shorelines and ferries was nothing compared to staring out from the bow of a ship. When the meals were over, Neoma stood at the front to let the wind cut through her locs. It whipped her simple tunic playfully when she threw her hands up to welcome its embrace. Every morning the sea glowed, and every night it deepened until the stars winked awake across the surface of the waters. A newfound freedom settled into her bones, consoling the grief there. Her pain was not gone, but being surrounded—and distracted—by the world meant allowing her mind to dwell on things other than her son.

Aboard the ship were all manner of women, some from as far as the Erewildes. When Neoma spoke to Rho, who was a cattle herder's daughter in that faraway continent, the young lady wasted no time in despising the boredom of the largely unsettled land. *The Countess* beached for an emergency on her sixteenth nameday, and the ship, trapped by the withdrawing tide, barely noticed the young stowaway until they were back out at sea.

"That must be—Katy-bird, how long ago was that?" Rho shouted up the ratlines of the main mast to a woman with fiery red hair. Neoma strained her neck up to see the woman, Katy-bird, throwing her leg over the yardarm.

She paused only long enough to whip her mass of coils into a knot at the base of her neck. Then shouting down, she answered with, "Gods if I know, you were but a baby! Ask Nanette."

Rho let out a huff. "Nanette has a memory good as mold, that one. Anyways. It's been a while."

Others told the same stories, talking about a family who did not accept their change into womanhood, and a ship ready to set sail the next morning. For many aboard *The Countess*, it was a place that embraced their first steps into freedom. To Neoma's surprise, the women were her community in more ways than one.

She narrowed the original party down to a handful of quiet people. Viorel one of them, Neoma watched from the corner of her eye during meals to see who the master boatswain spoke with more often than the others. Yet, outside of the quartermaster that Neoma briefly engaged with on her way to prepare breakfast, Viorel never spoke at length to anyone else unless it was to remind them of their duties.

"Oh, she's always been private." Julien, a dockhand, said when Neoma gently voiced the question during dinner. "Ain't that right, Uma."

Uma, who bore the marks of the sun on an aged, weather face, only grunted.

During the first week of her new life, Neoma saw little to negate the chatter of her compatriots. Viorel indeed remained private, and the quartermaster, Cyra, was polite in passing but never stayed long past the first inkling of dawn. Neoma had yet to meet any of the night crew, or even see their abode.

It made sense for them to sleep in separate quarters of the ship, but a twinge of curiosity refused to let go of Neoma that night as she made dinner. The next day being her off one, she made sure to prepare a hearty meal that the crew might stock up on. When all were served, she cleaned up rather quickly, even putting out the cookfire before the crew was dismissed.

Viorel watched her, gaze flicking between Neoma and the crew. "Eager for an early night, then?" She asked when she turned in her bowl.

"I'm tired as a dog, certainly." Neoma chuckled, keeping her face towards the wash basin as she scrubbed each bowl when they came in. She was not sure if she should ask permission to observe the night crew, or just wander above deck to see for herself. Certainly, they did not forcefully contain them to the sleeping quarters at night?

The master boatswain nodded right before she shouted. "Hurry it up you lot! Let the woman take her gods-damned rest like she deserves. Up!"

Rising swiftly, the crew scarfed down what remained of their stew as they walked to Neoma. Everyone offered their goodnights before ambling out of the room. Viorel gave Neoma a kind enough nod before leaving herself. With the room now only punctuated by the creaking of the ship, Neoma got her work done swiftly.

After carrying the wash basin above deck to dump its contents into the sea, she hauled it back into the eatery and to the small room that held some of the immediate food goods.

"I suppose I've just missed Viorel." The captain's smooth voice drew fingers down Neoma's spine. When she turned, there Armonia stood, a hand on her hip while the other pressed her wide-brimmed hat to her chest.

Neoma, remembering her oversalted blunder from before, brightened with the gladness of dinner being over. She wiped the remaining muck stuck to her hands n a little rag, closing the door to the storage room with her hip.

"Yes. You didn't pass her?"

The captain *tsked*, shaking her head. "She flies off for *privacy* after dinner. She thinks I don't know she's resting. I wanted to try and catch her before then."

"Are you going somewhere?" Neoma blushed at the interest woven in her tone. The captain, half turned towards the steps to leave, shuffled around to face her once more. Neoma's face heated under the woman's heavy gaze. "I mean, you seem dressed for the evening."

"We're on open water." Armonia smiled. Accompanied by the little prickle of laughter in the words, she looked to be teasing Neoma.

"Right. Of course." Neoma cast her gaze to the cook room floor. "Sorry."

Armonia leaned against the counter, moving so quietly that Neoma only noticed her closeness when the captain's hand rested on the table. "Sorry for what? You're not wrong. I *am* dressed to impress."

Neoma opened her mouth, no idea what she might say. Armonia stood over her slightly, the heel of her boots putting her red mouth at the height of Neoma's forehead. Looking down at her, the captain carried an air of enthusiastic fascination.

Was she fascinated by *her*?

With a sigh, the captain took a deep breath. The sound startled Neoma and she jumped back, realizing with a strange lift in her heart that Armonia was *smelling* her.

The captain met Neoma's questioning gaze unabashedly. Before either one of them broke the silence on their own, *The Countess* lurched in a slow, choppy way that meant the ship dropped anchor.

"Ah. My guests." Armonia grinned, pointing her hat up to the boards above them. "Would you like to observe?"

In her crushed velvet vest and billowing sleeves, the captain's threads made Neoma's simple but well-made attire seem raggedy. Neoma was already shaking her head, the awkward encounter with Armonia *smelling* her casting a pall on the evening. But the captain rushed forward, arms outstretched to grasp Neoma's hand before she could step away.

In the half second before she touched her, Armonia thought better and placed a hand on the counter instead. "You're beautiful, if that's why you're worried. My guests don't care for these threads anyway."

Neoma chortled in disbelief, blushing.

"Truly." Armonia nodded, a solemn look in her eye. "It's all for me. They are fine people, and I want to impress them."

"Then maybe *don't* invite the cook to your meeting."

She was about to turn when, in an act of desperation, the captain grasped her wrist. It was not a hard touch, but it startled her enough to try and pull it away. Armonia relinquished her arm immediately, punctuating her shame by taking step backwards from the crime. Raising her hands, she looked just as shocked at the behavior. Neoma had a mind to scold her until she saw the shallow fear in Armonia's eyes.

I suppose I've missed Viorel.

Perhaps the dazzling captain feared meetings without a friend by her side. In some odd way, it felt that the captain searched *her* out, not Viorel. How did she miss her in the crowd of people leaving the eatery, anyways?

Neoma pursed her lips, uncertain. Every evening, she had been asking Ocean for a chance to observe the deck at night. This might be an opportunity to satisfy her curiosity.

"Just… give me a moment."

Turning away from the captain's grateful smile, Neoma untied her apron and managed to clean all the bits of food out from under her nails before a call went up of someone boarding. Armonia appeared equal parts morose and excited as she paced. Her gaze fell to Neoma, flickering over her locs, her hands.

You're beautiful.

The statement hitting her only in that moment, Neoma felt a piece of her soul brighten under the captain's eyes. Extending a hand, the captain's mouth quirked into a teasing smile. Gestures like this were simple, with no hidden meaning other than to help a person up the stairs—but it felt like a promise as Neoma let the captain's fingers encircle her own.

Armonia brought the back of Neoma's hand to her lips. Pressure lighter than a feather, it still sent a warm flush up Neoma's arm. When was the last time Urias kissed her so tenderly without expecting something in return?

"Thank you, my friend." The captain smiled, releasing her hand from its warmth, the kiss still humming against her skin. "I feel much more ready with you at my side."

Unable to respond, Neoma simply followed the captain out of the eatery and up onto the main deck. Nestled closely to *The Countess* bobbed a vessel whose sails climbed high above their heads. It dwarfed their cruiser by two, the beaming dark wood glistening with rows of cannon windows along its side. Neoma craned her neck up to see the rigging, the three sails cinched to prevent the boat from drifting as it dropped its anchor beside *The Countess*. Lanterns of every color hung from zigzagging lines over the deck, though the ship was so tall that Neoma could only see the three figures expertly shuffling down the boardwalk connecting the two ships. Music bellowed from above, jaunty with laughter as someone beat out a tune in a language Neoma did know.

Armonia left her side rather quickly for someone only just procrastinating the meeting. The captain bowed low, removing her hat as she did. Once the figures touched down on the deck she rose, slamming the fabric back down on her head. The three guests were draped in thick veils that drifted in beautiful layers, catching every small gust of wind as they crossed the deck, but their hands remained exposed. Silence passed in a long moment as the first person reached out to touch the underneath of Armonia's chin. Their arm was decorated with beautiful, layered designs of spirals and symbols, and when they released the captain the arm disappeared back under the veil.

The custom seemed odd, but Neoma watched on respectfully as each stranger touched the captain's face in acknowledgement. Across from her, someone was pulling up a crate from below deck. Some of the night crew, as well as Viorel, walked carefully towards the entourage. The master boatswain faltered for a moment when she saw Neoma, the clinking glass loud as she overcorrected her pace.

There was a box for each of the strange guests, who took them without a word. No money exchanged hands, and no words, either. Armonia only bowed once more, keeping her back prone until the figures were all climbing the boardwalk once more. Everyone on deck watched them move, a reverence Neoma did not expect hanging in the air. The singing aboard the larger vessel halted upon their arrival, and once the last guest returned to their ship they began pulling the boardwalk in.

Viorel came to stand beside the amused captain, who picked something off her blouse's sleeve. Her eyes cut to Neoma, though she spoke only to Armonia. "They seemed more pleased than last time."

The captain huffed. "That face thing, you mean? Nay. It's just another way for them to say they'll catch me the next time I'm up to no good."

"Who was that?" Neoma could not help the question, just like the grin on her face. That was the largest vessel she ever saw, even in her days of watching the docks at Con-Quarry.

Every head turned, as if forgetting she was there. Armonia blinked away the surprise, replacing it instead with that swarthy grin. "They're a superstitious bunch. The veils are what they wear when boarding a ship that brought them bad luck in the past, like a ward. But we have business with them, so they deal with us."

Neoma stepped forward as the vessel began to lift its anchor from the sea. Above them, people were clamoring to the railing. Faces bright in the lanterns waved down as they set sail, and, seeing the children, Neoma waved her hand gleefully back at them. Their guardians gave her a sharp look before pulling their children back from the railing, unexpected fear in their gazes.

Neoma dropped her hand, trepidation tingling her skin.

"Thank you for your company, Neoma." Armonia stepped forward, her hand briefly touching the woman's shoulder. Viorel quirked an eyebrow at the unnecessary gesture, pursing her lips to keep the words back. For a comical moment, Neoma wondered what the woman might have done had she seen the captain kiss Neoma's hand. "It's appreciated."

More questions danced on her tongue, but Neoma knew a dismissal when she heard it. Viorel gave her a polite nod before placing a hand on the captain's shoulders. Armonia bent her ear close to the mouth of her master boatswain, sending a surprising jolt of jealousy through Neoma's chest.

Hoping no one noticed, she quickly turned back to the eatery. There was more to clean, after all, and she never wanted to stay where she was no longer needed.

"Miss Cardea?"

Neoma turned, half on the step, to face the captain. Moonlight cut through the drifting clouds, casting a beam of silver over Armonia's features. Her hat cut a sliver of darkness for her, concealing the upper part of her face from the moonlight. But those steady, bright eyes peered out from the shade.

"If you don't have too long, I would like to make it up to you for not being present during your introductions to the crew. Meet me in my cabin, once your duties are finished."

Without another word, the captain turned on her heel and sauntered back to her cabin. Viorel stood frozen, her gaze jumping between Neoma and her supervisor. Neoma shrugged at the woman, even more at a loss than Viorel.

As she finished organizing her mess, Neoma tried to ignore the gentle burn left behind from Armonia's kiss.

Bathed in moonlight, the women who commanded the deck in the deepest of night stood communal, but a solemness weighed their posture. Only a handful of women were needed, it seemed, to take care of the ship during the long hours, and their eyes flicked uninterestedly from Neoma back to the sea. With their long swords, they seemed more like pirates than merchants, with a few even boasting a rare, beautifully shaped flintlock. Neoma saw some of the governor's guards walking around with the contraption, but never heard them fired off. She knew the weapon was most desirable, so much so that the Sovilian queendom enlisted the help of their best metalworkers and powdermen to furnish an entire brigade with the weapon.

"Come in, Neoma darling." Armonia chirped after Neoma rapped on the door to the private cabin with her knuckles. A crack of light broke out onto the deck of the solemn night crew, but she wanted to be polite.

Warm light trembling with the bob of the sea touched the dark cherry wood of the room in an amber glow. The effect cast a glistening sheen over the polished furniture, rich in money and looks alike. A long table stretched the middle of the room, proper for feasting and private meetings, with low backed chairs padded in blue velvet. A heavy curtain draped over the far wall, concealing what Neoma guessed to be the captain's bed, and the blue material was fringed with gold and crimson tassels. Deeply plush rugs hushed Neoma's footsteps as she entered the cabin, closing the door behind her when the captain requested so. The weave was bright in the colors popular with Thantis craftsmen, but the image held the sharp, archaic shapes of Esmarin design. Every wall not tacked with marvelously painted atlases proffered shelves upon shelves of volumes ranging in size, varying in their leather and cloth backs. Armonia sat at a studious desk whose edges were carved to mimic the unfurling of blossoming flowers, its top a shining slab of obsidian. Upon it were strewn a vast number of parchments and oddities which held down the corners of a smaller map that the captain stood over. She made a note of something in her journal after tracking the day's distance, the sharp edges of her umber features glowing in the candlelight.

Satisfied with her observations, she looked up at Neoma, sending a trill of eager wariness through the woman. However gorgeous Neoma thought the captain, there was something paradoxical in her gaze that made a note of caution linger.

"I promise not to keep you too long. I'm sure you're tired."

A curl of disappointed twisted in her belly despite the pull of tiredness settled on her shoulders. "Only the proper amount, I suppose," she admitted with a small grin.

Her answer teased a broader smile from the captain. With a final scratch of her quill, Armonia ushered Neoma to pull up one of the chairs from the table, sitting down in her own behind the desk on her guest was comfortable.

"I'm sorry if this is untoward," Armonia began once Neoma settled. "Viorel answered your initial letter for hire, but while I commend her for managing the crew during the day she isn't quick to be personal with anyone. You've been here a week almost, and all I've gotten as a report is, *she cooks*. So this," Armonia waved her hand at the space between them, "is an interview."

"Don't those usually come before you hire me… and before the promise of money?" Neoma could not help the tease in her voice, and hoped it was not untoward.

Armonia gave her that winter's bell laugh, crisp and sharp. "Yes. I always—oh, how does that saying go? I try to eat the sand before it's salt?"

"Something like that." Neoma smiled. It took days for sea water to dry. The reason her family's wares were so sought after was not only because of their patience, but because of the refining process sharpened by years of experience. Some seasonings were cheaper, but carried the risk of sand being mixed with the salt because the farmer rushed the drying and sifting.

When she looked up from her hands, Armonia's soft gaze moved quickly away.

“So,” Neoma pressed gently, unsure of the look, “what happens in one of your interviews? My work has always been with my family.”

Thankful to move the conversation away from her sneaking glance, the captain cleared her throat. “Well, *officially*, I ask you your homestead, the details of your payment, whether or not you require special assistance on the ship.”

Neoma narrowed her eyes almost playfully. “But, *un*officially…?”

“*Unofficially*, I skip the jargon and we talk as peers.” Armonia leaned back in her seat. Despite the comradery in her voice, a glint in her silver eyes reminded Neoma to know they were not equals, not really.

“I’ve pointed out that we’re already at sea, so I can hardly be rid of you now. Viorel’s already explained to you your income, and I know your family from the letter.”

“And you know I had a son.”

The captain’s face softened, the playful sharpness replaced with true gentility. “Yes. That, too. You need not tell me more. We can speak on something else.”

Her empathy swelled Neoma’s heart. It was a relief to know people outside of her family had enough room for patience around her grief. She gave the captain a nod to request a change in the topic, which Armonia did with grace.

“There is one question I like to ask any new members of my crew. And, I’ll admit, it’s the reason for the sudden invitation as well as the privacy. What do you think is the difference between destiny and chaos?”

Expecting a more vulnerable question, it took Neoma a moment’s breath to hear the words. Lifting her chin in eager expectation, the captain waited as her counterpart mulled over an answer.

The last few months felt equal parts divine intervention and randomness, beginning the moment her son walked into the sea. No words offered any true clarity, but underneath every current was a purpose. Neoma had simply lost hers, and was struggling beneath the waves.

“I suppose some say there isn’t a difference.”

“Of course. Those with grand faiths see it all as intertwined. But,” Armonia steepled her hands under her chin, “I’m asking about what *you* think.”

Silver eyes met her dark ones, moonlight and midnight. Pulled into the glamour of their shine, Neoma felt the narrow walls of her heart expanded to idea of something deeper, kinder, than what she had with Urias. When her lips parted, the captain’s eyes did not drop to her mouth in the way Urias' did when he longed for her body. Armonia *saw* Neoma when she spoke, breathing in the music that fell from her lips.

"Destiny is the sound of my mother's heartbeat. It's knowing that when my feet turn towards home, there will be arms to welcome me back. Sometimes it's utter grief when I don't have the power to change anything, and sometimes it's my cousin writing to a strange ship on my behalf."

Armonia's eyebrows lifted in amusement. The captain tilted her head, listening to every word. "And what of chaos?"

Chuckling, Neoma shrugged. "It's hardly different. Chaos is the ocean's call before a storm, but it also makes you weightless against its power to change everything you thought you once knew. They're the same," she decided, "but in the way every river eventually runs into the sea."

It's the uncertainty of desire, of fearing the feeling of sex against my skin but longing for the closeness of another soul.

Neoma pursed her lips, forcing such an admittance to stay within her.

"Destiny will always become chaos… and the like." Armonia gazed at her, a new feeling drifting across her features but vanishing before Neoma had the chance to name it. The air between them stirred with a respect of similar minds, and for a moment Neoma dared to think that the captain might really be able to see into her heart.

Comfort settled over them, the kind Neoma rarely felt outside of her family's embrace. Nervous at how it overcame her, she pushed to break the silence with a playful laugh. "Is my answer going to be written into my documentation? Are dockmasters required to know these sorts of theoretical musings?"

Armonia rolled her eyes good-humoredly. "Gods no, thankfully. I'd be waiting for a permit to dock for hours otherwise. No, this is just so I can see where someone's head is. You'll be glad to know you have a good one on your shoulders."

The compliment warmed her, a peace Neoma took like a dollop of honey on her tongue. Hoping to speak as peers, Neoma asked, "Earlier, you said you brought that ship bad luck?"

Armonia balked dramatically, placing a hand on her tattooed chest. "Oh, *I* did not, I assure you. But an offense was made, unfortunately."

"Who are they? I've never seen such a custom. The wearing of those veils—it's all so romantic."

A reprimanding crinkle appeared between Armonia's brow. "Culture is not to be romanticized, friend. But I suppose it's strange when you first see it."

The non-answer shifted the tone in the room quite dutifully. Neoma's question drew down a mantle of civility that made the captain sit upright once more.

"I'm not privy to discuss private matters with a subordinate, Neoma. I mean no offense by dismissing the conversation, and I'm sorry if my friendliness made you presume I freely give away my patron's secrets."

She only nodded once, the estranged word solidifying the professional distance between them. Even though Neoma *was* below the captain, it still felt like a nail tacking up a warning sign. *Do not cross here. High tide.*

Armonia's glittering eyes searched her face, and dared a genuinely apologetic smile. "We'll leave the rest of the paperwork for your off-day, yes?"

Rising from behind her desk, the captain walked around the smooth obsidian top to offer her hand politely to Neoma. Even though the offer came out of a place of respect, not indignation, Neoma smoothly rejected the outstretched palm and stood from her chair. With only the space of Armonia's hand between them, Neoma caught the tang of iron on her breath. Still, the captain's gaze did not drop to her lips when Neoma's tongue wet them nervously.

"Good night, captain."

Leaning away slightly, feeling the icy wall between them, the captain dropped her offered hand. Armonia stepped out of Neoma way, bowing her head in silent dismissal even though the flustered woman was already halfway to the door.

"Miss Cardea."

Neoma paused, hand on the door knob, and glanced back at the captain.

Armonia's hand rested on the back of the chair she had been sitting in, fingers curling over its slope. Without looking up, the captain said in a small voice, "I think I like your answer the best. Thank you."

The ice around them thawed slightly. Neoma said nothing, casting her gaze down to the floor. Like a nervous teenager she fled the cabin, shutting the door behind her so fiercely that a nearby woman paused the knot she was making. Neoma apologized, shuffling across the boards, not lifting her eyes lest the crew notice the bewilderment—and hopeless infatuation—twinkling in her gaze.

CHAPTER THIRTY-TWO

"Your name can't really be *Dice*, can it?"

"Why not?" She griped testily. "Yours is *salt*."

"Saltraroran. And it doesn't mean salt, it means *blood of the ocean*."

"Tell yourself whatever you like, love, but there's a reason I call you Rory just as there's a reason they call me Dice."

"Ah! So it isn't your name, then."

Rory raised his palms in defeat when she cut her gaze to him. They rocked unsteadily in a longboat some distance away from the *Marksmen* with a net thrown over the side to catch fish. The meat was growing low in the storeroom, and Brutis wasted no time in ordering Dice and Rory off as one of the fishing pairs.

After the painful conversation with him and Evander, the first-mate seemed better at keeping a respectful though ever-watchful distance…so long as she gave him at least a smile of reassurance. Dice, for her part, held normal dialogue with her guardians despite the throbbing anxiety boring into her chest.

Out on the ocean, she wanted to tell Rory about her vision since the moment they got out of earshot from the *Marksmen* but the words stayed lodged in her throat.

And yet, Rory knew by the scowl in the corner of her mouth that Dice carried a fresher burden. Perhaps the song in their minds, however different, tied them together.

It was not an uncomfortable thought.

"What is it?" He leaned, an elbow on the edge of the longboat.

"Come off it, Salt." Turning her back, she busied her shaking hands with refastening an already perfect knot.

"Your annoyance invigorates me." Rory sat down in the bench across from her, refusing to leave her line of sight. Folding his hands behind his head, he rested against the bow and closed his eyes against the glowing sun. "It means I'm wearing you down. What is it?"

"Where should I tell you to shove it, Spice?"

Rory opened one eye to stare pointedly at her.

"Oh, I'm sorry. You don't like it when people use the wrong name?" Dice plopped down into the longboat, lamenting the mostly empty net. "It's almost like… well, gods above, like I *prefer* Dice."

"Great Ancestor, I relent." Rory grumbled. Reclining back into his easy posture, he let out a satisfied breath. "I'm only trying to make normal conversation, but forgive me for wanting to talk about something other than your growing insanity. How is that, by the way?"

"Oh, wonderful. I'm two steps from the ledge now instead of the three."

Dice slipped off her tunic, adjusting the bindings around her breast. The sun bore down on them, unrelenting in its growing heat the closer they got to Lesser Syvon. Tying the cloth around her head to cover her black tendrils, she leaned back in the longboat, mirroring Rory's lazy posture. In truth, she felt more at peace with him than anyone else, hence the stripping of her top and the carelessness of it. She knew the strange journal connected them in a way, but she liked to think he enjoyed her company, however tainted.

Dice may never admit the same to him, though in the comfortable silence that followed their gentle bobbing, she figured there was no need.

Rory's carefulness around her did not go unnoticed. Though his words were teasing, and often did try to breach the gap in normalcy, she knew he wanted to ask her about what happened in the brig. Evander and Brutis could be dissuaded, encouraging Dice's sexual proclivities within reason, but Rory stopped her from running herself through with a blade.

Bandages still covered the palms of his hands despite him admitting the cut was not deep. He needed to hide the evidence of his strangely colored blood, so even when it began to scab over Rory bound his palms every day. The cloth was a glaring reminder of what he already chose to do for her, and it made her feel sick with unworthiness.

"I tried to find the book when I was in the brig." Faces turned towards the sky, it was easy to let out her thoughts. Dice pretended she was simply talking to the fluffy cloud that drift overhead. "I didn't. But you know that."

"Mm." Rory murmured, bare chest gleaming with sweat. The rigid skin along his neck flexed, the gills searching. He dripped his hand into the water and splashed his neck nonchalantly before reclining once more against the bow of the longboat.

"I saw… something." Her mind refused to recall the shape of the creature. Every time she attempted as much, a throbbing pain started at the base of her neck. "Storm clouds. A great world of blood. My mother."

The longboat rocked as Rory sat forward, but Dice knew that if she looked at him she might lose her nerve. So she closed her eyes, gazing at the orange glow of the sun against the back of her eyelids.

"She was pregnant with me. It felt like seeing the world through a mirror, but it wasn't a *reflection*. It was a memory. She drank something, but I don't think she really wanted to. I think someone made her believe it was her only option."

Dice cleared her throat, the tears gathering there a surprise. When she thought of her mother before the vision, she was a distant figure. *Before*, the woman had simply been a portal that carried Dice into the world. Now, there was a face filled with terror and worry and resilience, all corrupted by the figure in the hood.

"*Before our bones were felled in twine, our tails turned stems of flesh, we drank the blood of our Ancestor so that our words were shaped in our minds into the tongue of the Duathi.*" In Rory's voice was equal parts awe and horror. "You weren't conceived as Dua-Nythi—you were *created* with blood magic."

Dice opened her eyes at the sound of his dazed wonder. He stared at her, fear and confusion mingling with something profound, something analytical in his study of her. The skin of her palms went tight at his words, poised for an unseen threat, her heartbeat thrumming in her wrists.

"This means a Dua-Nythi caster is alive. Dice," Rory's hands came down to grip the edges of the boat. "This means they have another journal."

Hark.

"You said your people called them Godharkers."

Hark.

"Yes, but that's a formality. A Godharker was a vessel. They spent decades training to become a physical channel between the Ancestor, or the Duathi and its people. They—"

"Were *prepared*."

Rory swallowed his words. Dice's heartsong rose in her ears, a whooshing of crashing waves in her mind. Suddenly, sitting in the open water made her stomach tighten with fear.

Hark.

"I need to see the book."

"No, Dice. What if—"

"What if I start crying blood? Well, we're used to that by now." Dice reached into the water, fingers curling around the thick weave of the net.

Rory's hands caught hers, forcing the net back into the water. His eyes were beseeching, brows downturned in anger. "What if you try to *kill* yourself again?"

"It's better than killing someone I love because I don't know what in the gods-damned Aether is going on! Don't ask that of me, Rory. Don't ask me to just be all right with the possibility of running *you* through, or the crew, or Evander—"

Her breath hitched, thinking of the blade crunching the bone of her father's breast. Of her hand being the thing which felled him. "Don't you dare ask me to save myself when that could mean killing everything that was ever good to me. Let me die if I turn the blade. *Let me die.*"

With their hands twisting in the water, Dice felt his tighten against the flesh of her palm. Anger warped the unfairness within him, righteous in its fury as he surrendered. Rory gripped the weave of the net, a muscle in his jaw twitching when he gave her a quiet nod. Together, they heavied the measly catch into the longboat, slotting the oars into their notches before returning to the *Marksmen.*

Dice felt the tide change beneath the water, sensed the churning of the Duathi's gaze on her neck when they roped the longboat into its notches and were raised into the air. The crew pulling them aboard lamented the poor catch, but Dice and Rory paid little heed as they leapt over the railing.

Evander cast her a look that said he knew now for certain that she was not telling the truth, but for some reason his steps faltered when they passed.

When their eyes locked, she hoped he saw the apology there before she turned and disappeared with Rory below deck. He brought her to the hammock assigned to him, waiting impatiently as he worked at a floorboard underneath the swinging net. It came up easily, and Dice braced herself against the drop in her stomach when her gaze landed on the volume, but nothing could have prepared her for the shocking, unfamiliar wave of *relief*.

Confused, she left Rory to pick it up, adjusting her stance to prepare for any bloody tears or awful whirlpool of emotion as he flipped through it.

She froze, staring down at the pages that moved under Rory's thumb. Emotion tightened in her throat as she gaped at the twitching symbols.

"I don't know how we'll find anything. Neither of us can read it." He sighed, frustrated at his inability to understand the curling marks.

Her hand lashed out, gripping so tightly to his elbow that Rory jolted.

Hark.

The images swam together, bleeding, uncurling, ink in water as the shapes became a language she understood.

Hark.

Rory's grasp loosened as she took the book from him. His eyes watched hers for any sign of blood, muscles tense in the event he must save her from herself.

Hark.

Dice's eyes scoured the pages, fingers rushing over the ink that shivered under her touch. An oceanic symphony, complete in its cascading beauty, rang out in such a beautiful melody that it brought salty tears to her eyes. The Common Tongue wove the sentences together, secrets finally revealed.

A warm hand touched her shoulder. Rory's.

"Dice… Are you all right?"

"Yes." She gasped. Magic vibrated under her fingertips. It kissed the skin of her palm as she pressed her hand down onto a page. *Magic. Here.*

"Dice." Rory stared at her, his hand still on her shoulder. "Are you sure? You… you don't look right."

She laughed against his ineptitude. Could he not see how perfectly glorious it all was? Did he not notice the shape of the words on the page as they moved to form the Common Tongue? Another wave of relief flooded her, joy at not being commanded by some distant thing to cry in blood or shake with terror. It was just a book of magic in her hands, bending to her will.

Softly, Rory's other hand grabbed the edge of the book.

Dice's gaze cut to him. It shocked him enough that, when she snatched it from his grasp, he stumbled away from her in frightened uncertainty.

“I’m fine!” She growled, nails curving into the leather of the binding. “It’s okay, Rory. It’s *okay*.”

He stepped forward, one hand reaching for her, for the book, and Dice turned away from him. It was too much like that night in the brig, where he cradled her and she was a weak fool.

But she was not weak, not anymore.

And the book was not *his*.

She was chosen.

The Duathi spoke to *her*, called to *her* mind, allowed *her* to read its language with the clarity of her own tongue.

Hark.

No one could take it.

No one.

It was all meant for her.

All of it happened to bring her to the book.

To the Duathi.

“I’m fine, Rory, really—”

Her voice died on her lips. Sunlight, not the pale glow of a lantern below deck, struck her eyes as she turned. Brutis hunched over her, his large hand squeezing her shoulders so painfully that she made a cry of pain.

His eyes widened, watching the thrall of a god flee Dice’s vision just as his blood slickened her hands.

The world narrowed, black tinging the edges of her vision. A howling scream deep from her belly ripped through her when Dice looked down at the gored flesh of Brutis’ stomach. Her own hands gripped the hilt of the blade, her own arms had guided it. The book had vanished, and instead she held a long, gruesome blade.

A great cyclone of anguish whirred in her chest. *What had she done?*

Pink intestines slithered out around the knife, freed of their casings as they hit the deck with a sickening *thud*. Brutis clung to her as he dropped to his knees, the weight of him bringing Dice down, too. Her red hands released the dagger, breath quick and shallow as she let out another cry of horror and cradled his face.

“Shh,” Brutis gargled, blood leaking out from the corner of his mouth. “Shh.”

“No!” she begged. “No! *No!*”

Mouth moving, unable to shape the words he wanted to say, Brutis lifted a hand to hold her chin.

Darkness sliced through his vision. A voice not his own whispered lowly, a grumbled warning as the crew shouted in horror and sorrow around them:

"*Hark*."

He slumped to his side, body landing with the emptiness of death.

Everyone's voice dropped out, frozen in terrified bewilderment. Dice felt her knees dampen with Brutis' life as it soaked into the boards of the deck. The smell of his insides made her stomach roil, and her gaze lifted, jumping from the faces that looked on her with biting rage.

Evander's was the worst of them, slackened with unnamable pain as his eyes struggled to find a place to land. His best friend, his companion throughout the years, laid dead, felled by the child he raised as his own.

"I don't—"

The words died in her chest.

What happened? Where's Rory?

She slumped into the grasps of the men who, in their own fury, ripped her from Brutis' side. Pain radiated up her shoulders under their grasp, a pain she knew she deserved, a pain she did not fight to relieve.

Evander's lip trembled as he took a knee. Every weathered line in his face caught the tears that fell like rivers down his cheek. When he met her gaze again, Dice could not stop the sob of heartbrokenness that rattled out in defeat.

She did this. The Duathi *made* her do this—but who was she now if not a monster?

The captain's voice was hardly above a whisper when he ordered, "Lock her in the brig. Lose the key."

Dice sobbed. The men dragged her limp body away, but she forced her neck around to stare at her shame as her boots scraped across the deck. Brutis, a heap of only flesh, his last breath stolen by the creature who consumed her mind. The Duathi took everything, even those final moments that should have been sacred to him.

Tears slid over her reddened face as she cried an empty sound of regret. His intestines coiled like rope. His blood, deep and dark, pumping out the last beats of his heart. His lowered lids that, even as she gored him, gazed upon her with love, like *he* was sorry, like *he* held the blade.

Even then, Brutis knew it was not by her will that she killed him.

Even as he died, he forgave her.

Dice felt all that was left of herself shatter when the gate slammed shut, its grating iron the song of her fate. It did not matter if it was metal, or flesh—as long as she lived, a cage must be her home.

CHAPTER THIRTY-THREE

Votives laboring for the Tularin Baths wore the sullen yellows and ambers of the House of their employ. No matter their gender preference or sex, the uniform of long flowing trousers paired with an open-faced robe that dragged across the floor was the same. Those with long hair met the requirement of keeping it clean and in a long plait, and absolutely no jewelry was permitted. Sen never had a profession since their upbringing did not require one, but wearing the plain garments after growing up dressed in silks of the highest fashion made their stomach curl and skin itch. What was almost more embarrassing was the fact that, without their family's name, Sen had to *work* at all.

What pleased them about becoming a Votive was the housing and prepared meals, effectively taking care of those concerns. Since it was the off season for all of the Baths surrounding the enormous lake in which the Godharker's mirror deposited them, seasonal Votives returned to their homes in Dunhet or Con-Quary. There were plenty positions that needed filling, so Sen figured being someone who fanned the guests and folded their robes would be easy enough,

It took an age for the Shadam to finish laughing at Sen's rapid decline in fortune, though, before assisting them in filling out the proper documentation.

In a matter of perfectly divined fate, Sen's request for employment came only a week after the YeSara Clan officially announced Lon as the new heir. The public invitations to all Houses and Clans, save House Dermont, had been sent out, urging guests to join the YeSaras on the island at the start of Brite.

The Shadam, who explained their position as a guardian of the Votives, was not themselves of House Tularin. However, their status remained significantly higher than Sen's, and the Shadam had an excellent memory of all the bitter words the disgraced YeSara wove around the heir to House Tularin.

"I must thank you, friend." The Shadam said once they finished presenting Sen with their sleeping quarters. The entire tour of the secret passages the Votives took to keep out of sight was punctuated with the Shadam's strained laughter. "When I tell the mistress that the ex-scion of the YeSara Clan is employed under her House, I'm going to get a raise. This room is yours."

It was the smallest living space Sen ever laid eyes upon. The slab of white sandstone had a limp mattress thrown atop it, and the long window that cut across the top of the wall did not have a glass pane. Bugs hummed through the room, landing on the pillow, thankfully unstained, and on the single writing desk in the corner. Sen had no trunk, no clothing other than the robes they were given by the Godharker. *Those* they wished to be rid off immediately, changing into their Votive uniform as soon as it was relinquished to them.

The Shadam went over the laundry schedule, when the house meals were readied, and how long the Votives had to eat before their duties. Everyone woke together before the dawn to prepare the meal that would break the fast of their guests, then the cooks went to prepare the food for the entire Bath while everyone else split off to their assigned pools.

It was the most *exhausted* Sen ever felt in their life. During the first week, Sen kept their meager pay hidden under their mattress, as if it were actually worth anything. Payment came to little more than a few silver pieces a day—enough for food from a stall, certainly, but too little to buy them personal items or extra clothing. None of the other Votives responded to their request for mint leaves they may chew, or scented powders for their underarms and intimates. Sen reeked for that entire first week, until the Shadam took pity on them by way of small vial of body powder, and a strange stick.

"You strip the bark on one end," the Shadam explained, "and rub it across your teeth."

As toiling as the work seemed, it came along quiet easily. Sen kept their hours filled with the organizing of little drinks despite the lingering cloud of embarrassment that appeared every time the other Votives whispered when they passed.

Gossip spread quicker through the help than it did the Houses. Soon enough, everyone realized Sen was once highborn, and now they were a worker with no surname. People enjoyed the disgrace of others but Sen was dealing with something that, for once, made twittering rabble die in their ears. Even the Shadam commended them after a time on not letting their new position in life lead to an untimely suicide.

Sen did not have the energy to explain how their mindset so quickly changed, and the Shadam did not care to ask. Their memories of Valeska's flaying still shocked them awake at night. The Godharker's icy fingers scraping the back of their neck as they walked the halls alone made them jump, but it was only ever Sen's body reimagining their escape.

When they slept, it was never for longer than a few hours. During work, they gazed out over the lake, wondering if the portal remained or if the Godharker moved it. Their dreams became flashes of nothing more than the stoney underwater caverns of Ma'Ceste's resting place, but Sen was no longer sure if they were simply memories. A strange sense pervaded the images, like Sen was glancing through the surface of water to gaze upon the future.

They hoped to leave the Tularin Baths after the season. By then, Sen should have enough to buy a ticket to Sovil, or possibly further.

Nothing remained for them in the Isles, not anymore.

Heartbreak resounded in that official decision, rare in its achiness. Sen found themselves wishing they were a better sibling to Lon, not for the money or fortune it might garner them but out of genuine regret. The longer they considered what she endured because of their defense of Valeska, the more Sen realized it was not Lon's pettiness that separated them for so long, but her self-respect. No one who had true self-worth tied themselves to a person like Valeska.

They hoped from the pit of their belly that nothing other than goodness came from Lon ridding herself of Valeska's seed—that her healing was swift, surrounded by hands that always reached out to her with gentleness.

Looking out across the water, Sen quickly batted away the tears before returning to their duties.

"Well, I think it is absolutely ridiculous to be letting in so many people from Esmar."

Sen did not recall if the countess was of distinguishable repute as she took a drink off the tray they proffered. They were completely unaware of her House or name even though Sen knew she mentioned it four times already.

Turning to her companions without looking at Sen, the woman fixed the quaff of gray hair piled atop her head. She might have old Syvon blood in her, but whatever lineage distinguished her from her peers lost its money a long time ago. Sen heard some of the older Votives calling her a *permanent guest* with a sneer on their lips. They were interested to hear what might come of her peacocking, and waited obediently just outside of her little circle.

One of the woman's companions was a gnarled older man sitting in the nearby bath, his leathered limbs and exposed cock not an image Sen wanted transfixed in their mind, but such was the risk of a Votive. The other friend sat on the long, deeply cushioned chair in front of the countess, and her hair hung over the back because it was so long. She seemed younger than her counterpart, though not by much, and her face pinched together in an eternal scowl.

The countess sipped her drink—the third one she pulled from Sen's tray—before continuing. "I mean, *really*. Esmar is sinking, their king is mad, and the lot of them do… inexpressible things with… *you know*."

The gnarled man and the wispy woman nodded enthusiastically, and Sen's belly gripped with the trauma of witnessing the very act to which she eluded. On their flat palm, the drink tray trembled. Thankfully, the guests were too absorbed in themselves to notice Sen's pallor.

"I can't believe none of our governing parties thought to ask the opinion of the people," griped the younger woman, her voice a pitch above tolerability. "Instead, they let out an official proclamation stating that all arriving from a *disadvantaged kingdom* are granted passage! Farmers and herders and what-have-you. They have no papers," she scoffed, "for their king forgot to order a census since the last turn of the season! They come here, buy up all *our* land, and just muck up the place."

Sen wished to ask how poor farmers had money to buy anything at all, but a Votive's mission in the bathhouse was to be seen and not heard. The annoyance they experienced on the outside of the conversation was new, and they considered Lon's opinions when the topic of Esmar came up in nobler circles. Lon was always quick to admonish anyone who felt that innocent people should be the ones to face the consequences of a violent king's actions.

Clicking her teeth, the younger woman flicked her hand. Sen came to know this as a sign of attention, bringing the tray within the woman's reach the moment they saw her lift her wrist. She took her drink and a hefty swallow before continuing.

"I don't understand why it our responsibility to pay for all of this! They're ruining our eco-nomicky."

The older woman shrieked, the heinous laugh startling Sen so badly that they almost sent the drink tray crashing to the floor.

"It's *economy*." The countess barked, and her gnarled companion echoed her laughter. "I swear, Ingrid, you can't even pretend to be smart."

"Well, it doesn't matter how you say it," Ingrid mumbled indignantly. "What matters is that it's being ruined."

"Speaking of *ruin*," the gnarled old man rolled over onto his stomach, and Sen cast up a prayer of thanks to the gods. Floating to the side of the bath, he crossed his arms on the stoney edge of the lip. "Have you heard what's happened with the YeSaras?"

Sen felt the blood drain from their face. At the same time, their neck grew so warm that they nearly gulped down one of the drinks. However, none of the three whom they served were high enough in station to be invited to any Clan gathering. Sen knew these people thrived off of anyone richer, poorer, better, or worse than them meeting utter ruin. Any morsel of another person's pain was a distraction from their own.

Sen made bedfellows with that desire often in their old life. They braced themselves for any detail that might slander them, considering the irony of being present for the gossip around their own name.

"Oh!" Ingrid flapped her hand excitedly at the man. "Oh! I read about it in the *Dismissed Damsel*—"

"I'm so glad you've finally learned your alphabet."

"Enough of you, old bird."

"Now," the old man grumbled, "don't go disrespecting my Tilly like that."

"I can't believe the two of you do anything other than gripe all day—anyways. Don't interrupt." She looked at them both. "It's awful rude. But yes, I read in the *Damsel* that the heir—oh, what's their name—ran away with that awful white-haired fellow? The one you're always complaining about, Uncle."

Sen tried not to let their eyes get too wide at the expansion of Ingrid's family tree. While Sen's aunts and uncles helped raised them, they never cared to share a bathhouse with family, even in their private estate.

Worse yet, people are saying that they *ran away* with Valeska? They felt almost as sick as they did when they watched his flaying.

"Valeska." The man said the name like a curse. "He owes me more money than I care to admit."

Tilly sighed. "There's a reason they call it the *Dismissed* Damsel, dear niece. It's nothing but gossip."

"Yes," Ingrid agreed, "but it is *so* entertaining!"

"Oh, that reminds me," Tilly interrupted. "Did you ever get out to the Terraces to see that juggler I told you about?"

Ingrid lamented that she had not, and in a heart's beat Sen was just another story. The days of shame they endured as they ran their family credit into the ground and made a fool of themselves meant nothing.

For some reason, that brought them a semblance of peace. Let people gossip and wonder and titter like old birds. None of them would so much as scratch the truth, not of Valeska's violent death nor Sen's path into the arms of a goddess.

The more they thought about their life, the more it seemed like a dream. Sen bore another hour with the trio before they retired to their rooms, the gnarled old man walking the entire way without a towel and dripping everywhere. They cleaned up the various drink glasses, taking a towel to the puddles left behind as they considered how, to their surprise, they managed to keep their shame tampered.

Behind them, feet pattered on the glossy white stone. Sen kept cleaning until the footsteps stalled next to them.

"Votive?"

Sen exhaled at the damp towel quietly before rising. They cast their eyes down, hands folded before them in a demure posture. The man wore a dazzling gown of evening blue that made the deep brown of his skin richer. He flicked a hand, ushering Sen to raise their gaze, permitting their eyes to meet.

His beard was cropped short, and the sides of his head were shaved close to his scalp. He kept the remainer of his gray-streaked locks back with a leather strap, revealing the sharp, weathered angles of his features. Richness wafted from him, down to the solid gold bangle around his left and right wrists.

"Yes, my patron?" Sen swallowed past the attraction, the desire to taste the man on their tongue. "How might I be of service?"

Smiling, the corners of his mouth deepened. "I seem to be having a problem finding my room." The finger that ushered Sen to lift their gaze stretched across the space between them. Hooking it on the inside of their robe, the man slid it down the length of fabric until it fell from his grasp.

"Might I, perhaps, ask you to assist me?"

Sen's eyes glanced rather quickly around the bathhouse, but the off season meant only a smattering of patrons lounging at the southern pools. Even their fellow Votives moved on to meander about their other tasks. Sen was utterly alone with the handsome stranger, slowly overcome by a swell of desire that went uncared for since *The Silver Lantern*.

It was easy, nodding gently to the man who turned to boldly lead Sen out of the bathhouse and down a far corridor. They knew it well enough, having brought towels or drinks to the apartments that split off the hall, but every step felt like rediscovering the marble, the paintings. Sen was not sure if they should speak, but as they walked they took intense pleasure in drawing their gaze over the man's back and shapely rump.

"Oh, goodness me." The man teased when they came to a split in the hall. He turned, placing his hands on his hips in mock confusion. "I can't seemed to remember which way. Might you guess?"

Sen could not help the grin on their face. Tapping their chin, they stepped closer to the man, catching the scent of musk and tangerines. It sent a jolt into their stomach, the nearness of the stranger pulling a thread of yearning in their belly.

The man smirked, lifting his chin quickly towards the right. Sen pointed behind them, and the man clapped as if remembering.

"Ah, *of course*." He motioned with a long, muscular arm. "After you."

Working their bottom lip between their teeth, Sen turned gleefully on their heel. They walked slowly, knowing with certain enjoyment that the man watched them as they glided. For once, even their Votive threads felt luxurious under the heady gaze of the stranger.

"Stop."

Obeying, Sen paused in the middle of the hall. They turned their face, looking at the man over their shoulder. A hunger thrummed in his gaze, and when his eyes were done roving over Sen's body, they lifted to meeting.

"To the left," the man instructed, meaning the doorway into the apartment.

Sen reached out, taking the handle and shoving the door wide. Beyond was a standard apartment that all patrons were allowed to rent during their stay, with almost no personalized furnishings. Sen stepped in, and the man closed in behind them, his heat radiating across Sen's back. A trill of anticipation rushed over their chest, drawing heat down into their belly.

"So," they chirruped, turning gracefully on their heel to face the beautiful man. "What is it you do?"

"I'm a merchant." He reached out, letting his knuckle fall down the line of Sen's cheek, their neck, the hard shape of their collarbone. Sen relished the touch, feeling the ache of their body begging to be devoured.

They wet their lips, and the man watched their tongue. "What's your trade?"

Dark eyes hot with desire locked onto Sen. "Rare antiquities."

Their voice stiffened in their throat, the next question stalled by a heavy lump. Sen swallowed once, and again when the strain on their neck did not vanish. It wrapped around their throat, an invisible vice that did not tighten the flesh but blocked any sound from escaping.

Stepping out of Sen's grasp, the man dropped his hand from their burning skin as their fingers raised to their neck, prodding, finding nothing other than their warm flesh. Watching them struggle to make a sound, the man held their gaze as he slid the door's lock into its home.

Unable to even part their lips, Sen took a step forward. A cold feeling, sharp in its finality, slipped around their ankle.

Snapped tightly around their leg was a golden bracelet. When Sen's eyes jumped to the man, he flashed his bare wrists at them.

"I apologize for the deceit." Nothing in the man's voice made his words sound genuine. "I hardly believe you would've followed if I told you the truth."

Sen took another step, and once more a gilded cuff snapped around their ankle. The suddenness brought them to their knees, and the man remained by the door as Sen collapsed. Every attempt to struggle was thwarted when the golden cuffs lengthened, climbing like wine across a tablecloth up Sen's legs. Cool metal consumed their warm, panicked flesh as the man finally stepped towards them.

He took a knee, a sad look in his eyes. "I know this is terrifying, Sen, but trust me. It's better that I found you before Ma'Ceste, or her rotten little golem. Now, you might actually have a *chance*."

The man attempted petting Sen's hair but they jerked their neck away form his grasp.

Impatient, he took their chin forcefully, sending a shock of pain up their jaw. "You've sworn yourself to her, so she *will* find you."

Sen made a noiseless cry of terror, tears blurring their vision as they felt the gold reach their chest. Their limbs felt detached from their stumbling mind as they cast their will out, begging to any god that listened, even begging to Ma'Ceste and her gruesome Godharker. But they felt nothing other than the panic in their throat and the weight of the gold as it climbed their body.

"Your gift sings to her. To *me*." The Merchant groaned as if caught between pleasure and remorse. He gripped the sides of Sen's face as the gold stole all feeling from their body. All it left behind was bitter, painful cold.

"But your magic is rough, a pearl trapped within a clam. Her gift to you would be power, but mine is the awakening of old blood. I'm going to rip away the barrier between you and the world, Sen of the First Songs. Then you will be the most *glorious* gift."

The Merchant gazed down at them with a look filled with adoration as the gold slide over their vison.

CHAPTER THIRTY-FOUR

How many coats do you see, Pelagios?

Darkness, cruel and cold. Hands reaching up to a light just beyond the surface of murky waters. Bodies mushed into the softness of old farmland. Seeds taking root in flesh, feeding from what is left behind.

What is a man worth? A woman?

Thrashing in the night. Sheets, sweet with her smell and damp with her fear.

What of a child, Pelagios? What are they worth?

Empty cradles. Sickness, rot in the bones, twisted faces and muted cries. Mouths that cannot shape the name of the king or grab the tit that offers to feed them. Children who did not understand the shadows.

Babes who did not know the knife from the shade.

Aletta stepped into the circle of light. Pelagios blinked against the harshness of her rotting face, and the glow spilling down from above. Gone was the woman he stole from, the woman his heart refused to release from its broken grasp. Her murky hair hung in wispy strands over the splitting skin of her shoulders, the bones in her jaw and neck glowing like swords unsheathed from their scabbards. White clouds blotted out the color of her eyes, but those fearsome orbs landed on Pelagios' face with clear understanding. In the middle of her face was a hole where her sloped nose once perched, her lips peeled away, exposing teeth. She stumbled forward on sinewy limbs, her dress slipping off the shoulder to reveal the pustulous breast that glistened with swollen, black rot.

"What do you see?" Her shivering voice called out to him, powerful in its condemnation. "Am I coat or glove? Queen or whore? *What do you see?*"

Pelagios lifted his hands, begging Aletta for mercy as he tripped backwards. His body hit a fleshy wall; he barely dodged the hands that reached out for him from the dark. A boy in armor, no older than seventeen, opened a slackened mouth. He saw them all on the edges of the darkness then, creatures in varying states of rot, all of them testaments to his shame.

"Are we coats?" They called out in rumbling, scratchy voices. "Are we gloves? Are we your finery, your tunics?"

"My children…" the decay in Aletta's voice did not hide the ache of loss. "My children… *my children*… taken from me. From my arms. Their graves are but water, and I am severed from them forever."

The chorus of groaning rose as Aletta lifted her shredded throat to the light above them. She yowled, the gargled, unnatural sound striking terror into Pelagios. He felt the front of his trousers dampen, relieving himself against his will as the bodies around him screeched in unison with the rotten queen.

"Please," he cried, dropping to his knees before her. "Please, tell me what I must do to release you, phantom!"

All at once, the screaming stopped. Silence fell over the ambling, pitted heads of Pelagios' victims as they all set their gaze to the queen. Cold seeped up, chilly against his damp leg. The world of shadows observed him, and finally Pelagios understood he could never have been its master.

Alleta's white, cloudy eyes peered into his soul, and she found it wanting. "I am trapped here forever. You have stolen my children, and Esmar sits without a prince to claim his crown. *You have taken everything from me*."

She bowed low, bones creaking until she met his gaze. "You know what must be done."

Aletta's breath was hot across his face, strange against the blankness of her death. The closeness of the phantom made Pelagios whimpered out the word, "*Yes*."

"Yes," he breathed out, waking from the nightmarish vision to a bed damp with urine. Though the candle on his bedside table was lit and burning angrily, the darkness felt too deep in his room. Beyond the flickering light, Pelagios knew there stood hundreds of eyes upon him.

For the first time since landing on Esmar's shores, the darkness did not enthrall Pelagios as he walked alongside the stone and tapestries. A wind rushed forward, doing nothing to startle the dazed old man as it blew out the torches in the hall. The cobble beneath his feet guided him to the king's rooms, to the blood drying in front of the fireplace where Einar once bid him to speak with the queen.

Theon's body laid before it, the fur pulled from the mantle, sticky in his death's grip. A crack ran up the back of his skull, pinks and grays of the matter within clumped and dried into the fur.

Pelagios did not stop, emptied of everything save for his last task as he slipped into the secret hall.

The queen's room, always aglow in fire, smelt like a tomb. Pelagios stepped across the threshold, his gaze lowering to the putrid flesh that melted into the bedding. Aletta's body dripped across the fabric, her skin sloughing off as Pelagios reached to place his hand beneath her limp neck. Putrid liquids eased over his fingertips but it was no matter, he told himself they would be free soon. His other hand he placed under her knees, the tendons dry against his palms as he lifted the nearly weightless body off the bed. Her dress hung loose on her frame, no more than a bit of ruined cloth, and her gaping mouth revealed the row of lipless, shining teeth.

"The queen is tired, Pelagios." Sitting in the armchair by the fire, Einar gazed at the general from around its studded features. His eyes were ringed with bruises, sleepless nights claiming the sinking paleness of his face.

Sick grief threatened to draw Pelagios from his duty, but it was hushed as Einar smiled wickedly.

Esmar was lost. Einar no longer understood the difference between reality and bottomless fiction.

He would not even remember that his wife once slept in that stained, reeking bed, and the grief almost held Pelagios with that revelation. But the old man no longer saw the boy he once adored, nor the king he once would die to defend.

His voice came out flat, defiant, when he said, "Your son is dead."

Einar's wicked smile deepened, his eyes sad and hollow. "Which one?"

Resounding laughter followed Pelagios back down the hall, through the tunnels of Carn-Duhl. It bounced inside his head, rattling the memories of slaying the children that Aletta birthed before Theon—and realizing he had killed the prince that strange, bloody night, the memory whipping like a tattered flag across his mind.

Each one was twisted, gasping for breath. It was worse for her each time, Pelagios saw it in her waning features and slimming frame. Her body nearly gave up as it carried Theon, but something was left over from those heartbreaking deaths. Knowing Pelagios would be ordered to kill the child should it be mangled like the others, she fought to give Theon all that remained of her heartsong as if to spite him, to spite Einar. This caused her to always be sickly, to always retire early from parties or dinners.

She had been too weak to fight him the night before the king ordered the hunt for the Kahun.

Just as Aletta had relented beneath him, Pelagios did not dare fight against the current of his destiny as it pulled him into deep tunnels he never walked before. Its strange, marbled stone of deep blacks and blues brought him to a terrace untouched by the reign of Einar, of Mycin, the entire line of invaders and murderers hidden from its scared drop into the ocean below.

Pelagios climbed onto the edge of the railing, keeping the queen's body in his arms as he adjusted his bare feet on the wet stone.

Below, the ocean raged. Dark waters slammed against the base of the mountain, a great will from an unseen force struggling to break apart the rock.

With a trembling breath, the sounds of the waves disappeared. Pelagios heard only the murmur of his heart in his ears, seeing not the churning storm clouds gathering overhead but the flicks of wheat bowing in the wind.

A peace he never felt hushed the raging fear in his chest.

Releasing all the air from his lungs in a gentle sigh, Pelagios stepped out into oblivion.

Avenir rose from his quiet slumber when he felt the body break the waves, and the waves rip apart flesh from bone as it slammed Pelagios against the deep rocks. The mage rose from his bed in the chambers gifted by the king in full dress, his breath catching earnestly in his chest as he glanced into the shadows.

"Soon, my friend. Soon."

No other soul roamed the halls of Carn-Duhl, though he passed cracked doorways from which spilled the sounds of pleasure. Avenir did not care for these things, his mind and soul bent by powers stronger than lust or desire. Especially now, with the shadows opening to reveal his next task.

Lifting a torch from its sconce, the mage turned to follow the steps of the damned. Behind him padded the quiet feet of a woman lost to the world, her body freed from its earthen shackles. Avenir welcomed the queen with a respectful, heartbroken incline of his head when she came around the bend, almost faltering when she saw he awaited her., The haunting, body free of Einar's influence, wore the black gown of a mother in mourning. Aletta's rotten face was hidden behind a veil as she observed him.

"You don't need to wear that here, my lady."

Avenir's patient murmur touched the coils of evil intentions that still threatened to grasp at the queen's body. The sins Einar committed upon her rotten flesh would hang around her ghost for years to come.

Aletta gave pause, choosing to slowly lift the veil from her matted face. Her horror did not shock Avenir, nor make his stomach recoil. In his eyes, he saw a victim who had no chance to reclaim herself, even in death. Avenir treated her spirit as gently as the others who reached out to him since his arrival in Carn-Duhl. Making way for the queen to pass in front of him, they walked deeper into the mountain.

Their path split from Pelagios' as their steps wound further down until the pressure grew in Avenir's head. Aletta continued to walk with him for a time, her gown hushing over the stone until the sound of rushing water broke the courteous silence. The smoother hewn stone gave way to rough, harried steps made from crude tools, eventually becoming little more than boulders haphazardly stacked together as Avenir entered the scared cavern.

The torch light did not touch even the lowest point of the cavern's ceiling when Avenir stepped out of the hall. His feet caught on the rugged stone, his eyes guided towards the opening that led out to the sea. Magic pressed in from every direction, soft against the flesh of his stomach, rousing a sensation of interconnectedness that brought more joy than any physical pleasure. The stone sang its song all around him, promising that the tide would be out for as long as he needed to finish the ritual.

As one last gift, a wave crashed down on the edge of the stone shoreline. It left behind a broken, ashen body already mangled and waterlogged. Pelagios stared up at the cavern with dead eyes that reflected the torchlight, his skull crushed in on one side, eye missing from its socket.

Adjusting the torch between two stones, Avenir bent to drag the waterlogged body closer to the edge of the wall. Carved into the rough surface of beaten stone rose a mosaic as old as the mountain itself, the symbols uncurling from a central piece that depicted three figure. The middle raised her arms up, the shape of her full breasts and the curls of her hair separating her from the two plainer figures on either side.

Depositing Pelagios' body beneath the image, Avenir began to undress. His robe fell from his shoulders, and his hands worked to untie the knot around his waist. Fabric disappeared piece by piece until Avenir stood before the ancient carving in nothing but his vulnerable bareness. Etched across his skin, deep as night, were the beautiful curls of a language no longer spoken. Tendrils drifted over the muscle in his back, alive, twitching in response to the image of the old gods on the wall, the gods of his people.

Avenir felt the wind grow silent. With reverence, gaze drawn up to the middle figure, the mage placed his hands on the lines of her feet.

"Hyyke," he murmured, bowing his head. Power shook through his body, pouring out of the markings of the goddess' image. "Great Mother of the Sea. Blessed is the current that carried me from the womb."

Pressure bore down on Avenir's shoulders. Sliding his hands across the stone, he caressed the shape of the simpler figure to Hyyke's left. "Shaksa, Great is Her Name, great is the Land born from the Sea. Blessed is the soil which carries the seed."

Shaksa's gentle laughter spilled out of the carving, striking music in Avenir's chest. He could not help but smile at her welcome, at the murmuring of the stone, as he moved to give his final greetings to Hyyke's partner.

"Here in your secret meeting place I greet you, Shakkan. Blessed is the path you have given me, your Godharker."

Rising up from his spine, Avenir sensed his honorable greeting had been accepted by the deities, and was reward with a tremor of delight. Only then did he pull his hands away from the stone wall, backing away with his gaze returning to Hyyke's image. He motioned down to the soaking body of Pelagios, gray as the stone he rested upon.

"You've asked of me to bring you a general worthy of commanding an army." Avenir's voice trembled. The energy coursing through his limbs made him want to sing, to scream. "As your Godharker, I have answered. Here is the body. Give him the spirit."

With a moan, the torch went out, submerging Avenir in darkness but he was not afraid. In the black of the night, with the sea roaring behind him, he felt the shadows thicken with a new presence.

At his ear, a supple mouth brushed his soft skin.

Three voices hummed, one presenting itself more than the others. The roll of magic slipped over the mage's body, sending a trill of desire and fear into his belly that hardened the length of him. Such a reaction happened often, the thrill of power—of being in the presence of the gods—lit his body aflame.

"*My favorite*," Shaksa, her throat singing with the echoes of her mother and father, commended him. "*Well done. We will have an army fit to take back our land, the land of your brothers and sisters. Unkillable. Unsinking. Unmade, then made anew. Our blood to rule, and theirs to spill. Well done.*"

Wind sped around him as the goddess pulled away. Avenir felt her power draw forward, gathering into a point in front of him before it exploded with a surge of energy. The wind died down, and the energy once stirring in the room settled into an easy, quiet thrum.

At his feet, Pelagios let out a sloshing, gurgling moan.

CHAPTER THIRTY-FIVE

Reeling back as she opened the door, a bitter smell of rot hit the back of Neoma's throat. She thought she smelt something odd when she gathered supplies for dinner, but since then the smell only thickened. She cursed not having sought after it before, especially since the day crew upturned their noses at the stew as if it were unpleasant.

Neoma held her breath in intervals, checking the barrels for any indication of spoilage. It was only a handfuls of weeks since they left port, her next day off was fast approaching, and she was certain Armonia would not be conveniently busy this time.

Their last meeting kept the wall between them high. When Neoma was making her way to Armonia's cabin on her off-day, it was Viorel who stalled her with an apologetic frown. Even though the woman explained that these things happened, and that the captain often had to step away, Neoma knew that despite the mostly placid conversation that she had struck a nerve.

As if a plagued settled over them, the crew kept their to circles as Neoma struggled to decided between respect, and her desire for company. No one was cruel to her, and she did not doubt that her nerves only made it *seem* like she angered them, but it was hard to fight against such a nasty voice in her mind when the only greeting she received was at mealtimes. Had she truly overstepped to such a degree with Armonia that the rest of the crew decided to shun her in response?

Neoma scoffed, immediately regretting the action when the spoilage filled her throat.

Armonia Arlowe. There was never a woman more fickle, at least not that Neoma met. She thought there had been a sprig of connection between them, even one as simple as friendship. Surely, her life as a mother did not mean she forgot how to speak to others? No—that captain thought about other things when she looked at Neoma, things that the woman feared *might* be desire.

She pulled back the lids of barrels of grains and dried fruits, running a hand through to turn the contents over for any signs of mush. The further back into the little storeroom she went, the worse it got, and Neoma had to plug her nose as she dug around.

"Absolutely ridiculous," she muttered to no one. Maybe, in the end, she was projecting her hopes onto the captain. Her loneliness seemed obvious, a mark on her face revealing to everyone the tenderness of her heart.

The mind played awful tricks on the heart, especially in times of great need. Neoma was not even sure what she wanted from the captain, should there be anything other than friendly professionalism.

Approaching a darker crate that she did not recognize, Neoma pressed through to drop her hand on its top. Her palm hit something wet, making her jerk it back in surprise. A red smear streaked across her palm. Neoma groaned, mentally preparing herself for the spoiled meat when she placed her hands on the heavy lid of the crate. Lifting once, twice, a final time, the overpowering scent of blood and spoiling gore hit the back of her throat.

Neoma looked down into the crate to see a hand reaching out for her, its fingers gnarled and the knuckles shining through the torn skin. Terror gripped her heart at the dismembered body, the lid of the crate *clunking* onto the floor. Her bloodied hands trembled as she backed away from the wooden trunk filled with severed limbs, with *human* remains.

Was this their cargo?

Her back did not meet the wall as she tried to flee, but the soft curve of a woman's breasts. Whipping around, she gazed up at Cyra, who leaned nonchalantly on the doorjamb. Highlighted by the last embers of the cookfire and a single lantern, her silhouette stood imposingly above Neoma.

Lifting her chin, Cyra sniffed the air. Neoma did not know where to turn, or what to do about the animalistic urge to run that came over her when the quartermaster lowered her gaze.

"I didn't—I wasn't—" Neoma looked down at her reddened hands. "I didn't—" She tried once more, but the words were lost.

A body. Limbs, fingers, gnarled, shoved into a box.

Cyra did not speak. So still grew the air between them that Neoma heard herself swallow against the sound of her heart. The quartermaster waited, but for what Neoma did not know.

Finally, Cyra pushed off the doorway. Stepping to the side, half of her face lit up from the glow of the lantern. She smiled at Neoma, whose wild gaze dropped down to the long incisor that peeked over the woman's lower lip.

The day they met, she did not smile. Now, Neoma understood why.

"Captain Arlowe intended for a proper explanation on your next off-day." Cyra's voice was low and husky, rough from years of shouting. She glanced over Neoma's shoulder, letting out a disgruntled sigh. "Unfortunately, it seems we'll be interrupting her breakfast. Care to follow me to the cabin?"

Despite being posed as a question, there was no room to reject the invitation. Neoma wiped her shaking, bloodied hands on her trousers before following Cyra out of the small supply room. Before they left, Cyra bolted the door to the room shut.

"What's that thing about curiosity?"

Neoma turned slowly, cowardice flooding her veins. Cyra still had her hand on the door, facing away from her.

"*Ah.*" The woman nodded, turning now to bear her fangs in a gruesome smile. "It is better to be open-minded in wonder than to close yourself because of belief. So tell me, Miss Cardea…"

Only the twitch of the lantern's flame gave away the new presence in the room. Neoma turned quickly, seeing three other strangers resting against the wall by the stairs when it had only just been herself and Cyra. Viorel stood with them, her face pinched in disappointment and her arms crossed.

Cyra took another step closer, eyes brightening with the smell of iron in the air. "What do you believe about the Revkyn pirates?"

Armonia kept her gaze on the spray of paperwork on her desk as she took a sip from a hefty tankard. A thin red line darkened the spot where her lips met. Her tongue flicked it absentmindedly, and Neoma watched the pink muscle taste very last dreg of blood until, as if remembering herself, the captain padded her lips with a cloth.

"Pardon me." She smiled, her incisors shorter than Cyra's. Did she file them down to evade suspicion? "You did, however, interrupt my morning."

The captain's cabin was large enough to host a long table of gleaming wood, at which Neoma and her Revkyn escort sat. Viorel stood behind Cyra's chair, not looking at Neoma unless she bent to whisper something in her partner's ear. The others who appeared alongside Viorel earlier did not introduce themselves. In fact, other than Viorel's irritating whispering, the only one to break the silence of shuffling papers was the captain.

Without its sash, Armonia's plume of black locks sat like a cloud on her head. As her eyes poured over the documents, Neoma could not help but follow the curve of the woman's nose with her eyes.

The captain glanced up, meeting Neoma's tender, studious gaze.

She dropped it to the papers quickly, but not before earning a gentler grin from the captain. Neoma just found out she was on a Revkyn cruiser, and she was thinking about the captain's *nose*.

"Alright." Armonia sighed. Leaning back in her chair, she took up her mug and kicked her feet up on the corner of her desk. "Have away with it, then."

Cyra stood, the chair groaning as Viorel pulled it away from her. "Obviously, Captain, someone slacked their duties."

"I didn't mean to—"

"My quartermaster doesn't mean yourself, Neoma." Armonia interrupted. "And right now it might be best to wait your turn, if you don't mind. I'm sure you have questions, and they'll be answered, but first I must deal with *how* you found out, not *why* you're here. Cyra?"

Neoma swallowed her mingling annoyance and fear, mind blotting out Cyra's voice as she explained to the captain whose turn it was to prepare the *food*. She had to ignore them, the idea of eating a person's flesh rolling her stomach.

Her cousin got her passage on a *Revkyn cruiser*, one hiding in plain sight by swapping between a day and night crew. Of course no one suspected a ship that was active during the sunlight hours of harboring Revkyn, especially one that illegally refused to fly the proper colors. Did Viorel act as captain when they docked, or someone else?

In that moment, Neoma felt like the greatest fool for agreeing to take the next ship out of Con-Quarry. Part of her wanted to blame Talaya, but she knew her cousin and the others meant well in their actions. With how easily it had been to conceal the truth from Neoma, she could not accuse her relatives of knowing the reality about *The Countess.*

A plummeting sensation made her take a breath. Faintly aware that Cyra was still talking, Neoma found her whisper breaking their conversation.

"Am I safe?"

Cyra cut off her sentence, eyes whipping to glare at her. But Neoma stared at the captain, whose answer was the only one she trusted.

Armonia dropped her feet to the floor. The memory of their private talk nights ago struck Neoma with a sudden twinge of longing.

The captain seemed offended when she answered. "Of course. Why wouldn't you be?"

The eyes of the Revkyn, alongside Viorel's judgmental gaze, bore into her skin. "Well… I mean. I don't mean to be rude—"

"Be rude or don't be rude, no one here gives a damn." Cyra stated. "Say what you mean, and own up to it. You think we'll kill you because we drink blood to survive."

Neoma did not argue, earning a bitter scoff from the quartermaster. "Of course. Of *course* you think that. It's all they say now, isn't it? Never mind the fact we only hunt the damned—"

"*Enough.*" Armonia's voice sliced through Cyra's, the order landing heavily over the room. "Let's not give away all our secrets, hm? Neoma," her silver gaze was gentle but no less commanding. "As captain, I promise that my crew will not harm you. There are others aboard who, like you, are an everyday sort of person. *We* have our… systems in check, so to speak. We don't want for that which sustains us, but neither do we wish to keep you aboard should you be uncomfortable. I was planning to go over everything the *proper* way…" she motioned to the paperwork on the desk.

It eased her worry a little, knowing that the crew was not intentionally trying to hide the existence of the Revkyn on board. However, that did little to shake the terror of finding a dismembered body in the storeroom.

"Willow is already being reprimanded, Captain." One of the previously silent Revkyn assured with a gruff nod. "She's not fresh, and she was informed like the others of a new person on board, so she should've known better."

Armonia seemed pleased at this, deciding to turn her fullest attention onto Neoma. "I know you're most likely not in the mindset to make official decisions, my dear, but it's important that we discuss them. Now, not only is this ship in-part commandeered by Revkyn, but it's also *commanded* by a Revkyn captain. This means, should we dock and be discovered, *you* will be considered a sympathizer. There are a dozen things I could say about how ridiculous that is—being a friend with a Revkyn doesn't mean you suddenly drink blood, too—but that's unimportant. Do you know the Parliament of Shores?"

Neoma, head swimming, said she did not.

"It's the law that states, in part, that Revkyn must identify themselves while coming into harbor." Armonia's faced twisted for a moment into a scowl. "It's a target on our back and on our people, and an unjust discrimination that thankfully has not yet extended to the rest of Gildonais. However, with this particular issue, Revkyn situated in the Nameless Seas are at risk of starvation. They must remain at sea, or deal with the undue consequences of docking in a country that might set their whole ship aflame. So, where does that leave us?"

"Bending the law." The woman who mentioned Willow interjected.

Recalling the night of the veiled people, and the massive ship they came from, Neoma looked between Armonia and the woman who just spoke. They bore the same hooked nose and high cheekbones, but the latter gazed at her with eyes the color of syrup.

Armonia motioned to the woman. "Neoma, this is Myrnn, my first mate and elder sister. She's in charge of managing our correspondence with prison cruisers, as well as maintaining the ship in my absence."

"The people from before… in the veils?"

"They were Revkyn."

Neoma's eyes jumped around the room, still trying to solidify the word. "What was in the crates?"

Cyra answered, her voice sharp. "Food."

Myrnn made a sound of interruption, and the quartermaster downturned her gaze. To Neoma, Myrnn said, "One of the ways Revkyn are allowed to eat is by making a deal with a country to handle the overpopulation of their prisons. However, these documents are only awarded to a select few ships at a time. Each country is allotted two of these permits to give, according to the Parliament of Shores. In the meantime, every other Revkyn ship must either pillage, pirate, or kill for their food. *We* have a permit, though it's not tied to a particular ship. In essence, we take the bodies, bleed them, and cork them like wine. It makes it easier for shipment."

"This puts us in a dangerous spot, as both landless and hungry people." Armonia turned to Neoma, beseeching. "We aboard *The Countess* don't need much. Revkyn can last for up to eight days after only feeding the once, but that doesn't make the need any less important."

Overwhelmed with the information, Neoma found her hands forcefully gripping the armrest of her chair. Most of her mind reeled from the body, a fact that the other women in the room seemed to forget. But then why would it bother them, if they were the ones amputating bodies and drinking blood? Perhaps, since they picked her up in Con-Quarry, they assumed Neoma used to stepping over the bodies of beggars in the streets.

To her surprise, Viorel spoke on her behalf. "As the only other person here *not* sustained by blood, I'd like to remind the Captain and company that stumbling upon a dismembered corpse, only to then be bombarded by all this parliament talk, doesn't help." She glanced at Neoma then, an understanding in her gaze. "Perhaps we give Neoma her allotted day off before ushering in ultimatums?"

Cyra's hand touched the back of Viorel's gently. "My love doesn't speak often, but when she does, I've always found it best to listen. Captain?"

"Yes, yes." Armonia did not seem happy with dismissing the company without having a more foundational answer. She seemed nervous, worrying her thumb over the pad of her forefinger. "I know you're right, Vi. Quite right. And I will gladly free Neoma of my thrall as soon as the rest of the paperwork is done."

Myrnn cleared her throat. "Does it make sense to document her considering she might leave?"

Armonia cut her silver gaze to Myrnn. Neoma wondered if the unnatural color might be due to the strangeness of Revkyn blood, or if the captain's family came from a place where the startling color was common.

"Are you questioning me, Minnie?" She snipped.

Myrnn flicked her wrist. "Fine, fine, *captain*." She muttered, rising. "I'm only asking the very same things mother would, if she were here. But by all means, waste your good parchment. Gods know the cost of it rises every time we dock, but the captain wishes to do her *paperwork*. Good night," the woman offered to the room, being the first of the gathering to leave without the captain's outright dismissal.

The captain let out that long sigh that anyone with large families knew well. Pinching the bridge of her nose, Armonia told the others that they had her permission to return to their duties. Viorel gave Neoma an apologetic look, which made her smile a little at the standoffish crewmember. The others paid her little mind, the looks in their eyes made of worry or distrust. Should Neoma choose to leave, they would be releasing a person who knew an important secret. Trust did not come easily for the crew of *The Countess*, this Neoma understood despite the nervousness flooding her body every time the image of the dismembered limbs in the crate flashed across her mind.

The captain did not speak for another moment. Looking like she really was gathering her paperwork together, Neoma was taken aback by her first question.

"Do you want to go home?"

Neoma pressed her lips together. Yes and no, but how did she properly articulate that after having learned such a secret? It felt improper to say she felt unsafe when the only thing the Revkyn did to her so far was be honest.

"I… I'm not sure if I want to stay." She admitted. "I didn't know the risk."

A painful look hushed over Armonia's face. She grinned without humor, without light in her silver eyes. "Risk is definitely an important factor in making decisions, yes."

Neoma had touched on a sensitive nerve. There she was, rightly shaken but speaking to a rejected member of society about weighing her options. Armonia was responsible for an entire crew of not only the everyday person but Revkyn as well. Every decision she made considered risks that Neoma did not have the capacity for. Every morning, and every night, the captain woke up to thinking about whether or not she or her crew would die the next time they went into harbor.

It was grief, but a different kind than Neoma's. Still, she felt ashamed for not taking it seriously until that hurt tone in the captain's voice.

"The rest of the crew knows about us. They have to, in order for things to go well." Armonia, finally done with the mindless flitter of her parchment, pressed her hands flat against the desk. "A good ship is one without secrets."

"Are the other ships like this one?" Neoma wondered aloud, unable to hush the curiosity.

Armonia smiled. "Full of women, you mean? No… that's more of a preference. The others," she rushed on, "are more like villages. Like the one you saw the other night but sometimes smaller, sometimes bigger. They have their own hierarchies, but instead of a crew there are whole families. Ships like *The Countess* are the ones that touch the shores most often. The others… there are too many children. They can't risk it."

Neoma's heart twinged. She understood a mother's burden most of all. "I didn't know it was like that."

"Most of you don't. It's not like you bother to ask." The accusation was small, but no less sharp when it hit Neoma.

And it was all truth.

"So," Neoma tried to relax into her chair. "Does that mean ships like *The Countess* bring the… food… to these village-ships?"

Armonia snickered. "Village-ships. What a mouthful. They're called domiciles, officially. But yes, we do. And, just to make my statement earlier clear, Revkyn also don't turn others with our bites, or have powers to enthrall you. What creates us is in our blood, left over from… something." The captain shrugged, completely unknowledgeable, just as everyone was, in the origins of the Revkyn peoples. "But sunlight does give us a most unfortune burn, and hurts our eyes."

Neoma did wonder about those fables, and was glad to have one dismissed.

The captain set a hand on the papers, grimacing. "I hate to admit it, but my sister is right. I don't think we should continue with this until you know you want to stay. As such, I can answer no more questions without risking the safety of those in my care. Take the day to think of it—in fact, ask Viorel for her opinion."

"Viorel and Cyra, they're…"

Armonia smiled. "A plain red-blood, and a Revkyn, yes. Their pairing makes sense the more you get to know them. Which is why I suggest *Viorel's* council. Good night."

Neoma rose from her seat, jarred at the quick release but in no place to argue against it. Thanking the captain, she slid out of the cabin with a feeling of being in two places at once. One foot remained behind her, in a world she knew well. This world existed with the stories of Revkyn pirates just on the edge, solid enough to spot the bone-white cruisers but still within the realm of fables. Her other foot landed quite suddenly in a new place, ultimately shattering most of what she understood about the blood-eaters. The information she was given settled only half her mind, for even though she understood the need for survival, the thought of Revkyn drinking blood and consuming the flesh of the dead brought her great terror. These people were haunting stories told in the night, but the women in the cabin only sought what was best for the domiciles that harbored their people.

Would Neoma be revealing an insensitive side of herself if she chose to leave? Other than their diet, which the Revkyn could not help, what truly separated her family from theirs?

Out on the main deck, the sun long disappeared from the sky, the night crew took their tasks slowly. A dozen pairs of eyes observed her, the questions behind them loud despite not a word passing their lips as Neoma walked by. No one hungrily snapped at her—in fact, the day crew never seemed worried about the Revkyn on board. If Neoma had not stumbled onto the crate of body parts, then she very well would have gone on in ignorance until the captain called upon her.

Viorel stood off to the side, Myrnn grabbing the elbow of a young woman Neoma suspected to be Willow. She looked only a little older than fifteen, gazing up at the first mate with anxiety but not terror. As Neoma passed them, Willow's bright eyes met hers.

"Sorry!" She whimpered, obviously ashamed of the discomfort she caused Neoma. "Really, I can't imagine having seen—I'm sorry!"

"C'mon now, Willow." Myrnn sighed, annoyed at playing governess to the young woman. "You're dumping out the latrine tonight."

"No-o…" Willow groaned, and Viorel gave Neoma one of her rare little grins as the young Revkyn was carted off below deck.

She reached out, spooking Neoma when her fingers gently grazed her elbow. "If you're anything like I was when I found out, you won't be able to sleep tonight. And, if I know the captain as I do, she told *you* to find *me*."

"She did. And… you're right." Neoma loosened a sigh, feeling the knots already settling in her shoulders. After the body, and all the information shifting her perspective, Neoma's mind was running wildly in all directions.

Viorel nodded. "Good. I have actual brandy, not that blood-soaked stuff our counterparts drink. And, better yet, I know a good spot to drink it. Care to join me?"

"—and so I learned never to go near a pregnant Revkyn while bleeding." Viorel chuckled, brandishing a thick, jagged scar that ran up her forearm.

Neoma took a swig from the small bottle, the sharp brandy a comforting burn. "And you still chose to stay aboard *The Countess*?"

"Oh, the worst of this is from catching a knife to the arm—which was not entirely her fault," Viorel assured her. "It was, however, rather stupid of me to try and seek help from a starving, terrified young lady."

Underneath the bowsprit, guarded by the carving of a water spirit whose tendrils of wooden hair curved around them, the two woman sat on a net over the sea. Viorel assured Neoma that the iron loops and the knots within them were sound, but it took some time for the older woman to relax into the tightly strained hammock. Below them, *The Countess* sliced quietly through the water. Here, their words went unheard by anyone other than the waves. Their way back up was a single rope that Viorel tucked under her thigh to keep from swinging in the air, and it had been their way down to the hiding place itself.

Neoma's fingers still clung to the net, but she passed the brandy bottle to Viorel easily. The hour they spent sitting filled with stories as Viorel danced around the death pervading the ship. She decided to favor the lighter stories of her misfortune, however Neoma felt their comradery slowly leaning into advice when Viorel fell silent.

"Do you know why this started?" She said, motioning to the carving of the water spirit around them.

Neoma shook her head.

"So, the story is this." Viorel adjusted herself on the net. While Neoma felt a little bleary, the brandy seemed to energize the other woman. "A long time ago, the Dua-Nythi ruled the seas. They didn't take kindly to anyone in a big ship roaming their waters, disturbing their peace, so they began to attack anyone who might be a threat to them or their cities. This happened for Ages, all right. *Years* of ships being attacked out on the open ocean, then people going missing, then boats never reaching the shore. Eventually, some old broad from Esmar decided to capture one of the Dua-Nythi… and hang her from the bow of the ship."

The jarring detail shook the warmth out of Neoma. Instinctively, her gaze lifted to the carving above them.

Viorel cleared her throat. "They came to an understanding, the Dua-Nythi and us. And since then, the tradition carried on. Well, the carvings did, when the Dua-Nythi disappeared to the bottom of the sea so they wouldn't end up like that first one. There's a reason I'm telling you this."

Swinging her feet over the edge of the net in a daring manner, Viorel huffed out a breath. She took another swig, upturning the bottle with a scowl when she realized it was empty. Neoma waited patiently, her own legs crossed and a good distance away from the edge. She avoided asking anything outright about Viorel's own experiences with finding out there were Revkyn aboard *The Countess*, figuring the woman would come to the story on her own.

"Sometimes," Viorel finally mumbled, "the world isn't fair in how it deals its unfairness. It wasn't fair that the Dua-Nythi attacked *every* ship it came across, but it wasn't fair for that Esmarin to hang one from the bow. Or for the other ships to do the same."

Neoma figured her meaning, after a moment of thinking past the brandy. "So, you're saying it's not fair how the Revkyn have to kill in order to stay alive. It's just…"

"An unfortunate circumstance, anyway you look at it." Viorel finished. "Yes. They're good people. Gods, Above and Below, I've pledged myself to one. If you were to go back and tell me when I joined up that I'd fall in love—no." She shook her head, laughing at some version of her younger self. "No, I'd fight tooth and nail to prove you wrong. Me? I *killed* Revkyn. Their fangs are worth a lot of money in the blood markets of Sovil. When I joined up with *The Countess* years ago, I was following a lead."

The strain in Viorel's tone made Neoma look away. "Was it Cyra?"

"Look at you, catchin' on." She smirked. "It was. Little did I know that this whole ship had an entire gods-damned *second* crew, all Revkyn. I didn't get far with my measly little needle, and it was Cyra who made sure no one else got a chance to taste my blood first."

"I thought—"

"I *was* a murderer, Neoma." Viorel said, guessing her words with ease. With a pointed look, she spoke without shame but with little regret. "By the Parliament, they were in their rights to kill me just as those merchants in Sovil believed I was in the right to kill them—*and* take their fangs.

"But anyways," she went on, "since Cyra was my mark, the crew left me to her. When she bit me, it… it took us both by surprise."

Intimacy touched the corners of Viorel's eyes. Softness enveloped her, the memory that should be terrifying eliciting such a swell of affection that Neoma grew embarrassed. She looked away from the woman, and down at the water far below them.

"It doesn't happen often, the connection between a Revkyn and us red-bloods. But when it does, it's beyond lust, beyond *love*. Cyra took in a part of me, and when my heartsong swam across her tongue, she knew *everything*. She knew my mother, my memories. My desires—Ah. I'm sorry."

Neoma still could not look the woman in the face.

"I'm sorry," Viorel said again, placing a comforting hand on Neoma's leg. "I was too intimate. I didn't ask if you're comfortable hearing those things."

"I'm... *not.*"

The realization of being discomforted by sexual talk hit Neoma like a cannonball to the chest. But Viorel nodded, easily accepting this boundary, not having a single idea of how important it was for Neoma to admit as much to herself, let alone aloud.

"When *that* happened, I had the opportunity to taste her blood at well. It seals the connection, in a way. And since then, we've been inseparable. I won't be crass about it, but she still takes my blood at times. It's like... well, it's like talking to get to know one another, but deeper than that."

For some reason, Neoma thought of the captain's lips on her neck. Instead of the shame such a thought usually brought on, a flicker of joy stirred in her chest. What would it be like, to know someone so intimately without crossing into that realm of sexual closeness?

"Without thinking of Cyra," Neoma began, shifting a little on the net. "Without thinking of your connection to her... would you have stayed?"

Viorel responded quickly. "No, likely not. If I didn't have Cyra, I wouldn't understand what she went through first hand. What they *all* go through. I was pig-headed, boorish, and hungry for money and death. If I hadn't boarded this ship... if I hadn't met Cyra, then I'd still be the same. Sometimes, people bred in violence need something equally aggressive to shake them free. I was one of those people, but I don't think we need to threaten you with fangs to get you to see why what *The Countess* does is important, and that the Revkyn got the sharp end of a stick they had no choice in grabbing. Tomorrow is your off-day, yes?"

Neoma dipped her chin, thoughts making a spot behind her chest tight.

"You have to make a decision tonight, then." Viorel warned perceptively. "But don't wreck your mind trying to justify it all at once. You were told one story your whole life, now you have the other side of it. That's a lot for anyone to take in. For now, just enjoy the sea."

Their silence fell easily. Neoma thought of the world that created this past version of Viorel, trying to imagine, like before, placing her anywhere other than *The Countess*. But the woman seemed to have found her place not only in a duty that brought her honor, but standing next to a woman who brought her joy. Neoma wished to be able to feel settled on the ship, just like Viorel, but her mind was beginning to second guess every decision it made since Koa's death.

Should she have stayed with Urias? Should she have gotten to know Monty, who, she realized, was the first women with whom she was ever infatuated? Perhaps Neoma should have stayed in Kairdwillo—her family welcomed her, and it was *safe* there—and took the time to discover these feelings on her own.

You must be the bravest woman among us, then, for I can't think of anything more frightening than suffering a grief which might shatter me completely, and then sailing off to the middle of nowhere to face it.

"Viorel."

The woman turned to her, a hazy smile on her lips. It was a night made for sitting in a net over the ocean, drinking and talking, and the softness of the moment virtually chided Neoma for breaking it.

"What do you think of the captain?"

Smirking, Viorel's narrow eyes turned into gentle crescents. "I think... you and the captain are more alike than Armonia is willing to admit. In all my time, I've not known her to bring a new crew member into her cabin for a private talk. *Ever*."

Viorel cut her a look that dared Neoma to argue. Like the image of the captain drinking her heart's blood, Neoma held on to the words with a surprised thrill that gave her a warmth akin to brandy. Viorel's hand rested on the back of her shoulder suddenly, and the gesture was strange for her. Giving the bone an awkward pat as the world settled around them, Viorel, with a soft redness in her cheeks, began to hum a melody. Neoma focused on the weight of the woman's hand, the comfortable lilting of her voice, vague as to whether or not it solidified a friendship between them but still grateful for Viorel's presence.

The ship continued its hush over the surface of the water. It promised to bring Neoma to a world of new answers, a severance from what she once knew, should she be strong enough to let the tide carry her.

CHAPTER THIRTY-SIX

"I know there's only so much you can tell me, but I have questions."

Armonia looked down at Neoma from behind the massive wheel. Her dark hair moved freely in the wind as *The Countess* broke steadily through the night. Red blood singing, she was struck at how the captain's silver eyes glowed like the stars above them. Armonia Arlowe stood, a goddess of her own realm, with the air of an aristocrat not a pirate. So much was concealed by the fine brocade that donned her frame, bright silvers judging anything that passed. Yet, unrest sat behind that severity when her gaze acknowledged Neoma.

Placing her hand on the railing leading to the upper deck, Neoma awaited the captain's permission with a pit in her stomach. After her conversation with Viorel, and a full night of tossing and turning in her cot, Neoma struggled to make it casually through her off-day. Viorel appeared like a ghoul, standing in the corner of Neoma's gaze, or the eyes of the crew members who had been informed that she knew about the Revkyn followed her every step across the deck. Since there were few places on a ship she could hide without feeling like a bilge rat, Neoma returned to her bed to sit, arms folded over her knees in contemplation.

Once the sunlight beaming down the stairs turned gray, then pink with sunset, she attempted to settle the racing thoughts in her mind. She thought of Urias, and was startled to notice her bitterness turned to pity, and hope that he had not really gone back to his vile mother. Koa's childish laughter rung in her head, the tune of an old nursery rhyme humming over the faces of the children she saw looking down at her from the domicile.

Out in Linlocke, there was a woman washing clothing with sturdy, rough hands and heady soaps. A lighthouse smile ready for any stranger, she lived with a warm, open heart and a crooked-toothed grin. In some way, this was another path Neoma might have chosen; to become friends with Monty, to stay and see what might blossom or die. Linlocke would change, just as much as she might, if she had stayed to understand what this new feeling was inside her.

All day theses images churned—children with needled fangs, Koa's laughter as he kicked the foam of an incoming wave, Urias' red-rimmed eyes and his twisted mouth as he struggled to mourn his son, Monty's calloused hands—until in a wink of a flintstone they collided. Neoma had made her decision, shooting up from her cot just as the white beams of moonlight touched the steps, illuminating her black skin with blues and silvers.

It was all a past life, a part of herself she cherished but no longer felt pulled towards. Urias, Monty, even Koa. Even though the twist in her heart said she could not let her son go like the others, not yet, Neoma understood that going home mean walking backwards against the tide. Ocean pulled her onto *The Countess*.

Standing as though posing for an oil painting, Armonia quirked a brow as Neoma realized as much. She leaned forward on her elbows to meet Neoma's gaze, giving her the space to continue.

"I can't just make a decision like this, not without knowing the outcome. I'm not like you."

"Haven't you been listening?" Armonia sighed. "We all take risks. To sit and constantly weigh the options is to watch life pass you by."

"Yes," Neoma agreed sadly, "but I already lost one life."

Armonia looked away, her fingers picking at the wood grain. Neoma felt the emotion tighten in her throat as she continued. "I don't think I can handle just giving away another. I have to figure out what is best for me."

Viorel showed her that it was possible for more than friendship to happen between the captain and herself. Chaos swirled around her head as she decided this next moment, the fear of change gripping her heart.

It was the thought of Koa smiling at her from that whitewashed beach in her dreams that gave her the courage to take the first step up to the vestibule. The captain stayed quiet for a moment, watching her rise with a narrowed, daring look. Assessing, the captain let out a tight breath.

With a jilt of her chin, she welcomed Neoma closer.

Unsure of herself now that she stood in Armonia's company without the escort of the others, Neoma kept her hand on the banister for support.

For the last day, the closer circle of blood-eaters and Viorel kept Neoma at a polite but curt distance. Despite sharing an intimate moment, Viorel returned to her distant self from when they first met, though her gaze remained ever-watchful. Neoma understood why the friendship came to a standstill. Why should the other women invest in a person who might not be there come morning?

Armonia nodded after considering Neoma's words, though she quickly moved her gaze to the sea. "What have you, then?"

Neoma let out a breath, forcing the words to follow before she lost her nerve. "Are body parts a common occurrence? I don't know if I can accidentally find… *that*… again."

It was only a flash, but the image still haunted Neoma. She believed it was part of the reason sleep evaded her, and why she struggled to remain agreeable.

"That never should've happened in the first place." Armonia sounded genuinely upset that it ended up causing such an issue. Without looking at Neoma, she added, "But I can't promise it won't happen again. The bodies come to us like that—dead, I mean. We drain them, bottling the blood like wine to give to our people. The meat is used to feed the Revkyn here on the ship. Are you asking that we stop eating, Neoma?"

"No." She shook her head furiously. "I just… being notified that a shipment is on board would be nice."

"What else?" Armonia's tone was short, her annoyance at Neoma's questions mounting. Perhaps she expected Neoma to leave, frustrated at wasting her time.

"Viorel said we're crossing the Nameless Seas. Why?"

"Do you think it wise that I give that information to someone who might tell her tales at the next port?"

"You were the one who said a ship has no secrets."

"Aye," Armonia's tone begged Neoma not to get testy. "A captain does, though."

Neona bristled. "Why are you like this?"

The captain cut her gaze to the ocean, abashed. With a curt twist of her mouth, she mumbled, "These aren't the questions I was expecting, to be honest."

"*That's* what I mean." Neoma pointed an accusing finger, knowing that the frustration inside of her was climbing, that it might all fall on the captain like it had on Urias ages ago.

Armonia hooked an arm around the pegs of the wheel. Putting the other on her hip, she faced Neoma with the type of smile that she often wished to slap off of Urias' face. "I'm going to need you to be more specific, darling, or else I'll have to make your decision for you and drop you off at the next port."

Neoma tensed her jaw. In order to keep her tone cool, she dropped her pointing finger and let her hand grip the banister once more. "You find me when I'm alone, on my first night."

The captain lifted a shoulder. "I wanted to see you for myself."

"Because you trust Viorel's judgement so poorly, yes?"

Armonie's eye twitched. "*No*," She said through gritted teeth.

Neoma let out a bark of laughter. "Oh, that's convincing, *darling*. Well, *darling*, there's also the fact that you invited me to sit with you in your cabin. And before that, you allowed me to witness the exchange of… *food*… before I understood what was happening."

"I do that all the time."

"Not according to your master boatswain, you don't."

When Armonia looked away, pressing her lips into a thin line, Neoma knew her point was clear.

The captain's voice dropped when she next spoke, sending a shiver of caution down Neoma's spine. "My *dear*. You're beginning to mistake my cordiality for softness. I have half a mind to correct that ignorance."

"I have the other half to call your bluff."

This was not going the way Neoma wanted, not by any means, but just like with Urias all those night ago she felt the truth swelling up inside her until it unraveled from her tongue. In this moment, she was not a mother who lost her son but a woman whose heart craved a love beyond the physical expectations cast onto her by society. She craved experience, something new that remained far from her reach in Linlocke, and even in Kairdwillo.

"*You* seek me out. You do. And I won't deny that it's made me wonder."

Armonia's silver eyes jumped to her, widening at the softness in her voice. Her throat bobbed. "How do you mean… wonder?"

Heat climbed up Neoma's neck, settling in her cheeks. For a moment, she completely lost her nerve, terrified of saying anything at all. It was too soon for her to feel anything more than infatuation, but she was tired of letting moments slip through her fingers. She willed her life away to a man she once cared for but never truly loved. Every curiosity, every desire to try something different with a woman, she cut out of herself because she had a son, had a husband, so why did she dare reach for anything more?

Talaya heard the hopeful desire in her words, and so thrust her into a life where she might be free to test that curiosity far away from the prying eyes of a world that might judge her for it.

"I think about holding your hand."

The captain blinked. She opened her mouth, but Neoma interrupted, the words spilling out of her before fear locked them in her throat. "I think about your eyes finding me in the dark, but not in *that* way. I got this knot in my stomach when you were looking for *me*, when you wanted to talk to *me*. I thought, after everything, I might not ever feel so gentle again. After I lost Koa—"

Armonia's palm cupped her cheek, surprising in its sudden closeness. The coarse pad of her thumb swiped away the tear there, and despite herself Neoma leaned into the touch.

"You hadn't told me his name." Armonia's voice breezed across her, softer than the wind. "It's beautiful, like his mother."

Neoma struggled to meet her eyes. Through lowered lids, the captain studied her tears, her trembling lip, with all the patience that Urias never allowed such a still moment.

"This is the first time I've been hopeful in what's felt like an Age." Neoma admitted. Her fingers lifted, uncertain, to grasp Armonia's elbows. The woman hummed underneath her touch, the embrace enough for them to sense the drive of wonderment they shared. "I'm not begging you to give anything to me but your company. I have no right to ask for it. I'm just… I'm afraid of giving this feeling a name. I'm afraid of staying here, and I'm afraid of going home and missing whatever may happen. I'm afraid that you will refuse me when I ask that, should I stay, if I explore this feeling with *you*."

"Neoma…" the captain let out a low, sad breath. She dropped her hand, letting it hover uncertainly by Neoma's hip.

Then it fell to her side. "I don't *want* the way other people do. If you ask me to kiss you, I'll recoil. If you ask me to touch you in the dark, I might hurt you with rejection. All I can give—all I *have*—is a comfort to some but an empty cup to everyone else."

The hurt in Armonia's voice pulled tears of empathy into Neoma's eyes. Years of betrayal hung onto the captain's words, thick as regret. It was her turn to touch Armonia's face, lifting her chin to gaze up at the captain with a tender smile. The motion was new, she had never touched Urias so carefully, and she did her best to hush the curl of embarrassment around her heart.

"If I told you I don't ever want to take to the marriage bed again, might that change things?"

Armonia took her wrist in her rough hand, gently caressing it, trying to decide between pulling it away and pressing it closer to her cheek.

"You can't just say this." She drew circles on the inside of Neoma's wrist, feeling her heartbeat there with unthreatening focus.

"I'm not."

"I might hurt you." As if to make a point, she pressed her finger a little tighter against Neoma's wrist. Heart beating madly against the touch, it felt more intimate than a kiss.

"Yes." Neoma agreed. "But I might hurt you, too. That's what happens when you decide to be vulnerable with someone. It's life. And," she tapped her chin, lightening the mood with a comedic *harumph*. "What was it you just said? To sit and constantly weigh the options—"

Armonia dropped Neoma's hand and drew her into her chest. The warmth of skin rich with the smell of frankincense pressed against her cheek as the Revkyn captain drew her arms tightly around Neoma. With only the stars as witnesses, Neoma locked her arms around Armonia's waist, pulling her closer.

This was more than enough, the honest expression of simply wanting to be close. Neoma meant what she said; she would not require anything more of the captain than to explore this desire without physical solace, to nurture it safely into whatever it might become. As an adult, she knew that relationships of all kinds might flourish, or might wither. But for the first time since losing the life she had for over a decade, Neoma knew in her heart that seeds were taking root. In her chest, they burrowed down into the ashen soil of her old memories. In the arms of the captain, who drew her so close as though she must consume her, Neoma considered that *this* was what her soul longed for during those years of shying away from her husband's touch.

All the while, she thought something broke within her when really Urias was not the right piece for her heart. Could Armonia be, if she pursued this?

"I take it you're staying." Armonia whispered into her locs, as if reading her mind.

Not able to help the bubbling glee, Neoma nodded against Armonia's chest. Then, with a quick breath, Armonia broke the embrace. She kept her hands on Neoma's arms, not yet willing to sever the connection entirely. Those silver stars roved Neoma's face, weighing something behind them.

"You asked why our heading is past the Nameless Seas." The captain pursed her lips. Her grip on Neoma's arms tightened for a moment before they slid down to take her hands. "I seek a book that holds the record of the beginning of our world. I've followed the marks for it nearly my whole life, and one of our soothsayers woke to a vision of me finding it in the Isle of Adelhart. She said she saw a world of blood and food for all the lost Revkyn at sea. She saw me sailing to the library, and finding the book that would reveal how we were *made*. This is more than you asked for," Armonia admitted, "but if you're to stay, you need to know the truth. No secrets on a ship."

Neoma gazed up at the conviction in the woman's eyes. Armonia, she realized, was afraid that Neoma *would* leave. This was enough to quell her disbelief. Who was she, anyways, to say that the soothsayers of the Revkyn people were wrong? At thirty-six turns of the season, Neoma was still learning to trust her own judgement—to honor her own desire. So, even if it meant sailing around the Nameless Sea, chasing after a faetale, at least she got to choose it, and at least it got to be on *The Countess*.

Lifting her chin, she tightened her grasp on Armonia's fingers. "I've never been that far south before."

The captain breathed out in relief. "You'll stay."

"Yes." A string in her heart tightened, a final farewell to her life before. "I'll stay."

CHAPTER THIRTY-SEVEN

Dice felt the storm gather beyond the wooden barrier of the *Marksmen*, her skin tender with raw magic as it throbbed up from the sea. Low, deep chanting hummed in the back of her mind, every pounding note raking its fingers across her scalp. Each breath she took paced with the song, no longer fighting against it but melding it to the core of her being. It became her meditation, the rhythm of her heartblood receding to give space to the power of the Duathi.

Sleepless nights darkened her undereye, skin sallow as she reclined heavily on the bench in the cell. Two men brought her food, worrying they might have to fight against her when they passed the morsels of bread and jerky. After two days of not eating, only one man began to appear. Dice knew they reported back to Evander, who refused to see her until Hughie, a dockhand, offered her fresh clothing through the bars of the gate.

He grumbled when she did not rise, dropping them on the soggy ground. "I'd let you rot in those," he spat, meaning her blood-soaked garments, "but you'll have a visit from the captain later. I thought it proper he didn't see the carnage of his friend."

Dice remained seated until Hughie left, his words cursing her under every goddess he could name as he stormed up into the light. Eventually, she rose to undress with sluggish limbs that protested her mind. *Lift the sleeve. Tie the trousers*. An age passed before the bloody rags sat in a pile at her feet, and she returned to her stupefied posture on the bench as though she had not left. Her thigh ached with its ever obstinate pain, but it was nothing compared to the shattered emptiness of her heart.

As punishment, she replayed to moment of awareness in her mind, the shock of the immediate transportation snatching her breath every time. Brutis shushing her gently as his intestines slapped upon the deck made her sob horrid, broken gasps of air. Had she walked up from the deck, guilty knife in her hand, or had she materialized like a shadow before him?

Dice felt the warm blood on her hands, where dried brown crescents stuck to the underneath of her nails. And in the darkness, when it would be hours until someone brought her food, she spoke to the glowing memory of the Duathi.

"Hark," her dried, cracked lips murmured. At first, the sound did not shake the silence; then she felt It. Lurking, quiet, settling into the boards of the ship, waiting for the next summoning.

"Hark."

Gooseflesh pimpled her skin—acknowledgement. *Authority.*

Sullen with despair, she gave that flickering darkness what it desired.

"Hark, for the Duathi is awake."

Steps resounded down into the brig, another creature summoned entirely. For a strange moment, she imagined Brutis surging forward, his insides miraculously wrapped behind gauze and linens and his sad but forgiving eyes finding her in the dark.

It's all right, Odessa. It'll all be all right.

Evander appeared with a lantern outstretched. He scowled at the tears in her eyes, for she was not owed the space for grief, only guilt.

Moments slipped by her easily, time melting into nothing finite or trustworthy. Hughie must have brought her a change of clothing hours ago. In the meantime, the storm outside had worsened, her body acutely aware of the dip and lurch of the wood beneath her. Managing somehow to remain upright in her seat despite the tilt of the world around her, Dice met the gaze of her father from under her lashes.

Evander gripped the bars of her cage with his other hand. Staring through the slits of iron, his tired eyes dark with fury and confusion, he searched for any signs of brokenness. What he sought after was any evidence of the daughter he once new, releasing a tight breath when Dice remained the filthy woman before him.

"You're not eating." His voice was hollow, scratchy. It was a voice tight with unshed tears.

Slowly, Dice shook her head.

"Good," said her father. Hanging the lantern on a notch above the gate, the light cast a yellow glow on him at an odd angle, concealing his gaze. "If you were eating, I'd have reason to think you felt no shame."

Dice looked down at her hands. Along her palms, swirls of black ink twitched across her callouses. Once she washed the blood, *Brutis'* blood, from her palms, there they were. They matched the strange, jagged symbols of the bard in her dream, solidifying the fact the Dice had not imagined any of it. Not the bard's black gaze, or the drowning in shadows.

Or the stillness of her heart, and the receding hands of the death gods.

If she had the book, she might compare them to the scrawling within the pages, but it disappeared along with Rory. No one told her if they found him, but after Brutis died they did a sweep of the entire *Marksmen* and came up without a clue as to where Rory went. They did not know he was Dua-Nythi, that he likely returned to his home when he was unable to stop Dice from destroying what she loved. Or, she killed him and tossed his body overboard. At this point, anything might be true, and the crew chose to believe as much.

Visceral hostility peeled away any kindness from Evander's voice. "I've always dealt better with a captive audience. This time, you will tell me *everything*."

"Evander—"

His fist collided with the iron bars, knuckles splitting under the impact. Never in Dice's childhood had the man struck her, but she watched his fists cleave a jawbone or splinter a finger when needed. They were sailor's hands turned to thieving piracy, worn and tired and weathered.

Evander did not wince or check the wound as the sound reverberated around them. The look in his eyes told Dice that if she dared to argue again, he might wring her throat himself. And, as much as she wanted to die, she would not make her father take the life of the last of his kin.

The Duathi released its hold on her for only long enough to weave her tale. It *wanted* to be known, she realized as she began, even if only by association.

Every word that fell from her lips urged the storm outside to grow in its rage. Recounting the details of her last months in Stormshale ushered out of the darkness of her spirit the power residing there. Words slammed over Evander's head, his lips twisting into scowls, his brow knitting with tears as she described finding Evangeline's body. Dice admitted she felt an all-consuming misery in that moment, and did not fight it when it melded to her bones.

When she spoke of the book, describing Talamondin's death as his blue blood hit the water, realization sparked in Evander's eyes as he recalled discovering Rory and Dice. Still, he pressed his lips together, not interrupting her horrid tale as she described to him the strengthening chorus in her mind, and the way the book changed right before she murdered Brutis.

Even with the words outside herself, her body felt weighted and rotten. It was too late for her salvation.

The lantern creaked overhead, groaning as the ship tilted. Evander held fast to the bars, having seen his fair share of storms, and gazed at Dice through the gate.

"What have we done to be mocked so by the gods?"

Her gaze snapped up, locking with her father's. Evander's eyes freed their tears, and he did not wipe them away in embarrassment or anger. His bleeding hand tightened around the iron, the bone of its split knuckles shining in the low light. Dice felt emotion swelling in her gaze, awkward under Evander's passion. Unable to keep her lip from trembling, she wept heavy tears that left streaks in the grime on her cheeks.

"What did you do," he hissed, lip snarling in anger, "to deserve this, other than survive?"

"You don't want to kill me?" She cried, the noise a sharp gasp, and hung her head over her shaking hands in relief.

Evander let out a tight sound of pain. "I can't answer that. I can't let you walk free. From what you said, these bars won't hold you should it happen again. *I don't know what to do—*"

"*ALL HANDS!*"

Their gazes ripped to the stairwell, the screaming order barreling through the roll of thunder. The call went up again as the *Marksmen* titled so sharply that Evander clung to the iron bars just to stay upright.

Looking to her, Evander dug into the pocket of his coat. Dice ran to the cell, holding the gate closed as he slipped the skeleton key into the lock.

"Don't—"

"It's all hands, Odessa." The wrinkles in her father's forehead knit together. She knew he was weighing the possibility of what might happen should she go free. Would the terror of the storm satiate the Duathi, or would it have her kill another?

Darkness once tight with an unseen presence felt cooly empty. Dice lowered her fingers from the gate, a wave of tension hushing over her limbs. Could she stall herself if another possession overcame her?

Evander swung the irons open, holding the gate wide to gaze at the young woman who was as distant to him now as the shoreline.

"All hands, Ward." He repeated as the ship groaned around them.

Dice stepped through the gate, trying not to notice the pain in her chest when Evander matched it with a step backwards.

"Aye, captain." She nodded, feeling the magic of the sea twist around her ankles. "All hands."

Black rain poured into the belly of *The Jolly Marksmen*, water sloshing over the boards as a wave cracked down onto the deck. Evander gripped the collar of Dice's tunic to keep her upright as they stomped past the flood of water pouring down the steps from above. Shoving her forward into the dark, he screamed for a lifeline, hoping someone stood near enough to hear.

Hands shot out, emblazoned by the flashes of lightning cutting across the rolling storm clouds above. No one bothered to argue Dice's presence, even after such a terrible murder. At that moment, the only pressing matter was praying to all the gods that the *Marksmen* did not capsize.

Dice's stomach flipped as the ship's bow leaned and tilted. Barely knotting the lifeline around her in time, her hands clung to the biting fibers of the rope as the deck flew out from under her. For a moment she hung suspended in the air as the ship plummeted, riding along the deadly underbelly of a crashing wave; then she crashed down onto the solid planks with moans of pain singing around her. Shoulder cramped, bad leg screaming out, Dice rushed to her feet. Haste made them all scurry, the master boatswain's voice breaking as he tried to shout the order to tie everything down over the booming thunder. The rain grew heavier in response, slicking her hair to her forehead. She swiped at it, angrily cursing the long tendrils just as another wave came down and swallowed the deck.

Saltwater shot up her nose and filled her lungs. She came up coughing but was immediately attacked by another frothy surf. The force of the wave knocked her sideways, shoved her towards the railing of the ship. Dice flailed her arm out, nails digging into the boards for purchase, splinters catching the skin of her palms. Saltwater burned her eyes, her heart slamming against her chest, against the ragged, useless breaths she gasped.

With a painful jolt, she shouted as the lifeline caught her before tumbling over the railing.

The *Marksmen* lifted into the air as another wave surged up from underneath—Dice's mouth slackened when, in a flash of lightning, she saw the boiling sea pull away from them. They climbed higher, the tidal wave carrying the ship into the thunderous cloudbanks. Energy crackled around her as a white-hot bolt of lightning sliced through the air about their heads.

Screaming as the wave curved, the *Marksmen* and its useless crew slipped down, down, *down* until it slammed once more into the sea.

The water parted around the ship, rising, thundering overhead with a force that knocked the little breath out of Dice's lungs. Coughing, she pulled herself up with her lifeline, following the rope to the main mast in desperation. She knew storms, but what surged around them was a reckoning, not a beacon of nature. Shouts, hopeless and hopeful alike, called out into the splintering dark. Rain thick as blood misted her vision—she could not tell in which direction she stood. Evander disappeared, most of the crew nothing more than slanted shapes in the storm. Thundering in her chest, Dice's heart *pulled* as though called to be an unseen force.

A panicked voice jumped up from the stairwell behind her. "We're taking on water! There's a tear in the hull, there's—"

His scream was cut short with a cry of terror, the heavy sound of something thick landing on the boards. Dice watched as a lifeline next to her went taunt, her fingers instinctively jumping to pull at it with all her might in an effort to save him.

"Man overboard!" Her voice clawed past her raw, aching throat. No one came to help. She screamed into the night once more, the sound breaking as her voice failed to climb above the rage of the sea.

The rope went slack, the sudden lack of force sending her onto her rear. Yanking fervently, she puled the line in until her fingers splayed over the smooth, cut edge.

Instead of risking another sailor, the man decided his own fate.

Who had it been this time? Evander? One of the twins? How many more would the Duathi take? *How many more—*

Remembering the sailor's warning, she pushed aside her feelings of grief, standing, slipping as the ship tilted again.

"We're taking on water! We're taking on water!"

A death sentence, a final farewell. Dice clung to the mast as the call went up around her, the words making it past the storm. Her tears mingled with the salt of the rain as she pressed her forehead to the mast, knowing now it was only a matter of time. Pressure cloaked her, the many forsaken paths she took throughout her life making her wonder, just as Evander, what she ever did to deserve such an end.

"I'm so tired," she mouthed into the back of her hand. Rain pelted her, relentless in its condemnation. "Please, *make it stop*."

Closing her eyes against the storm, Dice prayed to nothing in particular. She hoped her end would be swift, at least, and that the force of the vessel sinking into the waves crushed her.

Leave nothing of this body behind. Don't let the rot fester anymore.

The only friend she made in the world was gone. One of her guardians, felled by her hand, slept at the bottom of the sea. Her first love laid buried in some forgotten grave in a land on the edge of the world.

Dice ruined all that she touched, spreading the rot long before the Duathi took her.

Eyes ripping open, Dice lifted her face to the sky. Lightning slashed across the clouds, uncaring for the creatures it illuminated below.

Blinking against the rain, she felt her damnation twine within her gut.

"If you want me," she bit at that endless storm, "then come and take me."

The sky cracked overhead, angry at her resilience. A wild grin split her face as she watched the dark clouds unfurl. All this time, the creature *wanted* her to take life, but if it dared to claim anything, then let it take that which was already rotten.

"Do you hear me!" A new fervor struck the rawness in her voice. She stepped away from the mast, opening her arms to the storm that aimed to split the world.

Let her end be violent, as long as it was truly the end.

"If you want *me*, you'll have to do it yourself! *Come and get me*."

Lightning cracked once more, but the boom of thunder went deaf in her ears. Another world away, another lifetime before, that silence made Dice terrified. Now, she closed her eyes against the inevitable, its energy rising from the raging sea.

Up from the deep came the great horn.

It shook the timbers of the *Marksmen*, aggravated, the intent of destruction swirling in Dice's mind. Rain slammed against her skin, melted her clothing to her body. The water in the air shivered as it fell, the horn vibrating the world with another mournful bellow that condemned her to the darkest part of the Aether.

Before the *Marksman*, a great wave parted, revealing the face of a god.

Rising from the waters, the Duathi shook its sinewy mane of long, spiked vertebrae that spread in a fan around its beak. The membrane shined with the reflection of the lightning storm, veins spiderwebbing through the soft skin as it continued lifting its face from the depths of the sea. Out in open water, the creature engulfed the horizon, waves breaking against the *Marksmen* as its scaled body shivered with relief, with fury. From its throat vibrated a guttural call that shook Dice down to the marrow of her bones.

Her eyes rejected the sight. Red pooled in her vision but she kept her maddening gaze on the humongous beast as it leaned away, its serpentine body moving like a curtain in the wind. Tentacles flicked against the waves, thumping against the broken body of the *Marksmen* in the drumbeat of battle. She saw a hundred eyes, bright as torch fire, peer down at her from the great height. The Duathi snapped its beak, the clicking sound like a body breaking on the rocks, before dropping its hinge mouth.

Its archaic screech drowned out all reason, dismantling the fiber of her being. Dice became undone, withered under its horror.

The memory of a cliffside far away touched her mind, a gentle song in the belly of the sea, as her numb fingers loosened the lifeline. Tossing the slackened rope away, she faced the Duathi as it angled its head to gaze at her.

The sight of fire and utter wickedness knocked the breath from her lungs.

The horn became something wretched, bellowing slinking into a cacophony of dismay. She heard the voices of people begging the Duathi to save them, and felt their terror when it instead ended their lives.

Swiping away the pools of blood gathering in the corners of her eyes, she lifted her hands once more. "Hark!"

The Duathi rumbled, an otherworldly light gathering in its throat, the sound of a hundred canons setting off at once as its tentacles slapped down into the water. Behind her, Evander shouted her name, his voice strained against the unnatural vision. His fear reached out across the deck, but Dice felt nothing under the gaze of the Duathi.

She licked her lips, tasting the salt and blood there. "Hark! Hark—"

Evander's hand took her by the shoulder, bracing her body as he shoved a blade up through her ribcage.

Above them, the Duathi split the sky with a scream of agony, of being cheated. It cut out the sound of the horn, rupturing Dice's eardrums with a painful *crack* that echoed in her skull. Evander's warmth slipped away from her, the cold of death making her body limp as he dropped his forehead to her shoulder. Slumped against the blade, Dice felt the knife jerk upwards until it caught painfully on one of her ribs.

Her fingers lifted to touch the edge that poked through the underneath of her breast, sticking through her shirt. A foreign thing, sharp and slick, the blood already washed away by the rain.

Looking up at the Duathi, she saw its maw open silently, a decision made. It came for them, for the ship, its glowing throat revealing not muscle but swirling purple clouds struck through with glowing green light.

A jolt rushed through her mind, the thrall of the Duathi fading as it drew its power in towards that glowing cloud. Weakly, she pushed Evander's shoulder, but the pain climbing up her chest slackened every limb. Evander, a sob wracking his chest, dropped to the deck, his arms tight around Dice as she fell with him. Warm blood rushed over her stomach, mingling with the salt of the rain and sea. Her eyes did not steady on Evander's weathered face, or the split on his forehead that cried with blood, but on the god descending from the heavens.

Evander took her face in his hands. Words shaped his mouth, but they were lost. Blood streaked into his beard from his ears—Dice tried once more with all her might to push Evander off of her as her limbs grew cold, but he caught her hand as his mouth twisted in sorrowful farewells.

"You…" she felt the rumble in her chest, unable to hear the sound of her voice. "You *idiot*."

The Duathi consumed the ship in its maw, a great whirlpool rising from the depths as it dragged its Godharker into the sea. Not a waterlogged board or a torn sail remained, and the *Marksmen* became hapless myth.

Thank You

Nothing about this book would exist without the help of my Love, Cullen. During the summer of 2023, I was unemployed and Cullen supported our small household as I struggled with the first two outlines of *Bloodwater*. I felt like a burden, but he never made me feel that way—and he supported this book at every step. I sat on the couch and regaled to him the dramatic scenes and every twist before a word was on the page, and he listened with pride.

My heart is full, and I have done the work I set out to do only because I have such a wonderful, kind, patient, and loving partner in you. My Love, thank you for all that you've done, and for your relentless support of *Bloodwater* from the moment of its conception.

Thank you to the team at Williston Boarding School in Northampton, specifically Grace, Chris, Annie, Gen, and the night crew. You all listened to me ramble about writing my book, and were some of the first to see the cover that I made in CanvaPro. And when I went on to other, better things for myself, you continued that support, some of you as beta readers! For that, I'm so, so grateful.

Speaking of beta readers: Ursula, Avery, Grace, Skylar, SapphyLore, Elizabeth, and Kat, I know I've expressed my thanks in my countless emails throughout the beta process, but *Bloodwater* could not have been this final product without you all. You survived the first draft, which takes nerves of steel in my opinion!

Ursula, Kat—not only were you two beta readers, but you helped make sure *Bloodwater* was *right*. I'm thankful for the emotional burden you both carried as sensitivity readers for this project.

And, dear Reader, I thank *you* for taking the chance on an independently published book that, from its conception to its publicity, was spearheaded by a dorky queer with her head in the clouds. Thank you for diving into this world that took two years to get to the shelves, and thank you so much for making my dream of becoming an author a reality. Don't forget to give others like me a chance—you might just find your next favorite book.

I wish I could go back in time to that teenager scrawling in her journal and say, *someone is reading what we wrote—we did it.*

Thank you.

Forrest Graey is a Queer disconnected Native (Anishinaabe) living in diaspora. Her first "novel" was a handwritten *Pirates of the Caribbean* fanfiction. The fantastical pirates series, along with *Lord of the Rings*, *Inkheart* and games like *Dragon Age: Inquisition*, heavily influence her love for fiction and worldbuilding—though she has a soft spot for science-fiction like the *Mass Effect* games and the *Alien* movies. Her pagan spirituality, trancework, and knowledge of the Tarot guide many themes within her writing, as does the arduous journey from monotheism into paganism. She lives in Western Massachusetts with her loving partner, Cullen, and their cats, and is an interior designer by day. *Bloodwater* is self-published, the first book in the Bloodhaker Series, and her first novel—that *isn't* fanfiction.

Questions posed by Lila Mary, author of *The Red King's Mystical Suitors* and more; @lilamarybooks on Instagram.

✣ *From the gorgeous illustrations to the chapter headings to the maps in the front matter, so much care has been given to the visual elements of Bloodwater. Can you talk a bit about that?* ✣

I knew I wanted to go all-in with as much detail as possible, at least as much as I could manage with my own income. It helps that I've always had an eye for design, but the vanity pages and maps didn't simply start off where they are now. If people have been following me long enough, then they'll remember that first draft of the cover that I made with CanvaPro and… *well*. It was certainly a first draft! But then I went to a bookstore and studied the fantasy section. What covers resonated with me? How were their colors layered? From there on I whittled away until the vanity pages, maps, and finally the cover revealed themselves.

This book is my first, so I wanted to set the bar high enough to be impressive but still show room for growth. My plans is upward momentum—I'm proud to say that I think *Bloodwater* sets the tone for my future fantastical projects in the realm of Gildonais.

✣ *Themes of the ocean, from its history to its personification, are a central force in this book that unites all the characters. Can you talk a bit about why you chose the ocean as the centerpiece?* ✣

A bit of personal lore: once upon a time, I was a Tarot reader and had my own shop, Pomegranates and Wine Tarot. I had a Patreon as well, where I taught a handful of people about a Tarot card every week alongside energy work. I'm emotion-forward, which is essentially what the Suit of Cups represents. *Emotion, passion, flow, depth, intuition*. The water has always called to me, and after studying what it represents in numerous beliefs and cultures, it just made sense that it's the through line for *Bloodwater*. Water cleanses and restores, but it can shape boulders into pebbles and swirl together to create maelstroms. It's a transitional element, and there's plenty of that in the book.

✣ The worldbuilding of Bloodwater is so rich and vibrant; it feels completely real. Do you have a favorite piece of worldbuilding? ✣

I love different pieces of it, certainly, but as a disconnected Native in the diaspora, the country of Esmar is incredibly important to me. Here is a country ruled by invaders—its Indigenous people hunted, starved, or forcible removed—suffering the consequences of taking over a sacred location and treating the land poorly. Writing Esmar in such a way feels like releasing transgenerational trauma in an environment I can control and mitigate. It's a direct reflection of matters in our real world while still holding on to the air of fantasy. It felt *good* to write it, to make the people of Esmar complicated and vile or simply victims of circumstance. I know on the whole, it's not the people of Farstone or Neighweather to blame, but the King and his Court, but as we saw with Pelagios, how far can such statements like that go before we start making excuses for the negative behavior towards Indigenous people?

✣ What would you say is the through line in all the characters and their vastly different experiences? ✣

All journeys, in fantasy and reality, begin with a shattering of preconceived ideas and beliefs. Each of them are *becoming*—but as to what, well… That's a question for another time.

✣ *How important was it for you to include the darker elements in the story, as well as making this book unapologetically queer?* ✣

Incredibly important! I didn't realize myself that I was queer until my early twenties, and then for years I was stuck on defining what that meant to me. Neoma was inspired by that belated journey a queer woman might have, because there are so many stories of people with whole families and even children who take years to make such a realization. I don't ever see that kind of journey represented. I haven't come across a similar topic in the high-fantasy genre, but maybe I haven't run into it yet.

And the darker elements? Metaphors with a sprinkle of shock value, yes, but important, nonetheless. I'm morbidly fascinated by the way we as people fall apart when we experience change, how every time it gets so dark we fear *that's* our new reality. And while there are suggestions regarding off-page situations, I chose to hone in on necrophilia because I saw it as an example of people in power taking that power however they want—even from those who have no power left to give. People like that, they become another creature entirely, no longer human, no longer moral. *Absolute power corrupts absolutely*, yes, but so does simply the *promise* of power.

✣ *What do you want readers to take away from this book?* ✣

Surface-level answer is, I just hope they like it enough to eventually return to the realms of Gildonais! I have plans for this series, for the realm in general, and having people as excited as I am to discover it is any author's dream. The world itself was half a year in the making, the book almost two, and, well, I don't plan to stop any time soon!

But *Bloodwater* is more than a dark fantasy novel. It's political, it's unabashedly queer, it's dynamic. I hope queer readers specifically leave it feeling that they *do* deserve space in the world. Queer authors like me are going to keep writing queer love and queer adventure because *we're not going anywhere*.

www.ingramcontent.com/pod-product-compliance
Lightning Source LLC
Chambersburg PA
CBHW020246030826
48979CB00030B/2633/J

9798218774745